Heroes on the Home Front

Annie Clarke's roots are dug deep into the North East. She draws inspiration from her mother, who was born in a County Durham pit village during the First World War, and went on to become a military nurse during World War Two. Annie and her husband now live a stone's throw from the village where her mother was born. She has written frequently about the North East in novels which she hopes reflect her love and respect for the region's lost mining communities.

Annie has four adult children and four granddaughters, who fill her and her husband's days with laughter, endlessly leading these two elders astray.

2

F

ANNIE CLARKE
Heroes on the
Home Front

arrow books

1 3 5 7 9 10 8 6 4 2

Arrow Books
20 Vauxhall Bridge Road
London SW1V 2SA

Arrow Books is part of the Penguin Random House group
of companies whose addresses can be found at
global.penguinrandomhouse.com

 Penguin
Random House
UK

First published in Great Britain by Arrow Books in 2019

www.penguin.co.uk

A CIP catalogue record for this book is available
from the British Library

ISBN 9781787462588

Typeset in 10.75/13.5 pt Palatino by Jouve (UK), Milton Keynes
Printed and bound in Great Britain by Clays Ltd, Elcograf S.p.A.

For Miss Delilah Dore
A joyous force of nature.

Acknowledgements

Of course there's a great deal of background reading when writing about the past. So huge thanks to Google and *Bomb Girls* by Jackie Hyams. Thanks also to a fellow bus passenger who was a bomb girl (filling factory) during the war – fascinating. And my mum's anecdotes from her time working at the Royal Victoria Infirmary in Newcastle, not just nursing miners, but those whom the nurses felt were munitions girls (this was never confirmed – secrecy was paramount). She also had a couple of pals who were indeed munitions girls, though it was only much later that they felt able to share their reminiscences with me.

My fabulous pal Betty was at Bletchley Park during the war and aware of the need for secrecy when I was teaching her writing group way back when, but she finally loosened up and told me much. Oh, how I miss her. She was sooooo clever, and so mischievous. Again, there are many books on the subject: *The Secret Life of Bletchley Park* by Sinclair McKay and *Station X* by Michael Smith are just two of them. Him Indoors, a computer buff, has also been really helpful. However for a few years we lived close to Bletchley Park and of course visited, and saw and learned much. Do go if you can. Talking of Him Indoors, he has, as an ex-submariner, been able to bring some sense to the munitions with which the girls worked, and the technology at Bletchley Park, so he may have one of my chocolates. As always, any errors are my own, and my eternal thanks to everyone who has shared their knowledge. I am in awe of their courage, endurance and humour.

Chapter One

Fran Hall stood on the back step of her family's colliery house in Massingham, wrapping her woollen scarf over her head and round her neck before tucking the ends down inside her shabby mac. The scarf was all sorts of colours and the latest her mam had knitted, the one her da had liked because he said it made him feel cheery as the days drew in. She looked down at the old chair beside the step beneath which her da's boots should have been. Aye, well, they wouldn't be, not any more.

She stepped out into the yard, leaving her mam and the Proggy Rug Co-operative, as they called themselves, busy around the kitchen table. 'You be good, ladies,' she called. 'Not too much fun and games. You've fresh orders to finish for the department store, remember.'

She heard her mam's strained laugh. 'Howay with you, pet. Don't teach us oldies to suck eggs. You just keep wrapped up and enjoy your time with the others at the beck. Your gang has always taken its troubles there, right from being bairns. Make the most of yer time while your Davey is still on leave. Sarah and Stan are cosy together, but remember Beth needs company, with her Bob still at sea.'

Fran smiled, knowing that the co-op – all Massingham women – would be working not just at their rugs for Briddlestone's in Newcastle, but at keeping things normal for her mam, and Sarah Bedley's. There was nothing else they

1

could do for the widows whose husbands – the girls' fathers – had been laid to rest the day before, following a fatal accident in the mine.

She shut the door behind her. Normal, eh? Aye, that was about right, for there had to be a new normality in the Hall and Bedley homes now. They weren't the first in the pit village, and wouldn't be the last.

'Aye,' she repeated to herself, looking skywards, her breath puffing out into the cold. She was a pitman's daughter and would get used to her da being up there on that great grey cloud that had settled over the pit village during the night, heralding rain later in the day. He'd be dangling his legs over the side, with Sarah's father, their bodies all mended after the roof fall, chatting over their big day yesterday. Smiling to one another at the memory of their sons and their marrers carrying them up the hill to St Oswald's, while they were tucked safe in their caskets. She reckoned they'd be laughing at the lads panting, longing for a Woodbine as they coughed and spluttered beneath the weight.

She laughed, too, imagining them, two old friends – no, three, for Beth's da, Tubby Smith, would be there too – and whispered towards the cloud, 'Bad do, you old beggars, chewing the cud while you've left our Stan to take your place in the Canary Club. Mark you, Da, it's the beer he'll have with Simon Parrot that's made him take it up with a smile on his face, leaving me to do the hens. Oh, and don't either of you be worrying about a roof over our heads. Mr Massingham says the houses are ours for as long as we need 'em, and the rent cut for the first month, just like always for the widows.'

She stopped by the hen coop on the left-hand side of the yard and scooped out grain from the covered barrel. She chucked it through the wire as the chickens clucked about. 'Young Ben'll maybe help me, but not Mam, so I say again, don't be worrying, Da, eh? We'll be keeping an eye on her, every minute, making sure she gets over this, like she did the babe she lost. Don't want you pushing your nib in, checking up one dark night and frightening everyone to death. You just rest. You've done your bit.'

Her voice faltered on the last word, but she swallowed and braced her shoulders. She replaced the barrel lid before walking to the gate and lifting the sneck to head for the Bedleys' house. There she'd pick up the girls and Davey Bedley, her beloved lad.

She strode along the back lane, quiet now except for the workings of Auld Hilda, the Massingham pit: the winding gear that was bringing up the coal and taking down the pitmen in the cages, the banging and crashing of the surface screens where the pitmen separated the coal from the slate and dust, the whistle of the train heading for the main line . . . She breathed in the smell of sulphur and coal. It was the air of her hometown, and she watched the wind whipping at the slag heap, where the coal dust and refuse was dumped. Aye, it was all the same, but not the same.

She looked back at the pithead and whispered, 'You keep my brother Stan safe when he's back on shift tomorrow, Auld Hilda, because you didn't do too good a job with our da. Aye, better ratchet up yer game—' She stopped, because at least her da hadn't died of black lung, which had been his and Tom's fear. She said now, but quietly, 'Ah well, maybe you did us a favour after all, Hilda. Da's cough was getting worse, so I'll let yer off this once. But don't you dare tek any more of me family, you hear me?'

Fran hurried on, thinking that if anyone heard her they'd think she'd gone mad. It was 9 a.m. and the fore shift had clip-clopped in their boots along the back lane long before it was light, their murmuring drowned by the hooter. Would Bell Seam, which her da and Tom had been survey-ing when the wall and roof caved in, be reopened? It had

3

only been half worked out and would be good for many more tons once they shoved up more props. So, probably – after all, wars needed coal.

What would the investigation reveal? Who knew. Probably nothing, for the heap of coal would have destroyed much of the reason behind the fall.

She turned up her mac collar and hurried into Main Street. Ahead was the shelter where she, Sarah and Beth would normally have queued at 4 a.m. for the bus to the munitions factory. Beth should really have gone into work today, for her da had died of black lung a few weeks before, but Miss Ellington, the senior security officer on their sector, had given her a dispensation.

'Of course she did,' Fran muttered to herself. 'We three come as a package.'

In her shoulder bag she had spam sandwiches left over from yesterday's funeral tea; the corners were curling, but they'd been outside in the meat safe where the bitter cold of December would keep the spam fresh enough. She turned right into Sarah's back lane, her boots clopping on the cobbles.

Ben, their twelve-year-old brother, would meet them by the turning that led out of Massingham towards the beck. He was with George, his marrer, right this minute, trying to crack a crossword that Davey had set to keep the lad's mind away from sadness and to keep things as normal as possible.

There it was again, that word. It was normal that her mam was a widow now. It was normal that her da was safe, out of the pit. She looked up at the clouds, grinned and shouted, 'You lot better behave, and not go throwing down any more snow, just out of devilment.'

She stopped because Davey, her Davey, had swung out of his back gate and was hurrying towards her, his cap set to the left, but then something in his face changed. He slowed and, when he reached her, hesitated. He gripped her hands when normally he would have held her close.

She stared at him, but he looked away. She started to say, 'Davey, why—' but stopped, for he was grieving too. It had to be no more or less than that.

'Bonny, bonny lass,' he muttered. 'God, I wish I'd never left for me war work, never seen a bliddy code, never been put forward for Bletchley. Oh, damn, forget I even breathed that, for no one should know. But you do, of course you do, I told yer, because you're me lass.' He looked so strange, so preoccupied. Then he muttered, 'Come on, Fran, they're waiting.' He sounded hopeless, though after the funeral they'd found their usual support and love in one another. But *was* it their usual love? Was he still thinking of how the boss's son, Ralph Massingham, had pursued her? 'Shut up, Franny Hall,' she muttered to herself. Their fathers had just died – nothing was the same.

Davey had turned around and was hurrying to the Bedleys' back yard ahead of her, but now he flung over his shoulder, 'You talking to yerself these days, Franny?'

Fran shrugged. Normally she would have assumed he was teasing her out of love – but now? 'I were chatting to your da, my da and Beth's,' she fibbed. 'Telling them not to throw any snow down out of devilment, then telling meself to shut up.' Davey swung round and laughed, walking backwards, a great booming laugh – the first since he'd rushed back from Bletchley Park for the funeral. 'Aye, right enough. Devilment, eh? Careful what you say or St Peter's likely to banish them all down to where it's dark and fiery.'

'Aye, well, they'll feel right at home there, eh? Like being in the pit.' They looked at one another, recognising the pain, the misery, but also the laughter. Ah, now it was as it used to be. Or almost. She held out her hand, but he turned away and her heart sank. So, he *must* be thinking of Ralph, but she'd only been 'friendly' with him because he had threatened to tell his father that her da had poached one of Mr Massingham's sheep, and Davey knew this. And all 'being friendly' meant was that she had let Ralph walk her home. Now her da was dead, so that wasn't going to happen any more.

Davey pushed open the Bedleys' back gate and entered his da's, no – Fran stopped the thought – his mam's yard. Stan was standing by the bikes, which leaned against the rusted downpipe on the back wall. He was smoking, watching his blonde-haired Sarah as though he was taking a long drink, something that would sustain him all day, as she pulled the scarf up over Beth's ears and the woollen hat down, until only Beth's eyes and nose showed. Sarah almost crooned, 'There you go, pet. Might not be the best look in the world, and you could rob a bank and not be identified, but at least you'll not catch your death—'

Stan interrupted. 'Howay, we've had enough of that to last a lifetime.' Beth said, pulling the scarf down again, 'What, Stan, robbing a bank?'

Sarah elbowed her. 'Aye, that'll be it.'

Stan dragged out his Woodbines and waved them. Davey took one, cupped his hands around Stan's match and both lads inhaled, the wind lifting Davey's cap just enough to show his hair, which was the same colour as his sister's.

Fran looked around. Here they all were, the gang that had been formed years ago, the Halls with their dark hair, the Bedleys so fair, and Beth Jones somewhere in the middle with her red hair, but it was almost as though they were floating. Yes, Fran thought, or so they'd all said to one another last evening whilst the neighbours were scoffing the spam tea at the club. Things weren't quite real, and that's probably all that was wrong with Davey. After the funeral, Fran and he had talked about the whelp's – Ralph's – unwanted attentions, and Davey had seemed to understand.

The three girls waited together, arms linked, their breath mingling, watching the two men untangling the bikes, each of them with a Woodbine dangled from the corner of his mouth, and Fran clutched at the thought that even when Davey returned to the south, the three of them would have one another. What's more, Ralph would really have to leave her be, for not only was her da dead, but the sheep her da had shared out amongst the villagers shortly before the accident had actually been Massingham road kill, and therefore not poached after all.

Sarah slipped her arm around her. 'Are you thinking of Ralph?' she whispered.

'Don't, bonny lass,' muttered Beth. 'He's no hold over you now.'

Fran looked from one to the other. 'But Davey's so distant this morning . . . it's as though he still blames me.'

Sarah pulled her close, whispering, 'Howay, pet, me brother's just bereft. We're all bliddy well struggling, all finding our way, but we're all together. And we've a good job an' all, earning enough money to keep our families, as long as we stay in the dangerous sectors and get the extra pay.'

'Oh aye,' Beth said, 'with the detonators that can blow off our hands at any time, eh, and bliddy Mr Swinson being bossy enough to stop the bliddy Nazis in their tracks.'

Fran joined in. 'No, he wouldn't do that, he *is* a bliddy Nazi, the way he behaves.'

They were laughing again and for a moment Fran rested her head against Sarah, who said, 'We'll all be fine, of course we will.'

The three girls turned to watch the boys as the lads ground out their dog-ends, seeing Stan punch Davey lightly on the shoulder and say, 'Come on, Davey, you've only a few hours with us, so perk up and join in. We're the cream, you know, not like that crowd you're running with down south.'

At his words, Fran saw Davey's face stiffen. Was his distance nothing to do with Ralph? Had he met someone else down in Buckinghamshire, someone smarter and more interesting? Perhaps it had made him realise how small Massingham was, how boring, and she with it.

Beth pulled Fran close. 'Stop mithering it in yer head, Fran. I can see it writ all over your face. Everyone's just in a do . . .'

Fran took her bike from Stan who said, 'Davey mended yer puncture, so tis as well you left it here before . . . Well, everything happened, eh?'

There was a silence. Everything? Aye, that summed it up, Fran thought, but said, 'Puncture?'

Davey smiled, his eyes meeting hers, but only for a moment. 'Aye, a slow one I reckon, didn't tek a minute. I were glad to do it, Fran.' He came to her, his hand out-stretched, and she moved to grasp it, but all he did was to drag her bag and gas mask from her shoulder. 'Lord above, what's in the bag? It's heavy enough to be the crown jewels.'

'Close, Davey,' Sarah smiled. 'It holds delicious and delightful spam sandwiches. Our Fran did as she said an' all, and snuck out some sherry and a bottle of beer from the tea, just for us. Our Fran always does as she says, you know. You can trust her in a way yer canna trust most people.'

The boys waved the girls through the gate. Stan said, 'Get a move on, then. Sooner we get there, the sooner we can have some, eh, Davey?'

The three girls rode side by side along the back lane and out onto Main Street, where the snow was still heaped at the sides, last night's scatterings flattened by what traffic there had been. Fran, in the middle, listened while Beth talked of the letter she'd received from her husband, who could not say where he was, or what he was doing, but he was safe. 'A lot of blacked-out words, but they left in "With love, Bob".'

They all laughed.

Aye, safe for now, Fran thought. Be safe. That's what the wives of pitmen in Massingham said as their men headed out the door, but now, in wartime, everyone else must say it too. Be safe, for no one was. But at least the three mothers would carry that fear no more as they worked on their rugs, did their ARP work or made jam for the WI war effort, or whatever they all did to keep the ranges burning. Or the home fires, as Ivor Novello's song had urged in the First War.

She hummed as she pedalled towards the beck road, keeping pace with the other two girls. Beth said, riding next to her, her voice juddering as she cycled over the frozen clods of earth that had dropped from tractor wheels, 'I wonder how the others are getting on at the Factory? And I reckon Davey must be wondering what's—Well . . . Down at . . .' She stopped. No one except Fran and his mam had actually been told what he was doing, but Sarah and Beth had gathered enough from both of them to have their suspicions about code breaking at Bletchley Park, but knew better than to say anything. So much war work was a big fat secret, just like their own at the Factory.

Sarah smiled. 'We've only been away for a couple of days, so they'll be pretty much the same, I reckon. I wonder if Miss Poshness Amelia is going to try and find a way to sing with our choir again, now Miss Ellington is arranging some Christmas canteen concerts and wants us to be the stars for our sector's fore shift.'

Beth nodded. 'By, I don't know about that Amelia, she had me right fooled, she did. So timid and quiet when she were new, but look how pushy she turned out to be. And talk about snobby when the *Workers' Playtime* lot happened along – and her face when we were the ones chosen to sing, instead of her group. I wish we'd never helped her in her early days, that I do, the way she turns her nose up at us factory girls, stuck-up southern lass.'

Fran pedalled harder as they struggled up the incline out of Massingham. 'Well, wouldn't surprise me if she's putting together her own group again, now she's transferred to the office. I'm sure she heard Miss Ellington telling us the pubs are getting singers in some evenings and to get in quick, once we felt up to it.'

The other two girls grimaced, but then Fran muttered that she supposed there was room for them all. At that, the others stared, but then nodded. 'Aye,' Beth said. 'I suppose you're right, we don't want to be as pushy as her.'

Sarah ducked as a crow swooped, then said, her voice almost a howl, 'I know you're right and we shouldn't be pushy, but howay, I canna help it. We'd better practise, and hard. Give the lass an inch and she'll tek a bliddy mile, or that's me thinking.'

Fran and Beth laughed, and Fran said, 'My word, Miss Bedley is firing on all cylinders today, and good to see it. And she's right, so . . .' She burst into song, there and then, as they tore round a bend: 'You better watch out, you better not cry . . .' The other two girls joined in and as they felt the wind shift and get behind them, the men hurried to catch up, joining in the chorus. 'Santa Claus is coming t'pit.'

At the sound of Davey singing, Fran smiled, and then all three laughed, so he sang louder and louder. He was pushing down on the pedals, his cap in his pocket, until he was alongside her, his blue eyes on her, his blond hair flying, and it might have been the same colour as Sarah's, but it wasn't streaked by the munitions chemicals as theirs was.

Fran dropped behind the two girls as he rode no hands, sitting up straight, yanking on his cap, tilting it to the right, grinning as he always had. He reached out, at last. She took his hand and together they rode on as Ben swooped out of the turn to his marrer's house and joined in, calling, 'I could hear the racket miles away, yer daft lot.'

Davey yelled, 'Enough of that. Have you two lads sorted the crossword I set yer?' Fran felt her heart soar with happiness. Davey was back again, her Davey.

Ben came alongside and the wind was almost slicing through them as he panted, 'Course we did. Even got the coded bit.' He overtook them and scooted past the other two girls, yelling, 'Stop yer racket, save yer breath and catch me up, I dare you.'

He set off on his bike and Stan tore after him, shouting, 'Race you, little toerag.'

Ben's laugh was shrill, not quite right. He was only twelve and his da would not be coming home.

Davey still held Fran's hand as they reached the beck. All he wanted was to hold her in his arms and never let go. Never leave and never go back to Bletchley Park – and Daisy. At the thought of Daisy he retreated into himself and let go of Fran's hand, pedalling ahead, his smile gone. He heard her cry, 'Davey, don't . . . Oh Davey, I couldn't help having to be friendly with Ralph, I've told you that . . .'

Stan was leaning his bike against the leafless hedge where birds' nests hung, abandoned until the spring, and Davey skidded to a stop, leaning his bike behind Stan's. He came back for Fran's, not able to look at her. He wasn't worthy. He had been led like a sheep into Daisy's bedroom, while Fran had not let Ralph lead her anywhere so damaging.

He heard the beck running fast and turned to see that snow still clung to the bank, just as it always did at this time of year. He propped her bike against his. The others had fallen quiet and the girls collected dead and rotting sticks for the fire, drawing Fran into their circle while Davey pulled knotted newspaper from his rucksack. He placed it on the bank, which was burned black from the fire they had set just before he travelled to Bletchley Park.

He built the fire with the girls' wood, and Stan lit it. Beth and Ben ran over the bridge to the tree rope that hung motionless on the sheltered bank and Davey watched, wanting to remember every second. This might be the last time he was here with them all, because he couldn't keep facing Fran. Neither could he tell her and risk losing all of this. So whichever way he turned, it was over for him.

Stan yelled across the beck to Ben, 'Don't you bliddy dare swing on that rope, for I'm not diving in for you if you fall. It's running too fast. Come and eat, for Davey's to get his train, so's we only have an hour here.'

Ben yelled back, 'Language.'

The girls laughed. Davey rose from the fire, his bad leg aching, and he was glad, for it took his mind off his stupidity. He watched the flames gain a hold. Fran stood near him, but not as close as she would normally have done. He didn't deserve any better. Stan and Sarah stood to the left of them. Fran whispered, 'Everything's all right, you know, Davey. Ralph's gone from our lives and we have one another, haven't we?'

It really was a question, and one she had never asked him before. What the hell could he say? Did he tell her how he'd woken up on Daisy's bed one morning, after he'd got drunk, the words of the anonymous note telling him Fran was carrying on with Ralph banging around in his head? How the hell could he have been such a fool as to believe that rubbish?

Her eyes searched his face and he turned away, staring

down at the crackling fire, treasuring every moment of her closeness to him, rousing only when Stan yelled, 'What the hell are you doing, Davey? The fire's going out. We need more wood.'

It wasn't just Davey he startled, but Ben and Beth on the farside bank, who stopped and turned. Davey saw Sarah step back from the fire, her scarf falling to her shoulders, calling to Stan, 'Howay, bonny lad, keep your hair on, there's a few more sticks to burn through yet.'

But Stan stormed across to Davey and gripped his arm. 'I said, we need more sticks, I'm bliddy freezing. You lasses, get the sandwiches out, eh, not to mention the booze, cos Davey has to go soon.' All the while he was tugging at Davey, forcing him along until they reached the gateway of Farmer Thomas's field.

It was here, out of earshot of the girls, that he backed Davey against the gatepost so the catch dug into his back. Stan gripped his lapels and shook him as he kept his voice low. 'For the love of God, what's the bliddy matter with you? You've a face like an armpit and that lass, my sister, has had a bliddy awful time balancing that bastard Ralph against keeping the family safe. Let alone almost making herself an outcast from the village for what they thought she was doing with the boss's foul rat of a son. And you, what are you doing, punishing her with your distance one minute, then slobbering over her the next? What do you want her to do, grovel? Well, hell will freeze over before our lass does that, and while we're about it, I've a good mind to give you a bliddy good hiding.'

He almost chucked Davey from him. 'If it's over, Davey, then tell her, but stop blowing hot and cold, and don't pull the grief card, we're all feeling it. Sort it out, lad, because I'm not bliddy well having it for me sister. She's a diamond.'

Davey was fighting for balance, his boots slipping on the

frozen furrows. He recovered and stood his ground, waiting for another go from Stan, all the while looking over the fields to the pit. He wanted to go back in time to when everything was simple, when he could be here for Fran and his family. But how, after what he'd done?

Stan just stood there, strong and quiet, blocking his way to the beck. It was as though they were bairns again – Stan the leader of the gang, knowing how to do everything, and keeping them safe. They trusted him like they had never trusted anyone before or since, for Stan solved all their problems.

He wanted to weep, but men didn't, especially when they'd been daft buggers. He started to speak, but his voice trembled. He swallowed, and Stan's voice was different now, gentle, kind. 'Come on then, our lad. Spit it out.'

Davey shook his head. Stan's voice hardened. 'I'll mek it easy for you. I'll not let you go till you do.'

Suddenly Davey was spilling the words, explaining how he'd had the anonymous note about Fran and Ralph happy together, how Fran had then called the telephone box as usual and wanted to tell him something. 'I cut her off, thought she were to tell me it was over, so I got bliddy drunk, didn't I? Falling over me own feet, I were, and this Daisy from work, she helped me, and took me back to her room—'

Stan grabbed him. 'She bliddy what?'

'I woke on the bed in t'morning, not in it. *On* it. She were making tea or something, and calling me sweetheart. I said she weren't, and she said I'd led her on. But how? I'd always said I were Fran's—'

Stan shook him again. 'For God's sake, Davey Bedley, are you bliddy mad? Come on, be honest, did you lead her on? Did you . . . you know what?'

That was the worst of it, because while Fran had done what she had to, to keep her family safe, he had gone back

14

to a lass's room because he was jealous. He stared at Stan and shrugged, then almost shouted, 'No, I divint. I told you, I were *on* the same bed, whilst from the look of the tumbled bedclothes, she was *in* it. But no matter, I were in the lass's room and my Franny would never have done that. What's worse is that this Daisy says I did . . . well, you know what, and I bliddy didn't.'

Stan let him go. After a moment, he handed him a Woodbine and they both lit up. 'How do you know yer didn't?' Stan asked.

Davey was back in the room, seeing himself, confirming his memory, as he had again and again since then. 'I had me drawers on, see.'

Stan shook his head. 'Yer could have got dressed, yer clown.'

'No, Stan, yer see, I had to sew me drawers up tight because the elastic had gone, and where the hell do you get that, in this bliddy war? To get out of 'em, I had to rip the stitches.' He paused, then said, 'I had odd socks on an' all.'

Stan stared, drew on his cigarette, then exhaled into the wind. 'By, lad, you must have looked a right sight. Odd socks?'

He pulled Davey to him and slapped him on the back as he hugged him. 'Aye, you're not safe to be let out alone, you aren't. Well, you'd best tell our Fran, clear the air, for it's such a bliddy daft story, it has to be true. Tell her, if you still love her. So, do you?'

Davey was fierce now. 'Course I love her, Stan. More'n life itself, but I felt I'd wronged her just by being on the bed with another lass. I know I have to tell her, but she's mourning . . .'

Stan flicked his stub away. It arced through the air and fell on to the ice between two furrows, fizzing before going out. 'Tell her. She's thinking you blame her for Ralph. Tell

15

her.' They looked at the end of Stan's cigarette and Stan muttered, his hands deep in his pockets, jangling his money, 'Bet you can't get yours within a foot of mine. Sixpence on it, eh, Mr Saggy Drawers?'

Davey couldn't, and handed over the money as Stan said, 'You mind, eh. She'll mourn more if you don't cough up the truth.'

They headed towards the girls, who were calling them, but then realised they had no wood to take back. They had a quick scavenge in the hedge, grinning and talking. But as they walked back, Stan said, 'Hang about, what about the note? Weren't there summat you said to me about it at the funeral? What with everything else, I weren't taking much in.'

'Aye, the note I got was anonymous, but at the funeral I recognised the same handwriting on some flowers. It were Amelia's. I've got to tell our Fran about me daftness with Daisy, but what about Amelia? Do I tell our Fran about that?'

Stan shrugged and in doing so dislodged a log from the top of the bundle he was carrying. He stooped to pick it up. 'The girls have their own ideas about her, so I reckon we let it lie, eh, unless it comes up. I'll keep an eye on 'em. Don't you worry. You just have to sort things out with our Fran, because we'll have to set off in twenty minutes if you're to spend some time with your mam. Race you, eh?'

Stan was off, tearing along the bank, with Davey catching up fast. When they reached the girls, they built up the fire before settling down on their macs. Davey pulled Fran to him. They kissed, and he murmured, 'I'm sorry. We'll talk, but 'tis nowt you've done.' Her smile meant everything to him. They ate, drank and toasted their fathers.

It was as they cycled home that Davey began to tell Fran what an idiot he had been. The wind was up and as they sailed down the slope she said nothing at all until he got to the part where he'd sewn up his drawers. Her laugh soared over the wind and probably right up to their fathers.

She held out her hand and said as he took it, 'You're a daft lad, but my daft lad and I've loved you my whole life, so I know when the truth is the truth. That Daisy's a minx, for I believe you. It's in your eyes, my love, my Davey, and what's more, Stan believes you, or you'd not have come back in one piece from t'field.'

Then, though he had said he wouldn't, he spoke of Amelia's anonymous note. Again, she said nothing for a while, but held his hand even more tightly, and as they came into Massingham she said, 'I'm glad you told me. It's best I . . .' She waved her hand towards the girls. 'We know. As the three of us have said before, we might learn to like her again, but we'd be daft to ever trust her.'

Cycling behind, Sarah watched her brother and Fran. They were so strong, so sure and matched one another perfectly. She heard Stan then, who was riding beside her, talking of the beauty of the fields, hoping spring would come early and the harvest would be good, but there was sadness in his voice. It was how she felt too – grindingly sad one minute, missing her da, and then back in the real world the next. As long as Stan was there, she felt safe. She snatched another look at him and he was smiling.

Sarah smiled back. 'I love you, my Stan, and now the Japanese have bombed Pearl Harbor and America's in the war, we're not alone. One day it will be over.'

He grinned. 'I love you, and I canna wait for an end, but we'll just drive on, so we will, and get there.'

And she wished with all her heart that she wasn't such a scaredy-cat. She wished she had the gumption of these friends of hers, and couldn't understand why she hadn't.

Chapter Two

The next morning Sarah Bedley struggled awake from the depths of sleep and lay listening to the pitmen's boots on the cobbles, and smiled. The clatter meant that there had been no fresh fall of snow overnight and the bus journey to work would be trouble-free.

She heard coughs in between the growls of 'Howay, lad.' 'Reet enough?' 'Bliddy cold.' 'I've said it before, and I'll say it again, tis good the Yanks are in it too.' 'Took their bliddy time. Needed a bomb up their arse first, eh.'

Soon Auld Hilda's hooter would sound, and life was as it had always been. She turned on her side, pulling the blanket up over her head against the chill, listening for the sounds of the house, but there were none. She struggled to sit up. What was she doing? The pitmen were on the way to the pit. She should be up for work by now. Why hadn't Mam called her?

She flung back the blankets and stood, feeling almost drunk with tiredness in the predawn gloom. Ice had built up on the inside of the window. Shivering, she dragged on her clothes, then stumbled to the window, waiting to see her da clomping across the yard in the moonlight in his boots, bait tin clanging.

Da? She shook her head. 'Da?' she moaned. For her da was dead. How could she have forgotten, even for a second? How could she sleep when she was heavy with sorrow and her mam was almost off her head with grief? She flew into her mam's room, but it was empty, the bed not slept in.

She took the stairs two at a time, fear clutching at her. Not only had there been no morning call, riddling of the grate or clattering in the scullery, but ... Sarah stopped dead. Surely to God her mam hadn't gone to St Oswald's to sit at the grave as she had wanted to do after Davey had left last night? 'I must go an' all, to sit with yer da,' her mum had screeched, rushing along the hall, 'for he mustn't be alone.'

Sarah had taken her by the shoulders before pulling her along to the kitchen. 'Now hush. We'll tidy the place, bank up the fire and sit together over a cuppa, and then I'll help you to bed.'

Sarah gripped the banister, feeling as though her legs had nothing in them. She listened hard, but there was no sound. Surely not ... This time she took the stairs slowly, trying to shake off her fear. After all, her mam had let herself be settled in her armchair while Sarah tidied up the scullery. Mam'd even wanted to help clear up the boxes of food and drink they'd brought back from the Miners' Club after the funeral tea, but Sarah had hushed her and dragged a kitchen chair over to the dresser. She had put the leftover bottles of sherry and elderberry wine right up on top, which is where, for some reason, her da had always insisted they put any bottles of alcohol.

Sarah had made a pot of tea and they'd shared some honey biscuits before they went to bed. Her mam had murmured on the landing. 'You get some sleep, pet. I'll be all reet. Just need a bit of time to get meself together.'

Sarah listened now, hardly breathing as she drew closer to the kitchen. She should have checked in during the night, but instead she'd slept while Davey had made his way from Newcastle to the south. How could she? How could *he* leave them? 'How bliddy dare he? How bliddy dare Hitler start this bliddy war?'

Sarah slowed, realising she'd spoken aloud. The house was so quiet it almost echoed, and still the fury was rising. It was all well and good for Davey to have hightailed off, but what about her? Please God, don't let her have gone out. Please, please. There looked to have been no more snow, but it was so cold. Too cold. Oh, Mam . . . Oh, Davey . . .

She had almost reached the kitchen door, knowing she must open it, but what if it was empty and her mam was lying frozen beside the road to St Oswald's? She'd have to rush out and search for her, bring her back, nurse her. She could lose her job, which meant losing the house. Sarah's mouth was dry. She tried to swallow, took deep breaths and at last thought of Stan, so strong and calm, and Fran. Fran would breathe in for four, like Mr Hall had taught her to do when she was vexed, and out for four. Sarah did just that, pressing her head against the door.

Calm now, she listened, but there was still no sound. She reached for the handle, wishing someone else was there to go in first. Opening the door just a crack, she peered in. The first thing she saw was darkness – the range was out, the blackout still drawn against the moonlight. Her eyes grew accustomed. Her mam wasn't in her armchair. She stood in the doorway and turned on the light; the clock on the mantelpiece showed three forty-five. Her factory bus went at four. Oh Mam, where . . .

Sarah entered and there her mam was, slumped at the kitchen table, snoring. Her head lay on her arms, she shivered, stirred, grew still. Dribble oozed from her mouth. A sherry bottle lay empty on the floor. The smell of stale drink hung in the air. Sarah spun round and saw the kitchen chair hard up against the dresser. She looked back at her mam and for a moment a dark, distant memory drenched her, but then it was gone. Sarah's legs shook. She reached out, leaning on the table to stop herself from falling. Her mam stirred and Sarah froze. The darkness was back and building, because she recognised something . . .

There was a clatter and she saw that her mam had nudged the empty bottle with her slippered foot. It rolled backwards, then forwards, and slowly she began to remember the noise of a bottle on the flagstones, these flagstones. She recaptured the shape of the table: she a bitty bairn, not even as high as it was, home from school. Her empty bait tin dangling from her hand, trying to learn her two times table in her head and worried for her da and Mr Hall, who were in hospital, hurt in a roof fall.

She had stood in the kitchen and her mam was there, just like she was now, with the bottle rolling at her feet. Sarah hadn't understood, and had picked up the bottle and shaken her mam awake. Her mam had turned and backhanded her, knocking her across the room. It was cold down on the flagstones, lying on the broken glass, which cut and hurt. The blood had run.

Her mam had stumbled up the stairs to bed, leaving Sarah bleeding. Davey had stepped through the door, whistling, but had stopped when he saw. He had run to her and asked what had happened. Sarah lied and said she'd fallen. Later, her mam had asked too and Sarah had said the same, repeating the two times table in her head because the test was the next day. Now, she found herself whispering again. 'One times two is two, two times two is four, three times two is six.'

She'd told her da too that she had fallen when they visited him in hospital and he pointed to her bandaged arm. Her mam had asked again when they'd returned home on the bus. It was as if she might have been remembering, but she hadn't. Sarah had told the same story so often that she had forgotten the truth herself. Even the terror had faded.

21

A terror that was with her now, though, as dark and sour as it had been then.

She watched the bottle, knowing she should pick it up, but instead she watched her mam. It was her da who'd stopped the drinking back then, for he'd come home, patterned with stitched cuts and a plastered leg. He had seen the stitches at the back of Sarah's head – the result of a second 'fall'.

Her heart banged loudly as she looked at her mam again, not wanting to be near this woman. Instead she concentrated on locking that time away again, but couldn't.

Again, she watched the bottle and listened to her mam's breathing. She could feel and smell her da's gentle, clean hands when he had touched her head. He had sent Davey to check the pigeons, and then sent her mam to her armchair. He asked Sarah questions and to him she had told the truth because he was her da and said she must. It was the first and only time she admitted it and he'd whispered, 'Reet, bonny lass, yer free to forget all that's happened, for the load's mine.'

He had sent her out to check the pigeons with Davey. They had fluttered in the dimness of the pigeon loft and purred. Davey said it was cooing. 'But when you're five yer don't know such things,' he'd said. He had tried to lift her so she could see better, but he was only seven.

'I like the word "purring",' she said.

Davey put his arm round her shoulder. 'Aye, well, I like "cooing", so I understand.' To feel his arm was normal. It was safe. So was the loft, which smelled of the birds. When her da limped out to find them, he guided them inside, his hands on their shoulders. The windows were open, the kitchen was clean and her mam was in the scullery, washing pots that had not been washed for days. The bottles were gone.

Her da told them that if they were ever rich enough to

have a bottle of sherry or anything again, it would go up on top of the dresser and though someone could stand on a chair and reach it, it was a matter of trust not to. 'Trust,' he had said. 'Trust is everything.'

Her mam had entered from the scullery and hunkered down, looking into Sarah's face. 'Oh, my poor bairn. I divint remember. I were lost, but 'tis not a good enough reason.'

Sarah had let her mam hold her, and yes, she had almost felt safe, as she used to. Davey had looked from them to his da, who said, 'Woman talk, lad,' and laughed, but it hadn't sounded quite right.

Now her da was gone, Davey too. It was just her mam and her. Her kind mam, for so she had become again, for Da had seen to it. Aye, in time the smell had quite gone and Mam was back.

'One times two is two,' Sarah whispered to herself for courage. Step by step she approached her mam. 'Two times two is four, three times two is six.' She was closer to her mam now. 'Four times two is eight,' she whispered, on a light breath, almost soundlessly. 'Five times two is ten.'

Sweat was sliding down her back. She stopped by the table. 'Six times two is twelve.'

Her mam stirred and Sarah wanted to run out into the cold and the dark. She must find Fran, strong Fran. Or Stan, strong, fearless Stan. Fearless Fran. But instead she whispered, 'Seven times two is fourteen.'

She stooped to pick up the bottle, but it rolled beneath her fingers just as she heard a tap on the door and Beth calling, 'Anyone up? The bus's here, Sarah. Get yer skates on, eh.'

Sarah's hand trembled as she placed the bottle on the table. 'Eight times two is sixteen,' she told herself. Her voice was strange, high-pitched and shaky, as she called, 'Let yourself in, Beth. I need your help, me mam's . . . Me mam's drunk.'

'What did you say?' Beth called, but Sarah's voice wouldn't

work, even though her lips moved. She waited, her hand on the bottle as at last Beth opened the door just a crack and peered round it, taking in the scene. She entered slowly, trying to hide her shock, and stood on the newspaper Sarah had laid down last evening. The ash and snow from the yard stained the print.

For a moment Beth just looked from Sarah to her mam, but then she nodded. It was *her* voice that shook this time as she said, 'By, it's me mam you really need. I'll fetch her while you pull yer coat on. The co-op women'll deal with this for we need to work, pet, now our das are gone. There's nowt else you or I can do here.'

With that, she was gone. Sarah riddled the range, seeing the ash fall through into the ash pan, leaving just clinker. Her mam always riddled the range, to perk it up after a night of being banked. The sweat still slid. 'Nine times two is eighteen . . .'

She shoved newspaper, kindling and then coal into the firebox, opened the air vent and lit the paper, not waiting for it to catch. Instead, she shrugged on her mac, pulling on her hat and wrapping her scarf around her neck, the scarf her mam had knitted; her nice, good and kind mam, the one she was walking across to now. She hesitated, and then leaned down, daring to put her arm across her mam's shoulders, but ready to run.

'Mam, Mrs Smith is coming. The co-op'll look after yer and you must let them. It's just a difficult time and you'll not need the drink again, really you won't. I'm here for you, but we'll have to watch the pennies, eh? No more booze, not if we want a roof over our heads, d'you see?' The woman stirred and Sarah froze. But her mam just moaned, then fell asleep again, a bubble of mucus blowing in and out of her nose. The smell of stale booze was everywhere, but she had not hurt Sarah, no, that she had not done.

There was another tap on the door and this time it was Mrs Smith who entered, Beth's mam. Sarah straightened.

'You best be getting along now, pet.' Mrs Smith stood on the newspaper, slipping her feet from her boots. 'I've sent Beth along to hold the bus and Bert had better take note, or the co-op will want to know why. Don't you be worrying now. Your mam doesn't mean anything by it. We all have our own way of coping, and the co-op'll help her.'

Sarah stood, looked at Mrs Smith and then at her own mam. 'I've just told her we couldn't afford the drink. P'raps that was cruel, but I don't know what else to say?' In her head she'd forgotten where she'd got to in the two times table, and decided to start at the beginning. One times two is two.

'Aye, no one does, not right now. Just like no one knew what to say when my old lad died. Nowt helps much anyhow. You've done well, pet. Now on yer way with you.'

The clock on the mantel showed two minutes to four. The miners on the wartime fore shift still tramped past. Sarah hurried to the back door, dragging her own boots off the newspaper, stepping into them. 'How can I thank you?' she whispered.

'That's enough of that. Your mam, me and Mrs Hall are marrers, so you just go and do your work.'

As Sarah shut the back door behind her, she heard Mrs Smith call, 'Be safe.'

At last Sarah smiled. Two times two is four. Was that right, or had she got muddled? She must start from the beginning again or it could be bad luck. She tore up the back lane, saying to the pitmen, ''Ow do?' and the pitmen murmured in reply, 'Be safe,' when it was the women who usually said it to them.

The world's upside down, she thought, finding herself rubbing her arm where the doctor had stitched her cut all those years ago. He had asked, but she hadn't said – not even when her head had to be stitched too.

She slipped on the cobbles. 'Sarah, sweet Sarah.' There he was, her Stan, jogging towards her, his eyes red-rimmed from his own grief. Behind him Sid and Norm slouched along, smoking their Woodbines. He reached her and held her as the hooter sounded. At the pithead the winding gear was grinding and the sulphur was thick in the air. No, the world wasn't upside down, it was still turning, as it always did. Three times two is six.

She rested against Stan, feeling his strength and his arms around her. No, the world hadn't changed, it was only their lives that had. Stan was here, and he loved her as much as she loved him, so she was not alone. But he wasn't her da, so who would stop her mam?

Stan held her, telling her that Beth had fetched not just her mam to Mrs Bedley but him to Sarah. He held her face and looked down at her. 'Never you fear, we're all together, you, me, the co-op and the girls. That makes us strong, all of us bound together by the glue of years, see.' She did. Stan's lips were dry and cracked from the wind but gentle as he kissed her mouth.

She nodded, wishing she really felt strong. Would she, ever? What about her mam? Would she ever? If not . . .

He hugged her then. 'You concentrate today. Be safe.' He dragged himself from her, and set off after Sid and Norm, turned around to wave, then hesitated, calling, 'Oh, my darling Sarah, don't look so afeared.'

It was not just love she heard, but pity. It was like a blow, and as she watched him backing away from her, she forced herself to stand tall, for her lad didn't need a piece of cling-ing ivy, sucking the lifeblood from him. 'You too, bonny lad,' she called. He hesitated, looked long and hard at her, so she added, 'I'm all reet, daft lad. Strong as a bleedin' ox.'

He grinned then, and looked as though a weight had fallen from him. He waved, caught up with his marrers and they hurried on together. Five times two is ten.

She went on her way, shaking her head at herself. A bleeding ox, eh? Where had that come from? But she didn't care. It had sounded as strong as Fran and if she could just pretend, then maybe she would become so. She refused to spend even a second thinking of her mam, because she was on her way to work and there was no room at the Factory for mithering about other things.

Yes, she thought as she approached Main Street, that sounded more like Fran and Beth. Six times two is twelve. Or had she already done six times? She'd best start from the beginning.

Fran and Beth waited at the bus stop as Bert kept the engine idling. Mrs Oborne stood with them, pulling her scarf around her head, tucking in her hair, which had been cut short. They all wore theirs short these days to prevent it catching in any ordnance machinery. Mrs Oborne said yet again, 'Reckon I should go and help our Maud?'

'Stop worrying, Mrs Oborne, she'll have a bliddy army banging on the door bearing proggy rug frames any minute now. Me mam and Fran's will be leading the charge. Anyways, you're expected at work,' Beth replied.

Mrs Oborne was now wringing her hands. 'I should have known our Maud would look at the funeral bottles that were left over and snaffle a few. I remember last time when Tom Bedley got caught in that rockfall – doubled over he and yer da were, with the weight of the roof on top o' 'em. By, did the lass hit the bottle, but she hid it well, and it weren't till Tom came home and saw how things were that he said he'd be gone and tek the bairns an' all, less'n she stopped. So she found some gumption and struggled and finally put stopper on t'bottle, which 'tisn't easy, if you have the call in you.'

'Call?' Fran queried.

'Oh aye, her own da liked it too much an' all. We should have all remembered just now, and watched her close. We should have taken the booze away from the club ourselves. We, or mebbe I, should have stayed wi' her. It's too much for just one person, especially if yer the afeared sort like yon Sarah.'

She turned as Maisie hurried up behind them. 'Getting on?'

'We're waiting for Sarah,' Mrs Oborne muttered.

'Howay, the wind's too sharp, so I will.'

Mrs Oborne didn't answer but continued, 'It'll be a shock, you lasses, a nasty surprise for yer marrer to have found her mam, for she won't remember the last time, bitty bairns don't, more's the blessing. Poor wee bairn, but come to think on it, p'raps that's what made her afeared. For she were a bit distant, careless, our little Sarah were, and got clumsy if I remember rightly, took a tumble or two . . .' Her voice cracked. 'Life's a right pain, in't it. Aye, we should have remembered.'

Beth slipped alongside and put her arm around Mrs Oborne, who was usually so strong. 'Hush, bonny lass. Sarah will be just fine, and with Stan to show the way she'll grow stronger, and so will her mam, for there's nowt else the woman can do, is there? She has to make rugs more than ever now, to help out Sarah, for it's our lass who has to bear the financial brunt.'

Mrs Oborne smiled at the two girls, though her eyes remained worried. 'Aye, like you and Fran.'

Fran shook her head. 'Stan and me're lucky and can put our money together for Mam and Ben.'

Beth grimaced as though the thought of being the

breadwinner had only just really struck home. 'There's Davey to help the Bedleys an' all.'

'Aye, but he earns bugger all at—' Fran stopped, then added, 'His work, but he'll send what he can, I know he will. Stan and me can help too . . .' She trailed away, her mind in a muddle as thoughts seemed to be rushing in from everywhere, too fast to grab tight. 'But what about you, Beth?'

'I've me allotment from Bob, remember, and we've summat put by and something'll come up if it has to. And I'm not paying rent for me own house now I've moved in with Mam. Get on out of the cold, eh, Mrs Oborne? We'll wait. Fran and me'll deal with it.'

Fran gripped her hand. 'Aye, you and me, pet, we'll deal. We're invincible.' They smiled at one another.

'And Sarah will be too,' said Beth, 'once all the mess is over. It'll maybe make her a wee bit tougher, but until then . . .'

Mrs Oborne bustled her way up onto the bus, stopping by the driver's cab to scold, 'Don't you dare move a muscle till the lass is here, Bert, and then drive like the bleedin' clappers, no toddling along. We've money to earn and a shift to get to on time. Can't have these three lasses going short, not now we can't.'

Bert looked up from his *Sketch* newspaper, his cigarette almost burned to a stub between his thumb and finger. 'You just go and set your arse down, and stop getting yerself all of a mither. Life'll turn out all reet in t'end, and if it doesn't, then it isn't the end. Or so some silly bugger said. Load of bliddy rubbish, if you ask me.'

Mrs Oborne flapped the ends of her scarf at him and set off down the aisle, calling back, 'I didn't. And what a bliddy ray of sunshine you are, I don't bliddy well think.'

Fran and Beth grinned at one another, but Fran muttered, 'It's a right mess.'

Beth stepped closer, whispering, 'Aye, and for a minute I didn't know what were what when I went in, but you could smell the booze. I were shocked because I thought all our mams were so strong, and listening to Mrs Oborne just then shows it isn't the first time. Poor Sarah. If we're shocked, she must be . . . I canna imagine . . . But if we'd known, we'd have stayed with her.'

Fran said, 'Aye, but that's just one night. What's to do about the rest of time?'

For a moment they looked at one another and Beth's eyes filled as she whispered, 'Oh, Franny, we're so lucky, but we'll do what we have to, to help.'

Fran turned, looking along the road for Sarah. She swallowed down the worry and sadness, and then felt Beth slip her arm through hers. Together they paced back and forth on the ash that had been spread to stop them slipping on the snow. Fran pictured the back lane cobbles, which had been cleared by the occupants of the terraces. It was what the Massingham neighbours did, and always would do, so no one was ever really alone.

She looked at the wasteland behind the bus shelter, covered in snow. It was clean, beautiful in a way it never was in reality. Thoughts of Mr Bedley putting his foot down with his wife kept intruding. He was gone. Davey too. Who could stop Sarah's mam this time? She swung round as Bert hooted and called, 'Here comes the lass.'

Sarah was half running, half sliding along Main Street and Beth muttered, 'Well, we canna worry about it, or let our Sarah, not when we're at the Factory, or we'll make mistakes. We've to trust the co-op ladies'll to sort it, they usually do.'

Fran laughed. 'Oh aye, better than a regiment of front-line troops, I reckon.' At the thought of their mothers, both girls pushed back their shoulders and walked to meet Sarah.

They heard Bert grinding the gears behind them as he followed them along the road, braking when they reached her. The two girls shoved her onto the bus, then followed in time to hear the women singing 'All or Nothing at All', which The Factory Girls choir, led by Fran, Beth and Sarah, had sung for the wireless when *Workers' Playtime* had broadcast to the nation from the Factory.

The women continued to sing as they smiled and waved. Mrs Oborne had saved seats for them a few rows from the front; Sarah sat with Fran while Beth plonked herself down next to Mrs Oborne. Fran eased herself on to the wooden slats. 'Why aren't I used to these seats? Why don't I ever remember to bring a cushion?' she asked Sarah.

Sarah dug her in the ribs. 'The same words fall from yer mouth most days, our Fran.'

She sounded firm, almost strong, and Fran half smiled as she replied, 'Aye, pet. And trouble is, it's the same ruddy slats and nowt'll change till I fetch that cushion.'

The two of them laughed together and Fran relaxed. She had thought she'd have to be brave for the two of them, and she wasn't entirely sure she could be. Not without her da at home, at least not for a while.

Bert picked up speed as they travelled towards Sledgeford to collect more for the Factory. Now the women were singing 'A-Tisket, A-Tasket', which seemed a good balance to the programme for the Christmas Day show at the Factory, in just a few days' time. Miss Ellington had arranged to have it in the canteen, making sure they were all down for the fore shift and could perform at the lunch break. There would be other singers from each shift for their own meal-break concerts. Sarah nudged Fran and tipped her head towards the other women. 'I know they've all heard about Mam.'

Fran stopped singing. 'Oh aye, the telegraph's been

buzzing, but it's kindly meant. I wish I'd known about . . .' Fran stopped, lowered her voice and whispered, 'Mrs Oborne remembered the last time yer mam got too involved with the bottle, yer see. Beth and me, well, we'd have stayed with you if we had known. Mrs Oborne said yer were only a bitty bairn, and got a bit worried like, said you were a bit clumsy and took a tumble or two . . .'

Sarah looked relieved and nodded. 'Aye, that's what it was. Tripped over me own feet . . .'

'Well, just look where yer going, eh.' Fran shook her arm. 'Don't want yer doing that with a pot of explosives.' She was grinning.

Sarah shook her head. 'I should have remembered clearer. I'd have tipped the bliddy sherry down the sink. But I went to bed, so I did, because I was whacked and I just wanted to think of me da for a bit. Then when I saw her this morning . . .' She petered out.

Fran listened to the singing for a while as the bus chugged along past the wall where the Massingham sheep had broken free and one had got killed – the one the village had eaten. Was it really only a few weeks ago? She closed her eyes for a moment, then said quietly, 'But don't fret. Our mams and the co-op'll come up with a plan, they always do. By, they could run the world, they could, with their arms tied behind their backs.'

Mrs Oborne called out over the singing, 'We need to talk to Miss Ellington. Mark you, we'll have to curtsey because she's been shoved up a rung of the ladder, did you know? Now she's the senior sector security officer. Meks little difference, the job's still the same, she says, just busier. Anyhow, we need to talk to the lass about how many songs we need for Christmas Day. She were waiting for you to come back to sort it. Won't be too many, eh, for only half an hour? But I'll need to get me conducting arm ready, an' all.'

Before the girls could answer, they heard Bert shouting from the cab, 'She needs to belt her old man a bit more, eh, girls? That'll sort out the auld besom's arm.'

'Old besom indeed. Less of yer cheek, you old beggar,' Mrs Oborne shouted back.

Bert yelled again, changing down the gears to slip-slide around the Hanging Tree. 'You want to walk, do you?' All the women were laughing now, the song forgotten, but then they hushed one another as Bert shouted, 'Hush yer noise, this is important. Hush it.'

When they finally settled, he said, 'Our Stevie at the Rising Sun in Minton has been let down by the group that was to sing on New Year's Eve. They were called up, or two of 'em were, so not much you can mither about. He asked did I know anyone? I said yes, Beth, Fran and Sarah'd do it, I said, if he paid. Don't you dare say no, for your das are gone and you need some more money to help with costs. What d'yer say? I haven't a tin ear so can hear you're all practising yer stuff for the Factory doings. I reckon you can sing those songs and a few more an' all. The rest of you can come and bring your blokes along, put summat in the bucket for the widows of this year's pit accidents, as is usual on Hogmanay.'

Maisie called from further down the bus, '*Stuff*, the man said. He called our songs *stuff*.'

They were all laughing again now, even Fran, Sarah and Beth. Sarah murmured, 'Yes, because that's what pitmen's daughters do.'

Beth looked across the aisle, puzzled. 'What do we do?'

'We laugh and we go on,' Sarah said quietly.

Fran just nodded, hoping that this really was how Sarah felt. The two of them sat quietly together and Fran thought she heard Sarah mutter, 'Ten times two is twenty.'

Then Fran heard Beth singing, her voice soaring loud and true, 'All or nothing at all,' and she nudged Sarah. 'Ready?'

The two of them joined in, and with Mrs Oborne making the drumming sound, the others on the bus hummed as they had done for *Workers' Playtime*. When they reached the end, they applauded one another just as the bus entered Sledgeford. Slowing down as he neared the bus stop, Bert flicked yet another Woodbine stub out of the driver's window, muttering about the ingratitude of women objecting to 'stuff'. He added, 'Me words is like pearls before swine.'

Bert drew to a stop outside the Sledgeford club, where the other Factory girls were waiting, and Mrs Oborne called that she had a sock she'd stuff in his mouth if he went on mithering like this. The girls were clambering into the bus as Bert yelled, 'Don't you bring yer sock anywhere near me mouth, Tilly Oborne. Just give me an answer, you three girls. I need to let Stevie know.'

Fran, Sarah and Beth looked at one another and nodded. Fran started to call out, then stopped. 'You tell him, Sarah.'

For a moment Sarah looked alarmed, but Fran urged, 'Go on, you know what to say as well as either Beth or me, and everyone's fed up with hearing our voices.'

Sarah nodded, breathed in and out, then called, 'Thank you, Bert. We're really thankful to you for suggesting us and aye, we'll be there. Just give us the time when you know it, eh? Will you tell Stevie, or will we?'

'Leave it to me. Just be there at half seven,' Bert yelled.

The Sledgeford women were asking what Bert was on about as they continued onto the bus. The Massingham workers got busy telling them about the Rising Sun at Hogmanay until Amelia climbed aboard and the talking stopped. What on earth was she doing on their bus? Fran wondered. The office hours were nine to five, so she shouldn't be there. The Factory girls' heads leaned in together as whispers gained ground.

Mrs Oborne called as Amelia drew alongside her seat, 'So,

34

what's to do, lass? Back in with the Factory workers, are yer? That'll be a blow for yer after telling the producer of *Workers' Playtime* you were no "mere factory worker", weren't it?'

Even the idling engine seemed to hush as Amelia flushed, forcing a laugh. 'I'm such an idiot, forgive me. It wasn't meant. No, I'm having to make up time for when I took Sarah and Fran's places in the sewing shop so Mr Swinton could have no excuse for not allowing them to go to hospital when Davey was hurt.' The whispering began again as Amelia moved a couple of steps along, stopping beside Fran and Sarah. 'I'm so pleased to see you back at work after your fathers' deaths. So brave, and such a moving funeral service. My commiserations.'

Fran looked at her and saw . . . what was it she saw in those hazel eyes? Contrition? Well, suddenly she felt it too. Amelia had indeed supported them. Perhaps she should let insults be bygones and forget that the girl had sent Davey the anonymous message? Amelia waited, pale and tired like the rest of them, but unlike them, she had no community or nearby family to turn to.

Pity dragged at Fran and she decided that she must give Amelia another chance and say nothing to the others about the note. After all, it was only things like the deaths of their das and Mrs Bedley's drinking that were real problems, so she said, 'Then thank you, from all three of us . . .'

Fran looked over to Beth and then Sarah, both of whom nodded reluctantly.

'I'm so glad,' Amelia said now. 'Life's too short to be petty, don't you think? And while—'

Fran winced, wanting to shake the girl. Bert's voice cut across Amelia: 'I'm upping anchor, girls. Got to make up time. And you three, remember that Stevie's pub is called the Rising Sun. Don't go to the Travellers' Rest, eh?'

The bus moved and Amelia was pushed from behind by

Valerie, in whose house she lodged. 'Shift along. We'll be tossed to the ground when Bert roars round the bends.'

'I 'eard that,' shouted Bert. 'It's our Cecil you need to worry about. Thinks he's on a bleedin' racetrack, he does.'

Again there was laughter and as though at a signal, the chatter began again. The women moved along the aisle and Fran heard Amelia ask, 'What's happening at the Rising Sun?'

Maisie replied from the back, 'The three of them have a booking for Hogmanay, so they'll sing the songs we've been rehearsing for Christmas. You and those other two office girls are doing something for Christmas too, aren't you, for the aft shift?'

The three girls heard Amelia say, 'Well, it's all changed, actually. I was worried that with the grief the girls might find taking centre stage at lunchtime too much. So I volunteered our group to share the burden of their concert. The deputy section manager, Mr Bolton, said we have ten minutes, while Fran, Sarah and Beth have twenty, but we're able to step in for longer if necessary.'

Over the rising tutts, Sarah muttered, 'I'll bliddy kill her for muscling in, so I will, and don't you dare talk me into being fair to her ever again, you daft woznot, Fran Hall.'

Chapter Three

It took another hour and a half to reach the Factory and dawn was not yet breaking when Bert pulled off the road, bumping in and out of the siding potholes. The workers trooped from the bus, variously calling out, 'Goodbye, me old duck' and 'Be good, Bert.'

'He canna,' called Mrs Oborne. 'Divint know what it means.'

Valerie shouted out from the bottom step, 'Then if he can't be good, he'd best be careful.'

Bert's loud blast on the horn made them all jump and then laugh as they hurried towards the guarded gates. Other guards patrolled the fence that ran around the complex, but Beth barely noticed them – they were part of the furniture now. She muttered this to the other two and Fran murmured, 'Strange-looking chairs.'

Beth grinned. 'Aye, with moving legs.' She was glad they were back at work and life could go on as normal. Then she shook her head, looking at the guards examining the passes and shoe bags of the first in the queue before lifting up the red and white pole to admit them. Normal? Aye, well, what was normal these days? But at least there was no one else left to die. Beth stopped abruptly and Mrs Oborne bumped into her.

'Howay, lass, what's up?'

Beth was dragged on by Fran and Sarah. 'What's the matter?' Sarah asked.

'Oh, nowt, just had a stone in me boot.' Because there

was Bob, her husband, who could die. There was Stan in the pit, and there was Davey, doing heaven knows what. There were all these women, including the three of them, filling or preparing munitions . . .

She looked up at the sky and could imagine her da shrugging, coughing and then saying, 'It is what it is, pet.'

It was their turn to show their passes to the guards and they were admitted. Ahead were acres of single-storey brick huts and the area that contained what looked like several sunken, turf-covered air raid shelters, but which were in fact where shells and bombs were filled with explosives. Sunken because an explosion would be more contained, thereby avoiding blasting any of the other munition workshops into oblivion. There were others further along too, near the woods, where the chemicals were stored on delivery. They were not supposed to know any of this, but they had eyes and ears, though they also knew better than to use their mouths in this age of secrecy.

Were they going to plant spring flowers over the top of them all once the snow thawed, as they had done with the Anderson shelters dug into gardens? One of the allotment holders had said he would grow tatties on the top of his, but he'd piled the earth so deep it had collapsed the roof. Beth laughed aloud at the thought. Fran murmured, 'Talking to yerself's the first sign of madness, and laughing's when we send for the men to tek you away.'

Sarah linked arms with Beth. 'Howay, pet, what's got you going?'

Beth told them as they followed the others along the wide roadway, which had been cleared of snow by the maintenance men. They had banked it up on either side, but snow still lay on the flat roofs of the Factory's blocks. The pathways that led to each sector's work areas were clear, though. They followed Mrs Oborne, Valerie and Maisie, who were screaming with laughter at something, and Amelia, who walked alone, her hands in her pockets.

Amelia called goodbye as she headed towards the office and Beth suspected that within her big handbag were the high heels in which she usually tottered about.

Once inside the changing rooms, they hung up their macs, scarves and hats and shoved gloves into pockets and boots onto the racks to drip on the newspapers that covered the floor beneath. Already hanging up on hooks were the night shift's outer clothes, but these wouldn't be removed until this fore shift was ready to take over at the workbenches, for not a minute's production could be wasted, such was the demand as the war progressed.

They removed all hairgrips, pins, matches and anything else that could create a spark, and checked one another, all of which was second nature by now. At last there were individual boxes provided for all these bits and pieces, instead of tatty envelopes. All the while the clock ticked on from five forty-five. Miss Ellington entered with SO Mrs Raydon, both in their black overalls, to check their clothing. Mrs Raydon said, as per usual, 'No underslips or stockings can be silk or nylon, which are capable of creating static.'

'Fat chance,' called Maisie, as per usual.

They no longer had to strip off and dress again, as had been insisted upon for a few weeks. It was too time-consuming and clothing could easily be checked before the blue cotton overalls were donned. By five fifty-three they were ready to follow Mr Swinton, the foreman, who had appeared at the door, his green overalls looking as though he starched and pressed them every morning. Beth wondered if he laid them beneath the mattress to give that impression. It was what her da had always done with his funeral suit the night before 'seeing off' a friend. She pushed the wrenching thought aside.

Mr Swinton stood in the doorway and put up his hand, as though stopping traffic. He pointed to Beth, Fran and Sarah, all the while looking as though he had the worries of the world on his shoulders; either that or he had a blinding headache, which was strange as normally he was ferocious. Whatever was wrong, he probably thought the three of them were to blame. They braced themselves, for this man had loathed them since his son, Tim, had been beaten in the Massingham scholarship exam by Stan and, of course, Davey, who had chosen to stay with his crosswords and the pit.

'I see Hall and Bedley have returned, not to mention Smith having had another day or two away. Well, due to their absence I feel I must go through all the rules and regulations in case their memories need refreshing. After all, it's my task to keep you all safe and up to the mark.' Up went his hand again as groans erupted. 'Not my fault, so less of that. If someone has been absent, then I have a duty to, well, refresh their understanding of the rules.'

His hands were now in his pockets, bunched into fists as they so often were. It was as though Swinton could hardly contain his anger or stress, both of which Fran in particular seemed to spark. But, Beth thought, it wasn't Fran's fault that Stan had been to Oxford University on the scholarship while Tim Swinton had liked dressing up in the uniform of the British Union of Fascists, or so it was said around Massingham.

Swinton was getting ready for his soapbox oration, rising on his toes as he always did. 'Safety is prime, and it's not my fault if today you are late to your workstations and your pay is docked. For that's what happens if people take liberties with their timekeeping in wartime. Rules are rules.' His voice wasn't as harsh as usual, though. In fact, it seemed as if he was sorry they might lose wages, but that couldn't be the case. Beth wondered if he'd had bad news, but Tim wasn't in the services. Though what the lad was doing, they neither knew, nor cared for that matter.

Swinton was dragging his hand across his forehead, as though rubbing away a thought. He rose on his toes again, his face back to being fierce, and barked, 'So, you'll listen, got it? Yes, that's right, listen.'

Beth sighed. Perhaps it had been indigestion? Miss Ellington was stepping close to him, her voice low but carrying. 'If this runs late, these women must be allowed their full wages because they were here well before time. You could waive the rules, for heaven's sake. The night shift will also need an increase in pay as they'll have to remain for the extra minutes. So, think on, Mr Swinton, for someone will need to sign off on the delay and it won't be Mrs Raydon or me. I presume you will consult with Mr Bolton?'

It only took a moment for Mr Swinton to make a decision, and with a snatched look at the clock he flew through the rules, ticking them off on his stubby fingers. 'Do not speak of your work or where the complex is situated and what it is that you do here. If it is discovered that you have divulged any information useful to the enemy it could mean prison. The country has enemies within as well as without who will thwart the war effort if at all possible. We are not a sieve, we're a factory, so make up your own lies to family and friends. Say you're making cooking pots, for all I care. But never, ever speak of what goes on, trivial or not. Never, for we don't know who is digging for details.'

For a minute he sounded scared, thought Beth, puzzled. What was the matter with him? He was up and down like the cages at the pit. Had there been a warning that was being kept from the workers? Well, it wouldn't be the first time. War was war.

But then he continued, 'Just do your work, that's all you have to do, safely.' He was jabbing with his finger.

41

Fran put up her hand. 'Please, Mr Swinton, surely to say we're making pots would give the show away? We've been asked to collect them up and give them to the Spitfire effort, so why would we be making them where we—'

Mr Swinton almost screamed, jabbing his finger Fran's way, 'There's always one with a clever blabby mouth and it's always you, so . . . so . . . just shut it.'

There was a general relaxation into smothered laughter. Good old Fran, Beth thought, moving up close to her. She could always puncture his pomposity.

Mr Swinton carried on, wiping his mouth as though to free it of his fury.

Beth wondered where Fran got her strength from, for it was the same as Stan's, the head of their gang. But she was just like her mam and da, of course. As Swinton continued, she found herself thinking of Stan, once her boyfriend, and cringed at what a fool she had made of herself, thinking he'd returned to Massingham from the university for her. No, he'd actually come back to work in the pit for the war, since his leg had been so damaged in the coal fall that had also hurt Davey that neither man was suitable for active service. Stan was with Sarah now, and they made a good couple. And so did she and Bob. Of course they did.

Mr Swinton coughed and Beth heard him say, 'Remember, you do not traipse about the premises alone. If you require the conveniences you will be accompanied, for who amongst the workforce might have been corrupted by our enemies?' Was he looking at Fran? Oh, for heaven's sake. But no, his gaze was travelling around them all until he snatched a quick glance at the clock, and finished in a great rush: 'You must concentrate each and every minute. Check yourselves and your friends for metallic objects that have not been removed. Carelessness costs lives – and limbs. Hold up your arm, Miss Ellington.'

Miss Ellington stared at him while the women gasped. Even Mr Swinton knew he had gone too far as the security officer raised her handless arm. Flustered, he waved it back down and rushed on. 'You are here to fill weapons with explosives. If you drop anything, or cause a spark, especially when working on something like a detonator, you will cause an explosion. To drop a tray of explosives is to tragically destroy your own life, and the lives or limbs of others.' For one awful moment Beth thought he was going to point to Miss Ellington again, but he swept on. 'Our walls between the uprights are designed to give way to prevent a total building collapse, but nevertheless vital war work would be interrupted. Therefore, you must *concentrate*, because as well as all of this, we can't have flawed weapons going to the front . . .'

He trailed off, glancing at the clock. 'Six o clock. Quickly now, to your designated workshops. Pellets for you three, and you too, Mrs Oborne, Valerie and Maisie.' He pointed at Beth and her two marrers, then shoved his hands back in his pockets. 'The rest are where you were yesterday.'

Fran snatched a look at Sarah and whispered, 'He's right. Today you must concentrate and not even think of what's going on with yer mam, for I'm not taking you back to our Stan in a brown paper bag.'

Sarah smiled, though it didn't reach her eyes. 'I don't want you to, an' all.'

Fran turned to Beth. 'And the same goes for you, madam.'

'Aye, and you,' Beth retorted. 'Our Davey would be in a right do if you weren't around to keep him on the straight and narrow. What's more, I don't want you dripping through the bottom of the soggy brown bag either. I've only got one mac.'

They laughed as they pulled on turbans to cover their hair and headed for the workshop where they would wrap fuse pellets designed to charge detonators, and Beth felt relieved to be back and busy; to have to think of other things, with no time to worry about Mrs Bedley or their das. But then she paused. She'd never heard Mr Swinton talk of tragedy or nag so much about safety and security. Had someone in his family died too? She realised that you never knew what was happening in the lives of others and it was a strange thought where Swinton was concerned. Or had his wife come back, having left him a year or so ago, and he was none too happy about it? Or was Tim in trouble? So many questions and no anwers.

They passed the same old posters on the walls exhorting them to Be like Dad – Keep Mum or to Dig for Victory, when Beth noticed there was a new notice pinned on the bottom of one. It reminded those in work on Christmas Day that there would be entertainment at the meal break of each shift. Sarah murmured, 'We should sing some carols as well as our programme, or take a few out to make room. It makes people sentimental, and if there's to be a bucket at the Rising Sun for all the pit widows, we should have one here an' all.'

Fran said quietly, 'By, that's a grand idea. The vicar can distribute it. Do you remember singing "Away in a Manger" at the school party, Beth and me wearing our mams' tea towels on our heads because we were shepherds, while you had a blue cloth on yours, Sarah, because you were always good, so you were Mary?' The girls were laughing as they walked along.

They walked into the pellet shop with Mrs Oborne, Valerie and Maisie, as well as others from a different bus, and took the places of the night shift, who managed weary smiles. Mary Adkins murmured as she passed the girls, 'All yours, and I'm sorry for yer loss, all three of you.'

The girls took up their places and immediately got to

work pasting the fluted paper around the inch-long cylindrical pellets that would eventually be put into the noses of shells or guns, they were never told which, or what. Beth hated the little beggars and tried to ignore the chemical mixture coating her fingertips, knowing that by the end of their shift they would be yellow, and that somehow it would aggravate the rashes they all still had from before the funerals. How could the chemicals travel so quickly through the body? And how had Mrs Hall known that sphagnum moss would help?

She asked Fran as music played over the tannoy. Fran placed a pasted pellet on the stand and started another. 'Ah, well, it's from the First War. Apparently, the families had been digging it up from the moors for years and years, drying it on racks to use as dressings to draw infection. It's an antiseptic and healer, too. Mam worked in the hospitals, you see, with the soldiers, and the nurses remembered it and used it there for septic wounds.'

On the other side of Beth, Sarah was busy pasting. 'Aye, so if we scratch and the rash gets full of pus, we'll just put on more of the mams' mixture.' She winked at Fran, who grinned.

Beth placed a pellet in her stand. 'Aye, well, that's just put me off me dinner, so I almost don't care what's on the menu.'

Maisie could always be relied on to know, though no one knew how. 'Well, I care,' she volunteered, 'and 'tis shepherd's pie, with a sight more pie than shepherd.'

Everyone along the workbench laughed. Beth asked, as she so often did, 'But how *do* you know?'

Maisie touched her nose with her finger and they all shouted, '*No.*'

Miss Ellington hurried over with her pail and cloth. She wiped Maisie's nose and hands. 'Don't do it again. Can't have it getting in your eyes.'

Fran asked, although she always got the same answer, 'So, what is it?'

'Ah well, that's for me to know and not you, canny lass,' Miss Ellington replied.

Beth called along to Maisie, who was rolling her shoulders to ease the cramps, 'Aye, but just tell us how you know about dinner.'

'I ask one of the previous shift, daft thing. Then I can hang on to the idea of it to keep me going while we get sticky and itchy and bliddy fed up. It's spotted dog for puddin' – without the spotted bits, and with sugarless custard.'

Sarah sighed. 'I wish I hadn't asked. They could find some honey for the pudding, yer know. Farmer Thomas who has the fields by the beck has hives.'

On they worked, thinking for a moment of a time when there had been sugar, bacon and biscuits. Hour after hour they pasted the fluted paper and wrapped it before placing each finished pellet in the stand. All the while they hummed and all the time they concentrated, though sometimes they might talk a little, for the talk never really took up their minds. Pasting, wrapping, placing in trays, hour after hour, that's what did fill their heads.

At dinner break, Fran rolled her shoulders as they filed into the canteen. They sat round a table, eating grey mince that was almost suffocated by the mashed potatoes. They added more salt, which didn't really help, but it was food and merchant ships were being sunk to bring in supplies, so they appreciated it. They listened to the tannoy, which was playing music. Around the walls a few paper chains were hanging, but not many. Were they a fire hazard?

Fran grinned and asked the others. They all laughed as Mrs Oborne called, 'Aye, reckon if a few shells go off, some idiot'll break his neck getting 'em down in case it makes things worse.' They drank the water that was in jugs on the table, glass after glass to sluice the chemicals through their bodies.

Fran had left a bottle of water for the home journey under the seat of the bus, as had most of them. She sat at the table and drank one more glass, then in answer to Miss Ellington, who was beckoning to their table, they went into the small rehearsal room, followed by the choir. Miss Ellington said, 'I'll leave you to it.'

The room was off the dining room and was in fact the huge canteen storeroom. They were surrounded by shelves heavy with cleaning products, not to mention buckets, mops and brooms. They avoided these, and sang their play-list for Christmas Day. They finished up with 'Silent Night' and as they ended it, Beth said, 'I love it, although it was written by an Austrian and sung in German. Do you remember Reverend Walters telling us that?'

Fran and Sarah looked at one another. It hadn't occurred to them. Fran said, 'Howay, should we sing it, d'you think?'

The choir discussed it, but just then Miss Ellington called through the door, 'Girls, quickly, come and practise on stage. There's time.' She walked with them to the steps, saying that she'd heard the three girls were to sing at the Rising Sun on New Year's Eve, so she'd make sure they were off early from the aft shift.

As they climbed the steps onto the stage, Fran looked at the others. 'Damn, I didn't realise we were working the aft shift.'

Sarah said, 'Well, we know now and believe it or not, Fran Hall, the sky didn't fall in on us just because we let something slip through. God bless Miss Ellington for sorting it out.'

Amazed, Fran and Beth just stared at her. Beth said, as

Mrs Oborne clambered up the steps after them along with the choir, 'By, our Sarah. That's telling us, so it is.'

Fran took her place beside Sarah, who whispered to herself, 'Six times two is twelve.'

Fran said nothing. Mrs Oborne, the choir's conductor, was standing in front with a pencil, just as she had done when they sang for the wireless, having pinched it from Miss Ellington again. Fran looked at Miss Ellington standing in the body of the canteen, and pointed to the pencil. Miss Ellington shrugged, laughed and patted her now empty breast pocket and mouthed, It's *her* baton, I gather. Fran grinned, as did the choir.

Mrs Oborne waved at them to be silent, then turned and said to those sitting at the tables, ' "Silent Night" is Austrian and a good many of them are Nazis, so we divint know if we should end wi' it or not, given the war. Let's be having a vote at t'end.' She snatched a look at the clock and shouted, 'Quick, quick, choir, off we go, at a bliddy canter – look at the time.'

At that moment, Amelia called from the doorway into the canteen, 'There are only twenty minutes before the shift starts again. I suggest that the girls cut the number of their songs for the rehearsal, so the Office Girls can rehearse too.'

There was utter silence as the women in the room spun round and then back to Miss Ellington, who grimaced, then shrugged and nodded. 'Reet,' Mrs Oborne shouted. 'Off we go, but mek it a bliddy gallop, eh.'

The applause was loud when they finished and the vote for 'Silent Night' was overwhelmingly in favour, for it didn't matter what language it was originally sung in, it was God's carol.

It was the office girls' turn and they clambered onto the stage. They sang for ten minutes, then continued until Miss Ellington leapt onto the stage and waved them to a ragged halt as the women began to rise from their tables. She reminded them all of the Rising Sun Hogmanay entertainment and went on to say, 'I've arranged for Fran, Sarah and Beth to leave the aft shift early on New Year's Eve. Bert has promised that he or Cecil will get their foot down to get the rest of you there as soon as possible.' Loud cheers echoed around the canteen.

The pellet girls headed back down the corridor towards their workshop, their heads full of the carols, some singing, some chatting, half an eye on the clock on the wall, seeing that they'd be at their benches when they should be. Fran turned to Sarah and Beth. 'Our mams'll be right pleased we're singing. It's just that bit of extra mon—' She stopped as the ground shuddered. They all clutched one another.

'Oh no,' Maisie cried out.

The posters fell from the left-hand wall just as the sound of the explosion reached them, and the wall cracked and slowly, slowly bulged. The ground shook, the noise enveloped them, and now it included screams from the detonator workshop. Sarah whispered, as they hung on to one another, for nothing was stable, 'The walls – they're designed to give way.'

They all tumbled to the ground as their whole world shook more violently, the wall bulging more and more and the crack racing towards the ground, widening. The screams grew, the alarm sounded, they tried to hug the ground. All of them, including Mrs Oborne, lay there staring at the wall, knowing they should crawl somewhere, anywhere, to get away from it, but they were frozen as the wall bulged some more and they were buffeted by noise and pressure. Fran could hardly breathe for the terror. Beside her Sarah was murmuring again and again, 'Oh Stan, oh Stan . . .'

It seemed to last for ever, but when Fran looked up the clock on the right-hand wall showed just ten minutes and now the wall seemed to be shrinking more and more, until the crack closed, but not enough to dull the screams, the cries, the shouting and the siren as help came. Mrs Oborne called too now, her voice strained like a cracked violin, 'Bliddy hell, oh bliddy hell. Look, girls, another wall must have gone – the pressure's off this 'un.'

'So it wasn't our turn,' yelled Maisie, 'not this time.'

'This time,' repeated Sarah.

Miss Ellington was running up the corridor as everything steadied, calling, 'Come on, up you get, nothing you can do here. No more lolling about as though you're on the beach. Back to work. Quick, quick.'

Fran swallowed, trembling, her mind running with the words 'This time.' But she forced herself to say, 'We should sing "Away in a Manger", you know.' She pushed herself to her knees and the others did too, then to their feet. Fran's legs were shaking, her whole body too.

Sarah gripped her arm. 'You're shaking. I'm shaking. Beth?'

'Aye, course I am, but . . .' Beth was as white as a sheet, her streaked red hair stark against her skin. 'But we've got to get to work, and we've got to sing "Away in a Manger" on Christmas Day. That's what Fran said.'

Fran swallowed again, clenching her hands into fists. 'No, I asked. But if you think . . . And no need to dress our Sarah up as Mary – why should she have to be a good girl all her life?'

It was nonsense, but everyone laughed hysterically as they leaned on one another and then tried to force their legs to carry them towards the pellet shop. Miss Ellington patted each and every one of them on the back. 'Come along, keep to the right of the corridor. Maintenance will sort out the wall, and everything else. Come on, come on.'

Mr Swinton was beckoning to them at the entrance to

the pellet shop. 'No time to waste. Don't let a little thing like this get you down.'

Mrs Oborne shook herself, straightened and walked towards him, as though leading her ducklings. She raised her voice over the diminishing screams. 'Bliddy little 'Itler you are, and mind, you're the little thing that gets us down.'

Mr Swinton held open the door as the girls all looked from Mrs Oborne to the foreman. What on earth would Swinton do or say now? Sack them? 'I daresay I am,' he said. 'But it got you going. Now, for God's sake, you lasses, tek care.'

They passed him, seeing the tremble in his hands, the pallor of his skin. He followed them in, closing the door on the noise of the injured. The silence was a relief. Sarah whispered, 'Four times two is eight.'

Mrs Oborne was muttering, 'Bliddy, bliddy hell. Not sure if 'tis the explosion or Swinton being human that's mithered me more.'

Beth made her way to stand at the workbench, swallowing, gripping her hands together, hissing down at them, 'Stop your trembling, damn it.'

Miss Ellington was walking up and down behind them as they took their places. She halted near Fran, calling, 'Right, that's your panic time over. Best thing we can do is to carry on.'

The three girls looked at one another, and at everyone else. They all nodded, and began to paste the fuse pellets with hands that slowly steadied, and minds that tried to shut out the shock of such pain and terror.

That same day, at Maud Bedley's house, Annie Hall took over the care of her friend from Beth's mam as midday waned. She stoked up the range, replaced the poker and listened to the simmering kettle. 'Tea now, eh, lass,' she muttered, turning. As she did so, she heard Madge calling from the yard. Annie walked to the table and laid her hand on Maud's shoulder. 'Up you get and let the lass in, it's good and cold out there. I reckon the tea's mashed for long enough, eh?'

Maud stumbled to the door as Annie poured the tea, carrying the tray to the table. She glanced up at the top of the dresser, which was now bottle-free, and prayed that it would stay that way. She watched Maud lift the latch to let Madge enter. Madge kissed Maud and shut the door behind her, easing off her boots. 'By, it's a cold 'un. Snow's falling again. Me neighbour – you know Mrs Sweatham – is keeping an eye out for the bairn in case they shut the school. Then she'll bring our Bobby along here and he can cut some more strips for the rugs, eh, because no matter what, the New Year orders for Briddlestone's department store have to be filled. By, I like saying the whole name, meks me feel reet important, meking rugs for such a place.'

Maud Bedley slumped on her kitchen chair again, staring at her hooky rug frame on the table in front of her. She reached for a hook, held it for a moment, and then let it drop as though it was too heavy. Annie and Madge looked at one another. How could they tell her everything would be all right when her man was six foot under and her lass was working in munitions?

Madge said, smoothing the dark red strips of material Maud had worked into her rug, 'I reckon you're right to do a looped rug. If you were to do a proggy with its short lengths, it might not work so well with a wave of colour. The proggies are best suited to the merging of colours. Oh aye, it'll be grand, so it will.'

Suddenly, sitting opposite Maud, Annie replaced her cup on its saucer, wanting to scream. Her man was with Tom and she weren't falling about the place, so why should

Maud Bedley? Instead, she, Annie bliddy Hall, was here having to be strong, but then she shook herself. Hush, for she was a pitman's widow and they lived with the threat, it was nothing new, and her Joe was not just with Tom, he was with their Betty, her precious babe born and died within hours only a little over a year ago. And Maud had been right kind to her then for they were marrers, so it were all right. Course it was. She picked up her cup again and made herself sip from it as though today was no different to any other day.

The tea was weak, made with tea leaves used several times already, but what did it matter? What did was that one day Maud would remember who she was. Annie sipped again and called, 'Drink yer tea, ladies, then let's get to work, eh.'

Aye, she'd be here for Maud, just as Maud had been by her side. She picked up her proggy tool while Madge dragged her own frame out of her large bag and settled at the kitchen table between the two friends. Her eyepatch was not the usual Monday one, but was coloured silver. Annie smiled. 'By, Madge, you got your days muddled?'

Madge grinned. 'I decided to break out of me own habits and live a little. So, 'tis silver today and whatever I fancy tomorrow, and come Christmas Day I reckon I'll be hanging bells on it an' all.'

Annie found herself laughing along with Madge, and then, glory be, Maud Bedley joined them, her laugh sounding unused and hoarse. Annie knew that it could be a while before another came along, but if she and the co-op had anything to do with it, Maud Bedley *would* come alive again, it was just a case of working out a plan.

Chapter Four

That same day, Stan hurried across the Halls' backyard after his first shift back at work since the funeral. He reached the door, then turned back on himself and made for the chicken run. His da had always stopped by the fowl and rattled the chicken wire until they hustled out of the coop, all of aflutter.

'Howay, lasses, all reet? Getting ready for laying some belters by the morning, eh?' He dipped into the barrel of grain alongside the run and chucked a couple of handfuls through the wire. Aye, it was Fran's task, but there was nowt to say he wouldn't help. The canaries didn't need that much looking after, and Simon Parrot was keeping an eye on theirs, and Tom Bedley's, as well as his own. There was clucking and a bit of mithering from the hens and a clattering from the cock, and as he watched Stan wondered if they knew it was the son, not the father?

He replaced the lid on the barrel, sighed and looked up at the sky. 'Weren't the same without you buggers storming along in front of us to the pit this fore shift. No coughing and growling from the three of you. By, I miss you summat rotten. Reckon the whole pit does, an' all. Hope you're behaving yerselves, or St Peter'll have you down in the depths soon as look at you.'

He heard Sid calling from the back lane, 'Howay, you 'ear that, Norm? The lad's talking to himself.'

Norm replied, 'Means he's as daft as always. See you tomorrow, lad.' He heard them clomping on, knowing they

54

had waited to check he wasn't a blubbering heap; if he had been, they'd have been in like a streak of lightning. He stared into the coop, wondering if he'd have been so cared for at Oxford University. He doubted it. Though Professor Smythe, Mr Massingham's friend who was in charge of settling in the Massingham scholarship boys, probably would have rallied in support. He was a good old boy, a bit dozy, but kind.

He opened the back door and called, 'Mam, I'm back.'

There was no answer, but he'd thought there might not be, for she'd be at Mrs Bedley's. She'd left the tin bath in front of the range, complete with bar of carbolic soap, God bless her. He'd have first dibs at the clean water for the first time, because—

'Shut it,' he said aloud as he levered off his boots by the door. He lined them up on the waiting newspaper, then padded across in his bare feet, pouring the big pot simmering on the range into the cold she'd left in the bath. He stripped and sank into the warm water, leaning back and sighing again. Clean water? He'd often longed for it, but it was always his da's prerogative. He let the tears fall and then rubbed his face hard, harder, until he'd sorted himself out.

He used the brush to scrub his back, which his da would normally have done. He stood up, pulled the towel from the ceiling airer and dried his body, trying to avoid the fresh cuts. Then he balanced on one leg and dried his foot, before stepping onto the flagstones and drying the other. There, no footprints. One day, maybe, he'd be coming in from the pit, black as the ace of spades, and his Sarah would be waiting. She would kiss him whether he was clean or not, and she'd wash his back . . . One day . . .

He took the clean clothes his mam had hung on the airer, pulled on his drawers, twanging the elastic, and suddenly he laughed. 'Bliddy hell, Davey, it were as well you sewed yourself in, lad, or you'd not have a clue what you'd done when Daisy said what she said. But socks, man. Bliddy hell, socks, and they didn't even match. Still canna get that picture out of me head.'

He pulled on the rest of his clothes, thanking heaven for a mam such as theirs. She cared for them all, not like Mrs— He stopped. Sarah, sweet Sarah, what could they all do for her while her mam was . . . out of sorts? He stared at the range. The kettle was simmering, all set for a brew of tea. What would Sarah have met on her return if she didn't have the co-op ladies stepping in?

He longed to hold her, to keep her close always and save her worry. 'How're we to keep that roof over yer head, lass, and yer mam safe?'

It's what had bothered him since their fathers had died. How could he help when his mam and Ben needed to be kept afloat too, though Fran was helping mightily? It wasn't Mrs Bedley's fault she was no help right now. It was just how the grief was taking her. 'But it divint change facts. Sarah's pay when she's getting extra for danger is just about enough, but there'll be no headstone money, and if she's put into the safe sector for a while, and the rent goes up to the full whack, the pay isn't going to cover their living expenses. Davey's earning peanuts, and there's his keep to pay for an' all. Aye, I can help them a bit, but . . .' He remembered Sid's voice calling from the back lane. 'Aye,' he added. 'You're right an' all, our Sid. Daft as a brush I am, talking to meself.'

He checked the clock. It wasn't yet time to meet Sarah at the bus shelter, so he thrust his feet into his boots and dadded his pit clothes on the outside wall, whacking them again and again, watching the coal dust billow.

He hung his pit clothes on the stand in the scullery for tomorrow's shift. He cleared the yard, then scattered ash before making a pot of tea. He finally saw his mam's note propped on the mantelpiece. It was behind his da's pipe and pain clutched him. He touched the pipe; it was so cold. Aye, they had his headstone to pay for, as well as Betty's . . .

He read the note:

At Maud Bedley's. Make yourself a brew after your bath and leave enough in the teapot for Ben, there's a good lad. I daresay your lass will be right pleased to see your smiling face when Bert screeches on the brakes. Hope your day back at Auld Hilda weren't too bad, and you didn't miss your da too much.

He slurped his tea, put the cosy on the teapot, then checked the clock. It was twenty minutes before the bus came, so just time to check on his mam. He took off, running down the back lane. He reached Main Street, then turned into the Bedleys' back lane, increasing his speed until he opened their gate. Breathing heavily, he walked across the yard, suddenly missing Davey. He knocked gently.

It was Beth's mam, Mrs Smith, who called, 'Howay in, whoever you are.'

He stepped into the kitchen, kicking off his boots on the newspaper. His mam was working on her latest proggy rug. All the women smiled and his mam put her finger to her lips, hushing him, pointing upstairs. He crept over to join them. His mam broke off to pour him a cup of tea and suddenly he felt parched, though he had just had one. He gulped it down, wondering why Sarah's mam was in bed. 'Is Mrs Bedley all right?' he whispered.

Mrs Smith pushed her hook through the hessian and said quietly, 'She'll be reet as rain, one day. We just need to keep one step ahead of the lass on the drinking. She had a bottle we didn't find till too late.'

57

His mam nodded towards another empty sherry bottle by the door. 'Tek those out to the basket I put by the back step when you go, lad. Madge'll tek 'em back to the club, if that's where she got them from. We've poured away some elderberry wine we found upstairs.'

Stan looked up. 'Where's she getting it from if not the club?'

Madge shook her head at him. 'Where'd yer think? Plenty'll who'll sell it on the black, at a price. And first, that price'll be too high, so she'll be getting it on tick. Second, it'll feed the habit, so it's got to be stopped. What's more, we have to be reet wary not to rattle our Sarah wi' the worry of it all, for the tab'll be gathering interest.'

Mrs Smith said, nodding to the empty bottle, 'Tipped what were left down the sink, an' all, we did. Shame, would have made a nice fruit cake, if we'd had the fruit.' She laughed quietly.

Madge chuckled. 'And the sugar and eggs.'

Stan looked from one to the other, shaking his head. He was in the company of goddesses.

His mam rose. 'Yer need to be waiting for Sarah at the bus shelter, lad. I'll walk to the gate with yer.' She wrapped her shawl around her as she waited for him to put on his boots. She said as she watched, 'You tie 'em up proper from now on, our Stan. No more of this halfway business so you can slip and break yer neck. You're Ben's example.' Her smile was strained. 'Got to cross the t's and dot the i's from now on.'

They walked to the gate together, she pulling her woollen shawl over her head, and he slipping his arm round her shoulders. She was still too thin. 'You can't be keeping an eye on Mrs Bedley twenty-four hours a day,' he said. 'And neither can the other co-op lasses. Fran or me must be here for the night. Sarah were right scared her mam had taken off for St Oswald's, and she canna be up guarding her through the night when she's to work. I know Mr Massingham cuts the rent for a month, which is a grand help, and seeing you all at work I've just remembered that her mam's rug money could help, if she keeps at it. Do you reckon Mrs Bedley can get going on them properly?'

He opened the gate, but his mam pushed it shut again. 'We've been working it all out, Stan. You and Fran can sleep in the Bedley house until it's all calm again, which it will be. It canna be you alone overnight with our Sarah here, for 'tisn't seemly, so Fran can be with Sarah upstairs and you can sleep in the chair by the range. If you keep the front door double-locked and even put a chain on it, Maud canna leave that way. Then if you're in the kitchen, she canna get past you if she has a mind to head off for St Oswald's. Or go poking about for the bottles she's hidden. For I fear she has some, but we canna find them.'

Stan whispered, 'Or should we have her at our house?'

His mam shook her head. 'We co-op lasses feel Maud needs to stay in her own home where she has to be responsible for it, and besides, I don't want Ben seeing all this. We reckon what's happened is she's lost her reason, and the drink makes life bearable. So, she has to be guarded against herself until she's back on an even keel.' His mam shook her head. 'As for money, the co-op will have to help.'

Stan said, as the cold seemed to dig into him, 'But what about you, Mam? You lost our da an' all.'

'Aye, but I have the comfort of him being with Betty, and I have our Ben to look after, so I won't be alone to mither myself into despair come nightfall. But while we're talking, lad, we co-op ladies were thinking of Sarah too, and we reckon t'best thing for her would be the upcoming hope of you two being wed. Some light in a dark time. Some sort of belonging for all to see.' She repeated, 'For all to see. Yer see, lad, word's just come that Moira Sinclair's lass who works at the Factory has just been taken to hospital. Been a *bit* hurt in an accident, she were told, so she's gone to see her. But one of t'other girls involved and who were sent home, whispered that it was, in fact, a *bit* of an explosion, and Moira's lass is more'n a *bit* hurt. And it's a right shame, but two other lasses have bought it. They were from south of the Hanging Tree. We shouldn't know this, but Moira's one of our own, so we do, and I wouldn't be mentioning it further but for the fact our girls were close by, Moira said, *our* girls, lad. They were in the corridor and the wall near gave way on them. But yer know to say nowt to anyone, lad, just ponder it.'

Stan felt his lungs close, or that's how it seemed, and he could barely breathe. His Sarah. A bulging wall? A bliddy explosion? And this is what it was, day after day, for his Sarah, for Fran, for Beth. And one day, it might be them. Them, her, his Sarah.

His mam was speaking again as he found he could just about draw breath, but he was panting as though he'd run a mile, and his mouth was dry. 'So, we reckon our Sarah, with all her other woes with her mam, could do to belong. Really belong to yer, to the love you both have, and to know she's to be wed sooner than later. Sooner, do you hear?'

Stan found his voice as he reached out and gripped the gate to steady himself. 'I've asked her already, Mam, you know that, and she's willing, but I haven't a ring and there's no money for one, neither. Oh, I don't know, it's all so bliddy difficult and we're all so bliddy sad, and I can't bear to lose her, to have her working there, to—'

His mam shook his arm. 'Stop your mithering. It's war-time. She'll work where she needs to be, and you having a tizz isn't going to help.' She dug deep into her apron pocket, bringing out a six-inch length of fuse wire. 'We've been thinking on this today, Mrs Smith, Madge and I, and we brought Maud in on it too before she nipped off for a nap. Believe it or not, it were Maud's thought to use a bit of wire, so I dug about in yer da's box of bits and bobs when I went home to sort out yer bath.'

Stan didn't understand. His mam tutted. 'You're a clever scholarship lad and haven't a thought in yer head. We reckon you should make a ring with it and ask the lass. She can wear it and then everyone knows, eh? We're not sure you can be wed quite this minute. But soon, eh? 'Twouldn't be right, so near to—' She stopped.

Another voice called out, 'The grief is still roaring, so yer ma's reet, it wouldn't be seemly.' It was Mrs Smith, Beth's mam, on the doorstep, flapping her hands at him. 'Don't look so gormless, lad. Off you go, and fiddle with the wire on the way, eh?'

His mam was opening the gate and pushing him through. 'Don't you be late for yer lass.' She shut the gate in his face. He looked from the fuse wire to the gate, then ran like the clappers, rolling the glinting wire round his little finger.

Sarah, Beth and Fran sat on the back seat, reluctant to be split up by the aisle, prepared to put up with the stotting and jigging, which always seemed so much worse at the rear. They were quiet, busy with their own thoughts, their own aches and bruises. They left Sledgeford and headed towards Massingham and Sarah bit down on her lip. What would greet her at home? But at least they weren't dead like the two in the detonator shop, or hurt like Moira's lass, Enid. Who would keep a roof over her mam's head if that were to happen?

Fran and Beth reached for her hands, which she had balled into fists, and Fran whispered, 'Doing a Swinton impression?'

They all laughed. Sarah thought that life was so strange – one minute so dreadful, then they were laughing.

'He didn't seem the same,' Beth said. 'A bit bothered, not as angry, almost as though he was pretending rage, but then almost nice ... Howay, probably had a hangover.' They laughed again, but they could still hear the high pitch of the explosion.

Still holding hands, they talked of the Rising Sun concert, which would really help the three of them, for not only would it mean that they would have enough money to put aside for housekeeping, but word might get out about their singing trio. Then hopefully they'd be asked to do more, so even if they were put in the sewing department with lower wages until they recovered from the itch from 'the yellow' – as they all called it – caused by the chemicals, the bills could be paid. Besides, maybe the money for their singing would also help pay Mrs Bedley's booze bill, for it would rise and rise until they managed to stop her.

It was four o clock when they drew up at the bus shelter and Mrs Oborne stood, groaned and stretched. 'Seemed like a fair old slog today, eh?'

Yes, thought Sarah, that was the sum of it all.

Everyone was gathering up their bags and heading down the aisle. The three girls were last. At the front, Maisie began to sing 'Away in a Manger' and by the time they reached the pavement they had all joined in. They stood together singing until the final lines, 'And tek us to heaven, to live with Thee there.'

'But not yet, eh God,' Maisie added.

Silence fell for a moment and Sarah looked for Stan, but he wasn't there. She felt the ache of her bruises, and the dread and loneliness of going home. One times two is two, she told herself, and two times two is four, and everything is quite all right. Then she heard Stan call her name and he was running along the pavement from her back lane, slip-sliding on the snow.

'Bliddy hell,' he cried as he almost went over. 'Sarah, I've got to . . . Hang on a minute, all of you.' He sounded frantic.

She stared. 'Oh no, what's happened?' The others were clustering around her and even Bert came out of his cab to stand in front of the bus to see what all the fuss was about.

Sarah watched her love, her Stan, trying to run on the slippery pavement, and was fearful of his news. Mrs Oborne yelled, 'Howay, lad, she's not going anywhere, steady the buffs, eh. What's amiss? Come on, best out wi' it.'

He had almost reached them. Just a few more paces and he was there, in front of Sarah, panting.

'What?' Sarah asked. 'What's happened?'

He stared at her, then at everyone who stood waiting. No one spoke, not even Maisie, who was never lost for words. He shook his head, swallowed, and knew he had to do as his mam said. He sank down on one knee, holding out his hand, feeling all sorts of a fool. 'Will you marry me, sweet Sarah? For I love you and will till the sky falls down. I will share your worries; I will do whatever I can, because I do so love you, Sarah Bedley.' Suddenly he didn't feel a fool any longer, he just felt full of love, and fear, for he couldn't rid his head of the thought that she could have been the one hurt, or killed, and instead of meeting her here he'd be heading for the hospital, or worse. His Sarah. His beloved Sarah.

'For the love of all that's holy, lad,' groaned Bert, 'you asked weeks ago and she said aye, so no need to mek a meal of it.'

'Shut your noise, Bert,' snapped Mrs Oborne.

Sarah smiled. 'Get up, Stan. Your trouser leg's all wet.'

Stan looked at her. 'I know it is, but I love yer so much, I don't give a damn. I'll get up, but only when you put this ring on your finger and promise we'll go down the aisle once the grief is better, and bliddy well hurry, lass. I'm freezing to death here and if I get the rheumatics it'll be your fault.'

Everyone laughed, but not Stan and not Sarah. She took the ring, which was gold, but not as she knew it. She held it up.

'Holy Mary, fuse wire,' said Bert. 'Now I've seen everything.'

This time all the women yelled, 'Shut your bliddy noise, Bert.'

Sarah thought she'd die of relief, of love, and of happiness. 'Aye, of course I will,' she said.

Stan got to his feet, took the ring and pushed it on her finger. It was a bit loose, so he squashed it.

'It's too bliddy painful to watch,' muttered Bert. 'Time I were away.'

'Aye, it is an' all, and mek sure you're on time tomorrow – and Bert, you tek care, bonny lad,' yelled Maisie.

Stan took Sarah in his arms in front of everyone and she felt his warmth. She heard his words of love – and heard from him that she would not be alone until things were better, for he and Fran would be with her every night until it was.

'Oh I will, will I?' said Fran.

Mrs Oborne shouted, 'And you can shut your noise an' all, Miss Fran Hall, you know damn well you will be. She's yer marrer and you three lasses are joined at t'hip.'

Fran was grinning, Beth too, as the four of them walked back to the Bedley household. Sarah knew that as long as she could earn enough, everything would be all right, for she hadn't died today. And now she wore Stan's ring. And now she really would be his wife – once the grieving was done – and that thought would keep her safe. She was sure it would – almost sure. Sure enough.

She felt the ring on her finger, her hand in his, and looked around. She lived in Massingham, where everyone was family. What's more, soon she would wake each day to her Stan. She would cook for him and he'd check the hens, and they'd have . . .

Stan opened the back gate for her. 'I'm away to check on our Ben, lass. But the co-op's in there.' Fran and Beth walked towards the back door while he kissed Sarah's hand, and her ring finger. 'There'll be a way for you and me to find enough money to keep yer mam until we're wed,' he said, 'and after, no matter what section you're in, lass, so don't you worry. If you fancy being in a safer one all the time, I'll make more money somehow.'

She ran his words over in her head as he held her close. But no, the two of them would find a way, the two of them, not just Stan. She could be strong too. She would work in the more dangerous places because her friends would, and his love would keep her safe. Yes, she was sure it would.

By the time she'd reached the back door, she had reached twelve times two is twenty-four, because the closer she drew to the house, the less she knew if her mam had been drinking, or how to make her stop.

She entered the kitchen, finding the co-op women sitting round the table, and in the armchair was her mam. Sarah went to her and knelt down, holding out her hand. Her mother looked at the ring, then closed her eyes. 'By, I'm right pleased.'

Her breath was heavy with the fresh smell of sherry. She must have some in her room, for the co-op wouldn't have let her have it. Fran came to sit on the arm of Mrs Bedley's chair and started to speak, but Sarah took hold of her mam's hand, saying, 'When we're all sorted Stan and me'll wed, but not until then, so we all have to play our part to get calm, Mam.'

Sarah rose and sat opposite in her da's armchair. Although he was gone, *she* was still here, and her friends were too. Sarah fingered her ring. Four times two is eight.

'It were yer mam's idea to use the fuse wire, lass,' called Mrs Hall from the table. 'Right clever an' all.'

Fran sat on the arm of Sarah's armchair now, with Beth on the other. Beth leaned over, whispering, 'There, you see, she's already getting some gumption.' The girls smiled at one another.

Chapter Five

The next morning Sarah woke feeling as though she had only slept an hour, but when she checked her alarm it was three thirty. She turned over and met resistance. It was only then that she remembered Fran was sharing her bed and they were lying top to toe. She felt her friend stir and then whisper, 'I've just woken too. I didn't hear any movement from yer mam's room. Did you?'

'No, but are you surprised? She was sozzled off her feet,' Sarah whispered in return.

She heard Fran laugh, the bed shaking as she spluttered, 'By, Sarah, that's a picture you've just painted, so it is.'

Sarah didn't know why but she was laughing too, and it felt so good. She'd thought she'd never relax enough to enjoy anything in her own house again. Finally, she muttered, 'Poor Stan, downstairs in Mam's armchair, when at least we can stretch out.'

Fran was sitting up now. 'He won't mind, if it's for you and yer mam.' She swung her legs round, grabbed her pillow and set it against the wall, leaning back. 'Three thirty, eh? We should be moving.'

Sarah joined her, sitting close, and pulled the blanket over them both. 'Do you remember how we used to do this, sleep top to toe, when we were bairns? It was when our mams and das were chatting downstairs. Life were simple then.'

'Aye, maybe, but don't forget I were sleeping here some nights just a year or so ago when me mam were strange after wee Betty died. Life doesn't get simpler, seems to me, but

67

things just come in waves. Our poor old mams have a lot to bear, what with their old boys striving in the mine, getting hurt and maybe black lung, then their sons following 'em into the pit. And worse, their lasses muckin' about with explosives. No wonder they give way – who wouldn't? Maybe we will an' all, and when we do our bairns'll come to one of the three of us to help sort it.'

Sarah listened to Fran, wonderful Fran, and now she too could see them ahead in time, talking of the past as though her mam's drinking had just been a bit of 'giving way'. She felt herself relax and could have fallen asleep again, until Fran pointed to the clock. Three thirty-five. Aye, time.

For some reason she thought of the concert then, and like they so often did, they seemed to be thinking the same thing, for Fran said, 'I've been mithering this Christmas concert and I expect yer'll think I'm daft, but for the sake of peace, why don't we just share the programme with Amelia's office group? Fifteen minutes each and be done with it. Aye, it was to be our moment because we won the *Workers' Playtime* competition, but if we're generous, she won't sing on and on, getting everyone right mithered.'

'Aye, I were thinking on it, too. That Amelia's a reet pain in the bum, but she's miles from home and her real friends, and it'd be the right way to behave – but you tell her, Fran. I get cross when I see that sort of sniffy smile she does when she gets her own way and want to land one on her stuck-up nose.'

They were laughing again as they dressed, stopping when they heard the riddling of the range, and Sarah's heart warmed, for it would be Stan. But tomorrow she'd be up to riddle the range, for he had the pit and she wasn't helpless, no, she wasn't. There, if that wasn't gumption, she didn't know what was.

*

Stan had eased himself out of Mrs Bedley's armchair and hunkered down to open the range vent, riddling the grate until the ash fell through and the embers glowed. He added coals from the bucket; coal perhaps he had produced. It was quite something that it was still issued free to all the pitmen by Mr Massingham, even though the pit was under government management. How had the boss managed that? he wondered, grinning. But Mr Massingham managed most things, like getting Davey a better wicket when his leg was buggered to smithereens in the pit accident a few months ago, no doubt through Professor Smythe, who had fingers in many pies. Or so Stan suspected after working as the Prof's assistant in the university vacations.

Stan watched the flames. He wished Davey was still in the pit, for he missed the lad something chronic.

He winced as he stood, feeling as though he had been squashed into the shape of an armchair. Not that he'd slept much anyway. He'd come awake at every creak, thinking it might be Mrs Bedley creeping out to sit with her man or find more booze. When would it end, he wondered, now that old Tom wasn't here to sort her? Ah, but the co-op was here, he told himself, and they'd pull Mrs Bedley out of her mourning quicksand any day now.

He checked the clock that hung over the mantelpiece, then shoved the kettle onto the hot plate and stretched, his back clicking just as Sarah and Fran entered. He lowered his arms and drank in the tousled, blonde-haired lass he loved. She was the most beautiful sight there'd ever been, and what's more, today she looked rested. As the kettle lid began to rattle, he raced to the scullery ahead of them while Fran said, 'Aye, and this is the man you love, eh, Sarah, pushing ahead of us?'

He washed, did his teeth and snatched up the threadbare towel from the hook to dry himself before throwing it at Fran as she called from the doorway, 'Howay, lad, get a wriggle on, we've a bus to catch.'

'And I've tea to brew.'

Sarah laughed and it warmed his heart as he speared his way between them and told her, 'And I've dripping from Mam in the meat safe an' all. Just need to cut some bread before you go. I'm not having the pair of you off out to the Factory without something to warm yer.'

Sarah grabbed hold of him and kissed his mouth, and he wanted to hold her and never let go. But she pushed him away and followed Fran to the sink.

He poured water onto the tea leaves, then pattered to the back door, moving the empty pail he had rested there just in case Mrs Bedley made it past him. He'd reckoned if that was knocked he'd be awake in a jiff. He leaned out, reached the bowl of dripping from the meat safe and hurried to the table to cut the loaf his mam had baked, but the slices were like doorsteps. He stared. 'Oh bliddy hell.'

Sarah's arms came around him and she pressed herself against him. 'Oh, lad, yer'll have to wash yer mouth out with soap if this goes on.'

She stood beside him, took the knife, lay the loaf face down and cut thinner slices. 'It's too fresh,' she explained. 'It'll be easier tomorrow, that's if you haven't had enough of sleeping in the chair and rushed off home to yer mam's?'

He spread dripping on the slices she had cut and thought about what it must be like being wed, except when that happened, he wouldn't be sleeping in a chair. He grinned to himself and whispered, 'Not yet, our Sarah, but I'd much rather be in the bed wi' yer.'

Sarah flushed and before she could answer Fran was at the table, flicking him with the towel. 'Any more of that and it really will be time to wash yer mouth out, Stanhope Hall.'

She nipped back to the range, poured the tea and brought it to the table.

'Who'll be mam?' Stan asked as they sat.

He watched as Sarah poured. One day she and he would be mam and da to their own family. He sat back on the chair and longed for it, but the worry about keeping two families wouldn't leave him.

Though the war might be over by then, he mused, and Davey home to look after Fran and the Halls. That still didn't sort out the problem of him needing to help his fiancée and his own family right now. Or the problem of getting Sarah to accept his money when he could finally work out how to juggle what he had.

He ate his bread and dripping, though it stuck in his throat because Sarah, Fran and Beth were going back to the Factory, and God knows what would happen today. It was Enid yesterday, and the two dead girls, and they were only the ones they happened to know about. There would be others, for so much was kept quiet. He gulped his tea, which helped, then looked up as he heard a click and the door from the hall opened. Mrs Bedley stood there in her dressing gown, looking bewildered.

Sarah rose. 'Mam, come and have a cup of tea, eh?'

Mrs Bedley just stared, then left, shutting the door behind her. They waited. Would she try and leave by the front door?

'I've wedged it shut, don't worry,' Stan whispered. 'And Beth's mam will be here by the time we leave. Our mam will tek over when Ben's off to school, and then they've got their co-op rota, so nothing to fret about.'

He checked the clock. 'You have to leave in ten minutes for the bus. I can stay on if Mrs Smith isn't here on time.'

Mrs Smith arrived within the ten minutes, and Stan joined the two girls to walk along the back lane together.

The chill was grim. The pitmen walked like a tide against them.

'Ow do?'

'Be safe.'

'Like brass monkeys.'

'Wrong way, Stan, lad.'

'Aye, just seeing the lass I'm to wed to her bus,' he replied.

The pitmen laughed, waved and carried on towards Auld Hilda.

There had been more snow, but only a light fall, and their breath puffed out as they talked about Mrs Bedley. Sarah worried that her mam was taking so much of everyone's time, but it was Fran who beat Stan to the answer. 'It's grief, that's what it is. Last time it were when yer da was poorly, and something will stop her again.'

Sarah nodded, pulling her scarf over her head. 'I reckon she's worried about money too, but I can earn it. That's if she keeps on with the rugs and stops the boozing . . .'

Stan snatched a look at Fran. They had to find out where exactly Mrs Bedley got the booze, for there were no shops or pubs that would sell to her, or so they'd all promised the co-op yesterday.

As they reached Main Street they saw Sid and Norm heading towards them, striding past the Factory bus, which was idling and huffing out exhaust.

'Howay, lad,' called Sid, a Woodbine stuck in the corner of his mouth. 'Up and out from the land of nod, ready to face the day?'

Stan grimaced. 'Oh aye, rarin' to go.'

Sarah shot Stan an anxious look. He repeated, his eyes on her alone, 'Rarin' to go, slept like a log.' But Stan was really wondering if he could drag Tom's armchair over and stick his feet on it tonight. He looked up at the sky, asking silently, What'd you think of that, our Tom? And how the bliddy hell are we going to get your missus out of the darkness, eh? Put yer mind to it and float down your ideas, why don't you?

'I think we should bring in the box Mam keeps her Christmas decorations in,' said Sarah. 'She won't have any up this year as she's mourning. We can put a cushion on it and then you can at least put your legs up.'

Stan smiled and stroked her hair, then pulled up her scarf. 'You're a mind-reader.' He looked up at the sky. Or you've just floated the words down, eh, Tom?

They reached the bus. He tugged on the ends of her scarf and she came to him. He kissed her and murmured, 'I love you. I love you and everything will be all right, we just have to keep things going, eh, while we make a plan.'

Bert hooted and Mrs Oborne appeared in the bus doorway. 'Put yon lass down, bonny lad. And get yerself to the pit. Where's our Beth? She went running off to fetch something she'd left at home. Don't you go, Bert, till she's back or I'll have yer guts for garters.'

Beth ran up then, panting, with some sheets of paper rolled up under her arm.

'What've you got there, for heaven's sake?' Fran asked.

Beth grinned and handed them to Stan. 'Tek these to the pit and make sure you pass 'em out to yer marrers to pin on trees – posters for the concert at the Rising Sun on Hogmanay. Might as well get a good turnout, as we're being released early that day. I did it last evening. I should have been an artist, that I should.'

'No,' said Sarah. 'You can't be a singing star as well as an artist, bonny lass.'

The three girls looked at one another and laughed.

Mrs Oborne said, 'Aye, you'll have to decide – one or t'other, our Beth. Now, get on board, for the love of Mike, or pay'll be docked.'

Stan reached for Sarah again, but Sid and Norm took an arm each, and quick-marched him towards Auld Hilda. He called over his shoulder, 'Be safe. Even you, auld grump bag Oborne.'

She yelled after him, 'I'll skelp you, so I will. You're just being cocky cos you've given yer lass a ring. Well, she'd best behave herself an' all. And you lads get them posters up. The Rising Sun's collection'll be for *all* them widowed this year, as usual.'

Auld Hilda's hooter was sounding as they clambered on board. Sarah stood on the step, looking after Stan, and sure enough, even though the three marrers ran, he tore free and waved, blowing her a kiss before disappearing round the corner. It was only then that she made her way up the aisle as Bert complained, 'Bliddy women, natter, chatter, natter . . .'

'I canna wait for 1941 to bugger off,' Fran whispered, 'not only so we can sing in the New Year and get a bit of money, but . . .' She trailed off.

Sarah smiled. 'Aye, reet enough.'

Beth added, 'Then in a new year I *can* be an artist and a star, and you can admire me from afar. Aye, while I'm about it, I might as well be a poet, an' all.'

They hit her.

At the end of the fore shift at Auld Hilda, Ralph cycled home, wishing he was driving his red roadster instead. He hated the bike, but rode it to appear like one of the pitmen. He remembered the chauffeur, Alfie Biggins, who owned the bike, suggesting he pay a hire fee. In response Ralph had said, 'How about trying not to lose your job? Time you knew your place,' though actually he'd thought the lad had a point.

Biggins had asked if he'd decided he didn't need the bike

after all. Ralph had given him a warning for his cheek, of course he had. It was what Ralph Massingham did. But since the accident which had killed Bedley and Hall he hadn't really wanted to be that person any more. For it had been no accident, rather his own act of sabotage that had gone wrong. Sabotage ordered by Tim Swinton, the head of the Fascist cell he had been so damned foolish to join when he was home from school one holiday and it had seemed so exciting.

He'd liked the black boots and the secrecy, and it was such a thumbing of his nose at his father's marriage to Sophia, his stepmother. Now, though, it was something which had become so traitorous, so cruel and powerful, that he hated it. But it was so difficult to escape from and he'd only realised that once the coal fall had killed two fine men he hadn't known would be there. He sighed, head down, pedalling hard. What a fool, an idiot, a bastard he was.

He, Ralph bloody Massingham, was a killer; he was hateful, superior and a bully and always had been, but he had changed after the accident, utterly. The trap was that he dared not appear to have done so, for what if Tim Swinton realised 'the whelp' had doubts? Well, Tim'd damned well kill him, and the Massingham family too, for that was what the bugger had said to him at the start of all this. Ralph had laughed, thinking it was just words; it was only now that he believed him. After the accident at the pit Tim's only concern was that the collateral damage would cause an investigation and he didn't want questions to be asked. He couldn't give a damn about the loss of life. In fact, he seemed to relish it and when Ralph had demurred, Tim had warned against betraying the cause adding that the family of the traitor would have to suffer, as well as the traitor, for order to be maintained.

Ralph toiled out of the pit village into the full force of the wind, which, judging from the roads, had carried a bit more snow while he'd been grubbing at the black furnace of the face. God, he hoped he'd sleep properly tonight, but why would he, and why did he deserve to? Sleep brought the dreams and the cries of the men beneath the coal, so he preferred to lie awake with only his guilt and sorrow to keep him company until dawn.

As he pedalled he cursed Tim, for all the good it did, for he had promised Ralph over the telephone that there would be no one in the seam. 'So, you'll block the seam in aid of the cause. We have to hold up production – anything to thwart the war effort and help bring Britain into the German empire. Just place the fuse where I told you and it'll be put down to flawed props or roof planks.'

'*We* have to hold up production?' Ralph had asked. Who? he wondered, and not for the first time. Who did Tim take *his* orders from? Were they around Massingham, feeding Swinton information? Well, they must be.

'Drip by drip's the way to hurt the British,' Tim had insisted, ignoring Ralph's question.

But now the funerals were over and pit gossip had it that Mrs Bedley was struggling with drink. The girls and Stan were grief-stricken and Ralph didn't want to be part of the *we*, not any more. His mouth tasted sour and the wind snagged at his cap. He thrust his head down and pushed on the pedals. No, he didn't want it any more. The men beneath the coal had been kind to him when others called him 'the whelp'.

Tom Bedley, Davey's father, had clapped him on the shoulder more than once and told him he'd 'get t'hang of it soon enough, lad, and not to fret'. Joe Hall, Stan's father, had said, 'It'll get easier, lad. Not many'd come into the pit from yer boss class. Yer'll learn, lad.'

'You shouldn't have been there,' he whispered now. The

wind took no notice, and neither did the sheep. He yelled it again: 'You shouldn't bloody well have been there.' But even as he shouted he could still see their faces and feel Tom's hand on his shoulder.

'Yes, it was a bad mistake,' Tim had said when Ralph reported in, telephoning from the Massingham telephone box to the number Tim had given him in London. It was a number that changed all the time and it usually connected to a public telephone box.

'Oh God, what have I done?' he whispered as he cycled alongside his father's land. He had said the same to Tim.

'Don't make that mistake again,' Tim had replied, 'though thinking about it, it means two fewer experienced pitmen, which can't be bad.'

'They were people. They're dead,' Ralph had repeated. 'Dead. You said no one—'

Tim had snapped, 'As I said, collateral damage. It happens in wars. Remember what we're fighting for – a different system where we are governed by those who understand business, and order. Always order. To achieve this requires discipline, obedience and punishment. You do understand punishment, Ralphy boy?'

'I don't want—' Ralph started, only to be interrupted by Tim again.

'Now, Ralphy boy, I do hope you're not going to say you don't want to carry on just because of a silly mistake, eh? It's war, remember. You can't just walk away. You've killed two people, remember.'

Ralph braked now, placed his feet either side of the bike, and stared up at the sky, hearing his own response. 'As though I can ever forget,' he'd murmured.

Tim had laughed. 'You will, it's just a bit raw. Remember, under Greater Germany, our country will drive forward, those who have fought to bring our success about will be rewarded – property will be re-distributed, power will be taken from those who have it now, and handed to us, the Fascist fighters. Now you just have to remember that you are Ralph Massingham, son of Reginald. You're tough, rude and angry, not weak or a crybaby. Your job is to stay just like the Ralph people know, or questions will be asked. If you don't feel angry, pretend. Your other task, if I have to remind you, is to get access to the munitions factory. The Fran Hall access has failed, so make it happen with someone else. America's in the war now, so we have to try harder to achieve success. Got that? If not, lad, it might become known that a fuse was set, two men were killed, and lo and behold, it was all done by the boss's son, and a bit of a drop from a rope for you, eh? Or if one accident can happen, so can several more. Oh dear, no more Massinghams. Goodbye, Reginald, goodbye, Sophia.'

Ralph cycled on, his mouth still dry, his sweat still icy as he turned into Massingham Hall drive. He looked ahead and to either side at the hills, then behind to Massingham village and on to the pit. Now, and only now, could he understand Stan Hall's love for it. Now, when it was too late.

His foot slipped on the pedal and it caught his ankle. 'Bugger,' he shouted, then again, and again. He dragged his arm across his eyes. Bloody wind. The bike wobbled and he pedalled faster. He made his mind settle as he passed the oaks, counting them.

He must watch the road. Concentrate. He was going home. His hands were sore from the pit, from producing coal for Britain, so at least today, and many other days, he'd done something for his country ... He must work something out, pretend he was going along with it all and find a way—

Ralph braked and became aware that he had been squashing the rolled-up poster featuring the Hogmanay concert at one of the Massingham-owned pubs, the Rising Sun. Had Stevie asked for permission? he wondered, digging for the Ralph Massingham rage he needed to portray. How would that Ralph Massingham feel about Fran Hall swanning about and singing in one of his family's pubs after she'd got the better of him? All that attention he had paid her, all that manipulating with the poaching to make an opening to dig for information about her workplace . . . all come to nothing. But she wouldn't have said anything, he knew that now.

He'd talked to Stan when the hewer gave him the poster to put up on his ride home, which he had forgotten to do. Stan had looked bloody awful, which wasn't surprising because Ralph had heard that the pitman had been sleeping in an armchair at Sarah Bedley's house because the mother needed help to stop drinking. No, don't think of that. He lifted his head to the sky. The wind was harsher. Don't think of Stan's words. 'It's grief,' Stan had said. Grief, because her husband was dead. He pedalled hard up the incline.

He heard the sheep, they were close to the dry stone wall, and they were Massingham sheep and he was a Massingham. He'd get out of this hell he'd made for himself somehow and repair the damage he'd done, somehow. And keep his family safe, somehow. Until then he had to play the game.

Cycling round the corner of Massingham Hall into the yard, he bumped over the cobbles, slowed and stopped before dismounting and pushing the bike into the garage.

He stared across towards the house, the poster still rolled in his hand. He rammed it in his pocket because it was what the old Ralph would do.

He loved this house and had feared he'd be sent away when his father had found the British Union of Fascists uniform. It had been hanging in Ralph's wardrobe when his father had decided to help him pack for his last term at school. He had stared in disbelief when Ralph had told him it wasn't his, that he was looking after it for someone. He could still hear his father hiss, 'That appalling Fascist Tim Swinton, I suppose. Time his father did something about him, but I doubt he knows. Swinton's many things, but he is a believer in democracy.'

After that, his father had checked Ralph's every move and, being extra cautious, had forbidden his attendance at Fascist *and* Communist meetings. A bit late, young Ralph had thought, smug and sure. Now, as he went round to the front of the house, Ralph wished he had listened, but instead he had gone to Berlin for the Olympics with Tim when his father thought it was a school trip to the sporting event. He could remember vividly the cleanliness, the order, the friendliness and excitement of the Games. What a fool he was.

He walked in the front entrance because that's what he had always insisted on doing, although he was filthy and Sophia preferred that he didn't. She was passing through the hall, looked at his boots, and the footprints, but merely said, 'Oh, Ralph, darling. You have just missed a call from a young lady called Amelia. She sounded so nice but perhaps a little sad. She's in digs in Sledgeford, she was telling me. Wasn't that the girl you met at poor Mr Bedley's and Mr Hall's funeral? I wrote down her telephone number on the pad. She said she knew you from Oxford.'

Sophia pointed to the hall table. 'She will be at the telephone box at five.' She checked her watch. 'There is time for a bath, don't you think? You might care to use the bathroom in the staff quarters. So much easier for Mrs Phillips or me to clean when we're working in the kitchen. You know we have no staff beyond Mrs Phillips.'

There was silence as he looked at her, wanting to do as Sophia wished, though the other Ralph wouldn't. But then his father called from the study, 'Entirely up to you, as I've told you before, Ralph. But would you be so kind as to sweep the stairs if you use your own bathroom? And then clean the bath afterwards.'

Ralph felt the anger rising and was glad . . .

The front door slammed open and in came the evacuee lads from Newcastle, who wiped their feet only after Sophia pointed to the large doormat. They rushed past Ralph and one of them leapt up, knocking his cap off.

'Howay, mister, you should know 'tis rude to wear yer cap inside, you being a toff, an' all.'

Ralph stamped across the hall, leaving the cap where it lay until his father roared, 'Pick up that cap, Ralph, and have your bath in your mother's preferred bathroom. She has also laid out clothes for you. And then you might like to dadd the filthy ones you're presently wearing on the back wall, or if you don't like, ask Mrs Phillips if she would mind most dreadfully. One or the other.'

The boys were rushing up the stairs, and his stepmother, who had originally been his nanny, followed them. He longed for her to look at him again as she looked at them.

At five o clock Ralph telephoned Amelia and found some relief in chatting to the girl he vaguely knew from the time she had worked in an office in Oxford. He hadn't realised she worked at the munitions factory until he'd met her again. On and on she'd gone, against all the rules, showing off about the dangers and the courage needed. Could Amelia be his way into the Factory? If he got in, perhaps he could somehow foul up his sabotage attempt, escape, leave the area and finally get Tim Swinton off his back. He continued with the call and for the first time in years, he actually sent up a prayer.

At six, his stepmother called him into the drawing room for sherry. His father was there, standing by the roaring fire. In the corner of the room a spruce tree that had been cut down from the estate was trimmed with some of the decorations he had made with Sophia before his real mother died. After her funeral, he had been sent back to boarding school. On his return for the Christmas holidays he'd discovered Sophia and his father were married. He had never been able to see a Christmas tree without a spurt of pain and rage. But since the deaths, he could. That was all over.

His father handed him a sherry and for a moment it was peaceful, as life should be. Outside, the snow was falling.

Ralph sat opposite his stepmother and lit a cigarette, but then the boys burst in. Sophia laughed and said, 'Quietly now, play snakes and ladders over by the window.'

The boys knelt down on the carpet, taking turns to rattle the dice, until one looked up and called, 'When are the girls coming, Mrs Massingham?'

Sophia exchanged looks with her husband, then replied, 'We're not quite sure yet, Tommy, but probably in the New Year.'

Ralph looked from Sophia to his father. 'Girls?'

'Aye,' bawled Tommy, 'we're having some who've been evacuated but who ain't got homes yet and are stuck in an 'ome. They'll get on reet enough 'ere, that they will.'

'I'm sorry, Ralph,' Sophia said. 'I was going to tell you in just a moment.'

Ralph drained his glass. How would old Ralph respond? He knew, of course he did. '*Tell* me, not *ask* me. You've just *told* me we have no staff beyond Mrs Phillips, but you intend to fill our house with more riff-raff, so who the hell will look after all of them?'

'That's enough, Ralph,' his father snapped.

Sophia frowned as the boys left the game and crept from

the room. She rose. 'Ralph, I repeat, I was going to tell you, and then we could have discussed it. You are right, we have no staff, but I have an excellent idea and let me tell you about it now. As you know, we have some wonderful women in Massingham who are talented rug-makers and who I'm sure will be happy to pass on all their household craft tips to the children, as well as want to help in other ways. Of course, we will pay for this help, which might prove useful to the widows amongst them. In the meantime, please don't call anyone we welcome to this house riff-raff – it's not worthy of you, or this family. We are at war and we have to do all we can.'

He relaxed into his role, and why not? After all, this was who he had been for so long, and was horribly familiar. 'This house is my father's, not yours. You were just the bloody nanny, you idiotic woman.'

His father roared louder than Ralph had ever heard: 'How dare you speak in that way to your stepmother? She has tried to care for you without attempting to take your mother's place. Sophia is right. We are at war. You are doing your bit in the pit, which is very much to your credit, and therefore *we* must do what we can as we have this cavernous house. I insist that you understand that. I insist that you behave as a Massingham should.'

Ralph stood now, squaring up to his father, seeing the rage he had felt for so many years in the older man's steely grey eyes, and why not? How would anyone feel differently if he had Ralph Massingham for a son?

He spun round. 'Forgive me, Sophia. I don't know what came over me. And at Christmas-time too. You're quite right, of course, we must all do what we can. Count me in on that, eh?'

Sophia smiled, but her eyes were wary at such a sudden capitulation. His father patted his shoulder. 'Good man.

Strange and stressful times – we say things that on reflection we regret. The lads have spirit, and I feel that is something to be prized, eh, even though it might grate from time to time. Remember that the Massingham family never takes the privilege of its position for granted, eh? We've worked damned hard over the last two generations to build the family up from nothing, and our ethic is one of fairness. Now, another drink, everyone, before dinner, which is rather special: the gamekeeper, our very own Mr Eggars, managed to bag a few pheasants. Makes a change to rations, eh? And we even have a goose for Christmas.'

Ralph poured the sherry with a shaking hand. Things were back on track, but never for a moment could he, or must he, forget about the promise Tim had made regarding his parents if Ralph reneged on his commitment.

Chapter Six

New Year's Eve, Bletchley Park

Davey checked his watch as he decoded the last message that morning, knowing there'd be a flood of them by the time he arrived back from lunch. All around were the sounds of clicking, whirring, coughing and sniffing as the men and women of the section worked on the machines, which were copies of the German Enigma.

Every twenty-four hours the German settings for the codes changed, but the amazing machine devised by minds such as Turing's computed them, the hut adjusted their machines to that day's setting and the decoding work began. On and on, hour after hour, they pressed keys and decoded the latest intercepts. He was getting good at recognising a signaller's 'signature' and passed on the information to Norah, the elderly woman in charge, who would trot off to disseminate the information to someone else. Who, Davey had no idea. He knew better than to ask.

He saw from the corner of his eye that Daniel, who shared his digs, was on his feet, beckoning him over and pointing at his watch. Davey wanted to telephone Fran before she took the bus to the Factory for the aft shift. He needed to wish her luck for the pub concert, and hear her precious voice. Davey swallowed, the usual longing for her sweeping over him. He walked out with Daniel and grinned at Norah, who said, 'Tell her to break a leg, eh? That means good luck, in case you ignoramuses don't know.'

'Aye, I do an' all. Not sure about Daniel. He's a shilling short of a nine-bob note—Ouch.' For Daniel had whacked the back of his head. As he rubbed it, Davey said, 'I'll let her know, Norah. She'll be reet glad, and do an encore for you.'

Norah was waving him away. 'Get on with you, daft lads.'

Daniel, a step behind, said, 'Ignoramus yourself, Norah. Of course I know, so very there.'

'Is this a kindergarten I'm in charge of?' Norah called to the closing door.

They laughed as they walked down the gravel path and Daniel slapped Davey's back this time. 'She's a good sort. Too bloody clever by half, of course.'

They headed for the canteen hut, but Davey diverted from the path towards the Victorian mansion.

'Give her a big kiss from me, eh?' Daniel called after him.

'Aye, you've got to be daft to think that's even a possibility, you beggar. Grab me a plateful of whatever's going, eh, lad?'

Daniel's laugh reached him as he went inside, glad to be out of the chill. He hadn't known it got so cold down South. He hadn't known a lot of things, but especially how much he'd miss Fran and his marrers – and Massingham, always Massingham. He headed for the public phone box to the left of the hall, checking his watch again: 11.50. Aye, she'd be at the phone box. He waited to be put through, put in his money and pressed the button. 'Bonny lass,' he said. 'Norah says to break a leg, but I say good luck – not that you need it. Just do yer stuff.'

Her laugh was loud. 'Stuff? That's what Bert says.'

He heard his sister Sarah. 'Howay, our Davey, you behaving, eh? What about Daisy? Is she still saying Daniel led her on? Bit of a daft one, eh. First you, and then him. Sounds a wee bit lonely—'

'A wee bit summat anyway.' Beth had clearly snatched the phone. 'You all reet, bonny lad?'

Before he could answer, he heard Fran again. 'Tek no notice, our Davey. They've gone for the bus now.' She was laughing.

'Have you got yer clothes for tonight?' Davey asked. 'The taxi's coming as you arranged at six? It won't tek him long to get to the Rising Sun. Are you word—'

Fran cut through. 'Davey, dearest Davey, we've got it all sorted, never you fear, bonny lad.'

'I just wish I were there, pet,' he murmured. 'I miss you with such a longing.'

She replied quietly, 'Aye, me an' all. If I look ahead I canna bear the length of it, for how long will it be? But then I think we're the same as everyone else. War is war.'

The pips sounded. Davey fed in more money. He could hear her breathing and wanted to hold her. He wanted to cheer her this evening, wanted her to be wonderful, but how could she, along with the other two, be anything else?

He asked, 'Is yer mam and Stan going to be there, and Ben?'

He could almost see her shake her head, her chestnut hair bouncing as she did so, as she said, 'Not Mam or Mrs Smith, for . . .' She hesitated, and he took over from her.

'My mam, you mean? The co-op's still on guard, are they? You said it had got a bit better when I rang at Christmas and two days ago. I suppose you're still no nearer to finding out where she's getting the bliddy stuff from? I know I've said it before, but I'll say it again: I'm sorry it ruined Christmas.'

'And I've said it before, and will say it again: no, it didn't. We had to work anyway, like the rest of the country, and the concert went off all right, and Ben went to George's, which was a damn sight happier than staying at home, but next year it will be different. Hey, the war might be over.'

They laughed. Fran went on, 'But back to your mam: the pub and off-licence are still selling her nowt. She just says she's having a little bit of a nip now and again, barely nowt, she says, but we reckon it's more than a nip. She has to be getting it on the black, but who?'

Davey sighed. 'I wish I were there to sort it.'

They'd sworn to one another that there'd be no secrets ever again after he'd made a fool of himself with his stay over at Daisy's and she'd struggled with Ralph, so when he asked, Fran answered and that was the best way, but it still made his heart sink into his boots.

'Aye, but it's early days. We're all getting over the missing of our fathers, and them their husbands, in our own way. I think the Christmas concert helped us, gave us confidence, and this one tonight will, too. We just need something to help *her*.' There was a pause, and she began again. 'Just think, Davey, we can give out the collection to the area's widows like the Reverend Walters did with the money the canteen gave on Christmas Day, and have a fee to divide up to help at home, and with the booze bill when we find the damn thing. She's hidden it, says she doesn't know what we're talking about. Don't worry, it'll all be grand, so it will, and yer mam'll get straight.'

Davey checked his watch again: it was midday. 'You best be going, sweet canny girl, or you'll hold up the bus and Mrs Oborne will carry on like a tornado.'

Fran was laughing quietly. 'Aye, you're right. I'll sing for you tonight, my love.'

The pips were going again. 'And one song for Norah, eh?'

Again, he heard her laugh, then she shouted, 'I love you, to the sky and back. Now America's in the war, it'll get better.'

He shouted 'I love you,' then realised that those in the foyer had stopped what they were doing and were listening. He replaced the receiver, saying as he left the booth, 'It's me lass.'

Miss Downes, a sort of boss amongst other sorts of bosses, who had been passing, turned at the door to her office and raised an eyebrow. 'No, we'd never have guessed, would we, everyone?'

Davey laughed as he scooted across the hall and crunched along the gravel path to the canteen hut, drawing the scarf his mam had knitted before . . . Well, before the grief got to her. He blessed the co-op women who were still taking shifts, and Fran and Stan, who were staying every night.

He entered the canteen, which was muggy and warm and smelled of lunch. It was the same smell every day, and what's more, though the food was different, it tasted much the same every day too. Daniel was beckoning him. Colin, who was another boarder at their digs, was sitting with him doing the newspaper crossword.

Daniel shifted along the bench. 'You're so late it'll be cold.'

Davey grimaced. 'Ah well.' He ate the congealed mince as Daniel asked what songs Fran, Beth and Sarah would be singing. Davey answered with his mouth full.

'That's disgusting.' It was Daisy, who was squeezing in opposite with a full plate. 'So, it's the concert tonight? Shame it's not here, you could have taken me, Daniel. After all, we got on so well while Davey was away.'

Daniel sighed. 'I walked you back from the pub. I'm not sure you could call that getting on so well.'

Daisy winked. 'So that's what you call it, is it, walking me home?'

The three men left as one, no longer bothered by Daisy's

nonsense. Everyone had realised she exaggerated. 'See you later, Daisy,' called Colin.

There was no answer.

Fran, Sarah and Beth each carried their bottles of water in one bag and their best clothes in another as they found places on the bus for the aft shift. There was no Stan and his marrers to see them off, because the men had wangled the fore shift again so they could be there for the whole of the Hogmanay concert. They'd cycle over, each wheeling another bike so they and the girls could cycle back together.

As Cecil roared off, Mrs Oborne called, 'Yer lad got through on the telephone then, our Fran?'

Fran smiled, hearing Davey's voice all over again. 'Oh aye, wishes he was coming, and I wish he were too.'

She looked out of the window at the lightly falling snow and Beth called across the aisle, 'Here's hoping it doesn't keep going, or people'll stay away.'

Sarah grinned. 'Never mind the audience, it's us who'll not get through to Minton.'

Fran nudged her. 'Our lad'll crawl through drifts to hear you, and if you're not there, he'll set off to find yer, don't you fret.'

Cecil's windscreen wipers were scraping backwards and forwards because the snow lay so heavily on them. The women fell into quiet chatter, for the aft shift didn't suit them. After all, everyone had already done a morning's work in the house or with the ARP, then had to set to and work for eight hours and not be home till midnight.

Beth leaned across the aisle. 'Me mam's going to get your mam to finish her rug today, Sarah. The co-op are trying to keep her busy and it'll be good for her to be square with the Briddlestone's orders. Bring in the usual money too.' She spoke quietly because they didn't want the whole bus to know the details of Mrs Bedley's troubles, even though some did.

Mrs Oborne leaned forward, speaking from the seat behind. 'Aye, she's a grand hooky worker, and to finish'll give her summat to be proud of.'

They ground up the hill and around the corner into Sledgeford, where the women were stamping their feet against the cold. Cecil called as he drew to a halt, 'Quick as yer like. 'Tis starting to lie now, so I have to tek it a bit slow on the bends.'

The three girls looked at one another and grimaced.

Beth murmured, 'I hope it bliddy well stops before we have to leave at six.'

'I were just thinking of the Factory Christmas concert,' Mrs Oborne whispered. 'It were snowing like this, remember, then it stopped. But it looked magical. I expected to see Santa in his sledge any minute.'

Maisie leaned forward, saying, 'It were right good of you girls to give Amelia, Brenda and Rosie fifteen minutes, but it still weren't enough, were it? That Amelia took twenty. I don't know what yer do with someone like her.'

Fran sighed, remembering Miss Ellington's face when she had finally stormed on stage and announced, 'Now for The Factory Girls' in the middle of the Office Girls' rendition of their rivals' song, 'All or Nothing at All'.

'Mebbe Amelia just couldn't see the clock,' Sarah muttered.

'Aye, and mebbe elephants fly. Next you'll be saying she couldn't see Miss Ellington's face and gestures which said clearly she was a second away from strangling the three of them. Well, if she could with one hand. Or maybe she'd have ripped their throats out with her teeth.' Even as Maisie said it, she started laughing and soon they were all at it.

They arrived at the Factory on time and all hurried in

with their glad rags in a bag. The rest of the aft shift would go to the Hogmanay celebrations at the pub straight from the bus at the end of their shift because only the three singers could be spared to leave early. Their men would bring their bikes or they'd walk home at the end of the evening.

As they headed for the gate, the snow stopped. 'Just a shower then,' Maisie said, looking up at the sky. 'Don't look as though there's much more. Me bairn'll be sorry, but me mam'll be reet glad, for all the bairns'll want to head to the slope with their sledges or trays, but they'll not let the schools out early if it's not falling heavy.'

They were smiling as they showed their passes and made their way to the changing rooms. They were on bullets this week and after checking one another for 'contraband', as metallic objects were called, they headed down the corridor in their overalls, with Miss Ellington clucking like a mother hen behind Fran, Sarah and Beth.

'You must rush to the canteen when break is called at five thirty,' she said, 'and grab some food to eat in the taxi. Yer can change your clothes at the Rising Sun. It'd be good if the others could go early too, but they can't. Too much to do, but you know that. I left the collection bucket with Stevie at the Rising Sun on my way home yesterday.'

At the entrance to the bullet workshop, Swinton gestured to the three of them to move down to the other end where the task was to press detonators into the tops of the bullets. They replaced three of the fore shift, who grinned, muttering, 'We'll be there tonight. Need a bit of a sing-song and knees-up to kick this bliddy year into the back of beyond. The war canna go on much longer, can it?'

Fran sat on the high stool. She never liked someone else's warmth, not even on a bus, and pulled a face. She shrugged, picked up a small detonator and pressed it into the end of the bullet, then placed it carefully into its tray. Then the next one, and the next, and again and again while the tannoy played music, and then 'All or Nothing at All' came on and she found herself singing, quietly at first, then on hearing the other two join in, the whole bench started singing.

She knew they shouldn't, for they must concentrate, but they had been working carefully for so long, she was sure they could do both. As they sang, she suddenly felt so happy, so excited and so in love. She just wished Davey could be there tonight. She looked along the bench at Beth and as the song ended called, 'Aye, our Sarah's a lucky lass, having her man there tonight, eh, our Beth? Have you written back to Bob yet?'

She pressed in another detonator, then another, as Beth replied, 'Oh aye, we're getting into a pattern. I write most days, he writes once a month.' She was laughing. 'But I lay it under me pillow and dream of him, so it's part way close to having him home and with me.'

They fell silent as Sarah and Fran each wondered what it would be like to share a bed with their man.

On and on they worked, but then the belt that took away the trays and brought empty ones juddered to a stop. The groan from them all rose above the music from the tannoy. They stepped away from the belt as the fitter was called.

Fran stood, checking the clock. It was four forty-five. She was nervous now, really nervous, and wished they were working to keep their minds busy. Beside her, Sarah was humming, and soon Beth joined in, and they did the steps they'd learned in time with the music. The whole row copied them until Swinton came along and bawled, 'This is a workshop, not a bliddy music hall, and if you think you three girls are getting off early if this belt failure goes on and on, think again. What I want to know is – is it sabotage?' He stalked off. 'I've things to do. I'll be back. And get on and mend the bliddy thing, Alan.'

They all waited and the clock ticked on. Swinton's words had resonated. But he couldn't keep them here, not when he'd promised, surely? Beth pressed against Fran. 'It isn't fair.' Fran just kept looking at the clock as five ten was reached.

At that moment the fitter stood up and put away his tools. Swinton was back, and Alan said, 'There you are, gov'ner, fit to go. Just a bit of a maintenance problem, bound to happen sometimes, no one's been fiddling. Reckon it'll probably be all right, but we need that part. T'beggar still baint come yet.'

Swinton listened, his hands in his pockets. Fran said, 'About thirty minutes, Mr Swinton, that's all it took.'

'Aye, that's as mebbe, but that's a lot of bullets lost. Your section needs to make its target, and what's more, I canna risk it happening again this shift. We're too short-staffed with the flu going round to make up the shortfall, so it's all hands on deck and work like the devil from now on. You heard the man, they really need a new part, and there's a war on, you know. Our lads need them more'n you need to sing, so best get on with it. The deputy section manager Mr Bolton's been on the case and tells me that's that.' He wasn't shouting as he usually did, and he didn't rise onto his toes or meet their eyes either.

Fran stepped forward, but Miss Ellington had come in on the heels of Mr Swinton's order and held up her hand at Fran, pointing to the belt. The girls returned to the bench and the bullets. To her horror, Fran's eyes were filling, for they had the tab at the corner shop to pay, and bills and headstones to save for, and Mrs Bedley's booze debt, once they found it, and all the time the interest would be mounting . . .

She stepped back from the belt, dragged her sleeve across her face, keeping her back to Mr Swinton and her two

94

friends. They must not see. They needed her to be strong, but that wasn't all, for what they also needed was to sing tonight, to show off their skills so they would be booked by others. It would make all the difference now their fathers were no longer providing for the families.

She returned to the bench, where Sarah was openly weeping. 'Step away. It's dangerous,' Fran insisted quietly. 'Don't worry, Miss Ellington will sort it.'

Beth was crying too, and she stepped back with Sarah. They stood arm and arm. Fran worked on, glancing towards Miss Ellington, who was talking earnestly to Mr Swinton, who, to Fran's surprise, looked as upset as Miss Ellington. Finally, the SO nodded and Fran thought she heard her say, 'I'll see what I can do with her.'

Miss Ellington then stormed over to the girls. 'Stop that,' she snapped at Sarah and Beth. 'You have work to do. I'm going to see Amelia, see if I can work me charm and get her to take yer shift. Just work on. I'll come back soon.'

They worked and the time ticked by. They didn't sing now, no one did, and at five thirty the meal break was called, though Miss Ellington still hadn't returned. The three of them didn't want food but they sat with their usual friends, Mrs Oborne, Maisie and Valerie, and listened as the others on the table shouted across to the table on their right and told them what had happened. Each table shared the news. The clock was nearing six when Miss Ellington and Mrs Raydon entered the canteen, weaving their way between the tables towards them.

'Hey up, lass,' said Mrs Oborne. 'What news?'

Miss Ellington stood there, her one hand in an overall pocket, her truncated arm hanging by her side. It was as though she had to force herself to look at the three girls. 'I asked. I've spent all this time asking, cajoling and begging Amelia. But as Mr Swinton said, he had already asked her, and she repeated, somewhat brusquely I have to say, that she was otherwise engaged, and so were the other two office girls.' Miss Ellington looked up at the ceiling and cleared her throat. 'They have Hogmanay plans which cannot be broken. I have spoken to Mr Bolton, who said that Mr Swinton had already spoken to him about the problem and had tried for replacements unsuccessfully from other departments. Bolton insisted the first priority was the war and that you can catch up with the Rising Sun at the end of the shift. I'm so very sorry—'

Mrs Raydon interrupted. 'I offered to take your places, but Bolton refused and I suppose he's right, I do have my own role.'

Fran swallowed, for even Mr Swinton, usually so awful, had tried and that made her really want to weep. Across the table Mrs Oborne mouthed 'Gumption', but looked so grim that Fran feared for Bolton's life if he appeared this minute. Fran smiled and shrugged. 'Well, you can't win 'em all, eh, girls. There might be other bookings – this isn't the end.' But she thought perhaps it was.

Miss Ellington looked relieved. 'I have telephoned the taxi and asked it to be here on the dot of ten. You will be at the Rising Sun by elevenish to welcome in the New Year with your singing. I have also telephoned Stevie.' Her voice broke. 'He knew. He said he'd had an offer of a singing group who telephoned him on the off chance just twenty or so minutes ago. They'd had a change of plan, apparently. He will make sure a collection is taken for the widows.'

Mrs Oborne snapped, 'Who is the replacement? Bit bliddy convenient, weren't it, someone contacting them just as it were all kicking off here. Have we a bliddy name?'

Miss Ellington just shook her head. 'Well, let's face it, life is very strange these days, isn't it, Mrs Oborne? It was someone whose own booking had fallen through, it seems. But at least let's concentrate on the good news that there'll be a collection.' She and Mrs Raydon began to walk away, then stopped, and Miss Ellington said to the girls, 'Try not to fret. You can take over when you get there, and remember, there'll probably be other pubs, other evenings, other . . .' She stopped and the two security officers marched towards the door, but Fran ran after her.

'Cancel the taxi, if you would. It'll be cheaper. We'll go on the bus with our friends. Cecil drives like a lunatic anyway, so we won't lose time. Come with us too.' She hugged the security officer, determined that Miss Ellington wouldn't see how upset she was, how much they worried about money. The security officer was right – they'd have a bit of a turn once they got there, and that might be enough to spread the word.

Chapter Seven

Stan, Sid and Norm brought the girls' bikes to the Rising Sun, cycling by moonlight. They arrived at about eight and propped them up in the backyard, amongst plenty of others. Their caps were coated with snow, and their hands felt frozen. They hurried to the back door along the path, which had snow banked high on either side, and ash scattered along it.

'Bad enough I left me bicycle clips behind and me trouser bottoms are soaked,' grumbled Norm, 'but to get a wet arse cycling home if it snows again will be the bliddy end.'

'Sid, give him a whack and end all his miseries, especially if he's going to mither all evening,' grunted Stan, reaching the door first. Behind him Sid slipped on the snow and crashed into the dustbin, which tipped over. The lid rolled in a circle and the rubbish spilled out. The clatter set the village dogs barking.

'Bliddy hell, lad,' Norm groaned.

The three of them gathered up the rubbish and finally made it into the blacked-out lobby, vaguely hearing the lasses singing over the raucous chat and laughter. It was Stan's fault they were late, the others had mithered as they pedalled like fury to get here, but he'd had to wrestle Sarah's boozed mam to her armchair, and his mam had to come to get her up to bed. As he'd said to his mam, it didn't seem right for him to do it. As he left, Mrs Smith had arrived, so between them they'd manage.

Stan was still trying to fathom where Mrs Bedley had

got the drink as he felt for the door handle into the bar. Bliddy blackout. He went on feeling for the latch as he wondered. Well, on the black, obviously, but who from? He had been given the task of finding out by Mrs Smith and his mam as he left. 'Easier said than done,' he'd grunted.

His mam had just stood there, arms akimbo, with that look on her face which meant 'Don't mither, just get on wi' it.'

Norm said, as Stan continued to run his hand over the door, 'Mebbe yer could ask Stevie tonight, quiet like? He's likely to have been offered some, so might have a few names.'

Stan laughed. 'Mind-reader now, are you? Just what I were thinking.'

'Nay, lad, but I've been mithering on t'way over, cos what if it were me mam going under? I'd be right worried, so don't tell your Sarah about Mrs Bedley this night. There won't be nowt she can do and it'll put her off her stride. But by, all them bottles must be costing a fair bit, so Sarah'll likely need all her fee and more just to begin to pay the tab her mam's building up.'

Stan nodded. He'd been checking his own funds and still had a bit left over from his university vacation work for Professor Smythe that would help, but it made him angry. It was such a waste to chuck money down your throat instead of getting on with things. 'Where's this bliddy latch?' he muttered. He heard louder laughter from the bar and it made him even angrier, for the drinkers weren't listening to The Factory Girls, and he'd not have it.

'What're yer doing, Stan?' asked Norm. 'Get on in, lad, for the love of God. I want to wet me whistle.'

Sid struck a match. They saw that the latch was high on the door. 'Bliddy silly place to put it when you've thirsty pitmen breathing on the hinges,' he muttered. 'I'll tell Stevie that an' all.'

'It's a Massingham-owned pub,' said Norm, 'so just tell the whelp when he's shoving his tub full of coal, eh.'

At last they walked into the light and warmth of the bar and tried to thread their way through the drinkers to the girls. 'Excuse us,' Sid shouted, dodging Eddie Corbitt, another pitman at Auld Hilda, who swung round, a tankard in his hand.

'Load of rubbish them singers are,' Eddie shouted.

Stan just stared at him. 'Watch yer mouth, Eddie. That's me girl you're talking about.'

Grabbing him by the arm, Eddie hauled him aside. 'Yer gone daft or what, lad?' He pointed to the end of the room where the singers were performing.

Stan stared at Amelia and her two friends. Alfie was on the accordion, squeezing out the tune. One of the girls was a beat behind, and another didn't know the words.

'Bliddy hell, what're *they* doing here?' spluttered Sid. 'In't she the lass who wrote that anonymous note—'

Norm hushed him. 'That's between us, not the whole bliddy room, lad.'

Eddie nodded from the girls to Stan and the two lads ranged beside him. 'Best talk to Stevie about why they're here. He got shirty when I did and said he were sick of hearing us mither about the "entertainment".'

Heading over to the bar, Stan signalled to Stevie, who was busy dispensing his elderberry wine, the one that had a kick like a mule. There was beer on tap too, which old Mr Oborne, who was propping up the bar, pointed towards. 'Howay, our Stan, have a pint, eh? Mek sure he pulls it from the pump on the right. It's a special, just for regulars. It'll tek yer mind off that bliddy racket. What're them girls doin' here anyway? 'Tisn't what our Tilly said were to happen. It should have been yer lasses, shouldn't it? But Stevie took the 'ump when I asked.'

Behind the bar, Stevie was working his way towards them, dodging behind his missus, who was wiping beer tankards. He didn't look at Stan, just busied himself dragging the tea towel from his shoulder and wiping the bar free of beer spills as he said, 'Afore yer ask, yer lasses couldn't come off shift, and Miss Amelia Cartwright phoned from her office, said they'd offered to tek the girls' places on the line, but were told no. Summat broke, a belt or something, not that they best be putting that about like they are, when there's a bleedin' war on. So, she offered and I accepted. Nowt more to say. Put yer money in the collection for the first drink, 'tis only fair.'

He jerked his head towards a large pot on the bar. 'I have to pay these girls, see, so I want a collection for The Factory Girls, for 'tisn't their fault they let me down.' It was only then that he looked up. 'Sorry, lad, truly I am, but 'tis done now.'

Sid was putting money in the pot, making room for Norm to do the same. They both looked from Stevie to Stan as Stevie drew their beers from the right-hand pump. He slapped the tankards down. Stan tossed a bob into the pot and said, 'Not your fault, and the pot's right good of you, Stevie.'

Further along, Josie, the lass who helped Stevie and Mildred, was pouring glasses of elderberry wine for some Minton women who'd just come in through the front door. Snow lay on their headscarves. Their money went into the pot as Stevie muttered, 'The elderberry is me own makings and cost nowt, so we'll keep the pot going all night for that.'

Now Stan knew why everyone was talking over the singers, and why Alfie on the accordion was looking as though he'd sucked a lemon. Though where he'd get a lemon in this war, heaven only knew. Stan started to laugh, his beer slopping, as Mr Oborne raised his eyebrows at Sid and Norm.

'Howay, lads, what's up wi' yer marrer, eh? Got a touch of the hysteria, eh? Needs to get his beer down quick, I reckon, or someone give him a slap.' His guffaw made him cough.

Stan sank half the pint in a few gulps, wiped his mouth, then said, 'Aye, well, it's the end of a bliddy awful year for them girls and now they're missing out when they've practised so bliddy hard, when life's dealt 'em a load of rubbish. And tek a look at Alfie's face and tell me it doesn't sum up the whole bliddy shambles, eh?'

They were all laughing now, even Mildred, Stevie's missus. Stan raised his glass to her, then made his way over. He wasn't quite sure how to ask about things that came off the back of lorries and the people who sold them on.

'Now,' said Mildred, 'don't yer mither at me about letting them girls sing, our Stan.'

He shook his head. 'There's nothing else yer could have done, Mrs Pertwee. No, 'tis something else . . .'

'Penny for 'em, lad,' said Mildred, 'though I canna give you any work, if that's the thing. I know you're to marry, but—'

'No, it's nothing like that, Mrs P. The thing is . . . I was wondering just who you got yer best beer from?'

She merely looked at him and patted the side of her nose. 'Hey, lad, that's for me to know and you to find out, and keep your gob shut while you're at it. 'Tis just for tonight.'

He paused, then leaned on the bar as she dried some wine glasses. 'You see, I've a problem, and I'll tell you if *you* keep *yer* gob shut.'

She roared with laughter and leaned closer to him, serious now. 'I reckon 'tis Maud's supplier yer need to find, eh?' she whispered. 'It's nowt to do with this beer. It's Timothy's, yer know, lives by Minton almshouses. Just one brew a year, and where he gets the hops and yeast, I don't want to know. Nothing black market about it, not really. But wait one.' She disappeared out into the kitchen and came back with a scribbled name. 'The bloke I reckon you want's in Massingham in about three to five days' time, nasty piece o' work – no heart. We don't have no truck with that sort of thing. Reginald Massingham's a good landlord and he won't have diddling, so why go there? This bloke'll keep feeding it to her, he will, and let her have it on tick with a great wad of interest tied to it. She'll get no better till she's off it and can see her grief clearly. So, aye, best to get shot of this beggar, eh, but no names, no pack drill, got it?'

Stan read the name: Norris Suffolk. He stuffed the paper in his pocket and said, 'If I'd a diamond, I'd give it to you, and me lips're sealed.'

Mildred smiled. 'I reckon you've got a diamond in that Sarah, and you need to keep her close, for she's a stayer, she is. What's more, she . . . Well, they wanted the booking to help keep the families, but never fear, we'll ask the three of them again. I don't like that little minx Miss Cartwright, no I don't, not one bit. For she were quick enough to phone to take their spot tonight, and I doubt any of 'em warblers will share the fee wi' our lasses. 'Tis said by the wife of one of the maintenance blokes that the Cartwright girl were asked to tek their places by Swinton, can you believe, so he could release our girls. But she weren't having none of it, said she were committed elsewhere. Well, here she is, eh, committed my Aunt Fanny.'

Stan shook his head. 'Your bloke'll have got that wrong, there's nowt Swinton'd do to help a Hall. Stevie said she offered and were told no, which is more likely . . .'

'Aye, well, he forgot to tell me that. Oh, hang about, more wine needed down the end.' Mildred waved at some women who were beckoning and laughing. 'Sort out Maud Bedley, will you? There's enough bliddy nonsense going on

103

wi'out that, and one day the Americans'll come and we'll really be on the way.'

Stan smiled. 'Thanks, Mrs P.'

He headed back to the lads, but was waylaid by Madge, who was wearing a red eyepatch covered in sequins. 'Give an auld lady a dance, lad.'

Stan laughed, handed his tankard to Sid and danced a sort of two-step, for there was no room. It was what everyone else was doing anyway. While Madge chatted about the snow, the war and the co-op, all he could think was that Mildred had given him a name so he now had something to go on. He checked the clock over the fireplace. It was a while before his lass would be dropped at the pub by the bus, but once she was here and they were dancing . . . But no, she'd be singing in the New Year, course she would, and the thought made him smile.

Madge said, 'Aye, well, I'm not going to offer you a penny for yer thoughts, that smile says it all. Sooner you get wed, the better, lad.'

He spun her round again and she shrieked with glee. 'Aye, the minute everything's sorted, we will, Madge,' he said.

Steve yelled over the singing and the conversation, 'Stan, lad, put Madge down and give us a hand behind the bar. I want to give our Mildred a spin round t'room till her head swirls.'

'That'll be the day, lad,' called Mildred. 'You'll crush me feet and put me out of action for a week.'

Stan took Stevie's place behind the bar and pulled pints while Madge topped up wine glasses. The singers had a break, but Madge said they had to pay for their drinks. Amelia looked along the bar and saw Stan. She flushed, turned her back and the three of them threaded their way to the fireplace. They chatted amongst themselves, for no one welcomed them into their circle. Alfie continued to bash out tunes, and several people joined him for a singalong.

Stan worked on, a Woodbine in the corner of his mouth, and Madge chased Josie from behind the bar to have fun, while she continued to dole out the elderberry. At about half-past ten the door opened and in walked Ralph Massingham, immaculate in his suit, shirt and tie. Slowly and steadily the room became quiet, even the accordion wheezing to a stop as Ralph made his way towards the bar.

Stan sighed and forced a smile, squinting through the smoke that rose from yet another Woodbine. 'Evening, and happy New Year, Ralph. Thought you'd have been with your family on such a night. What'll you have?'

As he reached for a tankard from the shelf above the bar, he caught Stevie's gesture from the edge of the room. He was pointing to the pot and shaking his head. Stan gave a slight nod. He pulled the left-hand pump and passed over the pint. 'That'll be sixpence.' Stan rang it up on the till, watching Ralph lift the tankard, sip it, raise his eyebrows.

'Not too bad.'

'Aye,' Stevie said from behind him. 'And one day we'll have good beer again, but at least we've got through another year, so drink up – that fact's worth a celebration.'

Ralph looked at him as he sipped again. Then he reached out and touched the pot. 'And this?'

'Ah, this? Donations – money goes in there for the elderberry wine I brew. Just about coming into its prime, it be. 'Tis me own make, me own gift to the regulars, which is good for business, and they'll keep coming. Cleared with your father, of course.'

'Donations?' Ralph asked, one eyebrow raised.

'The pot's for donations to The Factory Girls, who couldn't come cos Swinton wouldn't let 'em off, or so that

Amelia says. You see, we have to pay this lot who're warbling something chronic up there, but we don't want our own lasses short, given their new expenses.'

Ralph looked at the girls, who were back on. 'Well, I'm damned, I didn't notice Amelia before. She didn't mention it.'

'Well, it was all last-minute, weren't it,' Stevie said, then added, 'In touch, is she then?'

Ralph's stare was steely. He said nothing, just sipped his beer.

Stevie made his way behind the bar and waved Stan back into the room, but Stan was reluctant. He preferred to have something solid between him and the whelp.

After half an hour more, the girls' voices were becoming weaker and more out of time, so Mildred beckoned them over for another drink. The girls steered their way through to the bar, and as they did, Stan heard Ralph call, 'Oh, I say, good show, girls. Nice to see you again, Amelia, though I didn't expect you to be singing. What happened?'

Stan moved a little further along the bar to serve Sid and Norm. All three listened as Amelia explained that the belt had broken as the girls were putting detonators into the bullets. Brenda, one of the other girls, snapped, 'No, you mustn't say what they're doing, Amelia, for God's sake.'

Amelia pulled a face while Ralph laughed and bought each of them an elderberry wine, putting money in the pot. 'Go on,' he said.

Sipping her wine, Amelia grimaced at the taste. 'Urgh, quite disgusting, but I suppose for those who know no better, Ralph . . .'

Brenda raised her eyebrows and looked at the other girl. Sid leaned across the bar and muttered in Stan's ear, 'I have a right strong urge to slap that Amelia across the chops.'

'Nay, lad,' whispered Norm. 'We don't hit ladies.' Then together they said, 'But she ain't no lady.'

Stan hushed them and moved away because Madge was calling. She had a packet of Woodbines and was offering them around. Lord knows why she'd bought them, because she was a non-smoker. She winked at Stan when he arrived. 'Well, sometimes it helps the evening along just to offer people the little firesticks, and it is Hogmanay, so why not use some of me ration from time to time?'

Amelia sank her second glass of wine and smiled at Ralph as they leaned on the bar. They had first met in Oxford, when she was a secretary at an accountant's. They'd been ships that passed in the night, but she hadn't realised he was the son of such an important man. 'It's a good opportunity to sing here, for if people like us enough, word will get about, we will get more bookings and quite likely end up in London, where I have contacts. *Workers' Playtime* was up here, of course. I made quite an impression.'

Brenda looked uncomfortable. Rosie buried her face in her drink. Ralph was buying another three glasses of elderberry wine from Stevie, but Brenda shook her head and nudged Rosie, who had been listening to two pitmen and a woman talking behind her. She turned, saw the wine, and shook her head, then said to Amelia, 'I just heard someone say that you were asked to take Fran and the girls' places today but said no. That's not what you told us, which was that they'd refused your offer. We would have been happy to do that because they made sure we sang in the Christmas concert. It makes us look mean, Amelia. So who asked you?'

Amelia just shrugged and whispered, 'Be quiet, and no one will know anything about it.'

'But we will,' Rosie whispered back.

Ralph said, 'Put your glass down – the accordionist is playing my song. We should dance to it, because I like a girl who knows what she wants, and what's more, goes out to get it.'

He put his arm around her while Amelia thrust her glass at Rosie. Ralph urged her into the centre of the room, and slowly the other dancers ebbed away to the tables while Brenda and Rosie whispered together, shaking their heads.

Further along the bar, Stevie said quietly to Stan, 'You heard that? So, why not tek your lads over to them two girls, and see what's what.'

Stan nodded as Sid and Norm looked at one another. 'Aye, I will,' he said. Sid muttered something to Rosie, then led the way across to a table set at the back of the room near the fire. Stan gathered up enough chairs and they sat, but the girls weren't talking about the Factory, or anything to do with it. Instead they discussed the moors near Thirsk, and the beck that ran through the small market town, which was near where they came from.

Talk of the Thirsk beck brought their own to Stan's mind and the picnics they'd had, and how their das had taught them to swim. Them: Sarah, Fran, Beth, Davey and him, the gang. He stretched out his legs in front of the fire. At least Sarah would be there soon to sing in the New Year, yes, at least The Factory Girls could take them into 1942. He smiled at the thought, and the smile grew broader as Brenda and Rosie moved closer to Sid and Norm. It would be good if the lads found some love. But it was then that Brenda said they'd typed up the bullet rota today, before putting her hand over her mouth. 'Forget I said that.'

They all sat, watching the flames and sipping their wine. Bullets? Stan thought. God almighty. Bullets, explosives, explosions, seven-day weeks when needed, rashes, yellow skin. At that moment, Brenda said, 'We feel right bad, taking your girls' places here. We should have taken their places at t'factory instead, but we didn't know that . . .'

There was a pause. Norm and Sid looked at Stan, who felt his brain clicking round, for at least now they really knew the truth about Amelia, but had it been Swinton or Miss Ellington who did the asking? For some reason it was really important to him to know, but he wasn't sure why. Finally, he replied carefully, 'Ah, I see. I see. So who asked you?'

Rosie said, looking over her shoulder, 'I don't know, we knew nowt about it, just that she'd offered and been turned down.'

'Ah well,' sighed Stan, ''Tis what it is, and you've done reet well. People danced to your singing. I danced.'

Rosie laughed. 'I saw you an' all, with the lady with the eyepatch. I really like that she doesn't hide it, but shows it off. That's a dollop of courage, that is.'

Sid was gazing at the golden-haired Rosie as though she was some sort of angel, and if he thought she was, well, then she was, thought Stan, but she couldn't touch his angel, his Sarah, his love. He checked the pub clock on the wall; a while yet before the bus arrived.

After fifteen minutes the girls were back with Alfie on the accordion, Ralph taking up position near to them, tapping his foot as they sang 'A-Tisket, A-Tasket'.

Sarah, Fran and Beth had changed into their evening clothes before they left the Factory, sad only that Miss Ellington had come down with a terrible headache and couldn't make it. She had arranged for a taxi to take her to Simon Parrot's in Massingham so she could explain that there would be no Hogmanay celebration at the Rising Sun for her, and only then would she head home to Sledgeford. The girls smiled at one another as they neared the pub, for it seemed that Simon and Miss Ellington's feelings for each other were now confirmed. Why else would she want to let him know that she would not be at the pub? Perhaps Simon would pack Cyn Ellington off to the spare room to sleep rather than have her take a taxi home in this cold. It would be all right, because his sister would be there to make things respectable.

As they arrived, they cheered and clapped Cecil, who had driven like the wind. Mrs Oborne led the way off the bus, but hung back for the three girls, waving the others on. She said to Fran, Beth and Sarah, 'Yer keep up them smiles, no matter how yer feel, all reet. Don't show the replacements that you care. Our Stevie will rest 'em, and you can get on with yer singing, as you deserve.'

They followed Valerie through the lobby, but bumped into her when she stopped dead in the doorway to the bar. She turned when Mrs Oborne said, 'Shift yerself.'

'It's that bliddy Amelia,' Valerie almost wailed. 'The cow, the utter bliddy cow. And she's our lodger – how can I speak to her ever again?' She stepped into the bar.

Mrs Oborne followed, peering towards the singers, then turned to Sarah, Fran and Beth, who stood staring behind her, then looked at one another, dumbfounded. 'Slap a smile on yer faces, no matter what,' she rasped. 'Seems to me like no one's listening anyway. Bliddy cheek. It isn't the way to behave – to tek advantage of others' misfortune. It just bliddy isn't. She must have made a call and set it up when she said she couldn't tek your place. I could swing for her, I bliddy could.'

As Mrs Oborne stormed over to the bar, Sarah saw Stan making his way towards them, his arms outstretched for her. She kept the smile glued to her face, and had got to four times two is eight by the time he reached her and enfolded her in his arms. 'Don't yer mind,' he said into her hair. 'Don't yer dare mind, for they're not a bliddy patch on you. How could that bliddy girl be so stupid, so greedy? Don't she know she needs marrers?'

While all around them people talked, laughed and drank,

Beth said what Sarah was thinking: 'Aye, but there's three of them who came along, not just Amelia.'

Stan stepped away from Sarah, stroking her hair into place. 'Seems the other two didn't know till half an hour ago that she took advantage. Follow me – there's elderberry wine waiting, and a pot almost full of sixpence coins to be split between you three lasses. It's Stevie's brew, so it's up to him where he puts the money. He's cleared it with Mr Massingham – the elder.' He nodded towards the 'stage'.

Fran froze, staring at Ralph, who was standing close to where the girls were singing. Beside her, Sarah muttered, 'What's he doing here? Don't worry, Fran. Stan's here, and we are too.'

Stan tried to lead the way through the drinkers, but was getting nowhere until Mrs Oborne elbowed her own way through, dragging Valerie and the others. 'Follow me. I've done me share of jumble sales, yer see if I haven't, and I needs a word or more wi' our Stevie.'

They all grinned as Mrs Oborne's elbows worked their magic and the seas parted. When people saw the three girls they began clapping and soon were all cheering. Mr Oborne yelled, 'About bliddy time. We need a decent sing-song.'

As they reached the bar they were sore from all the pats on their backs. Auld Ernie from the surface screens at Auld Hilda raised his tankard, looking like an ancient pixie sitting on his bar stool, and started to sing 'All or Nothing at All'.

Fran waved him to a stop. 'Hush, the other girls are giving it their all. We'll do it later, eh?'

Ernie grinned. 'Reet you are, then. Mek sure you do. We've been putting money in t'bucket that's just gone round for the widows, and the wine money in the pot to make up yer fee. Who knows, you might manage a headstone for yer bairn Betty soon, and yer da, Franny, and you too, girls, or mebbe just pay t'bills.'

Sarah gripped Fran's hand, then Beth's arm was round Fran's shoulders and she was calling, 'That's right grand, Ernie, you've given us lumps in our throats, so it's as well the other girls are singing. And look at it this way, if they hadn't been here, there'd have been no music, eh?'

Grinning, Ernie raised his pint glass, but whispered, 'That's as maybe, but them're not as good as our own sweet lasses.'

Not far from them Mrs Oborne was hissing at Stevie, 'What do you mean, our lasses baint be taking over to tek us into yet another bliddy year? They bliddy are, you know.'

Stan looked at Sarah. 'Wait here. I'll see what's going on.'

Fran put up her hand. 'You stay with Sarah, lad, take her for a dance, eh. Don't waste the evening. Coming, Beth?'

Side by side, they threaded their way through to Mrs Oborne, but Sarah tore away from Stan and joined them in time to hear Stevie say, 'Aye, lasses, I'm reet sorry, but they stood in, and it would have been flat if they hadn't, so 'tis only fair they mek it to midnight.'

Mrs Oborne reached across the bar and for a dreadful moment Sarah thought she was going to grab Stevie by the throat, but instead she stabbed at him with her forefinger. 'It's the end of a beggar of a year, and I hear enough cater-wauling when the old man's in his bath in front of the range. For two pins—'

'Hush, Mrs Oborne,' Sarah interrupted.

'It's an opportunity for Amelia,' said Fran.

Beth grimaced. 'Aye, one she took like a greedy bat.'

Sarah shook her head. 'We've got to try and be fair.'

Stevie was looking from one to the other, one minute relieved, the next guilty, and Sarah suddenly laughed. 'It doesn't matter. Maybe we can just sing a few if they want a break, eh? Even if it's after "Auld Lang Syne".'

Stevie immediately looked cornered, but there was no

escape because the missus was at his side now, her eyebrows raised. 'You have to tell them why you can't have them singing.'

He looked around and, leaning forward, muttered, 'Orders from above.'

The three girls and Mrs Oborne looked up. Mildred Pertwee tutted. 'Oh, don't be so bliddy daft, Stevie, they'll think you have a line to the Almighty. Spell it out.'

Stevie looked hunted again as he whipped the tea towel from his shoulder and twisted it over and over. 'Yer see, this is a Massingham-owned public house, and the whelp is here. He's taken a shine, it seems, to the pushy one from the South, so 'tis more'n me tenancy's worth to go against him, and he says she's to sing till midnght. I tried, lasses – you tell 'em, Mildred.'

Mildred nodded, her mouth in a grim line. Stevie was wiping the bar furiously now, and Sarah reached across, laying her hand on his. 'Don't worry, please. It's our fault for not being here. Of course those girls must finish the booking, 'tis only right.'

Stevie looked at her hand, then up at her. 'You always were a grand lass, and you two an' all. Yer das would be right proud of you.' He paused, then looked at Mildred, who nodded. 'Right proud,' he repeated. 'You go and have a good time, and don't yer go without the pot money, eh? We'll put it in a sack and you can divvy it up when you get it home.'

The girls kept smiles on their faces as they danced with Sid, and Norm, and Stan, and Auld Ernie from the screens, although he could only do an odd sort of hop. He'd been fitted with a wooden one after losing his lower leg in the First War. It was fine and dandy, as Beth said to Fran, as long as he didn't step on your toes.

They continued to smile, checking the clock, praying

that it would move quickly to midnight so they could cycle home, but wondering how Miss Ellington was, and hoping Simon Parrot stayed with her to see in 1942, even if it meant he was sitting quietly beside her bed.

Mrs Oborne sniffed. 'Probably asleep, or better, nestled up at the Canary Club. Reckon there might be a bit of fuse wire put round another finger an' all soon.'

Chapter Eight

Midnight struck and Amelia, Brenda and Rosie started to sing 'Auld Lang Syne'. Alfie had gone AWOL and was downing a free beer, from the right-hand pump. The revellers linked arms and sang chaotically, then launched into 'Pack up your troubles in your old kitbag and smile, smile, smile . . .' Fran, Beth and Sarah sang too, and it was wonderful to be there, with their friends, putting their all into a few community songs.

Steadily the pub fell silent, even Amelia and her friends, as the three girls sang on. Everyone swayed as they moved on to 'Keep the Home Fires Burning'. Mrs Oborne and Valerie were doing the staccato drums they had devised for the Christmas concert. Finally they were back to 'Auld Lang Syne', with everyone singing along. They paused to let the girls sing the last two lines, then Fran beckoned Amelia's group to join in: 'We'll take a cup of kindness yet, for the sake of auld lang syne.'

The revellers sang the whole thing again, raising their voices for 'We'll take a cup of kindness yet,' looking all the while at Amelia, who sang on with Ralph, though Brenda and Rosie fell silent. As the singing ended, Stan kissed Sarah, while Sid rushed to Rosie and kissed her full on the lips and she clung to him. Beth smiled as Fran's arm slipped around her. 'I divint half miss me bloke.'

'You can say that again,' said Fran.

Beth pulled her close. 'All reet then, I divint half miss me bloke.'

They were laughing when Stan hugged them both, then Sid and Norm did the same, with Rosie hanging on Sid's every word. Stevie and Mildred hugged them too, whispering, 'So sorry.'

'Don't be,' Beth whispered back, and Fran added, 'It gave us a night off, and there may be other times.'

Stevie nodded. 'Any time you like, lasses. I'll spread the word an'—' There was a banging at the door and he groaned. 'First-footers, knocking on the door to bring good luck, and a piece of coal, and food, and a dram of whisky, to ensure we will be warm and eat and drink for the rest of the year. But it'll only be coal they bring, and it'll be me giving them the whisky, and maybe a bit of toast.' Stevie rubbed his chin, his eyes knowing. 'Let me guess who's first for the free dram of whisky.'

He headed for the door, but had barely reached it before Auld Ernie almost fell in. Stevie had been right, for he carried only a lump of coal. This he thrust at Stevie, then headed for the bar, where the whisky waited. Everyone laughed and clapped.

Amelia came over to the girls. 'No hard feelings, and a very happy New Year to you. I do hope you're not on bullets tomorrow.'

Fran saw several heads turn their way and closed her eyes. Bullets? Really? Here? She whispered, 'Do not mention—'

Amelia put her hand to her mouth just as Ralph reached them. 'Is Miss Frances Hall nagging as usual?'

Fran looked at him as people milled around them, shrugging themselves into their coats. Most of them had work at some point tomorrow, depending on what shift they were on, or cows that needed to be milked or . . . She let her thoughts drift. She was too tired to deal with Ralph tonight. Too tired and too sad, for this was the first Hogmanay without her da. She just shook her head at him and found her way to the peg on which she'd hung her mackintosh.

She reached for it, turned, and there was Ralph, too close. He took hold of the mackintosh, but she held on to it. He pulled it from her. 'Let me help you, please. Your work is so—'

'My work is just boring,' she snapped, 'and what's more, I don't need your help.'

She walked away, leaving him holding the mac. He came after her. 'I know you don't,' he said. 'You made that clear at the funeral. I just—'

He held out her mackintosh and she grabbed it. 'I told you, I don't need your help. Though you said my da had poached a sheep, your father agreed at the funeral that road kill wasn't poaching. So, Ralph, we need never speak at all, just as you never need to meet me off the bus. Just mek sure you remember, eh?'

Ralph was staring at her with an air of . . . what? She couldn't tell, but it looked almost familiar. Who . . . ? Good heavens, like Swinton when he told them they couldn't leave the aft shift—

Just then, as though coming to himself, Ralph muttered, 'You'd do well to remember, Miss Frances Hall, that the Massingham family own most of the pubs in the area and I'll make sure that you and your friends will not sing at any of them.' He turned on his heel. Fran looked up to see Sarah and Beth staring at her, and knew they had heard, as had others, including a couple of men she didn't know.

Amelia was beaming at Ralph as he approached her. Fran could have slapped her. She heard Ralph say, 'I think you deserve a lift home, Amelia, don't you, after entertaining us so ably? I think perhaps there will be many more such openings for you at the Massingham pubs.'

Fran stepped towards them just as Sarah tore herself

from Stan, who stared after her, puzzled. Beth, who had been talking to Norm, did the same, and together they intercepted Fran. 'I know that look,' whispered Sarah. 'Leave it.'

Fran pushed past them to Ralph. She controlled her voice so it was not quite a shout, but loud enough for many to hear. 'Such a good idea on such a foul night to take Amelia home. But surely you have room for the other two girls as well, Ralph? Don't you remember taking us all to visit Davey? Two in the dicky seat, remember?'

Sarah had caught up and nodded. 'Yes, of course. You could drop Amelia at Sledgeford, then take Brenda and Rosie on to Fordon Bridge, eh?'

'Put our Sid down, Rosie,' called Beth. 'We've a lift for you from young Mr Massingham.'

Stevie was behind Ralph, chatting to Auld Ernie, but he looked up. 'Oh aye, that's the way. Yer da'd be proud of you, young Mr Massingham. Good of you to offer.'

Fran met Ralph's look with one of her own. There you go, stick that in your pipe and smoke it, you jumped up little toerag, she thought, and in the turmoil of the next few moments, as the revellers shoved past on their way to the door, Fran thought she saw a flicker of amusement in Ralph's eyes, but then it was gone. How stupid. Ralph would never find anything she said the slightest bit funny.

It was only as they cycled home, with Stan carrying the pot money, that the girls decided the boys shouldn't know about Ralph's decision to stop them getting bookings. 'The less they know the better,' muttered Fran, 'for they've to work with him. The toerag really *is* their boss and they need their jobs in Auld Hilda. Well, we all need their jobs.'

Beth agreed, but said, 'I reckon that Ralph wouldn't dare cause trouble for Stan.'

They pedalled up the hill towards the Hanging Tree

corner and Sarah panted, 'Aye, the scholarship boys are favourites of Mr Massingham's.'

Her head down and standing to thrust down on the pedals, Beth gasped, 'And we'll see if we can get some bookings with the other pubs that Massingham doesn't own.' But all three knew those pubs were few and far between, and after that it was a quiet finish to the journey.

It was two in the morning before Ralph arrived back at Massingham Hall. He was freezing, and had barely had a peck on the cheek from Amelia, thank the Lord, because the other two were on the back seat. Someone called Valerie had squashed in too, because she was Amelia's landlady's daughter. Amelia, eh? It couldn't be better really, because she was a real chatty-catty, and empty-headed into the bargain, so it would be easy to get information. Then somehow he'd make his attempt to damage the munitions factory fail, and nothing would implicate the silly girl, or him. He felt like being sick with the tension of it all, and sicker still at being foul to Fran, but he'd thought he recognised one of the drinkers as a pal of Tim's. He was there with someone else, stone-cold sober too, it seemed.

He sighed and put his foot down, wanting to drive and drive somewhere no one could find him, but his family was still here and his flight would put them in danger. So instead he roared up the long drive, skidding on the bend that would eventually bring him to the garages. As the wheels lost traction, he drove into the skid, corrected and slowed to a more sensible pace. He was sweating, but it wasn't the skid, it was everything else, and as he drove on an owl flew across the moon.

What the hell was it all about? Didn't the owl know the world was at war, and that Ralph's world was falling apart, and why the hell had Tim Swinton told him to concentrate on queering Fran's pitch to get Amelia onside? He said it would make the silly girl feel special, more willing to impress the man who had made it possible for them to get other bookings. 'That's you, Ralphy boy,' he had said.

'I can try other avenues,' Ralph had protested. He had killed the poor girls' fathers and hurt Fran with his Tim-induced pestering, wasn't that enough?

Ralph braked near the head of the drive, the wheels spinning out gravel as he stopped, listening to the idling engine. Before him, the house stood firm, built by his grandfather. Was he to be the Massingham who brought it all down around their ears?

'There are other people I can soften up,' Ralph had suggested to Tim, but Tim was having none of it. It seemed that progress had to be at the expense of Fran and Sarah. Wasn't it enough they were working with bullets? Probably detonators as well. It was payback for the scholarship, of course, twisted bastard. Well, he'd been one too, so it was a case of the pot calling the kettle black. 'It is indeed, Ralphy boy,' he said aloud, knowing that the hate he felt for himself was growing more extreme by the day.

He could see no owl now. He wound down his window, listening for the sounds of the countryside. There it was, distantly, the hoot of the owl over the baaing of the sheep. It steadied him. Hate? Oh, yes, that was quite accurate now, though earlier it had been for the Halls and the Bedleys. That's why he'd been happy to go along with the targeting of them at the start of this bloody business, and all because as children they'd bet him he couldn't land the ball in the goal. A goal they'd chalked on the wall when he'd sauntered down the back lane with his posh football, given to him by his mother shortly before she'd died. When he failed, they'd taken the ball and he'd destroyed their own papier-mâché one in revenge. He hadn't known they were only teasing and were about to give his own one back.

No wonder Davey had stabbed Ralph's shiny new ball with his penknife, kneeling in the wreckage of the papier mâché, then tossing the deflated ball back at the boss's son. It had been easily repaired, but that had not touched Ralph's need for revenge. He felt the heat on his face, the embarrassment at his actions – now.

He continued to sit, looking at Massingham Hall and the shadows that surrounded it. He heard a fox calling. Was it prowling around the sheep? Tim always seemed to be prowling, with his secret gang, working for the enemy.

Well, since he, Ralph Massingham, had at last come to his senses, all he could do was try to keep one step ahead and do his best to thwart things. Which is why Ralph had told Tim on their last telephone call that he was waiting for a chance to get information from the girl, and only then would he access the munitions factory. For that, he'd said, he needed a wintry storm to be able to cut through the wire, when the patrol's visibility would be hopeless.

He could then fail, retreat, and he might be left in peace for a while at least, until he could work out how to do more to fail his tasks.

He accelerated up the drive again, and somewhere the owl hooted once more, and the icy draught from the window made his eyes tear.

The roadster's slit headlights picked out the vicar's car parked to the left and Ralph swore. Surely not at this hour of the morning. God, he was tired and just wanted to head up the stairs, and perhaps, oh please, yes, he'd sleep now that he was trying to be a better person. But first he had to make his call to Tim. Anytime before 3 a.m. had been the order. He slid round and into the cobbled yard, then another tight turn into the garage. He shut off the engine, dousing the headlights. Biggins would be bound to be asleep, and Ralph knew he would normally be furious to be awake while an underling slept. He vaulted over the car door, then hesitated. He decided to open and slam his door, then, for good measure, opened and slammed it again. There, that was typical Ralph.

He strode out of the yard, across the gravel, up the steps and in through the front door. He eyed the hall telephone, set on the antique side table, but it was too public with the world sitting in the next room. Instead he headed for his father's study, treading lightly, but his father called from the drawing-room doorway, 'Do come, Ralph. The Reverend Walters will be gone soon, but you're in time to wish him a happy New Year before he does so.'

Ralph sighed, changed direction, nodded at his father who stood to one side in the drawing-room doorway, and entered the softly lit room. The fire was only smouldering now, but the room was still warm. Ralph pulled off his driving gloves and pasted on a smile as the Reverend Walters stood to shake his hand. 'A happy New Year to you, Vicar. Is your sister not with you?'

Reverend Walters flashed a smile, and murmured in a voice scarcely louder than a whisper, 'Apparently not, Ralph. Unless I've hidden her beneath the Christmas tree. So strange what gets hidden these days.'

Ralph flashed him a sharp look and saw Walters' ice-blue eyes fixed on him. Ralph hesitated. What did the man mean by that? What could he know? Had Ralph let anything slip? Sophia was watching him too, but her smile was kind, though tired, as she asked, 'How did the three Massingham girls do? I hear they have lovely voices.'

His father came back with a glass of malt whisky. 'Here you are, Ralph. This'll warm you.'

Ralph said between sips, looking at Sophia over the edge

of the glass, 'Ah, well, they were held back at work, so another three took their places. Damned good too.'

His father settled himself on the sofa next to the Reverend Walters and looked up at his son, who still stood. 'Held back? What do you mean?'

'There was a rush on at their place of work, but on what, who knows? None of us knows anything about anything these days. As I say, another three took their place.'

'Oh those poor girls,' said Sophia, 'they practised so hard, their mothers said, and have the most wonderful voices. They were in St Oswald's choir, weren't they, Edward?'

The Reverend Walters nodded. 'Indeed they were. Glorious voices, but with shift work and the war, the choir has rather faded. Indeed, so has the congregation. There have been some faithfuls, though. Mr Swinton, for one, who I believe works . . . Oh well, one mustn't talk of what people do, or don't do, as you say, Sophia.'

Sophia smiled gently. 'It makes conversation a bit stilted, as one tries to remember what stepping stone one can leap to, if you see what I mean. But as you have mentioned Mr Swinton, I do notice he makes every attempt to attend, slipping in the back or having to leave early, as work dictates. He's looked rather fraught and grim since his wife ran off a year or so ago. I think we can say that quite safely, as it's not likely to be of help to the enemy.' The vicar laughed with her, quietly. Sophia added, 'He has a son, hasn't he? Tim?'

Reverend Walters was leaning forward, interested. 'Ah, that's a point. When Mr Swinton arrived very late to an evening service just before Christmas, he was all of a dither, poor man. If I remember correctly it was the day of the mine accident in which Mr Bedley and Mr Hall were killed. He stayed on for a moment afterwards, saying he wanted to ask me a question about what duty a father owed a son? I was about to bring him into the vestry but then he was gone. Strange, really, because I'm usually asked about the duty a son owes a father.'

Silence fell. Sophia yawned. The clock said two twenty-five. Ralph gulped his whisky down in two, forcing himself to stay calm. Did Mr Swinton suspect his son? And if he did, and made a fuss, would it lead to the truth of the roof fall? And Ralph's part in it? Well, retribution was fair, he supposed, almost unable to breathe. He watched the flames flickering. He could still taste the whisky. Yes, if he, Ralph Massingham, was hanged, one couldn't possibly argue that it wasn't fair, and his family, though shamed, would be safe. Perhaps that was one way out of this mess, and would keep Sophia and his father safe from Tim. But would it?

The vicar continued. 'My sister mentioned to me that as she tidied up the hymn books he'd confided in her that he'd seen his lad on his motorbike that day, heading from Massingham to Sledgeford, but Tim had never called on his father. No doubt Mr Swinton felt he should.'

Ralph shifted and continued to watch the flames, knowing he should make the call to Tim. But it was the last thing he wanted to do, and if he did, should he tell him his father had seen him? Why bother, though, for Tim would want to know how he knew that, and then heaven knows what the bugger would do to those chatting about such things, let alone to his own father.

One of the coals in the fireplace fell and sparks flew. It was strange that for a few days after the roof fall he'd felt nothing. But then had come the horror, the dreams, the regret and the fear of Tim bloody Swinton. He shut his eyes against his thoughts, but that just made it worse.

The vicar said, just after downing the last of his drink, 'Didn't the lad get involved with the Fascists? But that was when so many were curious. If it wasn't the Communists, it was something else and they grew out of it. Or most did.' He placed his empty glass on the side table and checked the clock. 'Mercy, is that the time? I must away. So sad that the Hall and Bedley families were without their estimable fathers to see in the New Year. A most unfortunate accident.'

Ralph stared down at his empty glass, needing another drink, wanting to scream, 'Yes, it was. Arrest me, put a stop to it all.' He did nothing of the sort, of course.

His father was over at the drinks table and brought the decanter to Ralph, leaving it on the side table. 'Tuck yourself into a little more of that, lad, while I see our friend off. You look strained. Not surprisingly, the pit is a hard taskmaster.' Reginald Massingham looked at his guest. 'That's if you feel you really must leave, Edward.'

To Ralph's surprise, there was real regret in his father's voice, for the vicar seemed such a fuddy-duddy. But then Ralph looked again at the reverend, as though for the first time, and allowed himself to see an upright, thoughtful man, one who surely was barely forty. He was seeing so much more these days than he ever had. Was the vicar someone he could talk to? He shook his head at himself. Mea culpa wouldn't help – it still left his family vulnerable.

He rose and shook hands. The vicar wished him a happy New Year and Ralph reciprocated. Sophia and his father led Reverend Walters into the hall and waited until he drove away before closing the door. Sophia called from the hall, 'I'm off to bed. I have youngsters who won't be sleeping in. Happy 1942, Ralph dear.'

His father came to the fireplace and poked ineffectually at the fire. He made to put more coal on, but Ralph demurred. 'Leave it, Father. I'll finish this, damp it down, and then head up the wooden hill myself. You'll be up early with those boys, and I need to be up too, as there's an extra shift tomorrow.'

His father straightened up and smiled at him. 'Well, if

you're sure. We've had the most pleasant evening with Edward. He's made of such sterling stuff. A real hero, though not in it until 1918. I doubt he was even eighteen then, but he always swore he was, and never time to check, and he wouldn't have thanked me anyway. We found ourselves fighting alongside one another, 'whence all but we were dead.'

His father stared into the fire, then sighed. 'So many, and here we are again . . .' He stopped, then said, 'Yes, a very pleasant evening, but suddenly it catches up on one. I trust all went well with you? The Rising Sun, was it? Good to show your face around the locality. I do think that Stevie Pertwee is a forward thinker. We could do with more entertainment to cheer us through the war. Trotted out his elderberry wine, did he? He asked if he could, and donate the proceeds to the three fatherless girls, though of course we have helped with the funerals as usual. Well, off I go. Sleep well, Ralph.'

The two of them stood facing one another and for a dreadful moment Ralph thought his father would hug him, which he couldn't bear. Ralph mustn't feel he could talk to *him*, for he couldn't involve his family. That, at least, he could do for them until he had found a way . . .

They shook hands.

He watched his father walk to the door and listened to his footsteps crossing the hall. Sipping his whisky, he stared into the fire, feeling unutterably weary, then walked across to the drinks side table. There were photographs of his mother. He picked one up and sipped his malt again.

He could only remember her coming and going; each time there was a brief wave, a kiss that didn't touch his cheek, her perfume wafting. He had always thought she didn't like him, but Sophia had said that of course she did, she was just busy and had friends to visit in sunny climes, and wasn't he lucky because he had three people who loved him very much – his mother, his father and his nanny. Then his mother had died – TB.

The mantelpiece clock chimed three. Bloody hell, he should have phoned Tim to report on Amelia and to confirm that his plans must be to go in under cover of a snowstorm, for there'd surely be one.

He gulped down the remains of his drink, replaced his glass on the silver salver and headed for his father's study. He made sure to shut the door quietly behind him.

Sitting in his father's chair, he raised the receiver, asking the operator for Tim Swinton's number.

It rang. Tim answered. 'Yes.' No name, no pack drill, as always.

Ralph cleared his throat and said, 'Just me, old son, to wish you a very happy 1942. I hope you had a good evening?' Did he sound his normal self?

Tim said, 'Hello, old friend. Aye, indeed, quiet but pleasant. What about you, did you meet a girl, as you'd hoped? You were at the Rising Sun, I gather?'

Ralph grimaced at the 'I gather'. So, Tim was definitely keeping tabs on him. Was it the man he'd recognised as Tim's friend? He didn't ask, of course. Instead he answered, 'Do you know, I think I might have. She's a chatty little thing, busy at her war work, of course. We seemed to hit it off.'

After a pause Tim replied, 'Good. I'm reet pleased for you. Keep me in the picture. Mebbe 1942 will be a productive year for you.'

Ralph found himself nodding. How many more bodies would make a productive year? He shook his head and straightened his father's unblemished blotter.

Tim said into the silence, 'All well with you, is it, Ralphy?'

'Yes, of course. Just a bit tired, you know what Hogmanay is like. But just wanted to touch base, as arranged.'

Ralph was sweating. He remembered he had to bank up the fire. He hung on to the normality of that, for he didn't want to touch base; he had been ordered by Tim to do so.

Tim laughed. 'Tell you what, Ralphy. Give me a call on yer way to the pit. I had something to tell you, but 'tis too late now. It'll help with yer love life. Got a splitter, so need to get to bed. Too many bliddy beers tonight, eh? Though no doubt you've had a fine old malt.'

Ralph heard the bitterness in Tim's voice. Had it always been there? 'I'll telephone tomorrow, early,' he said. 'Happy New Year.' That was all.

'I look forward to hearing from you, and again, a happy New Year, Ralph.'

Ralph replaced the receiver and sat back in his father's swivel chair. He'd phone Tim at the usual Thursday telephone box in London – though where in London he hadn't a clue. Just as he had no idea where the other phone boxes were that Tim used on different days of the week. So, what did he have planned? Something that would help Ralph get close to Amelia, no doubt.

He made his way back to the drawing room and banked up the fire, adding ash. It would probably stay in. He stood, dusted off his hands and thought of the vicar, and about Tim being seen in the area on that dreadful day. How many others in the cell were here in the area, day after day? Were they in the pits or – perhaps and? – factories, obeying orders? Did any regret it as he did?

He left the room, switching out the lights, wanting to sleep without hearing the sounds of the two dying men.

In Massingham, Annie Hall was sitting by the range, home at last. Ben was staying with his friend George, way over at Pit Terrace. The pair of them would probably have finished the crosswords Davey had sent them. She smiled, looking up at Joe's pipe on the mantelpiece. 'Aye, lad, they're all settling, slowly but surely. We miss yer greatly, but we're managing.'

It had been a bit of an evening for her and Audrey Smith, what with Maud refusing to go to her bed and staring at the range like a mad thing until they'd set up her rug frame. They had stuck a hook in her hand and told her there was no time to waste, for they had orders to fill and money to make if they were all to survive. It seemed their words had penetrated, for she did as she was told and sat working with them for a good while. Annie shook her head, wondering how long it was going to take to get her friend sorted.

She looked up, imagining Joe listening to her. 'Happen it'll tek summat big, summat that's a bit of a shock, eh, our lad. Or a few shocks, for Tom isn't here at her side to say he'll leave with the bairns if she doesn't stop. Remember how she stopped, then he found she hadn't and he had to be there to keep her on the straight and narrow? So it's bound to be a longer job, and we'll all have to pitch in and take his place.'

Annie leaned back against the armchair, pushing the stool a bit nearer the range and resting her feet on it. 'But what shock?' she asked aloud. Well, whatever it was, she hoped it would be soon. At least Stan had told her that Mildred at the Rising Sun had given him the name of the black-market beggar who was selling her the booze, and would be doing his rounds in three or so days. Well, it was the last time he'd be calling, because Stan would put a stop to it. What's more, he'd find the amount on the tab and somehow he and the lasses would pay it off.

She allowed her eyes to close, wishing her bairns were here with her to see in 1942, but at least they weren't on the front line, which was more than could be said for many. Though there was enough of a front line here, come to that.

*

That morning Ralph was up and out by five. He cycled to Massingham, propping Alfie's bike against the wall before making the call. It would be short, it always was. He listened as Tim explained that it had been arranged for Fran Hall and Sarah Bedley to be transferred to Scotland temporarily. This would give Ralph time to get close to Amelia without the other girls there to muddy the picture.

'There's no need to take the daughters from the families at a time like this,' Ralph protested. 'That's cruel. I can manage Amelia.' Outside the telephone box the snow was falling again. He was cold but he welcomed the physical misery, for it helped mask the despair within him.

Tim laughed. 'Aye, maybe you can, but best to make it easier for Amelia to cosy up. Besides, we're leaving Beth Jones here, mainly because my contact can only justify transferring two. So she can look after all the widows – does that soothe your troubled breast?' There was an edge to Tim's voice, and his laugh was harsh and unamused. It was clearly a real question.

Ralph gritted his teeth. So, Tim *was* out for revenge against Stan and Davey? Well, weren't he and Ralph just two bloody peas in a pod, or had been once. 'Not a question of soothing my breast. I'm not that troubled. It was a fleeting thought.'

'Report in when there is something of interest.' There was a click and Tim hung up.

130

Chapter Nine

Sarah woke to the sound of the range being riddled and though she had only slept for two hours, she smiled. Stan, oh Stan. She imagined him hunkering down before the range, his strong hands, his precious face heavy with sleep. Fran's cold feet were resting against her shoulder. She tweaked the toes and Fran groaned.

'Aye, 'tis that time. Up we get,' Sarah whispered. 'Swinton wants us for the fore shift today, remember?' Their door was ajar so that they could hear if her mam rose and blundered into the empty bucket. It was Mrs Smith who had suggested it be moved from the back door to the landing, so the girls could get her back into bed more smartly.

Stan had said, 'By, Mrs Smith, we lot've been going around the mulberry bush and here you are, getting straight to the heart of the matter.'

Mrs Smith had answered, smiling, 'Aye, well, this way it only needs one of you to stay over.'

She'd winked at the girls as Stan opened and shut his mouth, then murmured, 'Aye, maybe you're reet, but that's not going to happen any time soon, eh, lass.' He'd put his arm round Sarah and kissed the top of her head.

Sarah stretched as Fran stirred and muttered, 'It can't be time. I've just got to sleep.'

'It can and it is.' Sarah shoved her out and then followed her. 'Quick now, for Bert'll be in a grump. He'll have been first-footing his street – you know how he likes to make a night of it – so he's likely come straight from that to the bus.'

Downstairs, after making their way to the netty and back, they washed, then gulped down the bread and dripping Stan had prepared. Then they filled their bottles with water while Stan packed his bait tin. It was Madge on duty at the Bedley house this morning, and she knocked on the door dead on five minutes to four. She entered wearing the same eyepatch as last night, and looked as pale as a ghost.

She shrugged off her coat and hat, left her boots on the newspaper and groaned. 'I'll swing for that Stevie. His elderberry wine should be locked away for good an' all. Me head's going to explode, so 'tis.' She held the door open and waved them out. 'Beth's staggering, aye, staggering up her back lane, so she is. Better hurry, girls, and you too, Stan. Hooter's going, or have you gone deaf?'

Sarah kissed her. 'How can I thank you?'

Madge held her for a moment. 'Nay, no need for thanks. Your mam was reet good to me when me old bugger took off, all the women were, and let's face it, always are. They helped look after not just me, but Bobby, making sure he got to school. Briddlestone's needs that additional order in by Monday, so New Year's Day or not, we work, like the rest of you. And I can do it just as well here as at me own home. We have another group working from Maisie's back room at the shop to keep pace with the orders. So, me point is, lasses, it's not all down to yer to cope. Yer have all of us, always have, always will.'

She held open the door. 'Quick, quick.'

In the Factory changing rooms, they were all checked by Miss Ellington and Mrs Raydon, both looking the worse for wear. Beth heard Fran say to Miss Ellington, 'Ah well, if you must stay up late with Simon Parrot when you've already got a bad headache, what do you expect, eh? Bit of a thumper again today is the least of it, I reckon. Bit of a dicky tummy too, if he brought out his home brew.'

'Shut up,' Miss Ellington whispered back, sweat beading her face. 'I was feeling better by midnight, so I got up and we saw in the New Year with his sister. You just concentrate, eh?'

Beth started to laugh, but her own headache soon put a stop to that. Miss Ellington wagged a finger at her, then at the rest of them in the changing rooms. 'And nowt from you lot, either, if yer don't mind.'

Mr Swinton arrived with his clipboard. He announced that the three of them were not to work in the bullet section today, but in the more dangerous detonator-filling workshop, which meant real concentration.

Beth, her headache thumping, shouted, 'Why us again?'

He ignored her and said, 'Come on, you lot, get to work. You had Hogmanay at least.'

The women grimaced, but Beth had had enough. 'That's not fair. Why is it always us who have to move around?'

Mr Swinton shook his head as Miss Ellington approached him, looking none too friendly either. 'Yer have to tek the place of three no-shows,' he said. 'Each one says it's sickness. I say, my Aunt Fanny. It's nowt to do with sickness, it's too much Hogmanay. So, get to yer workshop, if you please.'

Miss Ellington didn't bother to keep her voice down as all the others filed past into the corridor, holding her hand up to the three girls. 'Just stay there.' They did. 'Why does it have to be these three? Why not choose others for a change?'

Mr Swinton backed up a step. 'Because they're . . .' He stopped.

Miss Ellington was toe to toe with him now. 'They're what? The ones whose lives you like to make a misery? I thought we'd gone beyond that after—'

Beth, who was standing between Fran and Sarah, sighed and said, 'I need to get to a workbench, any workbench, and sit on me stool. P'raps I should have drunk the whole bottle of water.'

As one, they turned back to their pegs and dragged their bottles from their bags, gulping the water down. Beth wished she'd sipped it, as it seemed to swim in her stomach. At least she had Bob's voice to cling to, for he had telephoned that morning. He was in a port, he'd said, and hoping she'd hear the telephone ringing in the phone box as she went to the bus. She hadn't, but Mrs Oborne had and had answered, yelling for her to get to the box before the pips went.

Beth had run, slipping on the snow, but that didn't matter for it was her Bob. He was alive, he loved her and she loved him. She replaced the half-drunk bottle and longed for him to be waiting at home for her. She longed for her da too. She leaned her head against her mackintosh, gripping it. She must not cry. Must. Not. Cry.

The other two had already made their way back to Miss Ellington and Beth joined them just in time to see Mr Swinton whisper something to Miss Ellington that made her step back, surprised. Beth didn't want to know what the bastard had said. What difference would it make? They did as he decided, and that was that. She breathed deeply, as Mr Hall had shown them when they were bairns.

Miss Ellington turned to them. 'You best head on to the detonators, girls.' That was all. Mr Swinton turned on his heel and swished off down the corridor on his rubber-soled shoes. The three of them did the same after changing their shoes for the felt ones, passing the posters asking them to Dig for Victory and to Make Do and Mend, as though they did anything else.

They hated the detonators, the copper shells used to

initiate a shell's triggering process, which they had to fill with the highly sensitive lead azide, which looked so like the sugar that was now on ration, or fulminate of mercury. The fulminate of mercury was so sensitive to friction, heat and shock, it could break down into mercury that could leak into their skin or be breathed into their lungs . . . Mad as hatters, yes, that's what they were afraid of – becoming mad, or being blown up, losing a hand, a foot.

'Maintenance repaired everything so quickly after the explosion, damn it,' muttered Fran.

Sarah nudged her. 'Aye, well, let's just be safe, eh, as we say to the pitmen, and they say back to us now.'

'I hate the rash,' complained Beth. 'Drives me mad enough without the mercury making it worse and worse.'

They carried on to the doorway.

In the detonator workshop conversation had been forbidden since the accident, so no one spoke as they entered. The three girls made their way to the workbench and the stainless-steel barriers with the Perspex windows. They put on their masks, which Beth loathed because the cotton wool it was padded with grew hot and itched. They collected their small containers of fulminate of mercury from the hatch and carried them back to the workbench; it was too dangerous to be carried through doorways.

Happy New Year, Beth Jones, she thought to herself as she pulled forward the first tray of tiny copper detonators and sprinkled mercury in them. The tannoy broadcast the usual music programmes, made announcements, and her head continued to throb. She would never drink Stevie's elderberry wine again. How Bob had laughed when she told him. How she had loved to hear that laugh. How she longed for him . . . But she mustn't think, only work. Concentrate, concentrate. She hated Swinton, for he was a miserable soul.

As she worked, she could almost feel the powder seeping into her lungs despite the mask. From her lungs to the rest of her organs, not to mention back to her skin. She'd itch tonight worse than ever, but as long as she didn't make a mistake, as long as there wasn't an explosion, she'd be alive enough to scratch. Did the hatters really go mad from working with mercury? Well, Miss Ellington said they had, and Miss Ellington was always right. And how was Moira's daughter, Enid? Still in hospital, last she'd heard. Beth snatched a look at the floor, as though trying to see where the lass had fallen, the ceiling joist on top of her.

There was no sign, daft nelly, she told herself, glad it was Enid and not her, then ashamed of the thought.

What was it Mr Swinton had said that so surprised Miss Ellington?

She carried another finished tray of detonators to the hatch, and brought another small container of powder back. She had a rhythm now. Was her headache improving? She felt a cough coming so she lay down the powder container and spoon-like sprinkler, and stepped back. Fran looked, checking she was all right. She nodded, then coughed. She knew Fran was smiling behind her mask, because her eyes crinkled. On the other side of Beth, Sarah stepped back, whispering, 'Yer made me want to cough, an' all.'

Then Fran joined them, coughing. They were smiling at one another under their masks, waiting for the coughing to stop. Only then did they return to work.

Lunch break was called at midday, and in the half an hour after they had finished eating, Mrs Oborne dragged the three girls and the rest of the choir onto the stage while the others smoked or played cards or dominoes. The Factory Girls sang some of the songs they would have sung last night.

As they sang, they laughed at Mrs Oborne's conducting

and Valerie's staccato drum noises. They gloried in the humming of the rest of the bus women who made up the *Workers' Playtime* choir. As they did so, Beth felt her headache dissipate, along with her anger at Mr Swinton for transferring them to detonators. What did any of it matter? Here they all were, all their friends, singing and loving every moment. At the end, the applause was wild, and everyone hugged everyone else, wishing all and sundry a happy New Year. For her, this was the real Hogmanay.

They returned to the detonators, and at two, when the aft shift arrived, the fore shift hurried along the corridor, absolutely exhausted. They longed to get on the bus and fall asleep, but outside the changing rooms stood Mr Swinton, and with him was Bolton, the deputy manager of the sector. They were both looking towards Beth, Fran and Sarah, their expressions grim. The girls linked arms.

'Accident somewhere in one of the workshops?' Beth wondered.

'Could be,' replied Fran.

They kept on walking, past posters wanting them to Go Forward Together or declaring Still More Rags Wanted for Salvage. Sarah said, 'Try taking the rags the co-op's piled up to cut up for their rugs, and yer'll have another war on your hands.'

Mrs Oborne, who had joined them from the passageway to the pellet section, said, 'Aye, and I'll be leading the charge.'

They began to laugh, but still looked fixedly at the men, who had been joined by Miss Ellington. Sarah muttered, 'Are they counting us all in to make sure no one's done a runner?'

Beth murmured, 'We'll know in a minute because it can't be an accident, come to think of it. Why would they tell us now? Why not get us out when it happened, if we needed to be got out, that is? It'll be something bliddy Swinton's cooked up. Think about it, there he was, muttering to Miss Ellington before the shift began. She looked right surprised, don't you remember?'

'Aye, I do an' all,' said Fran, thoughtfully.

They were nearly at the door when Mr Bolton pointed to Sarah and Fran. 'Follow us,' he said. Fran and Sarah hesitated, not understanding. Mr Swinton tutted. 'Quick now, the aft shift's begun, we haven't all day.'

The three of them followed, trying to fathom what they wanted, but Bolton snapped at Beth, 'Just these two. Off with you to the bus, Mrs Jones.'

Beth continued to follow, saying, 'Where they go, I go. We're marrers.'

Miss Ellington barred her way. 'They'll be getting the bus back with you, so don't worry, I'm assured it's only temporary.'

Beth looked after Sarah and Fran and her headache returned. 'What's only temporary?'

Miss Ellington didn't answer, just shrugged. Mrs Raydon looked out of the changing rooms. 'Come along, Beth, into the changing rooms. We need to check everyone, as always. Can't have anyone taking anything out that they shouldn't, and please don't shout. I have the worst hangover the world has ever known, and the girls will tell you what's going on in a minute.'

Fran and Sarah followed the two men, with Miss Ellington catching them up. Fran shot back over her shoulder, 'Howay, scared we'll beat a retreat or run amok?'

Miss Ellington shook her head, but then winced. Sarah whispered, 'By, she looks like I feel.'

Fran whispered back, 'Me mouth's dry, me headache's worse, and I swear I'll never, ever drink again. Never even want to smell elderberry wine, or see berries on an elder tree, as long as I live.'

What she didn't say was that all she wanted was to head home, to her own mam, her own range, a pot of tea waiting for her, with nothing to worry about. No tannoy playing, no chemicals, no Mrs Bedley to guard . . .

She stopped herself and gripped Sarah's arm, who looked at her in surprise. Fran was thinking that it was far worse for her friend – she had no mam to turn to, no calm certainty. She straightened her shoulders and lifted up her chin. Her friend needed her, and in Massingham they all pulled together. She stared ahead at the men, knowing she and Sarah had not made mistakes during the fore shift, so how could they be in trouble?

Sarah was saying, 'P'raps they want us to sing at a concert for the whole Factory?'

They smiled at one another.

'No, can't be that,' said Sarah, 'all that applause'll hurt Mr Swinton far too much. Besides, that would mean all three of us being marched along.'

They passed the same posters all along the corridors whilst the men marched, Swinton's green overalls and Bolton's white ones swinging in time. Swinton's clipboard was held tight to his side, and neither man was saying a word. Well, Fran thought, if she and Sarah were in trouble, the two men should try working hour after hour with chemicals, or detonators that could blow your hands off, or . . . Suddenly she was furious, and heard herself say, 'Bliddy fed up, I am. Just bliddy fed up, and I could bliddy run amok.'

Mr Bolton was the one to shoot a look over his shoulder and say, 'Well, young woman, you're not the only one. You try managing a wartime factory, eh? Then you'll know all about feeling ruddy fed up, or running amok, so know your place, and keep quiet.'

Sarah whispered, 'Oh no, no, Mr Bolton, such a mistake.' She put out her hand to hush Fran, but it was too late, for Fran had already started to reply.

'You try being a worker in a wartime factory then, eh, instead of piddling about being one of the bliddy bosses shouting the odds.'

Fran increased her pace but Sarah pulled her back, hissing, 'Hush up, we'll lose our—'

But they heard the laughter then, as the deputy manager's shoulders shook, and he muttered, 'I take your point, Mr Swinton. Oh, indeed I do.'

Miss Ellington was close behind Fran now, muttering, 'Oh Lord, oh my Aunt Fanny, I really thought you'd been and done it, Frances Hall, but seemingly not.' They continued on down the corridor, then the men did a quick right turn into a sort of anteroom, still in step, and then into an office with Mr Bolton's name on the door. There were steel filing cabinets lining the walls and a desk in the centre of the room. It had one chair behind it and one in front for visitors. Or those in trouble more like, Fran suspected.

Mr Bolton, who was middle-aged with a belly that looked as though it was familiar with pints, propped himself on the corner of the desk and crossed his arms. He nodded to Mr Swinton. 'I'll do it.'

It was the sack, Fran knew. That's why the beggar had been laughing, for now he had grounds, but why? Beside her she heard Sarah whisper, 'Two times two is four.'

Fran was glaring at Mr Swinton, for he must be at the bottom of it, but strangely Miss Ellington was standing beside him, pressing her truncated arm against his as he stared at the concrete floor.

'Sorry, girls,' said Mr Bolton, 'but we've had a request from a factory further north for a couple of our best girls who are able to adapt to change and handle themselves and who are excellent workers. I have been through our sector's files where I keep the foremen's reports.' He waved towards the filing cabinets. 'And I am forced to agree with the reports: you are those two girls.'

Sarah blurted out, 'I canna, me mam—'

Mr Bolton nodded. 'Aye, so I gather, but I happen to know that Massingham pit village has a good, supportive community. I hear tell of a terrifying regiment – the co-op women?' It was a query. Fran and Sarah nodded dumbly. Mr Bolton sighed. 'And we must always bear in mind that the war's needs must come first.'

Mr Swinton looked up at Mr Bolton. 'But as I said, I have others who're as good, who are not recovering from their da's death. Beneath coal, it were, a fall. These're girls who're—'

Mr Bolton held up his hand as the two girls studied Mr Swinton in amazement. Mr Bolton's voice was like ice as he said, very slowly, looking from the girls to Mr Swinton, 'We've discussed this already.'

Mr Swinton stepped forward then, his hands bunched in his pockets. 'Aye, well, with respect, Mr Bolton, 'tis you who've discussed it. I haven't been allowed to put my side. 'Tisn't fair, 'tisn't the time – they even missed their evening at the Rising Sun because an office worker refused to tek their place on the line. Refused me, she di—'

Bolton's hand was up, his face set.

Miss Ellington, who had stepped forward with Mr Swinton, now said, 'I know you said they'd been asked for by name, Mr Bolton, but how? I mean, who knows them at—' She stopped. 'Well, at the unnamed Scottish . . . I mean, northern factory? Though it's only Scotland north of—'

Mr Bolton sliced his hand through the air. Fran and Sarah stared. So Mr Swinton *had* asked Amelia? He was fighting for them now? What on earth? Mr Bolton had moved round to sit behind the protection of his desk. He picked up a pencil and studied it as though it had all the answers. At last he said, 'Look, I only know what I'm told from above. There's been a request from someone who worked here temporarily – a Tony Plomer. He was moved from here, to help set up another . . . er . . . establishment. Ah, Miss Ellington, I see you remember him.'

Miss Ellington was nodding, her mouth tightening. 'Yes I do. He stayed for a few months. Never very friendly, in fact, he was mightily officious—'

Mr Bolton put up his hand again. 'I merely asked if you remembered him. I did not ask for a reference. Besides, he's not even at this particular establishment now, but in London, orchestrating things. He remembered the reports on their ability to adapt to new situations far more quickly than others. Look, young ladies, there's no need to become agitated. This will only be a very temporary assignment, one that will terminate just as soon as the factory can recruit more permanent staff. It has been extended, d'you see? Needs must.' There was a snap as the pencil broke in half. Mr Bolton laid it down.

'Oops,' said Fran.

Mr Swinton, Miss Ellington and Mr Bolton looked at her. Mr Bolton laughed, then, remembering the task in hand, sat back. 'Of course, Miss Ellington, if the two girls wish to resign in protest, or, indeed, you or Mr Swinton do, I will put that forward, but it would be like deserting in the face of the enemy and will rule you out, I dare say, for any future war work. Which you will probably want, especially the lasses now they have each lost a father and need the money, as you have explained, Mr Swinton, rather forcefully. And which, I gather, is what you also said to the young woman you approached to fill in for them yesterday. You must understand, I am not unsympathetic to the situation, but as I say, orders have come down.'

Again, the two girls looked at Swinton. He had protested and fought to keep them. Why?

Mr Bolton was leaving the room. 'Five minutes, then I need an answer. I need a word, Swinton, now.'

Both men left, Swinton slamming the door behind them. Miss Ellington looked after them, then back to the girls. 'I'm more sorry than I can say, girls. Trust me, Mr Swinton and I have both tried. I know he was a complete arse to you in the early days because he resented your brother over the scholarship. He still says he holds no brief for you, but I'm not so sure. Something's changed since your das' accidents. It's as though . . . Oh, I don't know, it just seems something's gone out of him. We tried to get Bolton to include Beth, in case you're wondering, but only two are needed.'

Fran was trying to absorb this. She and Sarah looked at one another, confused. Miss Ellington was nodding at the clock. 'Quick, you need to make a decision, for it'll be this transfer or I reckon it'll be the worst jobs for you, because Bolton won't be made a fool of. There must be some satisfaction for you in knowing that you are well thought of by Plomer?'

Fran was shaking her head. 'I don't remember him.' Sarah didn't either.

Miss Ellington frowned. 'Yes, you do. The young bloke with red hair and freckles. He used to be a friend of that little rat Tim Swinton's, though our own Mr Swinton wouldn't give him the time of day when he was here. Clearly couldn't stand him, but then he can't stand many, if one thinks about it. But it's your decision, really it is.'

The door opened and Bolton swept back in, alone. Fran and Sarah shared a look. They needed the money. Fran leaned close to Sarah and whispered, 'There's a war on, it's not for long. Your mam'll be looked after. After all, Beth and Stan are still here, and the co-op. Besides, could it help yer mam? Your going somewhere might be the shock she needs.'

'We've no choice,' Sarah whispered back. 'We can't desert.'

This is what they told Mr Bolton, who nodded, then looked embarrassed as he said, 'I'd really rather you didn't have to go. We need you here, and I'll push for your return, never fear.' He handed them an envelope. 'Train tickets, passes. When you arrive, transport will pick you up from the station. It will take you to the hostel. Your role will be explained once you arrive at your workplace. You may pass on the hostel postal address to your nearest and dearest, but just to them, and no more information.' He nodded to the door. 'Hurry and get your bus. You leave in the morning.'

'Tomorrow?' Sarah whispered.

Mr Bolton nodded. 'Be safe,' he murmured.

'That's what our das would have said,' Fran said.

Mr Bolton nodded again. 'I'm so sorry.'

Miss Ellington followed them out. Mr Swinton was waiting by the changing rooms, his hands in the pockets of his overalls. He stopped them. 'You do yerselves proud, eh. Just keep yer mouths shut and yer smart-alec remarks to yerself, Miss Hall.' But now Fran realised what she hadn't seen before – there really was no venom in his voice any longer. Instead, there was a softness, or was it a duty of care?

'Aye,' Fran said, as Sarah waited beside her and Miss Ellington went ahead into the changing rooms, 'but our Beth's still here to keep you in order, Mr Swinton, and by, she'll bliddy need to.'

He reached out his hand. She hesitated, then realised he wanted to shake hers. She did and he held it for a moment, whispering, 'Yer tek care. Yer going somewhere more dangerous.'

Fran looked at him as he gripped her hand tighter. 'Explosives – mixing them?' she whispered.

He nodded, to her and then at Sarah. 'I don't want to have to train up another few lasses to be top of the team. Waste of me bliddy time.'

He held out his hand to Sarah. 'I'm right sorry it's come now. You're the best, you three girls, but they only need two of yer. Be marrers to one another. Yer das'd be proud. Well, are proud, cos no one really dies, not in here.' He whacked his chest. 'It's a good thing to be able to be reet proud of yer bairns. I wish . . .' Looking strange, worried, he stared at them, not quite seeing them. He walked off, not strutting as he usually did, but with bowed shoulders and his hands clenched together behind his back. Neither of the girls could understand.

Chapter Ten

The two girls rushed in their felt shoes to change for the bus. 'Bert'll be getting restless,' Miss Ellington shouted. They threw off their overalls and shoes, grabbed their macs, bags and water bottles, and slammed their feet into their boots, then ran to the gates behind Miss Ellington, who chivvied the guards to check them through. 'Quick, quick.'

Sarah saw that Bert had drawn the bus right up to the front of the siding, and that the exhaust was huffing out into the cold air. More snow had fallen. She saw all this, but . . . She turned back to look at the brick buildings. There was hardly anyone walking along the roadway between the workshops, just three men: one pushed a trolley full of shells, while fifty yards ahead and to the rear the other two walked with a flag each to warn others to keep clear.

She remembered how young Jimmy from Sledgeford had died when a bomb had fallen off a trolley and exploded, and Sylv had been hurt when the nearest wall imploded in the blast, though she was back at work now. Sarah shivered but it was only because the wind beat against her and snow had started to fall again, that was all, and not because they were going to an explosives factory. Still she stared at the brick buildings.

This was almost like home, and they were leaving and Sarah was scared.

Bert hooted. Fran grabbed her and they leapt on the bus. 'Shift yerselves, lasses. We've homes to get to,' Bert yelled.

Fran's voice was strained as she whispered, 'Oh, Sarah. When will we do this again?'

Sarah just followed her down the aisle of the bus. Fran was scared too, and that made everything wobble. Who would take care of her mam, take the bottles off her, guard the doors, make her come to her senses?

Beth had saved the seats in front of her while she sat next to Maisie. They slumped down onto the slats. Fran groaned. 'One day I'll bring a bliddy cushion.'

Sarah laughed, and laughed, though it wasn't really funny.

Bert revved and drew out of the siding and as she laughed she was so glad it was Bert for the home run, for he was more their friend than Cecil. She'd miss him, and Mrs Oborne, and—

'Well?' Beth asked, leaning forward, her arms along the backs of their seats. Would the Scottish factory have a bus? Would the seats be slatted? Would Fran go on about a cushion? Would the snow be worse up there? Would the hostel be nice? Would her mam be safe? Sarah swallowed and let Fran answer Beth.

But as Bert drove off, they heard Miss Ellington running alongside, shouting and waving her arms.

'Stop,' everyone shouted. Bert slammed on the brakes. The bus skidded, just a bit. Miss Ellington clambered on, shaking the snow from her hair.

'Thought I'd grab a lift to Massingham. I have someone to meet.'

As Miss Ellington found a seat near the front, Mrs Oborne yelled, 'Howay, pet, summat to do with canaries, I reckon.'

'Now you're here, Miss Ellington,' shouted Fran, 'perhaps you'd tell everyone the news. We're still trying to get our heads around it.'

Miss Ellington stood up as Bert drove and told them of the temporary transfer of the two girls to another factory.

Behind Sarah and Fran, Beth groaned. 'What? Without me? For how long? Where?'

'Not for long, and not far,' Miss Ellington replied.

'It's that bliddy Swinton, in't it?' shouted Mrs Oborne. 'He's no soul, that beggar hasn't. First he could've got Amelia to tek their place so they could sing. And now this. Anything to bugger up the Hall family, and our Sarah's. They've just—'

Miss Ellington held up her hand. 'I have to stop you there because that's not the whole story. Amelia was asked by Mr Swinton to stand in on the production line. She refused, and then turned up at the Rising Sun. Amelia told me the same lie she told Mr Swinton, that she had another commitment. Well, she had – she booked herself in at the Rising Sun as a replacement the moment she heard.

'I tell you now that our Mr Swinton fought Mr Bolton to keep our girls with us, but they were asked for specifically. I have to be careful here, for we don't want any big heads getting off the bus at Massingham, but you might remember that snotty, ginger-headed bloke called Plomer?'

A few nodded. Miss Ellington continued. 'While he was here, so Swinton told me, his role included checking the reports Mr Swinton had written on you all, and Fran and Sarah were requested on the strength of them. It made it tricky for Mr Bolton to refuse. There really is a shortage in personnel at the other factory at the moment.'

'And why not me, too?' called Beth.

Miss Ellington shook her head. 'Beth, only two were needed, and given the circumstances, it could be considered a blessing. At least one of you remains here to keep an eye on your mothers.'

'Aye,' said Maisie, 'that makes sense, and we're all around too, so don't yer worry, Fran and Sarah. The Factory Girls will ride to the rescue.'

Mrs Oborne bellowed over the roaring of the engine as Bert urged it up a hill, 'And the co-op, so there's nowt to worry about.'

Suddenly everyone was chatting about Swinton, the change in him, and the three girls were stunned, amazed, and everything else, but puzzled too. Yes, everyone was puzzled. In the end Mrs Oborne yelled, 'Aye well, everyone grows up some day.' Now they were laughing and soon the singing started.

Beth tightened her grip on Sarah's and Fran's shoulders. 'Don't worry, there's everyone helping, plus me and Stan too. All of us'll keep an eye on things together.'

Sarah felt the weight of Beth's hand on her shoulder. She didn't want Stan and Beth to look after anyone together. What if their love started up again? What if . . . She looked at the ring on her finger and pressed it tight, deeper and deeper. One times two is two, she thought. Two times two is four. On and on she went in time with the wipers whilst all around the talk was of the war, the upheaval, of Bolton and Amelia. And Swinton.

She became aware, as they stopped at Minton, that Beth and Fran were talking about Mrs Bedley. Beth said, 'You mustn't worry, either of you. I'll move in.'

'Not if Stan's there,' Sarah blurted out.

Beth looked shocked and opened her mouth, but Fran patted Sarah's leg. 'Howay, steady, keep yer streaked hair on, pet. We've just been saying that it's not right for a man to stay, didn't you hear us? Beth's going to talk to her mam, see if she'd be all right on her own if Beth moves in with yer mam for the time being, but Stan's on call. We were saying that it's not fair to ask Beth's mam to keep an eye on some-one who's . . . well, who's not herself. Beth is more able to cope with things that crop up.'

'Crop up?' Sarah asked.

'Oh Sarah, don't be bliddy daft,' Fran snapped, then lowered her voice so that Beth couldn't hear. 'What I mean is, if your mam goes on drinking, of course, and gets silly, or starts fretting to go and see your da at St Oswald's. The co-op can manage in the day, but Beth says she'll be there at night. If she's on night shift, then her mam will *have* to come, and if it ever gets too tricky, they'll just have to run out for Stan. Don't worry, your mam'll be looked after, and that's what you have to remember.'

At last they reached Massingham. Sarah followed Fran and Beth off the bus and there was Stan, her Stan, not Beth's, not any more. She ran to him and felt his arms around her, his kisses on her hair. She heard Fran telling him their news. Miss Ellington stopped by them. 'Come to the Canary Club, girls. Simon'll have his brew and I reckon it'd do you good before you have to go home and tell your mams. I know it's only four o clock, but special times call for special treats.'

They headed towards the allotments with Miss Ellington and Stan. His arm was around Sarah's shoulders, and he gripped her tighter and tighter as she told him they would be staying in a hostel, and he could have that address but not the factory's. He whispered, 'I canna bear the thought of you being so far away, and what if it's dangerous? Well, of course it is. But it's so bliddy far. That beggar Swinton, I could swing for 'im.'

Sarah leaned into him and they walked in step through Massingham. She told him that it was not Swinton's fault, and that he had asked Amelia to take their place on Hogmanay. That it was not Bolton's fault they were going to another factory, but someone-or-other Plomer, and it meant they were good at their jobs, the best. She tried to sound strong.

As they neared the allotments, Miss Ellington began

walking faster and faster, drawing away from them. Fran laughed. 'Bit eager, eh, Miss Ellington?'

Miss Ellington waved her hand and laughed, but didn't slow her pace.

Beth, walking beside Fran, called, 'Aye, Miss Ellington, I reckon our Simon might let you stick chickweed through the wire if this visiting goes on. Best prepare yerself for the honour.'

They passed one plot after another, finally arriving at the Canary Club shed, hunkered down beneath an ancient apple tree, and there was Simon at the door, calling, 'I heard yer a mile off. You chatter more'n the birds.'

While Stan laughed, the three girls sighed. Once it had been their three fathers and Simon Parrot, then two fathers, now just Simon. 'At least there's one to carry on the birds, with Stan and Ben's help,' Sarah said.

They watched as Simon and Miss Ellington smiled at one another, then shook their heads as Simon held out his hand and Miss Ellington shook it. Stan called, 'Is that what she gets for rushing out of work, man? No hearts and flowers?'

Fran took over. 'Aye, flagged down the bus, almost throwing herself in front—'

'Bert skidding—' interrupted Beth.

'And then the woman had to stand in t'aisle while he rattled along, telling our friends what was what,' Sarah interrupted too. 'Lurching this way and that, and anyway, how's she going to get back?'

Simon Parrot muttered, 'Empty vessels, empty vessels . . . Less from you all, if you don't mind. I reckon I'll cycle her to Minton on me crossbar, or mebbe . . . Oh well, I'll sort it.' Now he kissed Miss Ellington's hand and waved them all towards the shed as laughter cut through the chill of the darkening afternoon.

As they waited for Simon and Miss Ellington to enter, Fran whispered to Sarah, 'Reckon he might put her up in his house, eh?'

Sarah smiled. 'Aye, mebbe, or more like in one of these cages. But we'll have gone, and we'll never know.'

Beth heard. 'Aye, you will. I'll get off a letter to yer hostel, or we can sort a time for you to phone the Massingham box. I'll need to talk to you, for I'll be all alone here.' Her voice broke.

'No you won't. I'll be here,' said Stan.

He followed Simon and Miss Ellington into the shed, but Sarah dropped his hand and stared about her. Her da's canes were tied into pyramids over on the neighbouring plot, with the remnants of runner beans still entwined. There were the sprouts that she had forgotten, because it was her da who had always picked them. Well, it was something she should do before she left. She stepped towards them, but was pulled back by Beth.

'Remember what I just said,' said Beth, her words little more than a breath. 'I'll be here to get yer mam right, our Sarah. You'll be gone doing the Lord knows what and you're not to worry. You're to be safe, and trust me to do me task. Trust us all and you just concentrate, eh?' Beth brushed aside the blonde strand that had fallen free from beneath Sarah's headscarf.

Sarah only now saw the lines beneath Beth's eyes. They hadn't been there before Mr Smith died, coughing his lungs up. Shame drenched her. These marrers of hers had lost just as much as she had, and were doing all they could to help *her* mam. Aye, *her* mam, even though they had their own to support. And what was she, Sarah Bedley, doing? Buckling, just like her mam, and it must stop. She whispered back, 'I'm right sorry, I just—'

Fran was in the circle with them now and murmured,

'You just don't want to leave your lad, or your mam, who is a bliddy worry, and yer can't think straight. Just like the rest of us. So enough now, eh?'

Sarah looked from one to the other, and nodded. 'Aye, but you know, there's something we need to do – pick the sprouts, or our das'll be shouting down from their cloud and frightening the life out of us.'

They just looked at her and roared with laughter. 'I reckon you're right, our Sarah,' Fran said, and the three of them hunkered down and picked what they could from all three plots, stuffing sprouts in the pockets of their macs. Stan arrived, bringing a sack from the shed. All four of them harvested not just sprouts, but cabbages and parsnips, enough for the week. They made plans for Stan and Ben to pick more as time went on.

As the three girls dusted off the soil from their hands it felt at last as though the healing of their grief had begun.

They all crowded into the Canary Club shed, where seed husks lay on the floor and the clean smell of sawdust filled the air. It was the first time the girls had been back since their das had died, but instead of feeling sad, they were comforted. Simon gestured to the bench. 'Park yerselves on that, you lasses. Stan, on the tub, and mek yerself useful – run yer fingers through this lot. See if you think there's enough hemp, but maybe too much red rape, eh?'

Stan ran the seed through his fingers, and it was as though each of the girls was looking at their da. They heard Miss Ellington and Simon laughing quietly as the pair of them pushed chickweed through the wire and into the cages.

Stan turned and smiled at Sarah. 'Remember being here, with us, you two lasses. It'll keep yer warm at night, and it'll do the same for me, Ben and the mams. Before we know where we are, you'll be back safe and sound. Safe, remember, and sound.'

Simon turned. 'I have a bit of sherry, only a bit, and a beer for thee and me, Stan. We'll toast 'em on their way, for Cyn's just told me all about it.'

'Sin?' Sarah queried, trying not to grin.

Fran didn't even try not to laugh. 'Really? Full of it, is she?'

Miss Ellington looked from one to the other, her eyebrows raised. Beth was leaning against the shed wall, laughing fit to burst. She tried to speak and at last she said, 'That's for Mr Parrot to find out, I reckon.'

The girls returned to the Bedley home after dropping off Beth with her mam. Stan had joined Sid and Norm at the Miners' Club to take in the sickness dues, as his da and Tom Bedley had done before him, and Simon Parrot and Cynthia Ellington were cycling home. Sarah opened the gate into the backyard, not sure what she would find, and heard Fran right behind her.

The wind caught the gate, slamming it shut. The back door opened and there was Mrs Hall on the step, calling, 'Come away in, lasses, for we've heard your news, course we have.'

Mrs Bedley was sitting at the table, her hooky frame set aside, her face quite calm. There was no smell of booze as Mrs Hall went on, 'The co-op's gone home. We've heard that this time it weren't Swinton, or so Mrs Oborne said. 'Tis just the war and its needs, and I heard too that Beth will be here, and Stan on hand. Mrs Smith says she'll be fine on her own – nice to have a bit of peace, she says, so she's right pleased Maud's borrowing the lass till all's tickety-boo. Or that's what she says, which is right kind.'

Sarah was looking at her mam, who was staring at the range. Mrs Bedley turned and held up her hooky frame. 'What do you think, lass?' The rag rug was a mixture of dark, flowing colours. ''Tis for the floor, not t'wall, Briddlestone's says. So these colours'll not show the dirt.'

It was the first proper conversation Sarah had had with her mam since the drinking had begun, and she ran her fingers over the loops as she had always done. 'It's right grand, Mam.'

Mrs Hall was putting on her coat and scarf. 'Yer tea's in the range, our Sarah. Stan'll eat with us when he brings the accounts back, then be along later to see yer, of course he will.'

They left, with Fran calling, 'I'll be back an' all to sleep, and I'll bring me carpet bag and we can cycle to the station together at the crack of dawn, or mebbe well before. Stan and Sid will bring the bikes back for us, or I'll skelp 'em.' She laughed, but it was strained.

Sarah dished up the meal and they ate in silence, her mam merely picking at her bacon and tatties until finally she reached out to Sarah. 'I'll miss yer, lass, sorely. Your da would say be right careful, be safe. Shame he weren't, eh?' She dropped her fork to her plate with a clang.

Sarah said nothing, just finished her own meal, and all the while her mam was restless, looking around the room. Sarah settled her by the fire, handing her the frame. 'Do a few more rows, eh, Mam? I have to pack, then we'll have a cuppa.'

She went to her bedroom, folding up every warm piece of clothing she had in the family's old carpet bag, and stuffed it in with her favourite book, *Black Beauty*. As a child, her da had told her stories about the Galloways that were used in the mine, and one Christmas he had bought her the book.

Sarah put in her nightgown and a pair of socks, for she couldn't abide cold feet. Through the bedroom window she could see the winding gear in the moonlight, and the snow lying on the hills. Would it be deeper in Scotland? At that, she gripped the handles of the bag, finally facing what she had been pushing from her mind: explosives? Well, she wouldn't tell her mam that, though Stan knew, and had paled.

She returned downstairs and was heading along the hall when the letter box clicked. She retraced her steps and picked up the piece of paper, but it was too dark to read, so she hurried to the kitchen. She shut the door behind her and then read the note. It was a bill. The drink was item-ised, and so was the interest. She looked up, but her mam wasn't in her chair. Sarah heard a clatter from the scullery.

'Mam?' She hurried to the scullery doorway in time to see her mam straightening up from the cupboard under the sink. She turned, as though barring Sarah's way.

'It were only a little nip.' But her words were slurred.

Rushing across, Sarah shouted, 'For pity's sake, get away from the sink, Mam. Get away.' She waved the bill. 'Just get away and stop it. You must stop it.'

Her mam side stepped. Sarah shoved the bill in her pocket and hunkered down, shoving aside the bucket, cloths and brushes, and there, at the back, was a sherry bot-tle. She grabbed it and stood, turning to see her mam trying to slip out into the kitchen.

'Don't you move, Mam. Don't you bliddy move. I'm throwing this away. How could you?' Every fury, every fear was there in her as Sarah dropped the bottle in the sink, the sherry splashing out.

Her mam rushed her, beating her about the head. 'That's mine, mine, yer hear.' Sarah put her hands up, pushing her away, but not quickly enough, for her mam backhanded her with all her might. Sarah fell against the sink, cracking her head. The bill for her mother's drink fell from her pocket to the flagstones. The pain ricocheted around her head. Her mam reached down. 'Sarah, oh Sarah.'

There was a knock on the back door, a draught, and Stan shouted from the kitchen, 'Howay, what? What the hell?'

Stan, always Stan, lovely Stan. He came. He picked her up. Her mam backed into the kitchen. 'What?' he shouted. 'What? Did you fall? What?'

She felt sick, and heard her mam crying. Her head was swimming. Stan's arm was around her. 'Come on, to the table.'

She leaned against him, but she was bleeding, she'd stain him. The seat was hard, cold. She clutched the table; the oilcloth was cold too. She was sitting in her da's seat. Stan was helping her mam to her armchair. Her mam was weeping and how could the smell of booze be so heavy in such a short time? Sarah thought. Such a short, short time.

Stan came to Sarah. 'There's a broken bottle in the sink.'

'Aye, and a bill on the floor. Read it, Stan, just read it. So much. How can I pay it? How can she still drink?'

Her head was stinging above her ear. She touched it. Blood stained her fingers. She looked at her mam, sunk down in her chair, her breathing heavy and drink-sodden. How could she? And how could she, Sarah Bedley, pay for it all? She levered herself upright. Her head swam, sickness swept over her, but none of that mattered. She was screeching, 'How bliddy could you, Mam? How can I pay for it? How? How?'

Stan was by her side, holding her. Then Fran was there too, her bag in her hand, the back door wide open and the cold howling in. 'What?' she said. 'What happened?'

Sarah was staring at her mam and said quietly now, 'How, Mam? Tell me how can I pay for it all?'

She slid from Stan's arms and onto the hard kitchen chair, holding her head. The blood dripped onto her collar. As Fran rushed over, Stan said, 'I found her on the floor, she must have slipped, hit her head. There's been a bill for the drink and her ma's been at it – again.'

He let the bill fall to the table.

'Get water and a cloth,' Fran snapped. He did so. Sarah looked from Fran to her mam, and then to the bill. Fran hunkered down as Stan dabbed away the blood, holding the cloth hard against the wound. 'Don't you worry. We've the donated money.'

'And I've some savings,' Stan muttered.

Sarah shook her head. 'Yer mam and Ben have needs, an' all.'

Stan touched her cheek, then wiped the blood from her neck. 'Aye, and they'll be answered. I'm earning, Davey too. And Fran. I can sort all this out, as is my right, for we are to marry.' He looked at Fran, who was checking the bill.

She nodded and said, 'Aye, we're all in this together, Sarah. You, and me, Davey and Stan, and Beth. We'll share and share about, course we will.'

Sarah watched as Fran looked again at the bill, then at Sarah's mam. 'How can we put a stop to this, though, Mrs Bedley? 'Tisn't yer fault, it's a weakness, but it canna go on.'

The roaring was there again in Sarah, for Fran was right. It couldn't go on, none of it, for she'd not be hit again, she'd not pretend either, not any more. Her rage was roaring right over the top of Stan's words as he said, 'Don't worry, this *is* going to be stopped, for I will make sure of it.'

Sarah watched her mam get to her feet and scuttle through to the scullery again. She tore after her, for that woman would not drink again, not tonight, not ever. She caught up with her mam before she reached the sink and dragged her back, screaming, 'Don't you dare. Don't you bliddy dare go near that bottle, and 'tis as well I'm leaving, for if I weren't, I'd be out of that door, and you'd not see me again, d'you hear? You'd not see me, not touch me, nor hurt me, never ever again. I were a bairn then, and you hurt me, like you hurt me tonight. But never ever again. Clumsy little bairn, they thought, eh. Well it weren't me, were it?'

It was Stan's strong arms around her, not her da's now, and his voice. 'Oh, bonny lass. It'll be all right. I'll mek it all right.'

This time, though, Sarah pushed free. '*I'll* mek it all right, for I'll not come back here, else she's sorted herself out.'

She saw Fran dragging her mam from the scullery while Stan held her again. She heard the kitchen door shut. She felt Stan's arms around her, his kisses on her hair, his voice. 'Oh, I didn't know. Forgive me, I didn't know. They just said you got clumsy, worried as a bairn about the booze.'

But she was working out the two times table and she wouldn't listen, for she mustn't lose her place.

Chapter Eleven

Fran and Sarah woke to the riddling of the range. Stan. They checked the time, but didn't really need to because the pitmen were marching along the back lane. "Ow do?' 'Fair nippy today, eh.' 'Too bliddy warm where we're going, lad.' Laughter and coughing, always the coughing. The two girls stood at the window in the moonlight, breathing it all in. Fran muttered, her breath softening the frost on the window, 'We'll be back soon.'

Sarah slipped her arm around her friend. 'Aye, but until then we'll be together and you can write and tell Davey where to telephone. He sounded all reet, did he, when he telephoned the box yesterday evening?'

Fran wiped the window and together they peered down to the yard, and then the lane. Every back lane in Massingham led to the pit, so every lane carried pitmen, there and back. Well, back if they were lucky. 'We're in a hostel, so they might have a telephone box of their own,' she said quietly.

'We'll find one, don't you fret, Franny.' It was all so normal. But Sarah's head still hurt, her blonde hair was still stained red, for they couldn't seem to wash it out last night, and her heart was bruised because she hated her mam. They dressed, for they had a train to catch. They stripped the bed, knowing that Beth would bring her own yellow-stained sheets, for she'd likely as not be back in the stemming with the yellow powder sometime soon, and wouldn't want to mess up the Bedleys' sheets.

For a moment Sarah imagined herself back in that work-shop, pouring the yellow chemical, which they guessed was TNT, into the drum. The powder flying up into the air; the coughing as it caught in their throats and fell on their skin. It was used to fill shells in another sector, and wouldn't explode without a spark, they were told. The yellow came out of their skin at night, like some creeping animal, stain-ing the sheets, letting them know it was in them, on them . . . She hated it, though it was safer than most workshops.

They picked up their carpet bags and looked at one another in the moonlight. 'Torch?' Fran asked.

'Aye, ready in me mac pocket. D'yer reckon they'll be smart up there, posh?' Good, she sounded calm.

Fran laughed. 'Well, we're used to that, with Amelia. We'll just have to think of Amelia, and keep our wits about us.'

They stared at one another. Fran said, 'Be brave for a bit longer. We'll be gone in minutes. You'll be free. Oh, Sarah . . .'

Sarah shook her head. 'No, don't. We just have to go. I've written Mam a letter, did it after you fell asleep. I'll leave it for her, for I'll not be back unless she sorts herself. I truly won't, because it's what me da said to her an' all, when she were bad before. She won't remember me words last night, so she can read them, and mek up her own mind.'

After she had written the letter last night, she had moved from the two times to the four times table, working her way up through the night. Four times four is sixteen. Five times four is twenty.

As Fran set off down the stairs, Sarah looked along the landing to her mam's room. The door was shut. She hoped she was in there, and dug in her carpet bag for the letter, slipping it under the door.

Sarah caught up with Fran and whispered, 'I divint want to see her.'

They continued down. Sarah touched her head. It was still seeping, though Stan had eased the cut together and put a plaster on, tightly. Today Beth would take over here. Stan would warn her of Mrs Bedley's right arm and would stay until her mam was in bed. Stan? Beth? She closed her eyes, then carried on down the stairs and along the hall, following Fran, who opened the door and whispered, 'Howay, our Stan, that's our da's first day in the pit breakfast, and we're not even hunkering down, but swanning about on a train.'

Stan was by the range, a frying pan in his hand, and his laugh was quiet. 'Aye, but you're both off for a bit, so I thought I'd do it anyway. It'll put hairs on yer chest and keep up yer strength. Come in and shut the door.'

The girls entered and there on the table were slices of bread, fried in dripping. Fran sighed. 'Aye, there's an egg as well. Have I died and gone to heaven?'

Stan nodded towards the plates as he carried the pan into the scullery. 'Ben slipped the eggs round last evening after you were in bed because Da's hens gave you a farewell gift. The lad said he'd be back to cycle with you to the train because he's not having you missing it and he reckons you'll dilly-dally. Right old woman he's growing up to be, that he is.'

Sarah liked the talk, liked that her mam wasn't here, liked the sound of his voice, the normality. She wasn't hungry but ate. They washed in the scullery and Fran sponged her hair again, just as she had done last night. She wouldn't dwell on last night – she was leaving. They dashed across the yard to the netty as the snow fell. When they returned, Stan had done them a bait tin each, with a bit of cheese and bread and dripping.

'Mam says to eat your crusts, lasses, it'll make yer hair curl.' He kissed the tops of their heads and whispered to

Sarah, 'By, I'll miss you, bonny lass. You telephone at the times we said, eh?' He raised his voice and grinned at Fran. 'Getting to be a habit, all this telephoning to them red boxes, eh?' As he spoke, he shoved his own bread and dripping into his bait tin, and hung it on his belt.

Ben knocked on the back door and stuck his head round. Snow lay on his cap and muffler. 'Stop your mithering all of yer. We need to get to t'station and it's snowing fast.' They all left together, the girls and Ben cycling against the tide of miners coming along the back lane, hearing, 'Be safe,' 'Come back,' 'Tek care.' They shouldn't know the girls were leaving, but of course they did. Gossip was like wildfire, but didn't leave the back lanes.

Stan clomped the other way, towards the pit. Sarah did not look back. She cycled on, but felt as though she was somewhere else. Since her mam had hit her she had felt like this, suspended. Did her da feel like that on his cloud?

The snow was driving into their faces, settling on the carpet bags jammed end first into their baskets on the front of the handlebars. The bikes rattled along on the cobbles. They pedalled out of the back lane into Main Street. The Factory bus was leaving the bus stop, its wipers swishing. The three of them waved. Bert hooted, slowed and stopped for just a second. There were Beth and Mrs Oborne on the steps, and Maisie, Sylv and the others pressing their faces to the windows, all waving. Then there was a roar of the engine and they were gone.

For a moment they waited, their feet on the ground either side of the pedals, looking after it as the exhaust threw out vapour, but then Sid and Norm approached. 'Be safe, lasses,' Norm said.

'If you can't be good, be careful,' said Sid, reaching across and ringing Sarah's bell as he passed. She slapped his arm, doing normal things. But she was floating.

Ben muttered, 'Howay. We have to hurry.' But his bottom lip was trembling, and he cycled ahead as though the demons of hell were after him, only skidding to a stop at the station. The girls left their bikes in the shelter, and Ben walked with them to the platform. They waited for the train to Newcastle to huff and puff into the station, but when it did, he just turned away and stalked out of the door. He stopped and called back, 'There've been too many bliddy goodbyes, so there have.' He was only twelve, and he was crying.

'Language,' the two girls called together.

The guard called, 'All aboard, shift yer arses.' They boarded.

Mrs Hall and Mrs Smith sat either side of the range in the Bedley house. The pots were washed and the table wiped. Annie Hall checked the clock above the mantelpiece. 'They'll be on their way and Ben will be back at our house. I left some fried bread warming in the oven, for I divint want him here, not yet, not till our Maud's had sense talked to her.'

'And our Beth'll be halfway to the Factory.'

Silence fell between them. Annie Hall rose and collected up her proggy frame while Audrey Smith lifted hers up from beside the chair. Together they worked, for Briddlestone's would need more of the co-op's rugs for the January sales, not that they lowered the prices, but people came in to see the bargains and bought good stuff as well. Or that's what Mr Witherspoon had told them when he asked for an increased order. 'We're shipping them down to London too, for the "sale" demand will be heavy,' he'd said.

A percentage of the price still went to the charity set up by Mr Massingham and Briddlestone's for the bombed-out families of Newcastle, and that, thought Annie Hall, was a good thing.

She was about to prod her peg through the hessian when they heard a bedroom door slam, then a cough and a creaking of the stairs. Audrey had stopped work too, and muttered, 'I'm at a bliddy loss with her. One minute I want to wring her neck, the next I canna think how to help her. I never knew she'd hurt little Sarah. No wonder she's such an afeared wee thing. It shook our Beth when she nipped round last night to say goodbye.'

Annie pushed a strip of red felted blanket through the hessian with her peg. The red interrupted the grey something grand, but all the time she was listening to the creaking of the stairs. With each step came a cough or a groan. 'It's shaken us all, I reckon. The co-op's in a right lather. Course we knew back then Maud had taken it bad when Tom were in the accident, but not . . . Well, not taking a hand to the lass. We all just thought she became a nervous wee bairn, clumsy with it all. It makes me reet angry, Audrey, and I divint know where to put the anger, that's the thing.'

Audrey didn't reply, but put up her hand. 'Howay, that were closer.' They listened, and there was another cough from the bottom of the stairs. They looked at one another, their proggy pegs poised. Audrey Smith pursed her lips. 'Well, 'tis time she were up, it's after eight thirty.'

Annie got up, and slipped the kettle from the slow to the hot plate, where the simmer became a boil just as the kitchen door opened to admit a bleary-eyed Mrs Bedley. 'What? What?' she said, looking from the two women to the kitchen table.

'There's a bevvy on the way – tea.' Annie could hear the coldness in her own voice, but why not, her friend had struck Sarah, and not for the first time it seemed. That meant there was little patience left, not in her, not in Audrey, not in most people who knew.

'Sit yersel' down at the table, Maud.' This time it was Audrey who spoke, and it was an order.

Mrs Bedley looked around, her hair unbrushed. 'What? Where's Sarah? Ah, the fore shift. That's reet.' She slopped to the table in her slippers, all trodden down at the heel, and her dressing gown hanging open over her grubby nightgown.

Audrey had put down her proggy frame and came to the kitchen table, pulling out a chair. 'No, she's not gone on the fore shift. You'll remember last night, after you'd whacked yer own bairn, that she said if she weren't already being transferred, she'd leave. Her head were bleedin', our Maud. And 'twasn't the first time, though she were a bitty bairn when yer did it last. Now sit down.'

The last three words were such a shout that not only did Maud look startled, but the tea slopped into the saucer as Annie brought it across and placed it before their friend. Maud Bedley looked from one to the other, confused, shaking her head.

'Drink your tea, Maud.' Annie took the chair at the end of the table. It was where Tom Bedley had sat, dear, dear Tom. What would he think? Aye, well, Annie couldn't know that, but she knew what he'd done the last time Maud started with the drink. Had he known his wife had struck Sarah, and more than once?

There was a knock on the door and Audrey opened it. It was Madge, carrying her frame. She checked the clock. 'Dead on time, eh. So, the four of us are together to stop this bliddy nonsense, Mrs Bedley.' Her eyepatch was green.

Had Maud heard? Annie didn't know, for Maud was slurping her tea. She finished it, saw the tea that had spilled over into the saucer, picked up the saucer and gulped it like a bairn.

Madge brought the pot over and topped up the cup. 'Aye,

best get that down you, for this is the last hangover you'll be having – ever.'

Maud looked at Madge, confused. Madge ignored her and asked the other two, 'Who's going to tell her what she did last night? For if my old bugger's anything to go by, he could never remember what he'd done.' She touched her eyepatch.

Annie had felt exhausted; just wanting to be by her own fireplace so she could worry in peace and deal with her own grief but Madge's words stripped all weariness from her, and she sat bolt upright. Audrey was covering Madge's hand with hers, Annie thought back, and realised that perhaps she'd always known the truth about Madge's husband, but Madge had been insistent when explaining the injury. Oh dear Lord, there was so much wrong . . .

Audrey said, 'We did tell her, just as you've now told us the truth about the cycling accident. Oh Madge, you should have—Though perhaps we really knew . . .'

'No, I shouldn't have told you for there were no need, but now I have, since 'tis the time for some home truths. But look at our Maud, it hasn't registered.'

Madge's gaze was steely as it swept over Maud Bedley, who finished her second cup and placed it carefully on its saucer. Only then did Maud see that the three other women were staring at her. She ran her hand down her face, then dragged it through her hair. 'What? What happened? I need a fag.'

Madge drew out a packet of Woodbines, gave the woman one and lit it. Maud inhaled deeply, coughed, and Annie wondered where on earth the good and kind woman she knew as Maud had gone.

'Where's our Sarah?' Maud repeated. 'Oh yes, on shift.' She straightened.

Was she trying to look and sound normal? Annie

wondered as she took in the trembling hands, and the way the woman was running her tongue along her lips as though she already needed a drink, before nine in the morning, for heaven's sake. Annie shook her head. 'Don't you remember anything?'

Maud put her hand to her forehead. Her fingers were stained with nicotine. She looked from one to the other, and slowly, somewhere inside her head, a memory stirred. She picked a piece of tobacco from her lower lip and whispered, 'Howay, what did I do?'

Madge told her and Sarah's mother paled. She dropped the cigarette. Madge rescued it, stubbing it out on Maud's saucer.

'Me old bugger might 'ave hit me, Maud, but never touched the bairn. Not like you.'

Annie added, 'Sarah said, before she went, that she would have left, even if she wasn't needed somewhere else. You know, Maud, the lass is right. You're her mam, you hurt her in more ways than one, and we've learned that you did this before, when she was only a bairn of five. Had you forgotten?' In spite of herself, Annie banged the table, and then again. 'You hurt yer own bairn, and it were the drink. And that stops now, for your Sarah won't be coming back ever if it doesn't.'

There was a tap on the door. 'It's me,' Maisie's mam, Mrs Adams, who owned the corner shop, called as she entered.

Maud Bedley looked from the women round the table to Mrs Adams standing in the doorway. She put her hands to her face. 'What have I done? Oh, what have I done to my poor wee bairn?'

Audrey Smith said, 'You've hurt her. You've let yerself down, our Maud. If it wasn't bad enough that she just survived that detonator blast because the wall didn't come down – and don't anyone tell me I should say nowt about that because I'm not running me mouth off in front of the enemy, only me friends.' Her gaze as she looked at them all was fierce. No one said anything. Audrey continued. 'Well, Maud, you need to get things straight in your head. You could have lost the lass then, and now she's gone somewhere else, and God knows how dangerous that is, for we certainly don't. So, as I say, 'tis time to get things straight, and lucky for you we're your friends. Together we will deal with this. Together we will make you better. Come away in, Mrs Adams. I hope you've brought a few broken biscuits an' all, and your frame, for we've plans to mek.' Audrey was almost panting, for she'd scarcely drawn breath throughout her rant.

Mrs Adams shook out her headscarf. 'By, the snow is falling thick and heavy, and aye, I have a few broken biscuits, and will finish me rug today. What were it Mr Danvers said – were it the tenth of January for delivery? Or were it Mr Witherspoon said that? I always forget who's the buyer and who's the boss.'

While Madge answered, 'Mr Witherspoon said it,' Annie reached over and gripped Maud's hand, shaking it to gain her attention for she seemed almost asleep again.

'You go and wash yerself and so on. You'll need to get your rug done an' all. We have to earn money, and show Briddlestone's that even if we are widows, and grieving, we are still reliable.'

Maud washed in the scullery. The women talked and planned as they worked, but there was no clear way forward except that now they all knew the truth of everything. What's more, so did Maud.

Annie whispered, an eye on the scullery, 'Stan says he knows how to sort the supplier of the booze, but he'll have to use the donation money from the Rising Sun to help pay off the debt. He has some savings too, and Davey left some for emergencies. But he'll mek sure the beggar doesn't come back – ever.'

Madge leaned forward. 'How?'

The other women looked at one another and Madge just nodded.

'Reet you are, then.'

They fell quiet as Maud came to the scullery doorway, wiping her hands on the threadbare towel. She said, her hair all awry and her skin blotchy, 'I divint know if I can manage without me drink, and t'sherry's gone.'

The women turned and looked at her for a long moment. Annie murmured, 'We need to be careful with her. We don't want to make things worse.'

Mrs Adams said, clear as day, 'Aye, our Annie.' She put aside her proggy frame, then picked up the brown paper bag containing broken biscuits and seemed to count them. Then she folded the bag three times, carefully set it next to the frame, leaned her elbows on the table, drew in a breath and was ready.

'Now you listen to me, our Maud,' she said. 'My Maisie's Derek were smashed into bits on some bliddy beach at Dunkirk, fighting to keep you free of that bliddy Mr Hitler. So divint you think you can drink yerself silly just cos yer hurting. Yer man has a grave. Derek hasn't. What's more, our Madge has no man and no bliddy eye because he were too handy with his fists.'

She turned to Madge. 'Aye, I were at the door for a while, listening. Fell of yer bike, indeed? I never fell for that, and I reckon neither did no-one else, but that was your choice. A bairn's different, our Maud Bedley. And what's more, yer can work on yer rugs to find the money to pay back the donation, which was a fee for the girls' singing, or you can think 'tis better to pour everyone's money down yer gullet. But let me tell you, lady, yer'll need to think about that again, for we'll not allow it. Time someone told you you're an ugly drunk – aye, that you are, Maud Bedley. What's more, you're a lucky cow an' all, for you have us. And we'll get you right once you find a smidgeon of gumption. So stick that in yer pipe and bliddy well smoke it.' She turned to Annie. 'And that's me being careful, our Annie.'

'Bliddy hell,' muttered Madge as Maud Bedley stormed out of the kitchen, into the passage. 'Remind me never to cross you when you're not being careful, our Beatrice Adams, or I reckon we'll end up like them biscuits.' She nodded towards the brown paper bag.

At this the women laughed, and then couldn't stop. They laughed until they couldn't draw breath, then Madge produced a twist of tea and waved it at them. 'I'll mash another pot, then we'll try to sort out a plan again, for I like a plan, even if 'tis half-baked.'

The co-op women nodded. Annie didn't worry that Maud Bedley might head out of the front door, for Stan had wedged the bolts. Aye, poor lad. Torn between caring for his family and Sarah's. She snatched a glance at Beth's mam and prayed that nothing would spark up between Stan and Beth after the past they shared. She shut down the thought. There was enough to worry about without that on her mind.

She watched as Madge sorted the tea and looked at the clock: nine fifteen. How were those two wee lasses? Where were they? Would the factory be safe? Oh, Annie Hall, don't be so bliddy silly, she told herself. Since when were munitions safe, eh?

Later that morning Maud headed out into the cold of the yard to the netty. She didn't need it, but she did need to read the letter in Sarah's handwriting that she'd found on the floor by her bedroom door. She leaned against the icy

171

brick wall, and drew it from her pocket with trembling hands.

Mam
You've made me almost hate you. You're a drunk, you're a disgrace. You hurt me. I'm away from you now, and I won't be coming back till you're sorted. Howay, I might not be back at all, for where we're going is more dangerous. Did you read that, or are you too drunk? I *might* not come back, for I might be killed. And the truth is, I *won't* be back unless you make yourself better. That's all I've to say.
Sarah.

Maud Bedley read it again, pressing hard against the wall. The words jumped. She wanted Sarah home, and even more she needed a drink, but she'd try, really she would. She whispered to her dead Tom, 'I will try, but I need you to help me.'
But of course, no reply came.

Chapter Twelve

The train to Scotland stopped and started as it pulled into sidings every few miles, and all the while the snow fell and the carriage grew colder. Some passengers had to stand in the corridor, departing when they pulled into a station, only for others to get on. It was close on eleven when a woman with a toddler in tow and another on the way boarded, stood for a moment in the corridor, then peered into Fran's carriage, in case there was a seat.

'Let's shift, Sarah. She should sit down, eh?'

The man sitting next to Sarah buried his head in his newspaper, determined to ignore the situation. Fran trod on his toe as she left. 'Ouch,' he exclaimed.

Fran turned, making sure her shoulder bag caught his paper. It crumpled on his lap. 'Reet sorry, were that only one of yer toes?'

Sarah pushed her from behind and they stood in the corridor as the mother and her runny-nosed son sat next to the man. Fran sidestepped along, finding just a bit more space amongst the many others standing, and looked back into the compartment, whispering, 'My, my, a restless small child, and he thought *I* were a nuisance. Reckon he'll wish he'd got out of there while the going was good.'

The little boy was standing on the seat, waving his arms around while his mother tried to make him sit. The train lurched over points. 'Oopsie,' muttered Fran as the boy landed on the man's lap, crushing his newspaper.

They leaned on the window rail, their breath misting the

glass. The scenery was changing from slag heaps and villages to open country and hills, or were they mountains? Whatever there were, Fran thought, they looked freezing with the deep snow. Even the banks of the becks they passed seemed to run out over the water like ice shelves.

The girls wiped the window yet again, then leaned back against the compartment wall. The train rumbled on and they balanced as it swayed and rattled over points. They talked of Sarah's mam in low voices.

'We'll leave it to the co-op. They'll sort her, just as we would sort things for our bairns,' Sarah said.

They grinned at one another and Fran smiled.'Will yours and Stan's be dark or fair?'

Sarah raised an eyebrow. 'Howay, lass, what'll yours be? For 'tis the same difference.'

'Is yer cut still stinging?' Fran asked. Sarah shook her head. Fran lifted Sarah's hat, and checked. 'Nowt happening, no more blood. P'raps it's better, or mebbe just numbed by the cold.'

Sarah sighed. 'That's supposed to mek me feel better, eh?'

Fran laughed. 'Summat like that.'

They pulled their scarves up around their mouths and pulled their woollen hats further down over their ears. Smuts from the engine flew past the window, mixed up with tumbling snow. 'Why does snow sometimes look as though it's falling upwards or just tumbling about, when it's really cascading down?' Sarah asked, her voice muffled by her scarf.

'No idea, pet. I'll ask Davey, he'll know.'

Sarah nodded and nudged her. 'Likely he'll put it in one of his crosswords. D'you reckon he'll go back to setting them and sorting out a magazine after he's ... Well, after the war?'

An elderly man standing next to Fran peered round her and said to Sarah, his voice thick with a Scottish accent,

'We'll all be tae old by then to remember what a crossword is, or what things were like before the war.'

A young woman the other side of Sarah leaned forward and muttered as the train swept round a bend to reveal a frozen lake, 'Why is it that I always get a ruddy ray of sunshine standing near me, usually in a kilt?' She raised her voice. 'Oh well, if we weren't Scots with long pockets, I'd take a bet on it that you're wrong.'

The man laughed and passed them each one of his cigarettes. His fingers were calloused, and two of them nicotine-stained. Fran dragged out her matches and they lit up. An eagle soared above the lake and the mountains seemed closer, white with dark shadows.

'I do love a loch,' the man said.

Ah, Fran thought. I'm not looking at a lake.

They pulled into a siding yet again, waiting while a goods train rattled past, heading south. 'There was room for both of us,' Sarah complained.

The man said, 'Aye well, probably carrying a lot of things that go bang, so best to tek care.'

Munitions, thought Fran, then studied the clouds that were gathering.

One o' clock came and went. Fran and Sarah dragged their bait tins out of their bags and offered their bread and dripping around, but kept the cheese for themselves for later. The woman licked her fingers afterwards and said, 'My mother swears by bread and dripping, winter and summer.'

The elderly man merely grunted, halfway through his. Fran muttered, 'Don't you go leaving your crusts, young man. Howay, how else is your hair going to curl?'

The old boy whipped off his woollen hat to show a bald patch, much like a monk's tonsure. ''Tis a wee bit late for that.'

Sarah, Fran and the other girl burst out laughing, at which he kneed along one of his suitcases for them to sit on. The girl was dressed in trousers, boots and thick socks up to her knees and seemed content to stand, but after another hour of slow progress, Sarah asked, 'Would you really not like to sit for a bit?'

The girl shook her head. 'Och no, pet. I like tae see the trees now the snow has eased.' She pointed to the pine forests, which looked like a Christmas card with their snow-decked branches, though you wouldn't perhaps include the raptors that seemed to hover on the thermals.

The old man had been dozing, but leaned forward now. 'A Land Girl, are yer, lassie?'

The girl laughed. 'Yes, but I've been sent to cut down trees for pit props for the mines or whatever the war needs. Never been happier. Love it. They're setting up a special unit to do it so I'll side-step tae that when it's up and running. Used tae work in an office. Aye, this suits me better. What about you two?'

Fran had leaned forward at the mention of pit props. They reminded her of Stan, of her da, and of Davey who had escaped, for now. 'You'd better cut some good ones. We have family in the pits,' she said.

'Had,' Sarah whispered, but only Fran heard.

The girl looked at them. 'Ah, then I will cut good and true. And you?'

Damn, thought Fran, who had hoped to distract the girl, but it was Sarah who replied, 'Oh, we're factory girls. And we sing. We'll call ourselves that when we get a booking in a pub . . .' She petered out.

The girl was interested and about to reply when the wheels screeched, the train slowed, and they entered the environs of a small town. Smoke from chimneys was snatched away by the wind. The old man stood and tilted his head. 'I'm leaving now. So I'll be away, teking my suitcases with me.'

176

The girls clambered to their feet, and pushed his case towards him. 'Are you staying long? Family visit?'

The man just put his finger to his nose. 'Why, that's for me tae know, and you tae find out, lassies.'

He opened the door once the train had drawn into the station and they helped him out with the cases. Not only were they heavy, but they clinked.

The forestry girl raised an eyebrow. 'Och, I reckon it's a wee bit of grog that'll be spread about the town this evening.'

The two girls sighed. Fran knew that Sarah would be wondering if there was going to be a wee bit of grog spread around the Bedley house. The train lurched, the wheels found purchase and they set off again, but all the time the Lumber Jill was watching them closely. Fran cut across any questions that were brewing and instead asked one of her own. 'We didn't ask your name? I'm Fran, this is Sarah. We're heading for a town called Pitaul—' She stopped short. Should she have said even that?

The girl nodded. 'Aye, well, I'm Annis – Gaelic for "chaste". My parents must have had hopes for me. I got teased in England at the school where they sent me. Army, you know. They travelled about. I'm glad tae be home. I get off a stop before you, for 'tis Pitauly Dubh you're heading tae, I reckon.' She whispered the last half of the sentence. 'Good luck is all I can say, lassies, in that particular factory, and speak slow, for they'll not understand you. But then you'll take some time tae decipher them too. But enough of that. If you're singers, give us a tune.' She raised her voice, waving down the corridor. 'For I see a pair of bagpipes came on board at the last stop and I could do without a lot of wailing. I topped up with a clink or two myself last night and my head's hammering fit to burst.'

' "All or Nothing at All"?' Sarah asked. They were in

177

open countryside again and the sky seemed to stretch for miles as they sang. As they passed crofts whose peat fires were sending smoke streaming on the wind, Annis started to sing 'Keep the Home Fires Burning'. The girls joined in and others in the corridor did too. Annis stopped as the bagpipes started, groaned, then laughed, and the singing continued.

It wasn't until the day had faded into twilight that the train stopped at her station and Annis left them, slinging her rucksack over her shoulder. She'd given them her phone number and said, 'Phone me if you get time, which you won't. But just in case, there's a public booth just outside the hostel, so I hear. Someone in our foyer'll find me. Annis Campbell. Remember that. Always happy to share a wee tot.' She waved and was off, striding along the platform with the bagpipe player, who wore a kilt that swayed when he walked. It reminded Sarah of Mr Swinton and Mr Bolton walking along the corridor in front of them.

Sarah watched them to the gate, then muttered, 'I think the world's gone mad. The girl's wearing the trousers and the bloke a skirt. But I like the idea of trousers, Franny. Better than an eye pencil line up the back of me freezing legs, eh? Or up the back of *his* legs.' She paused because Fran was laughing so much. As the train moved off, Sarah added, 'I hope Mam ... Well, I shouldn't have said ... But I'm bliddy glad I've gone. There I've said it, though I shouldn't have really . . .'

Fran's laughter faded and she hugged her friend. 'Sarah Bedley, you can say what you like to me, for I'd feel just the same.'

It was really dark when the train slowed again, though the stars were bright and the sparks flying from the screeching wheels vivid. There were no lights showing, of course, nothing to say they were coming into a village, town or station. Was this it? Should they ask? The man standing next to them said, speaking slowly, 'I see yer wondering, and aye, 'tis the one you want, Pitauly Dubh, lassies. We get a few of you heading this way. Aye, we had a Geordie last week too. You take care now.'

Sarah smiled. 'Thank you.'

So much for secrecy, Fran thought. Two strange girls heading off to some little town and it was quite obvious to some just why they were going.

They turned back into the carriage and heaved their carpet bags from the rack. The man sitting beneath ducked as Fran's swung too near him. He tucked away his feet. Fran winked at the young mum whose son was asleep, resting on the man's arm. Fran's shoulder bag was lighter than it had been – the water bottle was empty and the bait tin too, and they clinked as the girls jumped down onto the platform. They followed the few people who got off and seemed to know where they were going. Fran felt frightened all of a sudden, and hurried to keep up with them. She could barely see and even the air felt different here. Well, of course it did, it wasn't a pit village.

They joined the queue to hand in their tickets. The guard said, 'About bliddy time, for there's a lorry waiting for you lassies. You hurry along now, there's a war on. Can't keep people waiting, indeed you canna.' Or that's what it sounded like, but the accent was so heavy it was hard to work out.

'Tell your timetable that, eh?' said Fran.

Sarah pushed her along as the guard grumbled about foreigners and how he couldn't understand a word.

A lorry was waiting outside. The exhaust was visible in the starlit night. Two men leaned against the cab, smoking, as the girls approached.

'About bleedin' time.' They were English.

179

'If I hear a third person say that, I will rip their throats out with me teeth, for me hands are full and I haven't a third, so aye, teeth it is,' Fran said.

There was silence. Then one said, 'We've got a right one here. Hop in.'

Fran made for the door of the cab. The young man said, his cigarette breath reaching her, 'In the back.' He thumbed her towards the rear of the lorry. 'Benches along the sides, pull the doors shut after you.'

'Oh dear, Franny, steady,' Sarah warned.

Fran shook her head, feeling exhausted and even more vulnerable in this strange new world. She wanted to be home amongst the slag heaps, the pitmen, the women and their families. She breathed in for a count of four and out for four, as her da had always said. And then she heard Mrs Oborne telling her to get some gumption. She looked up at the stars, so bright in the firmament, and where he, her da, had to be.

She clenched her fists and dug them into her pockets, which made her think of Swinton. For some strange reason he was no longer the devil he had always been, but a worried, almost nice old man. Well, he might not be the same, but she, Fran Hall, was.

She breathed in again, one, two, three, four, and out, then spoke slowly and clearly. 'We've stood for bliddy hours in the bliddy corridor and we've just about had enough. We have nowt to say about getting in t'back like a load of spuds except that it's not happening. So, we're getting in that cab, and you'd better sort yerselves out or I'll drive it meself.'

She reached for the cab door again. The men chucked their cigarettes on the ground. Fran looked at the stubs. 'There're a few more puffs in those. Made of money, are yer?'

While the men scrabbled to pick them up, the girls opened the door and clambered onto the passenger seat, their bags at their feet. They heard the swearing, then the laughter, and smiled at one another as one man got in the driving seat. The other squeezed in alongside the girls, shoving them over. As the men drew one last time on the stubs, finally throwing them out of the window, Fran said, 'Best be off. Can't hang about while yer dilly-dally. We're late enough as 'tis.'

The man next to her muttered, 'Me dad warned me about women like you.'

They drove off in silence and as well as feeling her heart beating hard and fast, Fran heard her mam hissing, 'Language, Franny Hall.'

It was a small town and they could see little of it in the light from the slit headlamps. Soon they were out of it and the darkness was complete, though the snow-covered countryside shone white in the moonlight. After a few minutes, Fran thought that she might as well hold out an olive branch and said, 'Nice to meet you both. We're Fran and Sarah.'

The driver grunted. 'And what's more, yer bite.'

Sarah nodded. 'But only when we're hungry.'

The man on Fran's right moved his arm and dug in his pocket for more cigarettes. 'I'm Roy, and driving yonder is Simon. We're medics at the factory and were picking up medical supplies and anything else delivered to the station. We also double up as part of the maintenance crew. Can't understand a word anyone says up here because I'm a Sassenach from Oxford way. You made yourself plain enough just now, but that was because you were speaking slowly and savagely, but best drop the savagely and just stick to slowly. I think you're probably from the pits, Geordies, hey? So they'll not catch on if you gabble.'

Simon changed gear to go up a snow-covered hill. Roy said, 'We took another lamb to the slaughter last week from your parts. Newcastle, she said. Nice lass. I reckon *she'd* have slipped into the back without a fuss, but there's room for one in the front. Not a squash like this. Simon can't hardly change gear.'

Fran wriggled round to stare at him. 'I think we leave all talk of the back of the lorry out of every conversation we have to have from now on.'

'Steady, Fran,' Sarah whispered. 'These kind men waited for us, after all.'

Fran pinched her and muttered, 'And you can stop being sweet an' all.' Sarah laughed and Fran went on, 'But, aye, thank you for waiting. Reet kind of you. We know a Simon. Simon Parrot. He breeds canaries.'

There was a short silence, then Simon started laughing, 'Course Mr Parrot breeds canaries, course he ruddy does. Tell me, are they all barmy in your neck of the woods or is it just you two, and Mr Parrot?'

Fran and Sarah were laughing now, laughing and smoking, and for the rest of the journey they talked of this new area: the loch along which they were driving now, the hill they were skidding down, the mountains in the distance, the heather the men said grew everywhere. On they drove. They nodded when they were told of the TB Simon had had and the crook knee Roy had, so neither could be considered for active service.

Instead, they had been given medic's training and sent up here, to the 'heathen wastes', as Roy called them, and when they weren't busy mending the workers, they were mending the fences.

The two girls sat quietly, thinking of the factory and its dangers. Apparently the hostel lay alongside the loch, but what was a hostel like? Fran wondered to herself. They'd never lived anywhere but their own homes. Sarah said this, and Simon volunteered that the hostel would be an experience. 'Just think of a prison.'

'What, it's got bars?' asked Sarah.

Simon changed gear and called over the noise, 'Oh no, just warders. They lock the doors at night, so don't get carried away and forget the time or you'll freeze to death in this neck of the woods.'

The girls fell silent.

The medics dropped them at the hostel, but as they began to walk up the path, feeling their way and wishing they'd remembered where they'd put their torches, they heard the crunching of gravel behind them. It was Roy, limping towards them, and he led them to the double doors, his torch lighting their way. He shone it on the bell. 'Password is, "Sorry we're late, it was the train and please speak slowly." ' He half bowed and laughed. 'Don't worry, you'll pick it up soon enough, just like I've had to listen hard to you. Good luck, girls.' He headed back down the path.

The door opened just as the lorry roared off. A voice said, 'Och, whit time do you call this to be arriving anywhere, lassies? In, quickly.'

By the time they'd worked out what she was saying, they'd been pulled into the darkness. The door shut behind them, and a light clicked on. The woman, wearing a grey skirt and cardigan, raised her eyebrows, sighed and tapped her watch. She shoved home the three bolts on the door, then took a key from the metal ring hanging from her leather belt and turned the lock. She clicked the key back onto the ring. It bedded down with several other keys, but was by far the biggest.

'Follow me, and you'll be quick about it.'

As the woman marched past them, Fran whispered to Sarah, 'Is there a pair of handcuffs in her pocket?'

The woman heard. 'Only when you lassies are so bad

that a good whack doesnae work.' She spoke slowly, with not the glimmer of a smile. Then she winked. They climbed the stairs, lit dimly by wall lights, and were shown the toilets at the end of the corridor before being taken to the door of their room. The woman whispered, ''Tis late. The new lassie that shares wi' ye is asleep, so no lights, no talking. You'll be up wi' her at five for porridge and the bus to the factory. There you'll be worked, fed and watered.'

She held open the door and they entered. The woman shone her torch onto two beds. There was a third, already occupied. They undressed silently, putting their clothes at the end of their beds. There was just enough light through the curtains to make out shapes and Sarah saw a wardrobe and a chest of drawers. An inside toilet, she thought, and just down the landing – no tripping out to the netty on a cold and frosty night, or using the bucket if you couldn't face it. They took turns to walk along the corridor, wash in a white ceramic basin with hot and cold water, and stare at the white bath with taps.

Sarah crept into her bed, lay on her side and gazed across at Fran, wanting to reach out. As though Fran could read her mind, she rolled over and stretched out her hand, meeting Sarah's across the space. For a moment they stayed like that, then tried to sleep.

In the corridor, though, Sarah heard girls' voices kept low, their Scottish accents making the words indecipherable. Doors opened and shut. Would the warder be patrolling the corridors? Would her mam be drunk at home? Would Stan be there, with Beth? *Shut up, shut up.*

The next morning they woke to the sound of someone saying, 'Howay, you two. Time to get up, we canna hold up the bus.'

A girl stood at the foot of Fran's bed. She was dressed in

a skirt and blouse. 'Aye, I'll talk slowly if you will.' She sounded nervous.

As they threw their clothes on, Fran said, 'You're the one from Newcastle.'

The girl's face cleared. 'Howay, you and all?'

Sarah, dragging a brush through her hair, said, 'Not quite. Massingham.'

The girl was opening the door. 'Quick, I'll show yer the bathroom next to the toilets. There's four toilets, and four basins with hot and cold taps. Four, and they're inside, for heaven's sake. Me name's Viola.'

Sarah didn't have the heart to say they'd already found them as Viola, towel in hand, led them almost at a run down the linoleum-covered hallway floor. They tried out the toilets again. They washed in the white ceramic basins with the hot and cold taps. Viola grinned across at them. 'Right grand, eh? Didn't have them in our Newcastle back-to-back. Just the netty, freezing in winter. Surprised we didn't get chilblains on our bums. And it were the scullery where we washed.'

They were laughing at one another. Sarah kept her hands under the running water, then scooped some up and plunged her face into it, laughing even more as she straightened up a little and dripped over the basin. 'Well, I don't know what it's like where we're going to be working, but this is so grand I could get used to it. Bliddy luxury.'

Viola shrieked with laughter. Fran grinned, then said, 'Language, our lass.'

Suddenly quiet, Viola handed Sarah a towel. 'Aye, me mam used to say that to me and me brother. Dead he is, Dunkirk, and me mam and da too in a bliddy bomb raid. I got out, they didn't, so I can say "bliddy" now, for there's no one to nag me.'

Sarah exchanged a quick look with Fran and said, 'Oh,

aye, there is, pet. Language, Viola, language, if you don't mind.'

All the while Sarah was thinking how dreadful it'd be if Davey were dead, and her mam and—She stopped, for her da was up on a cloud and her mam next to useless, unless Sarah's letter jerked her back to the woman she'd been. She handed the towel back to Viola. 'So, think on, lass, we'll keep yer on the straight and narrow, you see if we don't. We're three Geordies and Geordies are family – that's right, isn't it, Fran?'

Fran nodded. 'So we'll skelp you, pet, if you get out of hand.' The three girls stood looking at one another, smiling, but then others ran in, shoving them to one side.

'Och, we'll be late, and then the dragon will breathe fire, and that's worse than where we're going,' said one ginger-haired girl, splashing her face.

'Thanks for the use of your towel. We'll have to get ours from our bags,' muttered Fran. But then they were off along the corridor, snatching warm clothes and empty water bottles from their rooms before heading to the dining room downstairs, for the gong was sounding.

In the dining room there were what seemed like a hundred girls sitting at long tables and the clatter and chat was deafening. Viola headed for some empty places. They slung their macs and scarves on the backs of their chairs and sat down. No one paid them any attention. They ate the porridge that was set before them. It was salted, not sugared, and was barely warm, but how could it be otherwise when there were so many to feed?

There was bread and marge too, and Viola spread some of her porridge on a slice and made a sandwich. 'My mam used to, so I do. It keeps her with me,' she said as Fran and Sarah watched. They continued to spoon their porridge into their mouths, but Sarah left a little, and she saw that

Fran had too. They each made sandwiches, and they weren't half bad. A girl across the table shook her head.

'Och, can you see the Sassenachs are forming a tribe, our Anthea?'

The girl sitting next to her winked at Sarah and the other two, then said slowly, 'Everyone needs to belong. You watch one another's back until we remember to do it too. Newcomers get lost in the fray sometimes. But I daresay you already know that? I'm Anthea.'

She was talking to Sarah and Fran, who smiled back but said nothing, for it sounded as if Anthea knew they were experienced, but that was all she'd know, for they'd tell her nothing. They hadn't been born yesterday.

Anthea smiled and nodded. 'Aye, best to keep mum.'

It was as though the new Sassenachs had passed some sort of test.

Viola wiped her mouth and drank down her tea, which was pale and weak. The others finished a second behind her. Then a bell rang and the chairs scraped backwards. Like the others, they dragged on macs and scarves, pulled hats from their pockets and scooped up their bottles. But then Fran said, 'We need water.'

'But the buses are here,' Viola said, heading for the door.

Fran shook her head. 'No, we need to fill our water bottles.'

Viola just stared. 'Howay, why?'

'To sluice the chemicals.' They were being shoved along. Fran stopped and shouted, 'Stop yer shoving.'

Everyone did stop, and turned to stare. Fran said, 'I'll say this slow so you can hear me. I need to fill me water bottle, for it's what we know to do to help reduce the rashes, and how we know that is our business. And if anyone else pushes me, I'll push 'em back, but harder.'

Sarah looked at Viola, whose fear mirrored hers, whilst

187

around them the women shifted. One stepped forward, her flaming red hair hanging in two plaits. 'Och, 'tis a sound thought. We need to find some flasks or bottles tae. Here, follow me. I'm our floor captain, name of Morag, Glasgow born and bred.'

She was a large girl with a smile that creased her face. They followed her, with Sarah telling Viola she could share theirs.

At the factory, set in the shadow of heather-covered hills and nestled behind patrolled fences, the low, flat-roofed buildings made them feel they were back in their normal world at last. Sarah smiled to herself. How strange that preparing to work with explosives seemed so familiar it felt like 'home'. They showed their passes and walked with the red-haired Morag to a building set to one side of a wide roadway. She led them to the changing rooms and told them that they would wear the blue overalls on their pegs. The two girls drank some water, sharing it with Morag and Viola, whose hair was almost the same deep red, but short and curly rather than long and plaited. Even that made them feel at home, for Beth had red hair too.

Sarah thought of her for a moment, at home, with Stan. She closed her eyes. Stan.

'What's wrong?' Fran asked.

'Nowt, just trying to clear my head.'

Fran whispered, 'If you're mithering about your mam, you canna. You need to concentrate on the job. The co-op will keep an eye, they're miracle workers, remember?'

Sarah closed her eyes again, because she couldn't hope for a miracle. Why? Because her da wasn't there to hold her mam to task. But at least here she was free of her, for a while. Free of the fear and the worry, but when the security officer came to stand in front of her, she found herself silently running through the two times table in her head as she was checked for metal, silk and nylon, which they'd already put in the boxes on the side.

'You're not new tae this, eh?' the woman said. Her accent wasn't as thick as some.

Sarah shook her head. 'Not quite the same work, but not too different, it seems?'

They changed into the trousered overalls, wellingtons and turbans. The trousers felt strange for they'd not worn such things before. Sarah decided she'd wear socks tomorrow. The foreman came in wearing a green cotton coat. He was middle-aged, his face hollow with tiredness. He ran through the safety rules because he had two new lassies, he said. The rules were the same as the ones Mr Swinton parroted, and she imagined him there, his fists in his pockets. But instead of the fierce bully he had always been, she pictured him as he was before they left – worried, older, fighting for them – and suddenly she missed him. She turned to whisper to Fran, who was starting to say the same to her. They smiled at one another.

They learned they were to be in the guncotton-processing section. 'To get the lie of the land before you're moved to something . . .' Mr Bryant petered out. 'Well, something more . . .' Again he petered out. 'Och well, just something.'

The women laughed.

'Aye, well, something'll do us fine,' Fran said.

Sarah smiled, for Fran was so strong, so capable, so . . . well . . . like Stan. And no, she wouldn't think of Beth calling on Stan for help. Nor would she think of her mam. One times two is two . . .

'You'll be going with them as well, Viola, help them get the lie of the land,' Mr Bryant said.

'Well,' murmured Viola, 'just so long as it's the land and not the heavens.'

Mr Bryant continued: 'And you'll be along with the lassies, too, our Morag. Then off away to your own work. I'm told you'd like water on the tables at the break too, Morag. A sound idea.' He seemed to know to speak slowly.

'We can thank the Sassenachs for that,' said Morag. 'We'll be having it at the hostel now tae. I had a word with the kitchen before we left.'

'Aye,' he said. 'The prison guard called through to me.'

The women laughed.

They wore masks that were as itchy as the ones they had at their own factory. It was hard to think that there could be anything more dangerous than being here, so what did he mean it was breaking them in? Morag had explained when they entered the workshop that when very dry, the guncotton, or nitrocellulose, was highly explosive and could be ignited by heat, sparks or friction. 'Hence the wellington boots, my wee weans, and the permanently damp floor.'

She left them in the care of the supervisor, saying, 'Ye'll be speaking slowly, wee Cathy, for they're from the south, three Sassenachs, and one with a verra big mouth.' But Morag was laughing.

Fran said, 'But we're from the North.'

'It's South of us, lassie.'

They worked all morning with other women, about twelve in total. They put funnels into their machines, shaking in the powder until it was full. Sarah was sick, sore and tired of powders, because she could almost feel the itch beginning. Her mask was itching and the heat against her mouth was building. She closed the lid on the machine, pushed the handle to press it, and the guncotton came out in an oblong block two inches high. This process could kill her, and those around her, if she was careless. If she let a hairpin drop, if . . .

Just then Fran whispered, 'Aye, that could be me mam's flour, it could, and them a slab of pastry.'

The supervisor standing behind her muttered, 'Well, let's not even think of making a wee patty out of it, eh. And never, ever think of heating it in the oven, or you'll be on a short trip to the stars, but not quite in one piece. And never, ever drop yer mam's mixing spoon in yon funnel and pull the handle down, for the love of God.'

Someone else put the blocks on a tray to be carried to a pressing house. They continued working: powder, funnel, lever, powder, funnel, lever. The supervisor appeared behind them. 'I think we'll have you in the drilling room soon. That's where the shaped "patties" go, which is one along from here. Holes will be put into the blocks there, and the cores, and then they'll be dipped in acetone in a further section.'

They knew better than to ask what they would be used for, but could guess: detonators for something big.

This was confirmed by Morag over lunch. 'Aye, they'll be for depth charges and such like. So remember that. They blow up, so let it not be you, but you lassies know what you're doing from the look of you. You too, Viola, though you've only been here a week.'

Lunch was in the canteen and there was music on the tannoy here, though the guncotton workshop had been silent, for danger threatened with every movement and concentration must be total.

Sarah hummed along to the music. Fran too. Viola played the saxophone, she told them, and had brought it with her.

They caught the bus home at two, having reached their target, travelling alongside the loch in all its beauty, and traipsed up the path with the rest of the girls. Morag drew them along the hall to the dining room, where cups of tea waited for them. They sat and drank, almost speechless with the headaches that had grown while they concentrated. They had breathed in the powder and their lips were sore from the insides of their masks, which had been claggy with it. They listened to those around them and tried to understand some of what they said, which seemed to be about the pub in the village that was holding a dance on Wednesday, in somewhere called the Back Hall. The whole of the hostel seemed to be going, though they weren't asked.

They drank up, ate a biscuit each, poured themselves a glass of water, which Morag had arranged, and noted that the time for supper – soup and sandwiches – was six o clock. They headed to their floor, which was the Blue Floor. All the girls were on the same shift, Viola told them, to prevent disturbance. 'You sleep when others sleep.'

Exhausted, they flopped onto the beds and Sarah slept, dreaming of her mam, the hard floor, the cut on her head. She woke with a start as she heard the saxophone playing 'All or Nothing at All'. Fran was singing along quietly and Sarah sat up. The two girls were standing at the window, Viola's eyes closed as she played. Sarah rose and joined them and for a moment it was like home.

As they looked out across the snow-covered slopes and the few crofts with smoke curling up into the sky, and not a pithead in sight, she knew they had actually never been further from all they loved, and those they loved. Oh, Stan.

'It must be wonderful in the summer,' said Fran.

Viola stopped playing and shook the saxophone. 'Aye, I expect so. You'll be long gone by then, but I'll still be here, one Sassenach amongst a bevy of Scots.'

Sarah leaned her head against the windowpane. 'Aye,' she whispered, her breath clouding the glass. 'Aye, we'll be home by then.' Oh, Stan. But if Mam hasn't stopped drinking, where shall I live? She looked at Fran, and knew the answer. With Fran Hall and her family. Or maybe she and

Stan would be wed and have their own colliery house, and her mam could do what she must, and she, Sarah Bedley, would pretend not to care.

Fran muttered, 'It makes me think of Amelia and how lonely she must feel to be the only southerner amongst a gang of Geordies. Has it made her what she is? Should we try again? When we telephone Beth this evening, we'll talk about it, and try to keep her safe from Ralph at least.'

Viola shook her saxophone again. 'This is a girl at your other factory?'

'Aye, a bit of a minx it has to be said, but maybe we can give her yet another chance.'

Sarah asked why Viola was shaking her saxophone.

'Oh, to get the spit out.'

Sarah and Fran said together, 'That's disgusting.' Then they all laughed. They sang again, while the raptor glided above the loch and the snow glinted on the bank. After supper it would be time to telephone their men and Beth. Then, Sarah thought, she'd hear Stan's voice and imagine she was in his arms. She supposed she'd have to ask about her mam. She touched her head. The cut was healing, but the scar would remain.

Chapter Thirteen

Stan met Sid and Norm the next morning on Main Street, their caps leaning to the left, their eyes squinting against the smoke from their Woodbines. Behind them, the slag heap seemed to smoulder, though there was little wind to whip it up. Sid cocked his head towards the Bedleys' back lane. 'Aye, best we check up, eh? But grand to be in yer own bed and sleep sound, our Stan?'

Stan just grunted, for his sleep had been disturbed by the absence of Sarah, by the thought of her doing whatever it was she was doing, by the missing of her that hearing her voice had made worse. But at least he now had the telephone number of the office in the hostel for emergencies. The other thing that had cheered him was having a word with Fran, as feisty as ever, and hearing that they were sharing with another Geordie who played the saxophone. By, that took some backbone. He grinned to think of a girl on stage, giving it a bit of go.

As they clomped down the back lane, slipping on the cobbles, he handed over Madge's and his mam's Woodbine rations and told the lads, 'We'll split three ways, like normal, though if yer bad pitmen, I'll tek 'em back.'

Norm laughed. 'Good as gold we'll be, lad, and she plays a saxophone, yer says? Howay, I'd like to meet her, an' all. You've yer Sarah, Sid's hankering after that Rosie, and who's for me?'

Sid nudged him. 'There's always that snooty Amelia?'

The mention of her name reminded Stan of Fran's question

about Amelia being adrift in a sea of northerners, without a paddle or a lifebelt, and shouldn't everyone give her a wee bit of support? He asked the lads, as coal-dusted pitmen on their way off shift passed them, heads bowed. All called to one another, "Ow do?' And sometimes, "Ow's the lasses?' 'Mrs B all reet wi' Beth?' 'Mrs Smith all reet wi'out her lass?' 'Yer all reet wi'out yer two lasses?'

Stan answered them all. It was only when they reached the Bedley backyard that he was able even to think of Fran's question about Amelia again. As he began to ask the lads, Beth hurtled out of the gate, crashing into them. Round they spun, slipping on the snow, and all four of them fell, Beth on top of Stan. Stan looked up into her laughing face. For just a moment he was back to what seemed like years ago with Beth, her luscious body and her laugh that made everything all right. Sid hauled her off and Stan scrambled to his feet. 'Squash me bait, would you?' he laughed, brushing the snow from him with shaking hands. What the hell was the matter with him?

The hooter was sounding, the pitmen skirting around them. 'Get yerselves to t'pit, and the lass to the bus.'

'What's wrong wi' yer lugs, pet? Canna you hear Bert hooting?' It was Eddie Corbitt.

Beth called, 'Howay, Mr Corbitt, I canna hear nowt with Auld Hilda's hooter blasting out.' She turned to the lads then. 'I spoke to the girls, must have been after you, Stan. Grand they've got a good billet – hot running water, eh? And a nice friend they've found an' all, poor lass. No parents, which is tough going. I thought it were sad enough without me da, but she's lost both of hers and her brother.'

Stan said, 'Aye, she were saying about being kind to Amelia, just to see if support changed her manners. Did she say the same to you?'

Before she could answer, Norm, who was digging out a

195

cigarette, almost growled, 'I reckon she's moved on from our level – up a peg or two, from what the whelp were saying. There he was, fiddling with his pick at the face yesterday, and it seems them two's as thick as thieves.'

Beth was walking backwards up the lane. 'Aye, well, that's what were worrying them, I suppose. So, our Fran thinks we should make sure she doesn't get into daft ways, and herself into mischief – you know, not just personal like Daisy, but chatting and showing off about Factory stuff. You never know who's listening, or so we keep being told.'

'Well, that's your department,' said Stan. '*You* work with her, after all.'

She was turning now, hurrying along, then called back, 'Mrs B had a good night. Me mam's with her now. They said to tell yer there's no need to call in, they're in charge.'

Stan waved, but she was running, slipping and sliding, and they heard, carried on the wind, 'Bliddy hell, like a bliddy ice rink.'

'Language,' yelled Sid. 'You'll get yer mam's tea towel whipped across the back of yer legs.'

Beth's laugh was loud. 'Only if you tell her, our Sid, then it'll be your legs getting a whipping an' all, and that'll be from me.'

The three of them were laughing as they headed into the wind towards the pithead. They talked of Amelia and then Mrs B, for Sid and Norm wanted to know when Norris, the black marketeer, was calling for his money. Stan sighed. 'Beth told me on the phone he said in a note which came through the letter box that he'd not come for a few days, and because o' that, the interest was even more, the beggar.'

They headed up and into the pit yard, nodding at the gateman, who waved them through. They collected their two tokens, then waited their turn in the crowd for their lamps, putting a token on the hook and the other in their pockets.

'Where is he, then?' Sid muttered, looking over his shoulder as they queued for the cage. The whelp had been put back on the tub because all he did was fiddle about, trying to get the pick in.

Stan muttered, 'Think bad penny, then think he'll turn up.'

Just then they heard, 'I say, chaps, let me through. Got a bit held up, but I can see my marrers up there, ahead.'

Sid and Norm raised their eyebrows as Andy from Pitway Terrace murmured, 'Marrers, eh? He'll be bliddy lucky.'

Sid nodded, but said quietly as the cage rattled up from the depths, 'Aye, Andy, lad, but he's the boss's son, so we say nowt, though we can think what we like.'

Stan felt a heavy hand slap his shoulder. 'Here we go again then, lads. Into the murky depths to the beating heart of my family's mine.'

Stan wanted to say, 'Shut yer face, it's not as though we don't know that, you pathetic snob.' Instead he said, 'Got yer lamp and left yer token, and put t'other in yer pocket?'

'Come now, Stan, old chap. As though I don't know the routine by now, eh? Took you more than a short while to get used to the right cutlery for formal hall, I hear?'

Stan merely nodded. It was the whelp's latest poke and prod to bring up his days at Oxford. The cage gate opened and the men herded forward, squashing into it, Mr Oborne ahead of them. They stood in a line, with Oborne against the rail. He asked the back of Stan's head, 'The girls got there safe? I'll need to tell me Tilly, though I 'spect the co-op's filled her in.'

'Oh aye, safe and sound,' Stan murmured.

'Enjoying themselves, eh?' said Ralph. 'A change is as good as a rest, so they say.'

Stan just stared at him, while Sid muttered, 'Aye, I could

do wi' a rest, but not a change. Howay, lad, don't know where that bliddy nonsense came from in t'first place.'

The cage doors clanged shut and they descended. Ralph said, 'Oh God, I hate this.'

Sid nudged him. 'Bit of a change from Oxford, eh? Good as a rest, I dare say.'

Ralph's smile was weak. There was a general sigh as the lift approached the bottom of the shaft. Stan bent his knees. The cage whacked to a halt. The gates opened and the men poured out, heading for the coalface, but Stan heard the seam overman calling him.

'Stan, and the rest of yer fine bunch o' lads, I don't think, get yerselves over here, quick sharp.'

Stan led them across to Tom, who stood outside his office, a cigarette behind one ear and a pencil behind the other, his cap overshadowing both. 'Just warning you, lad, that Bell Seam's being opened today, to clear it proper and get it working.'

Stan just stared at Tom. Bell Seam? Where his da and Davey's had died? Bell Seam.

'You hear me, lad?'

Sid, his arm over Stan's shoulder, said, 'Oh aye, he heard yer. But I reckon 'tis not us to clear it?'

Tom was shaking his head. 'Wouldn't do that to the lad, but I want Ralph to be the putter. I reckon you can spare him.'

Ralph was shaking his head; he had paled, sweat beaded his forehead. 'Not me, not Bell Seam.'

Stan stared, for the whelp's voice was strange. Tom just shook his head. 'Don't be so bliddy daft, you'll do as you're told. Them weren't *your* da, after all.'

'No, but they were good to me.'

Now all four of them stared at him. Tom shook his head, his voice grim. 'There's nowt dangerous. Oborne's down there an' all, he'll see yer right. Besides, 'tisn't an invitation to a dance. You're best as a putter and a bloody nightmare on t'pick. There's a bliddy war on, so shift yer bleedin' arse and do as ordered.'

'Or what? You'll sack the boss's son?'

Tom put his hands on his hips, thrust back his shoulders and stared at the whelp. 'Nay, nowt like that. I reckon Albright, whose order 'tis, will send a message to Massingham Hall and what happens after that's between yer and yer da. So, what's it to be?'

For a long moment, there was nothing but the sounds of the pit reverberating around them and the heat building, the coal dust thicker too, kicked up by the pitmen clomping by. Ralph finally nodded. 'Best get myself off and practise me waltzing, eh.' His laugh was strained, but from the pitmen there was nothing. They just turned on their heels and followed Stan along the main seam, with Ralph behind, keeping to one side as the Galloway ponies hauled tub trains to the cages or coalfaces.

Norm muttered, 'Let him eat our dust, just fer a change, eh? Usually he's leading, kick kick, choke choke.'

Soon the lit roadway gave way to the dark of different seams and at Bell Seam, Ralph peeled off, saying nothing. Stan wouldn't look. His da had died down there. But he wouldn't think of that. Someone somewhere had thought it not worthy of an investigation; some props further down Bell Seam had been found to be substandard and it had been put down to that, and they were probably right. On they went, and as the roof lowered and they bent their backs, he thought of Sarah. He missed her, and as he thought this he heard Beth's laugh and saw her face, too close to his.

Ralph set off down Bell Seam. Thick cobwebs still draped from the roof planks, the same cobwebs that had caught at him and dropped blacklocks, otherwise known as cock-roaches, down his neck when he'd crept down here to set the fuse to bring the roof down. And those same cobwebs had torn at him as he ran with the others to help the two men.

Ralph dragged another cobweb from his face, shuddering. Ahead he could hear the shovels at work clearing the coal, and the banging as pit props were installed and the roof boarded. A blacklock fell down his neck. He scrabbled to grab it, then stamped it beneath his boot, just as the coal had crushed the men. Would he hear the screams and cries as he drew near? He bloody deserved to. He walked on, lifting his feet. At least he was learning that – lifting, so less dust was disturbed – but all he wanted was to be back in Oxford and never to have come, and what's more, never to have gone to Fascist meetings, met Tim and been such a fool. And never to have hurt poor Sophia with his words, and those evacuees, these pitmen. All he wanted was to stop being *that* Ralph Massingham, but he couldn't, it was too dangerous.

He kept going, finally reaching the fall. Oborne was there. He pointed at the tub. 'Get a bliddy move on, tek it to the roadway and get young Sammy to hitch it as he comes through. There's plenty more waiting here for yer to fill.'

The men had set up their lamps, so their shadows flickered and jumped as they worked to clear the coal he'd brought down. He couldn't look, but grabbed the tub and set off along the rails with it, his back bent, pushing. He made himself think of Amelia. He was to take her for a drink and tell her he'd fixed up a singing evening at another of the Massingham pubs. That would satisfy Tim, for now.

Sammy was bringing along the tub train as Ralph reached the main seam, the chains clinking and the tubs rattling. As Ralph hitched the tub to the chain and unhitched an empty one, he set off back down Bell, wondering if, by clearing the coal, he might clear his head, or please God, his conscience. He reached the coal fall, left the empty tub, grabbed the full one, setting off again. He wondered whether, if he got information out of Amelia and then failed to access the Factory properly, Tim would actually leave him in peace and let him go. He thought he knew the answer, but at least it would give him a bit more time to try and sort something out. But what? He had no bloody idea.

He bent over, pushing the tub in the darkness and the heat. The coal dust was in his mouth, gritty between his teeth. Some coal tumbled off. He stopped, jammed the wheels and picked up the coal. Was it tainted with the blood of Tom and Joe? Would it burn better for it? He threw piece after piece onto the tub's load, then pushed the tub onwards, punching aside the cobwebs. He cursed bloody Bedley and Hall for getting in the way.

But it didn't work, for he'd liked them, and he'd killed them. No one else, not even Tim, had done that. It was Ralph bloody Massingham all on his own.

Chapter Fourteen

Davey sat at the breakfast table the next morning, spreading the sliver of margarine they were allowed, and thought of his love. He couldn't imagine quite what Fran was doing, for all she could say last evening was, 'No more or less than before, bonny lad.' And all he could say was, 'Be safe.' But he knew that she held his heart in her hand, and he hers.

He had asked about his mam, and if she was still drinking. She'd said Stan would be writing to fill him in. She asked about Daisy, but he'd had nothing to add other than the fact that she was pale and preoccupied. He asked about the others at the hostel and the factory and she'd spoken of Viola.

He had asked about the countryside and she'd described it. He'd told her of the skaters on the Bletchley Park lake. They had then fallen silent, listening to one another breathing. Finally, she, the woman he loved more than life itself, had ended by saying, 'Oh Davey, I miss you so much, I love you so much. I want this war to end, right this minute. I want you to come home and I do so want to come home too.'

'Me an' all, my sweetest Franny,' he had said and had been glad the pips had gone, because his voice was breaking. He had replaced the receiver, pressing it down hard, looking out onto the dark street. He was sick of it all, but knew from the decoding work he was doing that the war was not even close to being won.

He realised now that he had only half spread his margarine.

'I'll be mother then,' said Daniel, 'since you haven't answered, but have instead been gripping that knife so tight I reckon your fingers have set around it.'

Davey grinned and finished before putting the knife down. 'Aye, you're reet, they do feel a bit stiff.' He flexed them while Danial poured the tea.

From his table by the bookcase, Colin called, 'Can anyone remember the real colour of a cuppa?'

Martin, who sat opposite him, groaned. 'Must you say that every morning? We voted on when to have the used tea leaves, remember?'

Daniel laughed. 'D'you think that's what marriage is? People driving other people mad day after day?'

Davey crunched the last of his toast and shook the crumbs from his fingers. 'Aye, well, yours will be I reckon, whereas mine will be grand. Every word I say will be right perfect, and I will be adored and—'

Martin rose, walked over and whacked him across the head with his rolled-up newspaper. 'Time for the bus. And your crossword's in the paper this morning, did you know? Under that rather strange name you use: Beckworth.'

Davey smiled. He'd forgotten, but that meant there'd be more money for the family finances. It could help pay Norris's bill. The smile faded. Such a waste. He'd pay in the cheque when it arrived, then send Stan the cash to pay the bills.

Daniel was pushing his chair back. 'Remind me, why Beckworth?'

'Because the beck's worth its weight in gold. Taught us to swim, gives the kingfisher a home and us somewhere to tek our lasses to give 'em a—'

'Stop.' Daniel rolled up his napkin, stuffed it through the

ring and threw it across the room. It missed the napkin basket. 'I shouldn't have asked. It's put my aim right off.'

Colin was rushing from the room. 'Come on, you two. Just for once, I don't want to have to talk a load of rubbish to the conductress to stall the bus.'

Daniel slurped down the last of his tea while Davey took his napkin to the basket, picked up Daniel's, then followed him from the room. They grabbed their macs and Daniel called to Mrs Siddely, 'Back usual time, Mrs Siddely.'

'Oh, really,' she called from the kitchen. 'Nothing usual about your timings, and I hope you've put your socks in the linen basket, young Daniel. But at least I won't have to hunt for them, they're so stinky they'll come if I whistle.'

Daniel was already half out of the door, so Davey replied for him. 'See you when we see you, he meant, Mrs Siddely. Have a good day and watch it – the socks are advancing.'

Her laughter was a good sound, Davey thought, as he shut the door. Her lad had been in hospital with scarlet fever, but was home now, a bit pale, but able to do the simple crosswords the four of them set him. It kept his brain ticking over, they'd said to Mrs Siddely, because the lad was being a nuisance pestering his mam with endless requests for this, that and the other.

Daniel was ahead of him, tearing along the main street, swearing as the bus drew up at the stop in front of the pub. 'It's bloody early. Hold it for us, Col.'

Colin was about to disappear into the bowels of the bus, but instead stayed with one foot on the pavement and one on the step. 'Deadly Daniel'll be here in a minute, take pity and ask Frank to delay the bus, there's a dear,' he called to Sylvia, the conductress.

'Oh God,' groaned Daniel. 'She'll get the bus to go with that sort of nonsense from the idiot.'

Sure enough, they heard the 'ting-ting' and the bus

started rolling, with Daniel and Davey running as though the hounds of hell were after them. Colin was losing his footing and falling up the bus steps, then sliding down again. As his feet dragged along the road, the bus stopped. Daniel spurted ahead of Davey, whose bad leg made speed impossible. As he brought up the rear, the postman cycling towards him shouted, 'I've one for you, lad.'

Barely pausing, Davey snatched it and rammed it in his pocket. 'Thanks. Got to rush.'

He tore on, while Daniel held the bus and Colin shouted, 'I say, that was a bit hard, Frank.'

Davey leapt on board to find Colin being pushed down the aisle by Daniel to join Martin, who always seemed to remove himself from their disasters without a backward glance.

Sylvia winked at Davey. 'One day that daft smart-arse will learn.'

Davey laughed. 'Aye, well, Sylvia, he hasn't yet. But he hasn't a bad bone in his body. It's just his way.'

She shook her head, put her hand out for the fare, and handed him a ticket. 'Your Fran all right, is she?'

'Franny's always all right.' The bus lurched as Frank took off. Daniel called down the bus, 'There was no need for that, Frank. You were actually early. Timekeeping's the name of the game.'

'Put a sock in it, lad,' shouted Sylvia.

'He couldn't,' replied Colin, 'not one of his. It would poison him.'

Davey laughed as he joined them. He'd never thought these lads would be his friends, but they were. Not his marrers, but his friends, and that was enough.

Davey's hut left work on the dot, just for once. They stood in the fresh air, then sauntered to the lake because the bus wasn't due for another twenty minutes. They smoked, watching the skaters whose laughter rang out in the fading afternoon light. Daniel muttered, his smoke-heavy breath hanging in the air, 'If I was an artist, I'd paint this.'

Davey's head was ringing from the clicks of the machines and the bustle. He could still hear the doors slamming, the screeching of chairs, the coughs and sneezes. The relentless bitter cold of the huts always gave him a splitter of a head-ache, and even made his teeth ache. He'd taken to wrapping a scarf over his head and Daniel and the others had laughed to begin with, but now wore woolly hats pulled down. The one-bar fire was a joke, they'd decided. Put there just to irri-tate, or tantalise, for it did no good at all.

As he looked at the skaters, Davey thought of the ice that had clung to the edges of the beck in the coldest of winters when they were bairns. They'd stamped on the bank to keep their toes warm. It was only Stan, Sid and Norm there now. He stopped; no, there was Beth as well. By, he bet she was lonely without the other two girls.

He tossed his cigarette butt to the frosty ground, watch-ing it fizz to nothing. He shoved his hands into his pockets, touching the letter he'd forgotten all about. It was from Stan. He hoped, as he opened it, that the lad had received the money he had sent at the beginning of last week. Read-ing on, Stan said that the money was tucked away in the pot at the Hall household, well away from Davey's mam. Beth knew to come to Stan when she needed provisions, Stan said.

He then told Davey of his mam's treatment of Sarah, now and in the past. As Davey read on, the words made no sense. He reread them, then looked at the lake as the skat-ers swirled and fell, only to pick themselves up and skate on, mirroring his thoughts as he tried to remember, but he couldn't.

He read on: *Sarah had forgotten. Your mam's off her head when she's on the booze. But I'm sorting it, putting a stop to the bloke who's selling her the rotgut. And Fran hasn't told you, because I said I would, for they have enough to think about at you-know-where.*

Davey folded the letter. Beside him, Daniel said, 'I skated on the village pond when I was eight. The ice cracked, I screamed. It was only a foot deep. I felt a right fool.' He was pointing at the frozen lake.

If I was any kind of a brother, Davey thought, I'd have remembered the past. But he hadn't dreamed of it, hadn't a clue. He should be there, keeping an eye on it. He closed his eyes, then opened them and looked up at the cloudy sky. *Da, I didn't know. You should have told me.* He could almost hear his da saying, 'You were nowt but a bairn, seven years old.'

They caught the bus and at the front of the queue was Daisy, all hunched over, her scarf over her head. She was smoking, not talking to anyone. She climbed aboard and sat at the front, staring out of the window. Davey hesitated. She looked so alone, but Daniel pushed him on. 'Oh crikey, don't get embroiled again, lad. Just take a seat, for the love of Mike, or we'll be left standing – again.'

They sat. The bus hurtled on, for there were fewer stops with the work bus, and Davey made himself ponder the coded signature he had noticed in a signal today. He couldn't bear to think of wee Sarah, alone, keeping it a secret. No, not that, leave it till night, till he could cope, perhaps. Now, it was work. That cypher signature – was it really the same person from last week? If it was, it would pinpoint where the German signaller was and therefore his brigade as they moved position.

He would have to stay alert tomorrow as he decoded yet more messages for the translators to put into English. But discovering the signatures was what made it interesting, and more helpful for the war effort. Aye, staying alert was what it was all about, as he had not known to do for his wee sister. He fingered Stan's message, wondering how he hadn't suspected, how he hadn't asked. He wondered how he could continue to love his mam.

Daniel was offering him a Woodbine. He took one. The bus pulled into a stop, the one at which Daisy disembarked. Davey could never bear to look over at the house where her digs were, and where he'd found himself. Daisy had started to walk along the pavement, keeping to the lee of the garden hedges, and in spite of himself he was drawn to watch, for she seemed so slow these days. The bus jerked and drew away, and as he passed he saw her stop, rest against the hedge, then crumple to the pavement. 'Bliddy hell,' he muttered and reached over Daniel, who sat by the aisle. He pressed the bell, then pressed it again.

Daniel stared at him as though he was mad. 'What the hell are you doing? It's not our stop.'

But Davey was pushing past him. 'It's her, she's fainted.' He rushed down the bus. 'Stop, Frank, please. I've got to help someone.'

Frank, too, looked at him as though he was mad. 'Just here,' Davey ordered. Frank jammed on the brakes and Davey jumped off the bus, running back along the pavement. He could hear footsteps behind him and Daniel yelling, 'Wait for me.'

Daisy was on all fours when they reached her. They put a hand under each arm and helped her to her feet. She stared at them in the gloom as though she didn't know who they were.

'Let's get you back to yer room,' Davey said. 'Come over queer, did you? Probably got a bit cold, eh?'

Daniel was sharing her weight. 'I feel sick,' she muttered.

Davey hoped she'd vomit Daniel's way, if she was going to do it at all.

They sat her on the garden wall and Daniel pressed her head down. 'It's supposed to help,' he told them.

They sat either side of her. 'Hangover?' asked Davey.

'Something like that.' Daisy laughed weakly.

Daniel nodded. 'Ah, the shepherd's pie. There was rather an overkill of gristle.'

Daisy straightened. 'Please don't talk about food.'

They waited. Daniel sneaked a look at his watch and Daisy caught him. 'I'm fine. Thank you. You go home, eh?'

'No,' Daniel said. 'We'll make sure you get back safely.'

They set off again. She was unsteady, but managed without help. 'Thank you,' she muttered at her landlady's gate. 'I can manage now.'

Davey thought of Sarah, managing without him while his mam belted her. He shook his head. 'Howay, pet, we'll get you inside at the very least.'

She shook her head, but they insisted. They reached the door, but before Daisy could put her key in the lock it opened and her landlady stood there, looking at them one by one, then shook her head. Davey said, 'No, we don't want to come in. She fainted.'

The woman just nodded and stepped to one side. 'In you come, Daisy, about time you got this sorted.'

Davey had taken Daisy's bag and now handed it to the woman. Daniel said, 'I think it was the shepherd's pie.'

Daisy was heading for the stairs, and the landlady just looked from her to the lads. 'Is that what you're calling it these days, eh? More like a bun in the oven left there by her pilot chappie. Probably six or seven months gone, squashed in by her corset, no doubt, and him took down by a German five months ago.'

The two men looked from her to Daisy, who had sagged

down onto the stairs, resting her head on the newel. 'I'm so sorry,' she said to them both. 'I wanted someone who'd be with me. I went a bit mad. Fear. I'm just so sorry.'

'Hell's bells,' murmured Daniel.

What would Fran think? Davey wondered. The girl wasn't crying, she was just sitting, looking so thin, sad and exhausted. Fran wouldn't leave someone on their own, and he'd done enough of that, leaving his little sister to be bashed as a bairn.

The landlady started to close the door. 'Well, she'll have to leave when it shows more. People ain't blind and there'll be no job, and no pay.'

Davey put his hand on the door and pressed back against the landlady's push. 'Where will she go?'

The woman shrugged. 'Not my problem. She's got parents.'

Daisy was clambering to her feet and they heard her shout, 'No, I can't tell them. I've told you before, Mrs Ackerman.'

Davey pushed harder and the landlady opened the door a bit more. She said to the girl, 'That's as maybe, but I can't be having people like you in my house, that I can't. When you start really showing, out you go.'

Davey stared at Mrs Ackerman's swollen ankles and her torn tartan slippers, but whose weren't in the war?

Mrs Ackerman let the door swing open. Davey called to Daisy, 'You're not alone. I'll be your friend. That's all, but I'll do what I can, though I'm not sure how much use I'll be.' Fran would understand. But even as he thought that, his mouth went dry with the fear of losing her.

Daisy just looked at him, all hope gone, only grief remaining. Then from beside him, Daniel said, 'Me too. Davey and me together, we'll help, and I might know somewhere you can go. But, for now, just head to bed. See, I'm a poet. Tomorrow a new day will dawn, and trust can be renewed. Carry on working for as long as you can, but sit with us at lunch and be not afraid. And for heaven's sake, keep wearing the long cardigans and eat something, girl, the baby needs food.'

The two of them stepped backwards off the step. The door slammed. They walked down the path as Davey said, 'Tomorrow's a new day and "be not afraid"? All yer need's a tambourine and a placard at Speakers' Corner, and an orange box to stand on. It's a right kettle of fish is what it is.'

Daniel shook his head. 'Nope, it's a bun in the oven, my friend. A pilot's bun, and if only for that reason it deserves something better than being out on the street just because we chose to walk by on the other side.'

They set off, walking to their village, and it was then that Daniel mentioned his father was a vicar and worked with places girls like Daisy could go. It seemed that wartime created a boom in babies and girls at the end of their tether with nowhere to go. They had the baby, a few kept theirs, but mostly a home was found for the child. The girls could carry on with their lives. Not perfect, but a solution of sorts. 'But she'll need friends until then. I am willing if you are, but I'm not a total idiot and I'm not stepping forward all on my tod, considering Daisy's predilection for the dramatic. Father and Mum, you see, would expect I do something. I expect your Fran would too.'

Davey slung his arm over the lad's shoulders. 'No, you're not a total idiot, just a bit of a Samaritan – a bliddy good one. I reckon you're right about Fran, and besides, I need to help her. What if it were Sarah or Fran? I'll tell my lass when we next speak.'

Daniel laughed. ' "Need"?'

Davey just shrugged. 'Me to know, and you not to bother to find out.'

There was silence as they settled in for the three-mile walk, and as he limped along, Davey wondered what Fran would really think. With Daniel involved too, surely she'd trust him. Well, whether she did or not, he had to make good what he'd failed to do for Sarah, and that was that.

Chapter Fifteen

A week later, Fran's mam, Mrs Hall, squeezed another chair around her kitchen table. It was two o' clock and the co-op ladies would be here soon. Some would bring a twist of tea to boost the pot, and even if the tea leaves were from yesterday, it would be warm and wet. Behind her the range was burning briskly, the cups were set out in the centre of the pine table, and her frame was lodged against the leg of her chair at the table's head. She sat down with a thump. Would Maud Bedley come?

Beth was still on the fore shift, but had slipped a note through the letter box as she headed for the early bus, saying that Maud had drunk sherry before Beth had woken. She must have got it from somewhere and hidden it, but where? She wasn't pickled but the smell was there, so the news was good and bad. But there was another bill put through the door too, which she'd show Stan if he called in tonight. On the bill the supplier had said he'd call 'tonight or tomorrow night'.

Annie had hurried round to the Bedley house straight away, of course, and Maud was on her feet, wiping the pots, not drunk, but the smell was there, just as Beth had said. She'd denied drinking when Annie had asked how it was going, saying she'd promised she wouldn't, 'So you have to believe me.'

Annie had just stared at her, thinking that because Maud wasn't drunk, perhaps it could be classed as an improvement? Poor Beth, when it had seemed to be going so well.

But had it been – was Maud just clever at hiding it? As Maud went on with wiping the pots, Annie had worried what all this was doing to the lass. Beth had said to her yesterday, though, that it was only fair while Fran and Sarah had been transferred, because at least she was working here, seeing her mam, being with people she knew.

But as Annie left, calling back that she would expect her at two, sober, Maud had smiled. 'Of course. I want me lass to come home, don't I?'

Now, in her own home, waiting for the co-op, Annie sighed, for Stan would be sorting out Norris tonight or tomorrow and she tried not to let the fear and anger at the trouble Maud was causing overwhelm her. Surely Sarah's departure should have stopped the drinking altogether, but perhaps it didn't work that way. Perhaps it was one step at a time?

Annie reread Fran's letter now, which had arrived that morning, saying that Davey had telephoned. That girl Daisy was in the family way, but Daniel's father was getting her into a home for girls who'd gone astray. Annie looked up now. Fran had written, 'I feel so sorry for her, because we all feel frightened, sometimes desperate, when our men go to the pit, and to have a lad die in his plane and never see his bairn – poor girl.'

From outside the back door, Madge called, 'Aye, our Annie, first sign of daftness, talking to yerself.' Annie hadn't realised she'd read it aloud.

The door opened and as Madge entered, Annie laughed, buoyed up as always by this woman, for if anyone needed her edges soothed with a bottle of sherry it was Madge, but she just kept soldiering on. Hot on her heels came Mrs Smith and – glory be – Mrs Bedley, who entered along with a smell of sherry, but it wasn't strong. No one commented, no one even exchanged a look.

Madge merely passed over her twist of tea. 'Get t'kettle on, then, bonny lass.'

Audrey Smith hurried to the range, calling, 'Ah, our Annie's not just a pretty picture, 'tis simmering nicely. Bring in the milk from the safe then, Maud. A cuppa's just what we need.'

Before Maud could, Mrs Adams from the corner shop knocked and entered, along with Beryl, Susan and Verity, all carrying their frames. They all had red noses from the cold. 'By,' moaned Mrs Adams, 'might not be snow, but that wind's raw, that it is. And I've no broken biscuits.'

While the new arrivals shed their macs, hats, scarves and, finally, boots, replacing them with slippers that had known better days, the others sagged. No bits of biscuit. 'Ah well, there's a war on,' muttered Audrey Smith.

Mrs Adams was grinning. 'So I've brought whole biscuits, one each. But no telling the ration man, mind.'

They all laughed and Annie said, 'Sit yerself down, before we strangle yer for disappointing us, then hug yer to death for being kind. Whole biscuits, d'yer hear that, ladies?' Even Mrs Bedley was smiling, and Annie thought, yes, there really is an improvement. If Stan could put the supplier off, then where would the silly woman get sherry? Not anyone round here or Annie would pay them a visit herself.

She made two pots of tea and brought them to the table just as Maud returned from the meat safe with the cold milk. Was it Annie's imagination, or was there a stronger smell of drink? Right, Maud wouldn't be sent out to the meat safe again, and if she could search the pockets of her cardigan, she bliddy well would.

They sat around the table and beavered on, with Annie going through the accounts, letting each woman know how much they were owed, and how much of a percentage divvy she had taken from each sale for the pot. 'As you know, it's for emergencies. If we need to buy more blankets or rags, or someone has a fall and needs attention, t'money's there. Are we still reet with that?'

Maud Bedley put down her hooky, and without looking at anyone said, 'Well, I need to pay me rent, yer see, and with our Sarah gone . . .'

Laying down her frame, Annie started to answer, but Audrey Smith shook her head. 'Howay, lass, you're forgetting our Mr Massingham gives it to pitmen's widows reduced for the first month of a death, and he's extended it to February, and for yer, too, Annie, because your lasses are on temporary transfer.'

Annie nodded and picked up her frame. She could have slapped Maud. A heavy silence had fallen over the table. Suddenly, for no reason, Annie started to sing, and as though it was a life raft, the others clambered on board and sang along. All except Maud Bedley, who was licking her lips, desperate. Annie poured her more tea, letting the others sing as she whispered, 'Drink this. Tea is the answer to everything.' She gripped Maud's hand. 'Drink it,' she insisted. 'Be like the rest of us, eh, lass. Bit of gumption needed, not just from your bairn, but you too.'

It was then that she heard a banging at the front door. The singing stopped. The front door meant trouble; telegrams about a death, police with bad news . . .

She checked the clock. Three thirty? Could it just be children door-knocking on their way from school? She rose. 'Keep singing. What is it the girls love? Is it "A-Tisket, A-Tasket"?'

She walked hesitantly to the front door. There'd been no hooter, so it couldn't be Stan in a pit accident. Fran – something at her new factory? Ben – something at school? There was no one else who could have been hurt, for he, her love, was already dead.

She opened the front door and parked outside was the Massinghams' Rolls-Royce, with Alfie Biggins at the wheel. Mrs Massingham stood on the doorstep, wearing a scarlet woollen scarf around her neck and a black coat. Annie touched her apron, trying to undo the strings.

Mrs Massingham put out a leather-gloved hand. 'Oh, please don't, Mrs Hall. I'm sorry to call unexpectedly, but it couldn't wait. You see, I am desperate. I have girls expected this evening. Girls evacuated from Newcastle for whom there are no billets, and so of course we said yes. It's been a bit on and off, and now it's quite definitely on, and they're on their way, and all such a rush.' She did indeed look flustered. She gripped Annie's hand. 'Oh, Mrs Hall, I do so need you and your friends.'

Annie heard the kitchen door open and the sound of someone approaching, then Audrey Smith's arm slid around Annie's waist. 'What's to do, lass?'

The two women stood close, for they were marrers, tight and close. Maud should be with them, for she was their marrer too. Annie swallowed; that wasn't for now. Instead, she said, '*You* need *us*, Mrs Massingham?'

Behind Mrs Massingham Alfie had left the car and was heading up the road, waving his cap and calling, 'Abraham, take the football down the back lane as you were told, and the rest of you boys too. I know school's over early today, but you still need to use yer brains. Main Street's not the place for a kickabout, for the love of God.'

Mrs Massingham put her hand to her forehead. 'Oh, Mrs Hall, Mrs Smith, I forgot. Is it all right if the boys play in the back lane whilst we have a little chat? They have a football and have orders to behave.'

'The boys? Football?' Annie had lost track.

'Little chat?' added Audrey.

Mrs Massingham shook her head now and gripped her

clutch bag, which she had been carrying beneath her arm. 'Oh dear, what am I like? I wonder, may I enter? I have a proposition to do with the evacuee girls.'

Annie shook her head. 'Oh, but I have the co-op—'

'I could tek one girl,' said Audrey, 'perhaps two at a stretch?'

'Oh no, no, I have room, I just haven't . . . Look, I know I'm a nuisance, but it was the co-op I needed and if they're here, I can talk to you all direct. You see, the nanny we appointed for the evacuee boys went months ago, and I have been managing, just. A slight issue about wet beds, which has now been rectified. But now I will have six boys and the five girls, and I have asked the billeting officer – a real dragon – if the girls would like to learn crafts. She said indeed they would. I feel that probably she hasn't asked them, but . . .' Mrs Massingham drifted to a halt.

'Oh dear,' she said, as though trying to catch whatever it was in her head. 'I believe I'm getting as bad as dear Professor Smythe who manages the Massingham scholarship boys at Oxford – the one who kept a close eye on Stan there, and supported young Davey with his crosswords, with my husband's connivance, of course. Between them they even found him his present post—Oh Lord, should I have said that? It's all so difficult these days, knowing what should or should not be known, though I didn't say what post. I keep losing the thread, there's just so much to think . . .'

Annie and Audrey leaned into one another. It was cold, but how could Annie ask the boss's wife into the kitchen? The front room would be just as freezing as the street and she hadn't dusted for far too long, but they couldn't stay here like idiots. She opened her mouth, but Mrs Massingham said, 'I need you and I believe that some or one of you might need – well, not me, but something different. I believe that when one is struggling, a distraction might be of help,

218

as well as earning more money to pay . . . well . . . unforeseen bills? Do I make myself at all clear?' Mrs Massingham's dark hair was escaping from beneath her hat and her brow was furrowed.

Madge's voice loomed from behind Annie, who jumped. 'Pet, nowt you're saying is clear, but I reckon what you're trying to say is that . . .' Madge lowered her voice '. . . some aren't handling the loss of a husband reet well and maybe could do with something different to keep 'em busy, instead of chucking booze down their throat – and ignoring the fact that somewhere along the line the piper will have to be paid. Am I reet?'

Annie gasped, Audrey stood to one side, gaping, but Mrs Massingham roared with laughter, her breath white in the cold air. 'That's rather what I'm trying to say.' She looked at Madge. 'Are your middle names "Fran Hall" by any chance? Lovely Fran, who we met properly at poor Mr Hall's and Mr Bedley's funeral and who stood her ground so ably when Reginald started to be slightly superior. I had to hide a laugh when he used her first name as though it were his right, and she, in her turn, insisted on using his. But then he shouldn't have been so surprised, since he is an admirer of Stan's, as he is of all the boys who win his scholarship. But I'm going on, again. I really must stop this chatter. What I'm trying to say is that I hope we might be able to help dear Sarah and Davey's mother, eh? But also . . .' she put up her hand '. . . also, I truly need the help of all the co-op, or as many as can manage, for craft classes, though any help you can give in support, perhaps cookery classes, just being there—'

Annie interrupted, for she was still thinking of Maud. 'Is there nowt you don't know, Mrs Massingham?'

'I seem to hear things . . . Perhaps they're brought on the wind.'

Audrey nodded towards Alfie Biggins, the son of a Massingham hewer, who was returning to the car. 'Howay, Alfie's never been called the wind afore.'

Mrs Massingham was shaking her head. 'Oh please don't blame Alfie. We like to hear how things are going with the pitmen's families, especially when there has been a loss. So, the hopelessly long and the rather lengthy short of it is that I need the co-op to teach the girls some crafts, and your rugs are a byword around here. Mr Witherspoon speaks most highly of you. Yes, I do happen to know him.'

She smiled shyly. 'The thing is, I find I simply end up chasing my tail with six boys, let alone when the total will be eleven. Without your help, ladies, I think I will sink completely. And I want to help Mrs Bedley. And I really would like to come in and stand by your range, because I am absolutely frozen. And please, if I may call you Annie, Madge and Audrey and so on, my name is Sophia, as lovely Fran established at the sad funeral.' She dug in her handbag and drew out a large twist. 'I have brought fresh tea.'

The three women looked at the tea, then at the boss's wife. Annie said, 'The tea is the password, and will get yer into the home of any pitman or his widow, Sophia. But wipe yer feet, if yer will, and follow us.'

As they led the way down the corridor, Annie heard Sophia laughing and calling, 'Ah, I see where Fran gets it now.'

Annie led the way into the kitchen, where the women were sitting like statues, waiting to see who had called. When they saw Mrs Massingham they stood in a flurry, except for Maud, who looked over her shoulder and seemed not to understand.

Annie shook her head. 'Sit down, you're not at school. Mrs Massingham has come calling, in need of a favour.'

Verity was watching as Sophia Massingham unwound her scarf and slipped off her coat. 'I'll hang 'em up for yer, eh?'

Sophia shook her head. 'No, please, just tell me where?' Verity, Mrs Adams' neighbour, pointed to the hooks on the back door.

While Sophia hung her clothes, Annie waved the large twist of tea. 'I'm doing another brew, thanks to Mrs . . . er, no . . . Sophia, while she takes a seat – have mine, Sophia. I'll pull up another. Now, you tell the ladies about the jobs you're offering us all, eh?'

At that, the other women looked at one another, and then at Sophia as she sat in Annie's place at the head of the table. She reached out, and ran her hand over Susan's proggy rug, which was almost finished. 'I used to make hooky rugs with my mother, but I can do proggy too.'

'*You* did?' Susan asked.

'Oh yes. Little Sophia Benton from High Wycombe, near London. But my mother was from Washington pit village. I missed the North, which is why I nannied at Massingham Hall.'

She was smoothing her gloves on the table and without looking up said, 'It's rather lonely, marrying a delightful but busy man. One doesn't quite have friends in the same way. Perhaps because . . .' She trailed off.

Madge was working her hooky rug and said, as only Madge could, 'Because you married the boss and t'others around can't quite forget yer not one o' them, eh?'

Sophia burst out laughing. 'Are you quite sure your middle names aren't Fran Hall?'

Across the general laughter Maud Bedley called, 'Of course they aren't. Fran's . . . Well, I don't rightly know where Fran is, or me lass.'

Audrey Smith spoke into the momentary pause as Maud

hiccuped, 'While Annie's busy mashing the tea, Sophia could tell us more about the help she needs from us.'

Sophia seemed to collect her thoughts just as Audrey collected up the used cups from the table to wash them in the scullery. Annie dug into the crockery cupboard and found the Christmas bone-china cup and saucer, her most precious possession, given to her by her mam when she married. She placed it on the tray with the others. 'I can't expect her to drink from our chipped cups,' she whispered to Audrey.

She placed the tray in the centre of the table as Sophia finished explaining. Maud leaned forward, her elbow slipping off the table. 'I divint understand. Yer want us to go to Massingham Hall to teach five girls how to cook and mek rugs? So how's we to get there? How's we to find the money for frames, for extra old jumpers and blankets for strips, and . . .'

Sophia smiled. 'I will send the car, of course.'

'Or if that goes wrong,' Audrey added, 'you can send the tractor and trailer, and us'll leap up and sit like duchesses on a bale of straw.'

'Howay, it'll have to stop while we get on,' said Verity, 'for I'm not teking a flying leap anywhere, that I'm not.'

Madge poured the tea and handed Sophia the bone-china cup and saucer, saying, 'Not sure if I should curtsey.'

Sophia giggled. 'Please, this is making me too nervous. Next time may I just have one of the same cups as you? I couldn't bear to drop something so precious. Now I come to the part about the payment for your time.' She discussed her thoughts, which were far more generous than anyone had expected.

They looked at one another and then at Annie. Madge shook her head, raising her eyebrows. Sophia saw and looked worried. 'Oh dear, is that not enough?'

Annie Hall looked around at the co-op, then back at Sophia. ''Tis too much, and will spark a bit of envy. D'you reckon you should just check yer lads are all reet in the back lane?'

Sophia sprang to her feet, flushing. 'Oh yes, of course. Do have a talk. Oh dear, perhaps I shouldn't have . . .'

Audrey slipped off her shawl and walked round to Sophia. 'Slip this round yer shoulders, nip out, check they're not up to no good, and come reet back in, and stop yer mithering, lass.'

Sophia grinned suddenly. 'You sound just like my mam.' She rushed out of the door and across the yard.

Annie looked round the table again. 'Thoughts?'

All the women were happy to do it.

'The money?' asked Annie.

There was a pause, then Verity said, 'You're reet, 'tis too much. She should just cover the materials and a bit more. When all is said and done, there's a bliddy war on, and we should help the bairns. We can still mek our rugs while we're there, and a trip in a Rolls-Royce would be grand enough, I reckon.'

The others thought the same, and Beryl slipped out to fetch Sophia back in, rather than have her loiter about in the cold. When they entered, Sophia handed Audrey her shawl, saying, 'They're having a wonderful time. Some of the lads from round about are out there too and they've got a couple of teams together. So, what are your thoughts?'

Stan had stopped off at the allotment on the way back from his shift to pull the dried dead runner beans free from the beanpoles, or Fran would nag him. He picked more sprouts, and cut a cabbage. Sid and Norm were doing the same on the Bedley and Smith beds, stuffing the vegetables into a couple of sacks from the Canary Club's shed.

As they walked towards the Halls' back lane, they talked of the whelp, who seemed out of sorts; quiet and almost polite. Sid rolled his shoulders. 'Made me feel reet uneasy. Him polite? What's the beggar planning, eh?'

Norm kicked a stone along the street. 'Lord knows, but I reckon it's summat we won't like.'

Stan hoisted the sack onto his shoulder. 'Maybe he's thinking of ways to get out of t'pit. He's not been right since me da and Davey's died. Could be he understands only too well now what it means to be a pitman?'

They turned into the back lane leading to the Halls'. Sid said, 'Howay, not heading for the Bedleys'?'

'Co-op's meeting at me mam's, so Mrs B will still be there. Beth'll not be back till four, so Mam or Mrs Smith'll keep her busy till then. Seems—'

'Well, would you look at that,' Sid yelled. Ahead of them were two teams kicking a football, trying to get it into one of the goals chalked on either side of the lane near the Halls' back gate. The three marrers knew the bairns on one team, but not the others.

'Put yer sacks down, lads,' shouted Sid. 'The Massingham bairns are outnumbered. You and me, Norm, for Massingham; you, Stan, for the outsiders.'

They laughed together, slung the sacks to the ground and ran down the lane, muscling in, calling instructions while the lads shouted back. Stan scored. The outsiders cheered and leapt in the air. Sid and Norm groaned and yelled, 'Foul.'

The outsiders shook their fists. They played again, and this time one of the bairns from the terrace near the bus shelter scored. He was mobbed while the men panted, bent over, and Norm grunted, 'Getting too bliddy old for this.'

'Language,' called Annie Hall.

They straightened up and saw the co-op standing there

at the Halls' back gate, laughing. Mrs Massingham was there too, but then she rallied her boys. 'Maybe leave the football for the other team, eh? You've another at the house. Perhaps you should all play up there, in the back field, on a Sunday. What do you think, lads?'

The outsiders were nodding. Mrs Massingham looked at Stan, Sid and Norm. 'They could do with some advice, don't you think? Perhaps if you three are free on a Sunday afternoon? Just an idea, no pressure. For tea we could have buns that the girls and the co-op will have baked.'

Before they knew quite what they were doing, it was decided that every other Sunday, if they were not on shift the three pitmen would train the boys, and the more the merrier. If Stan could round up some more Massingham boys to make up a team, that would be grand, or so Mrs Massingham decided. 'The tractor and trailer will collect and return you all. Now, lads, home we go. Round into Main Street, where Alfie will collect us.'

And she was off, leading the boys like a mother goose.

Stan bent down, hands on knees, still panting. Annie was laughing and so too were the co-op, even Maud. 'By,' Audrey said, 'somehow she's got us reet where she wants us, but so nicely done, we'd all do it again.'

Annie told the three lads what the plans were, and that Mrs Massingham had insisted they were paid. 'But keep them lips zipped, lads, for she hasn't had a chance to tell Ralph yet, and that needs to be done careful like.'

Ralph sipped his beer at the Old Oak while Amelia, Brenda and Rosie sang. He could hear they weren't perfect, far from it, in fact, but the accordion covered up a lot of it and Amelia had been pleased. He found a table, because no one at the bar spoke beyond a nod of the head and an "Ow do?'

He stretched out his legs and played with the beer mat, clapping when others did, nodding along to the music when he remembered. He tried to work out how he could drop the other two girls first and then tootle to Sledgeford with Amelia. She liked to chat, thank heavens, and wanted to please, but all he wanted to know from her was if the fence ever came down, perhaps for maintenance. He sipped again, looking round the bar. Some from the Factory were here, not that he knew them well, but Amelia said they used the bus. One he did recognise was Beth Jones. He'd heard Stan say in the pit that he was stopping by the Bedleys' this evening so Beth could go with some friends to the pub. She nodded to him, but that was all.

He sipped his beer, wondering how long someone could go with just flickers of sleep and half-waking dreams. He realised the singing had stopped; there was a bit of clapping and he joined in, beckoning the landlord for three glasses of elderberry wine. He'd kept seats for all the girls. They came, they sat, and did they think they'd conquered? Amelia sat next to Ralph, who said, 'I say, girls. Excellent. Really enjoyed it. A lot of talent there.'

Amelia smiled at the landlord, who left the wine glasses in the centre of the table. She took the one that was fullest. Ralph saw the other two girls share a glance and thought: Amelia is like me, or as I was.

'Thank you so much for helping us get bookings. I do feel we're becoming better known, you know, and could go far,' Amelia said.

Not a chance, Ralph thought. Perhaps if you were Fran, Sarah and Beth it might happen. He shut down the thought. 'So, how's work? Still busy?' he asked.

'Frantic,' Amelia said. 'So many targets, and some buildings are being enlarged. Makes things breezy as I bustle about the place with messages.'

Don't say any more, you silly girl, Ralph thought. Some-one will hear, someone will tell Tim, who will want me in there.

'Oh do be quiet, Amelia,' said Brenda. 'How many times do you need to be told? We're not supposed to chat about work.'

Ralph said, 'Oh, I didn't hear. I was listening to the land-lord. Some sort of a raffle, I think.' He was aware that Beth was by the bar and had turned around, but was now check-ing her raffle ticket.

Digging into her handbag, Rosie said, 'Aye, a pork chop for one lucky person. Better than a nugget of gold, I reckon.'

None of them had the lucky ticket and soon it was time for the girls to resume singing. Sitting by the fire, Ralph was so bored that he felt more tired than he had since the roof fall and relaxed as his lids grew heavy, and a feeling of drifting off to sleep consumed him. Steadily the noise faded and darkness fell. But then he heard crying from beneath the coal, and the smell of the dust filled his nose, the clash of shovels and the curses of the rescuers jerked him awake: the girls were still singing.

He wiped the saliva from his chin, knowing there had been no cries in reality, for how could the dead speak? There had just been the curses of them all, including him, the whelp, the killer, as they tried to save them, the shovelling . . . He stared around, then at the clock over the fireplace, which had only moved on another five minutes, and he could have wept.

The next Monday the telephone in the hall rang again. Ralph was in the sitting room, scanning *The Times*, feeling too weary to breathe even as the words danced before his eyes. He started to rise, but heard Sophia say, 'I'll see who it is, as I'm passing anyway.'

He began to read the latest war news again, but looked up as Sophia called, 'Ralph, dear, it's for you. Amelia?'

Ralph sighed. 'Thank you, on my way.' He folded the newspaper, laid it on the sofa and knew that Tim would like this friendliness. He took the receiver from Sophia, who was smiling as she walked away, and said, 'Good evening, Amelia. I thought you were on a late shift.'

She giggled. Ralph sighed more deeply. 'I am. I'm using the office telephone, just to say thank you once more for arranging the new booking. I do hope you can come to the next one?'

Ralph tightened his grip on the receiver. 'How could I possibly bear to miss you three songbirds?'

Even to his own ears it sounded false, but not to Amelia's, clearly. 'I hoped you'd say that,' she said. 'Oh, Ralph, I have to go, we have a delivery of chemicals arriving for the storeroom, or that's what they say is in the lorries. Such a lot of revving, and we're not supposed to notice. How, with all the noise? Chunter, chunter they go, along to the store-room dug deep into the earth near the woods. It always reminds me of an Anderson shelter. They'll be growing vegetables on it—Oops, sorry, I shouldn't have said that, so forget I mentioned it, there's a good boy.'

Ralph sighed even deeper. It seemed to come from the region of his feet. 'Mentioned what, Amelia?' His laugh was as false as his words.

She giggled again. 'You're so sharp, really you are. I must go. I just wanted to say thank you.'

'You're very welcome, Amelia.' There was a click, and he replaced his receiver too.

He waited for a moment. He should report the conversa-tion to Tim, but it was enough that *he* knew. If he was any sort of a saboteur he'd act on it, but only at the right time. The right time for failure.

Chapter Sixteen

It was the end of January and Sarah, Fran and Viola were gulping down their breakfast porridge with the rest of their shift. The previous night, their end of the table had spent so long at the hostel drama group's auditions for *42nd Street* that they had all slept until the last moment, Fran shaking Viola and Sarah awake and all three rushing to the bathroom and back to get dressed, then careering down the stairs, Viola in the lead.

'By, you're quick,' Sarah had called.

'I were called a streak of lightning at school,' Viola flung over her shoulder. 'Skinny little thing I was.'

Fran and Sarah had laughed. 'Aye, well, you still are.'

The pair of them had won places in the chorus since they would probably be home by mid February, when it was to be performed, and chorus singers wouldn't be missed.

Scraping her bowl after making a porridge sandwich, Morag now said, 'You were really good, you three – Sarah and Fran singing, and Viola playing the saxophone. I reckon you should have been put down for bigger roles, all of you. You two lassies singing somewhere towards the front and Viola flashing her sax right alongside you.'

Viola laughed as she gobbled her porridge. 'Aye, flashing me sax, eh? But we won't be missed if we're not able to play. Bliddy cheek. And I'm not going, anyway.'

'Och, neither would that old cow of a producer Isla Sinclair be missed,' Morag muttered, shoving back her chair.

'Too big for her boots is that one. If she were a man she'd have a giant of a sporran and nothing to shout about behind it.'

Everyone roared with laughter as they finished, picked up their bottles of water and followed her out of the room. 'Come on, come on,' called the 'warden', Miss Jenkins, clapping her hands. She held the door open and they tore out of the hostel to the buses, everyone trying to be amongst the first in order to grab a seat. Sarah realised that Viola was way behind but when she looked for her saw her talking to the warden at the front door. 'Hurry up,' she yelled. Viola was nodding, then she rushed to the bus. Fran and Sarah had waited, so all three had to squash into the crowded aisle and hang on to the overhead straps.

'Ready for take-off,' yelled Hamish.

Fran muttered, 'He should have been a pilot,' then felt bad, for Davey had told her that Daisy's boyfriend had been just that. Had Daniel's father found a mother-and-baby home for her yet? She must be showing, no matter how long and big the cardigan was. Nearly eight months she'd be, surely. By, the lass's legs must ache. Surely someone had noticed, or maybe they had and were ignoring it? How dreadful it must be to give up the child when his father had died for the country. Or died any old way. She thought of her own life, and was grateful for it.

Hamish tore off but missed second gear, as he so often did. The whole of the bus seemed to sigh as they heard the grinding of the gear and felt a faltering of the bus, a jerk, as he had another go. Finally, he got into gear and the speed picked up just as Viola yelled, to the amazement of them all, 'For the love of God, Hamish, how did you ever get this bliddy job?'

It wasn't just the other girls who stared at her, but Fran and Sarah, for Viola was never cross, never spoke out of turn. 'What's got into you this morning, our Viola? What did the warden want?' Fran asked.

Before Viola could reply, Deirdre, who shared the room next to them and had nipped into a seat just before they arrived, looked up. 'It's that bliddy wee Isla. I heard her this morning, telling the warden she had to tell Viola she's not to play the saxophone at all, but is tae sing in the chorus, off stage, like you two. And Viola's permanent staff, an' all. Isla's jealous, of course she is. She plays it tae, you see. Och, her screeching could wake the dead. Mark you, the warden tore her off a strip, said to do her own dirty work, but that Isla just swept off, as she's prone to do.'

Viola leaned into Fran as Hamish lurched around a corner. Sarah peered round at her. 'Is that it, Viola?'

'Aye, that's it. Right crabby it's made me, but it's also because it's the end of January and you're likely going soon and I keep forgetting, then I remember and I know I'll be back to being adrift in a sea of bliddy Scots.' She winked at Fran and Sarah, then at Deirdre, but it was an effort.

Deirdre laughed. 'Och, away wi' ye, you don't know how lucky you are, lassie. We'll tek good care of ye, and let's be having a song to help the porridge tae settle – "42nd Street" comes tae mind.'

They all sang as they travelled alongside the loch, which seemed dark and sinister beneath the solid grey cloud, though the raptors were still soaring on the thermals and the mountains glinted white with snow.

All those on the bus moved in time with the music, singing their hearts out: 'Come and meet those dancing feet . . .'

Soon all those in the aisle were doing the actions of the chorus line, as far as one could hanging on to a strap, and for a moment, listening to them all, Fran felt as though she was on the Massingham Factory bus.

She moved on to thinking of the co-op helping the bairns

up at the Hall, swishing up in the car like a load of Lady Mucks, as she had written to Davey. It had made Fran think of Simon and Roy telling them to get in the back of the lorry, something the lads never failed to speak of in loud voices whenever they met on the factory site.

She grinned at the thought. Viola said, over the singing, 'So are the evacuees, the girls anyway, already working on rugs?'

Sarah nodded. 'Aye, when they're not cooking or doing homework. The rugs aren't good enough to sell to Briddlestone's, but it's early days. The war'll go on long enough for them to get good and have their own junior co-op. Or they will if that little tyke Eva has anything to do with it. By, she sounds a right little tiger.'

Fran was laughing at the thought of them all beavering away together, and the best thing was that her mam was pretty sure Mrs Bedley had mostly stopped drinking. It was the 'mostly' that still worried her, though, because as her mam had confided on the telephone, there was no real way of telling what the truth of it was or wasn't.

Sarah was laughing now. 'Your mam was so funny on the phone, when she said the boys reckoned it was cissy to cook, but by the time Mrs Oborne had told them their fortunes they had pushed up their sleeves and set to. Fair frightened to death they were, but reet pleased afterwards when they came to eat the scones they'd all baked.'

As they sang on, Sarah peered out at a croft whose peat fire was sending smoke up the chimney. It rose straight as a die. It was a strange saying, until you knew that it meant a dice, and that straight meant true, or correct. She remembered her mam telling her that. How was her mam, really?

'She's getting better,' Beth had said. 'Not quite reet yet, but better. The black marketeer put off coming *again* – just keeps upping his bill and adding the interest accrued, then gets some lad to stick it through the door.' Sarah tightened her grip on the strap and it wasn't just because Hamish was swinging round a bend, for how could the bill be paid, if he didn't come to collect the money? She closed her eyes as Hamish roared round another bend, tighter this time, that ran on through the pine forest. Beth had thought Norris might come tonight, for that's what had been written on the latest bill, but the beggar had said that before.

Sarah then allowed herself to think of Stan, her Stan, her love who was looking after her mam with Beth. He wasn't staying overnight, but he sometimes ate there and . . . She fought down the fear and the jealousy.

Finally, they were nearing the factory, which had been built in the shadow of the forest in order to be hidden from aerial view as much as possible. On night shifts they had twice heard planes rumbling overhead, seeking like hounds, but so far not finding a scent. When planes had been heard, they had been escorted to the air raid shelters, but it held up production so it was a tricky call, the foreman had explained.

To the right of Fran, sitting near the window, Fiona, the girl who shared with Deirdre, cursed Hamish. 'I'm about tae see my porridge in me lap, you gormless kilted—' She stopped.

Deirdre, sitting next to her, handed over a paper bag. 'Hang over that, hen.'

Just in time Hamish screeched to a halt outside the gates. 'Off ye get. I've more to pick up as Donald is off sick.'

'Poor bliddy women,' muttered Fiona. 'They don't know what hell they'll have to endure.'

The women hurried off, showed their passes and opened their bags. The guards smiled at the bottles of water they all carried now. They hurried along the paths to get out of the bitter, howling wind. Morag groaned, 'Oh, not more snow.'

The flakes were light, swirling, but they still had to reach their blocks and it was growing heavier every second.

Fiona was walking beside Fran. 'If Hamish teks the roads on the way back at end of shift like he did coming, he'll have us in the loch, and I reckon I'll be right pleased, cos it'll put me out of my misery. He knows his driving meks me sick.'

As they sank their chins into their scarves they were hailed by Simon, the medic, who was carrying a large box with a red cross. 'Supplies for the clinic,' he shouted. 'Let's not be using any of them today, girls. Steady as you go, hey. Blood's too red against snow like this.'

Deirdre made a rude gesture, then hurried into the changing rooms, leaving Simon laughing. It was warm once they were in and had changed into their overalls. They put on their wellingtons, rubber aprons and turbans quick as a flash. It was then that the security officers entered to check them over, and they all began to drink as much water as they could before heading for their work area.

Whenever they saw the SOs, Sarah and Fran always thought of Cyn, and wondered how she and Simon Parrot were getting on.

They were all working in nitrates now, highly dangerous, but they had doubled their pay, which was a relief, and they followed the foreman, Mr Todd, to the section, which was housed in a large, cold building. They waited behind the night shift, who were using long prongs to move the cotton around in the pans containing the nitric acid that was used to create TNT. The cotton had been teased out of bales and fed into a machine that shredded it into fluff, then it was packed into numerous metal boxes and brought in here on trollies.

They worked in pairs, Sarah and Fran, Viola and Fiona, and each pair took turns with the prong. While one stirred, the other pressed the cotton between stone plates to squeeze out the acid. Water was then run on top, to help drain the acid away.

The tannoy played, but there was no singing. There was just total concentration. The masks itched as always, but better that than breathing in the corrosive fumes. They stirred and pressed pan after pan, making the cotton brittle enough to turn into explosives. Viola had said they could become professional boxers because it was such heavy work they were building stevedores' muscles.

Behind them Deirdre shouted, 'My face.' They didn't look, but kept on working as Morag ran with the girl to the large barrel of water in the corner and scooped water to dilute the acid that must have splashed up into Deirdre's face. Again and again Morag scooped until the stinging had subsided and the burn had been prevented. Last week Fiona had left it too long and had had to run to the clinic to have antiseptic powder put on her arm burn. She had returned to work immediately, of course. Only once had Fran, Viola and Sarah seen the massive water tank in the corner used. That day a worker had slipped as she put the cotton into the cake mixture – as the workers called the nitric acid – and sunk her arm into the acid. Screaming, she had run across to plunge into the tank. The medics took her away. She was not seen or spoken of again.

The itch was back and Fran longed for her mam's sphagnum-moss mixture, but as she stirred she wouldn't think of the nights she lay in their three-bedded room, itching but trying not to scratch or turn over one way and then the other, for she didn't want to disturb the others. She tried not to think of anything, stirring, pressing, sluicing, carefully, oh so carefully. 'Quick, quick,' called Francie, the leader of the team. 'Targets to meet, girls.'

Hour after hour they worked until at last it was eleven thirty and time for lunch. They traipsed out into the canteen.

They all had headaches. Was it the way they had to peer down, cricking their necks, or was it the fumes? What did it matter, it just was.

They queued for their meal, then carried their plates to their table. The talk was of the war, of their families, of the snow. Through the windows they could see it falling, much heavier now. Sarah looked from Fiona to Fran to Viola. 'Reckon we might have to curl up in the cotton-teasing room. It's warm there.'

Viola grinned. 'Some do, so they say.'

Mr Todd had entered the canteen and was making his way to their table. 'Uh-oh,' muttered Fiona.

'Bit of a turnaround, girls. I need you five.' He pointed to Fran, Sarah, Viola, Deirdre and Fiona. 'In the guncotton section. Not the teasing room. The guncotton section, so you can wipe that smile off yer faces, and I'll believe you're happy with that.' It wasn't a question. 'Quick as you like. We're short of a few, and falling behind.'

The five girls just nodded and continued to eat.

'Quick as you like, I said,' he repeated.

They gobbled down their food and went without pudding. As Fran passed Mr Todd she muttered, 'You owe us five rice puddings.'

'Thank you, Fran Hall. And while I have you here . . .' They were walking to the exit a pace or two behind the other four. 'We had a call from Mr Swinton, wondering how you were, and another one, a woman, butted in. A Miss Ellington wanting to know if you were behaving yourselves. I told them that you two were a disgrace and had another girl and her saxophone involved in your little posse.'

Fran laughed. He nudged her. 'I told them I'd keep you both if I could, but know I can't. We have more girls coming from the Labour Exchange and I told Mr Swinton that in all probability he'll have you back in a week. So, today's

Saturday . . . So, aye, you could be back to pester yer families not this weekend, but next. He says Miss Ellington will let the families know as she gets to Massingham most days. Mark you, it's not absolutely definite, but pretty close. It's into February, I know, but it's the best we can do. Best tell Sarah, and if the wee Geordie Viola wants to head back south of the border, Mr Swinton will find a place for her. Or so he agreed. Mark you, she's an orphan, as you know, so she'd need a roof over her head.'

Fran hugged him. He grinned. 'Och, put me down, lassie. Mrs Todd wouldn't understand, though she's knows I'm a magnet to women and have to beat them off. Run along now before I change my mind.' His booming laugh followed her as she set off for the guncotton section. She turned, knowing he'd be watching her; it was his duty to do so. After all, she couldn't go wandering about unescorted.

He called after her, 'We've a couple of new ones on the machines. The SO checked them for metallic objects, then fed them through, but casting no aspersions on the SO, we're right busy today, so keep an eye on them, eh? They've had the safety rules read to them, so all should be fine. They've come from another factory and have worked in similar, and they seem capable, or so their references said. Nonetheless, a mother hen . . .' He waved her on.

Mother hen? Fran thought, and then, as she walked through this Scottish factory, she was standing alongside her da, scattering the seed to his hens. *Oh, Da.*

When she arrived, Viola, Deirdre and Fiona were already at work at the machines, as was Sarah, who was also keeping an eye on the door. Fran waved and headed towards her, wanting to shout out the news that they'd be home in a week. A week. She passed the new girls, who were on machines situated between Fiona's and Viola's. Did the new ones know how dangerous it all was? There was the explosive powder to pour into the funnels, then the lever pulled down, then BANG if something sparked. She shook her head at herself. Of course they did, the foreman had just said they had been working in a similar factory, though he'd also said to keep an eye on them. Mother hen, eh? Well, he'd called her a sergeant major the other day, so perhaps mother hen was a better image.

One of the new girls looked nervous and Fran smiled as the lass poured the contents of the container into the funnel that was feeding the powder into the machine. Aye, she knew what to do. As Fran neared, she saw Viola, next to the new girl, accept the usual container of powder brought to her on a tray and start to pour it through her funnel into the machine. The new girl watched for a moment, then finished pouring her own. Had the SO told them they were dealing with explosives for the mines, or was it depth charges to blow up the submarines? He'd let it slip to Fran and Sarah by mistake.

Viola was pulling the machine handle so that it pressed the fine powder into a two-inch-high block. The powder made Fran think of Mrs Oborne and her scones. By, her mind was busy with Massingham, but that was because she was going home. Aye, that was it. But these powder 'cakes' were a million miles from Mrs Oborne's. One spark would see a lot of people disappear. She grimaced. A flash of flame, an explosion, chaos.

She saw the danger man, which was what Fiona called the senior security officer, walking behind several of the machines, checking the girls.

She found herself smiling. They were going home . . . home . . . So it was as well they weren't singing any solos, for now they wouldn't be singing anything. Isla could stuff that in her saxophone and squeak away.

All around her the eleven girls were working. It was as

though they'd never done anything else in their lives, so sure were they all, even the two new ones. One had freckles, and Fiona had freckles, perhaps it was a Scottish thing. Fran watched Viola, wanting to tell her that she could come south with them. But it would have to wait, for their concentration mustn't be disturbed.

Would she want to come to Massingham anyway? Would Mam like a lodger? Mrs Smith and Beth lived alone, so Viola might be better with them. Or if Mrs Bedley was better, she might like a lodger too. She'd need all the money she could get to make up for the booze bill. Aye, that would be best. What's more, it would mean Beth could go home and Sarah would still have support. Aye, that—

Fran stopped as she neared the spare machine – hers. But there was something . . . Her mind was clicking, searching. Something had caught her eye. She looked back at the girls, the machines . . . Something was wrong, but the girls were working as they should, pouring the powder into the funnels. Powder that was really guncotton, cotton that arrived by rail to be teased, fluffed, flaked . . .

What was it she had seen? She watched the danger man, dark-haired and elderly, progressing along. He'd almost reached the new girl next to Fiona, the one with freckles.

Oh, it was probably him she'd noticed. She watched. He had snow on his hair, just a few flakes. Was it snowing at Massingham too? She saw that Fiona was shaking the powder carefully into the funnel. Once it had been like snowflakes floating in the vat as it was stirred . . .

She grinned, and walked on. The clock was ticking, time's awasting, she thought. But there was still something niggling . . .

She turned, went back and looked just as the danger man peered over the shoulder of Fiona and her neighbour, the new girl, the one with freckles . . . The new girl's hair . . .

Something was glinting at the front. Or was it just a trick of the light? She drew closer. Yes, there was something he couldn't see. Her heart lurched, she opened her mouth to shout, but it was falling . . . A kirby grip?

'No,' shrieked Fran, but the word died in her throat as the blast took all the air from her body and she was flying, crashing, tumbling and hurting. Too hot. Too much pain. Another crash, louder, and then a rushing sound. A thick, dead sound, sucking the air from her. She was lifted and then tumbled. Another crash. Then silence. There was no more pain, no heat. A scream shot through the air, loud, louder. Then she felt the ground hard beneath her, the ground shifting. What? A kirby grip? A plane? A bomb from the plane? A kirby grip. What? 'Sarah,' she called as the ground lifted one more time and fell away from her, taking the light, the life, her world.

Chapter Seventeen

The dust filled Sarah's mouth. Something heavy and hard was beside her head, digging in. Water ran down her face and into her mouth, wet and warm. Warm water? So many bangs, then another. Crash. Whoosh. Fran . . . She tried to turn her head away from the sharpness, but there was no room for there was more sharpness there. A little, just move a little. No. No. Too sharp, too hot. A smell. Burning. A sound. Shouting. Screaming men and women. She heard the roar of a lorry. Was she on the road? Where was she?

She must look. Her lids were too heavy and wouldn't open. Her da was saying to Davey as they lay next to her, 'Turn your head under coal, then you can breathe.' 'Aye, Da,' Davey said, their voices fading. 'I canna, Da,' she said, as wet warmth trickled into her mouth, but her mouth was full of dust, so how could there be room for more? 'No, I canna.' But she couldn't hear herself.

And she couldn't hear her da, and she couldn't hear Stan. If Davey was there, Stan would be. Stan? 'Stan.' She couldn't hear herself, only the creaking of the coal, squeezing like they said it did.

But then it was quiet. She was tired, so tired, and calm. It was getting cooler, much cooler, and wetter. She woke with a jerk. She could hear shouting, something shifting, scrapes, more shouts, then nearer – whimperings. From the pit-head? Why was she under the coal?

She listened for her da, but heard Fran call. Ah, Fran was here too. Why? She tried to shout. Her mouth wouldn't work. Dust was in it. On her. She was still wet. There was darkness and sharpness all around. And dripping. The sound of water, shouts and cries. 'Sarah?' It was Fran. 'Sarah.' Like the wind on the beck. Faint, fading. There was crying, calling now, louder and louder, but not from Fran. Fran didn't cry. Who was it? Where were they?

Asleep. Perhaps she was asleep. A dream? Sometimes she dreamed she couldn't move. She could hear noises, but not move. Yes, she must be asleep. She could hear Fran calling. Then Viola. Why was Viola at Auld Hilda? 'But no, silly bairn, I'm asleep, in me bed.' She breathed and coughed, the dust moved in her mouth. Why was Viola in her house? Was it because her mam was drinking? There was a crash. Was it her mam throwing bottles? Oh, Mam. Now Sarah didn't want to wake or get up to meet another day. No, she wouldn't. She'd sleep and the dream would change. Perhaps to the beck, eh, and Stan.

She slept, but then Fran was calling again. 'Answer me, Sarah. Answer me.' Her voice was stronger now. It sounded strange. Was Fran crying? But no, Fran was strong for them all. Fran stopped them from falling, from stopping, from giving up. No, it wasn't Fran, because if she was crying, what would Sarah do? Why, she'd go to sleep and not get up. Then the noise of crying, whimpering and the calls would stop.

Fran was on her side, but she liked to lie on her back. She tried to turn, hearing her mam riddling the grate. There it was, scraping, scrabbling, knocking, a crash. A crash? What? Her shoulder hurt so much. Her arm hurt, her head hurt, her mouth, her lips. She tasted wetness, salt: tears. They stung. She heard a whimper, another, another, so many, and they were hers. She pressed her lips together, then stopped, for it hurt. But she mustn't make that noise.

She was strong. She had to be. People expected ... She breathed in for four, out for four, and felt herself fade.

Then the pain was back. She hadn't moved. She tried, but she couldn't. It was dark even when she opened her eyes, and dust fell into them. There was a smell, what was it? Burning. Something was burning. Da? Where am I? Da? Where are you? Come and get me, Da. Dig me out. It's squashing me. Did you bring me to the pit? Maybe the roof's come down on me, like it did on you. Was I with you, and you left me behind? Why did you leave me, Da? Why? When I'm lost and afraid. But I have to be strong ...

She pressed her lips closed. She lifted her hand to reach her da. It wouldn't move. She tried harder. But something was too sharp, cutting her. The weight was pressing, hurting. Da said the coal squeezed the props. She couldn't ... She must sleep ... She was fading. 'Da ... Da, I'm coming ...' But it was like a whisper on the wind.

Viola lay face down. Face down in the dust. On bricks, under bricks, bricks everywhere. She was drowning, sinking, choking, like she had when the bomb came down. Mam? Da? Why was she here again? They were dead. Her mam and da were gone. So, it wasn't the bomb, she knew what that was like. No, this wasn't so ... ? She didn't know. She slept. Then moved, something hurt. She was working, pulling the handle like Mr Todd said. Pull carefully, carefully. The tannoy ... No, not allowed, not here. Different noises. Scrabbling, sobbing, calling, whispers on the wind. No, it wasn't the bomb, it was the powder. It was the machine next to her, toppled over, and on her legs? Or were them bricks? Aye, it was on her hand. Cutting so deep into her hand.

She looked inside her head, seeing Fiona and the new girls, then a flash, a roar, burning and crashing as the machine . . . Fiona had screamed. The new girls were gone, just gone, disappeared as she looked, as she fell.

Fiona? 'Fiona,' she called, but couldn't hear her own voice for it faded on her breath before it had even left her mouth.

Simon and Roy waited with the firemen as Mr Todd and one security officer headed towards them. Only one SO, for the other was under this lot. Roy watched as the last of the workers from the end of the building were herded away in the snow. No one asked what had happened. They knew – it wasn't the first time, and it wouldn't be the last.

On they walked, their shoulders bowed, to the medical centre, where the nurses would check them over, but Simon and he would be first in here. It was their job. They'd been through the Hull blitz. Nothing surprised them, but they hadn't known those buried under the stinking piles of crock then. Now there was Fran, Sarah, Viola and Fiona, the lass with freckles, and the others.

A security officer from another sector passed, his white overalls almost black, singed at the hem. He was taking the weight of the elderly Mrs Flowers. She'd be checked over like the others and if unhurt would go back to work in a different sector. 'There's a bliddy war on,' he muttered.

Simon looked at him. 'You can say that again.'

He did and they grinned, but it didn't reach their eyes. Mr Todd was leaving the workers, who were still trailing past the fire engine and the emergency teams. So pale, Simon thought. Was it shock or plaster dust?

Mr Todd stepped over the hoses that the firemen had begun rolling up, while others on the emergency team examined the destruction, tested the uprights and talked of ways to clear a path to those who needed rescue. The chief fireman met Todd. 'One explosion set off another, like a row of dominoes. The walls came down, and the roof in places, but the uprights held. The roof shouldn't have collapsed.'

Todd shouted, 'Well, it bloody did.'

Butcher, the fire chief, pointed to the worst of the debris, from which acrid smoke was rising. 'The bricks doused the blast, the ceiling dust smothered the flames. The water from the hoses finished off the job. There's no gas, so all inert. Just checking the structure properly, then we'll get the lassies out and you medics in. How many lassies, Mr Todd?'

He was asking Todd to get his mind working, Roy thought, because they already knew.

Todd held up his hands, examining his spread fingers, staring as though the answer was in them. They were trembling like leaves in a gale. Roy sat him on a pile of timber. 'A few deep breaths, eh, Mr Todd? In and out. Slow like. Four in, four out, that's what the London firemen said. There we go, in and out.'

He was holding Todd's wrist. Simon raised an eyebrow. Roy said, 'Fast, but not leaping about more'n you'd expect. He'll be fine.'

Todd looked up at him. 'Aye, well, it'll never be fine, not for the lassies, nor for me. What did we miss? What did I miss? What set it off? What have I done?'

Butcher's voice was level as he said, 'That's not for now. We'll be asking questions later, but the security officers obeyed protocol, and you know yourself things slip through. You can take horses to water, but you can't make them drink. Everyone checks everyone else. Sometimes bad things happen; it just is.'

Mr Todd stared up at the man. 'Horses? What the hell are yer talking of, sonny?'

Roy laughed gently. 'He means, you can tell people what to remove, and you can check till the cows come into the byre, but if, let's say, there's a hairpin, or a grip lying forgotten, deep within the hair . . . An accident is an accident. It just is. So, answer the boss, how many lassies?'

Roy still held Todd's wrist and Todd seemed to find comfort in that, for he said quietly, 'With the SO, thirteen.'

Simon shrugged, his face grim. 'Of course it is.'

Butcher said, 'You shut your blether, laddie. Thirteen or three, makes no difference. No superstition here. We'll get tae them, never you fear. You medics be ready to go in on our coat-tails to check them over before we get 'em out.'

As Butcher marched towards his men, Simon called, 'Was that coat-tails or kilt-tails, Chief?' His team looked up and laughed.

'Me tae know, you tae find out, laddie,' Butcher called. There was more laughter, there always was, it was how they survived to do the job, but it didn't touch their hearts.

Todd stood up, brushing himself down. 'I must get on. Make sure the other workshops are meeting targets. Come tae find me when you need me.' He walked towards the other buildings where work would have continued as though nothing had happened, and all the time they heard Todd muttering, 'We all missed something. We have to learn from this, but all the wee lassies . . .'

Roy looked on as the emergency services tested the debris. The snow fell and began to settle.

Sarah knew where she was now. She had heard the voices, Simon and Roy, heard the laughter. It was all right, they'd be rescued. It was—She stopped. No. No. 'One times two is two, two times two is four.'

There was a crash somewhere. A cry, a groan. Why had Fran shouted 'No'? What had she seen?

Hadn't she, Sarah Bedley, looked up and seen a glint as something fell into the machine and the handle was pulled? Or had it? She still heard the roar and felt the heat, the pain . . .

'Can anyone hear me?' someone called. Who was that? Sarah tried to speak. But the dust was in her mouth still. She spat. Her mam wouldn't like it. Spitting was nasty. Drinking was nasty too, Mam. She spat again. Her mouth was clearer. Had drinking cleared her mam's head? Had their donation money cleared the bill? Or was interest still being added? Was Beth there, in the armchair, with Stan in the other? Oh Stan. She formed his name with her dry and cut lips, but it died on her breath before she could hear it.

'Can anyone hear me?' It was that voice again.

Sarah spat again but her mouth was so dry. She heard Fran then, and she sounded so tired, but she wasn't crying. Fran coughed and started again. 'I can hear you, Viola. How are you?'

Sarah ran her tongue round the inside of her mouth as Viola croaked, 'Never been bliddy better.'

Sarah tried to laugh. Viola called, 'You still with us then, Sarah?'

'Howay, canna get rid of me.'

'Fiona?' croaked Fran.

Viola wept, coughed. 'I don't know. I saw her, then I didn't. By, me hand hurts.'

Sarah smiled to herself as Fran replied in a whisper, 'Only yer hand? That's bliddy lucky, hinny.' Other voices were joining in now, coughing, choking and crying.

Someone said, 'At least I'm not cold. I'm wet, but not cold. But I was scorching hot.'

Roy called then, 'We're coming to get you, girls. It'll take a bit of time. We'll be working hard. Got to get you back to work.'

'And we thought Swinton were bad,' said Fran.

Fran still lay on her side. She was so thirsty, she could drain the beck. She sat and looked at it, and Davey's arm was round her shoulders, her head against his. It was so calm. The kingfisher darted along the water. A fish glistened in its mouth. A kingfisher didn't sing, did Davey know that? Do you, Davey, my love, my life? Do you know that a fish is glistening in our wee kingfisher's mouth? Do you?

Glistened, glinted. Fiona was so close to the new girl and to the kirby grip that glinted. And Viola was so close to Fiona? She called as the kingfisher darted back into the willow, 'Viola? Fiona?'

Viola said, 'Yes, yes, I'm here.' Fiona said nothing.

Davey asked, 'Why are you crying?' She didn't know. The beck darkened, and instead she tasted dust, salt and blood. Yes, warm blood. In her mouth. Her arm hurt deep down, her chest too when she breathed. She wanted it to stop. And to stop that pain she must not breathe. 'Me lips hurt an' all. Kiss 'em better, Davey.' She said it but she couldn't hear it.

Sarah called then, 'Franny, is that you crying? No. No, you mustn't. You need the moisture. Fran Hall, stop yer crying because you don't cry. You mustn't, for us.' She fell silent, then Fran heard her say, 'Two times two is four. Three times two is six.'

'Howay, what yer doing, lass?' croaked Viola.

Sarah sighed. 'I said it when me mam was . . . When me mam were unkind. I said it, and it were my words, coming out of my mouth. They only came out if I wanted 'em to and if I didn't want to, I'd stop. You see, the words did what I said, not what any other beggar said.'

'You're a right daft lass, our Sarah,' called Deirdre.

Deirdre sounded strong, not hurt. Now she shouted, 'They've got me out. The medic checked me here. No need for the bliddy nurse. I'm off tae get the bus. I'll have a bath ready to run fer you at t'hostel when you're back. And for Fiona – you listenin', lass?'

There was no reply. After a moment Deirdre said, 'She's just teking a rest, that's all. Just a re—' Then there was just the sound of running feet and Deirdre's fading voice, 'Bliddy, bliddy war.' Then the hoot of a bus.

Sarah heard Viola groan and then weep. Sarah took as much of a breath as she could and called, 'Come on, Viola, say it wi' me. You too, Franny, loud as we can, eh? One times two is two, two times two is four.' She coughed, choked.

'Three times two is six,' said Fran.

'Four times two is eight,' said Viola.

Other voices now, Scottish voices: 'Five times two is ten.' 'Six times two is twelve.'

'Seven times two is fourteen.' 'Eight times two is sixteen.'

Then Roy's voice could be heard: 'I reckon that's our two who wouldn't go in the back. Bad pennies, eh? Still alive and kicking. Nine times two is eighteen.'

Now Simon's: 'You can come in the cab from now on, you two, and any of you others. Sit on me lap if need be, eh, Viola. Come on, lassies, louder. Ten times two is eighteen.'

Viola called, 'He canna even bliddy count. 'Tis twenty, you galumph.'

Mr Todd called now, 'When you've finished with yer tables, you can sing us a song. Then, when we get you out you can have a good long drink.'

'Mek it snappy,' Viola called out. 'Me hand's bliddy agony jammed under the machine.' Her voice broke.

The girls continued, quieter now: 'Eleven times two is twenty-two.'

Roy called, 'I'm coming through to you as soon as we can make it safe. Don't want to dislodge more and make it worse. But you're first on me list, Viola.'

'Oy, oy,' yelled Simon, 'I'll race him. Just keep on with yer tables, there's good girls.'

Sarah led them into the three times table: 'One times three

is three.' They croaked with her, 'Two times three is six, three times three is nine . . .' On and on, and Fran was back on the bank of the beck, watching the kingfisher with its glinting fish, which fell from its beak when it sang. But a kingfisher doesn't sing, even when its glinting fish falls, hits the water and bursts into flames that roared and drowned the singing, and the trees falling into the beck crash, creak, groan.

Davey, thought her mind, while her mouth formed the four times table, and she was glad that for now Sarah was the brave one, the strong one. And she felt proud of her, so proud. 'Six times four is twenty-four.'

Chapter Eighteen

Beth sat on the bus next to Maisie, listening to the chatter but looking out of the window at the snow drifting lazily to the ground. It was as though it couldn't really be bothered, perhaps because it felt winter had been going on for too long. She tutted.

Maisie peered at her. 'What's up, hinny?'

'Howay, just a mithering winter, eh?'

'A bit more to go an' all, but the days are getting longer, so we mustn't grumble.'

Mrs Oborne sitting behind them said, 'Ah, but we do. When're the lasses coming back is what I want to know, our Beth?'

'Well, wouldn't we all, Mrs Oborne? I asked Miss Ellington at dinner time. Then I asked Mr Swinton. He said he'd put in another call tomorrow. Said he'd asked yesterday and a Mr Todd said he thought perhaps a week, which would tek us into February.'

Mrs Oborne nodded. 'And I reckon Maud Bedley's getting better at life? She were up at Massingham Hall with us yesterday afternoon, after school, teaching the girls to bake rock cakes. Strange ones, without sugar and dried fruit, but honey does the trick. You getting any sleep at Maud's place?'

Beth sighed. 'Aye, but I miss me own mam summat rotten of an evening, though I pop in, of course I do.'

Valerie turned around on the seat in front. 'And Stan?'

'Oh aye, he's on call. Nips in with Sid and Norm on his

way off shift, but I haven't had to yell for him. We lock the doors tight and there's been no slipping out.'

What she didn't add was that there'd been yet more bills, with more interest accrued, and there were times when she could slap Mrs Bedley with a wet fish, and do worse to the beggar she had bought from. But when did she do the buying? When had the woman become such a liar? At least she wasn't drinking near as much, probably because there wasn't that much to drink, and if Beth knew where it was hidden, she'd tip it away, then dare Mrs Bedley to make a fuss. If she did, she'd crown her with her own rug frame. It was better, no doubt about that, but it had to stop, really stop.

Mrs Oborne muttered, 'I heard Amelia asked you yesterday to be part of her singing group again.'

Beth nodded. 'As though I would. I'll wait for me marrers. They're the ones I sing with, and no one else.'

'Amelia's still getting bookings, eh?' asked Mrs Oborne.

Beth sighed. 'Why wouldn't they be, with the whelp leaning on the publicans? And to be fair, they're not bad, and with the other two in—' She stopped. 'Well, with the other two not here, why shouldn't they take the opportunity? That's what me mind says; me heart says I'd like to give 'em a good kick up their arses.'

Mrs Oborne laughed. 'I thought you were turning into a saint for a minute there, our Beth, and would have to spend a bit o' time polishing up yer halo.'

'An itching yellow one that'd be then, from the stemming,' Beth muttered.

They were all giggling now and Valerie called, 'Where'd you keep your halo, Mrs Oborne, in yer rug frame?'

Mrs Oborne crossed her arms as they came into Sledgeford. 'Aye well, it's with the family silver, lass, in the butler's pantry, waiting to be given a good going-over.'

Bert pulled up at the bus stop and shouted, 'We don't want to hear about you being given a good going-over, Tilly Oborne, if you don't very much mind.'

Valerie hurried down the aisle, jumping off last, waving to them when Bert got the bus in gear again. Beryl said, 'I wonder how long Valerie'll be able to cope with Amelia lodging with them?'

Beth whispered to Mrs Oborne, 'Reckon Amelia hopes she won't have to for too long, but instead'll be the one telling you what to teach the evacuees at Massingham Hall as she drifts about in a tiara, wife to the whelp.'

While the others were laughing, Beth chewed her lip. Amelia was such a fool and it was a worry. The girl said too much in public places. Aye, she'd have said where Fran and Sarah were working if asked, that was if she knew, of course. But what about all the stuff she did know, and all those hours she spent in the pub with the whelp, glugging down elderberry wine? And would she let anyone warn her? Would she, hell.

As he turned left out of Sledgeford for Massingham, Bert yelled, 'Soon be at home, girls. Yer can get yer feet up, have a cuppa and think of me cleaning the old cow back at the depot.'

'Well, our Bert,' called Mrs Oborne, 'just what do you think we lot'll be doing? Just t'same in our houses, you daft old mitherer.'

When Beth struggled off the bus, with a rug Mrs Oborne wanted her to pass on to her mam, she almost fell over Stan, Sid and Norm. 'Howay, lads, you're getting in the way of a working girl, so here, carry this for me.'

She started to thrust it at Stan, then kept hold as Mrs Oborne said from behind, 'Think again, young Beth. Them's done overtime from the look of them – black as pitmen they are. Now why in t'world should that be?'

The lads laughed and Beth nodded. 'Aye, you're right, so I'll tek it round meself.'

The boys walked with her, clattering along her back lane and talking about the allotment and what they should sow when the time came. When they paused, Beth said, 'Our girls might be home next week, or thereabouts. Only a might, though—'

'Yer what?' Stan swung round to stare at her. 'Where'd you hear that, lass?'

'At dinner time. Mr Swinton said he'd double-check tomorrow. But he phoned yesterday or summat, and it were looking hopeful, or so he said.'

She stopped at the Smiths' back gate. Sid and Norm tipped their caps. 'We'll be getting on. You sure you won't be needin' us, lad, for later, eh?'

'There's nowt you can do that I can't, but ta. See you at sparrow fart.'

Beth slipped into her backyard, calling back, 'What's happening later? As though I don't know. Canary Club, is it? Howay, I'll drop this off, then be on me way to Mrs Bedley's. You get on, Stan.' She entered, wishing that it was her and Stan coming in from work, for she'd heat the water and wash his back, feel his skin—She stopped. What the hell was she talking about? She meant Bob, course she did, and shook her head. She was damned tired, that's all it was.

Her mam came from the scullery. 'You all reet, pet?'

'Oh grand, but it's just so bliddy bleak. I see more each day how you and Mrs Bedley and Mrs Hall feel about yer men. They're gone, and nowt to put in their places, and I feel that about me marrers.'

For a moment the two looked at one another, then Mrs Smith said, 'Oh aye there is for you. They'll be back and there's you and Bob, and one day there'll be bairns, for this war can't go on for ever. Aye, and who knows, someone might come calling for me one day, and he'll be my Prince Charming.'

They laughed. Beth handed her mam the rug. 'In the meantime, this is from Mrs Oborne, so get yer mind round that, Mam. Best be off.'

Beth turned for the door. As she reached it, her mam said, 'You're doing a good thing with Mrs B, lass. You're doing your best to get her straight for your friend, and that's summat to be proud of. It's not a thankless task, for I was there this afternoon, and she's coming along, yer know. Booze is a painful thing to leave behind when you think you canna manage alone.'

Beth opened the door. 'Ah, but she's not alone, Mam, she has to remember she has the Spartans, the Trojans, the Amazons – in other words, t'co-op.'

As she shut the door, she heard her mam say, 'Ah, I'll remember you said that when I wake in t'morning, wondering why I'm bothering.'

Beth just shook her head, for the courage of these mothers kept her going. She crossed the yard. Her mam called, 'I've left a mess of pottage in t'oven over yonder. Just dish it up, our Beth. And some of Mrs Hall's lavender grease for your rash is on the mantelpiece, and some sphagnum moss if you think you'd rather. Bliddy stemming.'

The thought of the stemming made her itch even more as she stepped into the back lane to find Stan leaning up against the wall, smoking a Woodbine. 'Howay lad,' she said, 'that's not going to help yer footie practice with the Massingham boys. You'll be panting worse than ever on Sunday. Who're you playing this week? And I told yer to get on home.'

Stan walked along with her. 'The Sunday school, so we're borrowing some of them to make up our team.'

They talked of this and that as they headed for the Bedleys' back lane. Stan tipped his cap at her. 'Listen, lass, you might hear a noise later, for I'll be here nine prompt. I've had a message that Norris, the marketeer, is calling for his money, for definite, 'tis said.' He tapped his nose. 'I'm not having him mither you or Mrs Bedley, so I'll be in the back-yard. So, as I say, if you hear more'n a bit of noise, ignore it. I've the money from the Rising Sun, and that's all he's get-ting. He can shove his interest. Or rather, I'll shove it somewhere if he doesn't clear off.'

Beth felt the wind swirling around her and the snow seemed frantic rather than lazy, as it had seemed earlier. Or was she the one feeling frantic? She said, 'You need backup, don't you? That's what yer marrers meant, eh?'

He shook his head, throwing his fag end away. 'Howay, I'm so bliddy angry, he's the one will be needing help to keep me off him if he makes a fuss.'

Beth sat by the range, opposite Mrs Bedley. Sarah's mam had barely eaten, just fidgeted, picking occasionally at the stew of a tiny bit of bacon, carrots and parsnips. Beth had boiled up some cabbage leaves, too, just for a few minutes, as her mam insisted, because what was the use of boiling all the goodness away, she always said. Well, Beth thought, sitting back, scratching, she at least needed all the good-ness she could get, or so Mrs Hall had muttered when she left them almost the moment Beth arrived.

Beth had told both women then that their daughters might be coming home next week. Mrs Hall's face had lightened, but Mrs Bedley had merely hung her head and picked at some bits that still clung to her from the after-noon's rug-making.

Now Beth sat staring at the range, looking at the clock as it neared nine. Did Mrs Bedley know Norris was coming? Is that why she couldn't sit still, and why Mr Bedley's old jumper lay on her lap, half pulled? The woman was supposed to be knitting up something with it. Beth wondered if she should remind her, again. She didn't, for any minute now Stan would face Norris. Norris was a nasty piece of work, but then Stan was a pitman.

She swallowed. What if the beggar brought others? What if Stan was beaten black and blue? Would Norris come in here, swinging his fists? She looked around for a weapon, and hurried to the scullery for the rolling pin. She put it behind her on the armchair. Mrs Bedley didn't notice; she was somewhere else in her mind, probably down in a bottle of brew. For a minute she hated Sarah's mam, hated her with such a passion that she felt sick, sore and tired of doing Sarah's job. She stopped. No, that wasn't fair. Sarah was working, in explosives, she knew that much, and it wouldn't be a picnic.

Was that a noise, out in the yard?

She sat up and checked the clock. Mrs Bedley leaned forward 'Eh, what?'

'Nothing, Mrs Bedley.' Beth turned on the wireless, low, so Mrs Bedley wouldn't hear. There was someone talking, but Beth couldn't hear what was being said. She brought out the rolling pin from behind her, hiding it against her side in case Mrs Bedley saw, but there was no fear of that, for she was staring at the range again. Beth moved to the kitchen table, trying to listen to what might be happening out in the yard. Mrs Bedley dozed, and Beth crept to the door, opening it a crack.

She saw them then, two men fighting in the darkness, just the stars to see by. She heard Stan, as he pinioned Norris, for that must be who it was, to the ground. 'Yer stay away, for next time I'll have me marrers, and they'll help me give you a bliddy hiding, understand? You've had all the money you're going to get. We've paid for the booze and you can bliddy sing for the interest. Got it?'

The back gate opened, and another man entered, then another. Beth snatched up the rolling pin. Mrs Bedley woke and saw. 'What?'

'Sit down reet now. You've done enough bliddy damage to last a lifetime.'

With that, Beth was out of the door, brandishing the rolling pin, but then she saw Sid and Norm picking up Norris, brushing him down extravagantly and kicking him out of the gate. 'And don't come back.'

An ARP warden yelled, 'Shut that door, or put that bliddy light out.'

'Hold yer bleedin' horses, it'll be shut in a minute,' Sid called back as they helped Stan up, and Beth dropped the rolling pin into the snow.

Norm laughed. 'Aye, for a moment it were like you were Fran, storming to the rescue. Can you tek him in, dust him down? We're following the ratbag to make sure he goes, then we'll head off home. And shut the bliddy door.' He was laughing as he mimicked the ARP warden.

They were out of the gate before she could answer. She took the weight of the man she had loved, and lost. The man whose place Bob had taken, Bob whom she saw so seldom. In the light from the kitchen doorway she saw that Stan's lips were cut and bruised, his eye half closed. She said, 'Come on, lad, let's clean you up, eh.'

Her voice sounded unsteady even to her. Stan put his arm around her shoulders. Together they stumbled to the door, which Mrs Bedley now held open, looking confused.

'I said, put the bliddy light out.' It was the ARP warden.

'Aye, just doing it,' Beth called back.

They squeezed into the kitchen and Beth kicked the door shut while Stan clung to the back of a kitchen chair. Beth yelled, 'Mrs Bedley, a water and flannel from the scullery.'

Beth pulled out what had been Tom Bedley's chair at the

head of the table and steered Stan to it. Mrs Bedley brought the bowl and Beth bathed his face, dabbing his poor bruised mouth. The water grew blood-red whilst Stan regained some colour. He looked up, smiled and leaned into her, his head against her breasts.

Beth stroked his hair, gently. He mustn't know that suddenly, although she loved Bob, she felt she would never care for him as she had cared for Stan, and here they were, together, for a moment.

She bent and kissed his hair, then saw Mrs Bedley sitting watching from the other end of the table. Beth sighed. This was the mam of Stan's fiancée. Their eyes held, then Mrs Bedley said quietly, 'Howay, lad. 'Tis all my fault, all of this.' She still looked at Beth. 'But 'tis over now. He is paid, and I will work on me rugs and at Massingham Hall. And I will make money to repay you, really I will, and I thank you. Yes, 'tis over, and I will never drink alone again, not after this.'

Her eyes were still on Beth as she added, ''Tis time to think of tomorrow, and to remember we owe so much to so many, and that our families and friends are what keep us true and firm. I have shamed meself, and 'tis not a good feeling.' She nodded at Beth, who smiled weakly. For the woman was right. They must remember friends and family, marrers and family, Sarah and Stan.

Stan straightened. Beth patted his back and picked up the bowl. 'You're all reet, are you, Stan? Do yer need to see the doctor?'

Stan grinned. 'Don't be bliddy daft. I get worse in the pit some days, and Norris won't be back. Sid and Norm are reinforcing that as we speak.' He rose. 'I dropped me cap, so'll pick it up on me way out.'

Mrs Bedley rose and went with him to the door. 'I reckon, lad, 'tis high time you and our lass were wed. What say you, our Beth? Sarah will be home soon, and I'll be tickety-boo from now on, though how I could . . .'

Stan was smiling at her and bent and kissed her cheek. 'Aye, I were going to mek her set a date when she gets back, but I needed to mek sure she could relax, that you . . .'

He gaze was intense as he looked down at Maud Bedley, who said softly, 'Then be sure, our lad. 'Tis the start of being over, for good.'

She shut the door on him and turned. All the time Beth watched as Maud came to her, leading her to Tom's arm-chair. 'Sit yerself down, our Beth, for thee and me have to keep one another strong and on the straight and narrow, for what's past is past, and there's only today, and then another day. So you help me, and I'll help you, and you just see how pleased you'll be to have yer own man home, and yer mar-rers, for loneliness makes us hanker and believe more than is real. Yer have to remember that, and leave all else as . . . well, what? You and me, eh, we'll move on together, teking an arm from time to time, should we get mithered, eh?'

Beth was listening. The fire was crackling and spitting with coal from the slag heap. Auld Hilda's coal was good and pure.

At last she replied, 'Aye, I loved him, Mrs Bedley, some-thing sore and deep, I did, but I did him wrong. I know I love my Bob, but something tugs in me when I see our Stan. Tugs, it does, fit to strangle me. But it doesn't when me Bob is here, so I reckon you're right –'tis loneliness. Well, all too daft, eh, all this mithering. It's a bliddy nuisance.'

Mrs Bedley laughed, picking up the old jumper that needed to be pulled out. 'Aye, like me and the drink, and I'm sore ashamed for what I've done, and there's our Stan, and yer girls' money. So, you and me, lass, we'll mek an end of it. We can do it, together.'

It wasn't a question, and watching Sarah's mam starting

to pull out her dead husband's jumper in order to create something different made Beth go to her, kneel beside her and lay her head on Maud's lap. 'I reckon our Sarah and Stan should have the banns read when she gets back, then she can wear one of yer woollen hats you've knitted from this going down the aisle, eh?'

The pair of them laughed quietly. 'Aye, 'appen you're right, Beth.' Mrs Bedley stroked Beth's hair. 'What a pair, eh, but we'll get through, or Tilly Oborne'll have our guts for garters while she digs around looking for our gumption. And lass, how you've looked on and taken care of me . . . You're a grand lass, and don't you ever, ever forget it.'

They spent the rest of the evening sitting talking, glad that neither of them were alone.

Chapter Nineteen

They had fallen quiet under the debris and stirred when Roy called, 'Oy, you've only got to the seven times table. Slackers, that's what you are. Let's hear you – one times eight, eh? Come on, Sarah, you show them how. We're nearly there.'

Sarah heard him say quietly, 'Check 'em when they break through. Need to know they're all still with us.'

'Right you are,' Simon murmured.

'How're we doing, lads?' called Roy. 'Ready to get 'em out yet?'

'Nearly.'

Fran was calling: 'Forget the eight times table, let's talk about the wedding.'

Viola, her voice weaker than it had been, murmured, 'Wedding?'

Fran laughed, but it was strained and hoarse. 'Our Sarah . . . there's never been time to sort it out, so while we're here, with nothing else to do, let's get at it, eh, girls? No point in a ring if you don't wed.'

Sarah smiled to herself as someone called Susan said, 'Och, it comes tae something when we have to climb under a load of debris to sort out a wedding. So, what're you wearing, Sarah?' Susan's voice was weaker too.

Sarah longed for a drink, aye, she'd even lick at a puddle, so she would, and she could imagine the wetness on her tongue.

'Hey, wake up, Sarah. It'll not be long now.' It was Roy.

'Let's be hearing about the frock, eh, if you've ditched the arithmetic.'

She drifted for a moment . . . once eight is eight. She always found the eight times table hard, somehow. Why? 'Why?'

'Why?' called Fran. 'Because we want to hear.'

Sarah thought, hear what? She'd turned her head a while ago and had been able to spit out the dust, but it had hurt her head and it was bleeding again. She knew it was blood, because she could taste it. Blood had a taste. She didn't think she'd known that.

Susan said, 'My sister wore my mother's wedding dress. Married a soldier, she did – my mam, I mean, he's me faither.'

'Not long now,' Roy called. 'Can you hear the shovelling? The shifting of the bricks, the beams . . .'

They could, she could, Sarah thought.

'So, what was the dress like, Susan?' Sarah called.

'Yellowed wi' age, didn't fit, but somehow she looked like a wee princess, and she's got a face like the back end of a saucepan.'

They were all laughing, but then dust fell and they all lay quite still.

Sarah said, 'I don't know if me mam had a wedding dress. I'll ask her, but she might still be drunk? Two times eight is sixteen.'

Fran called then, 'Aye, I reckon your mam has a dress. Think of the photograph – it were on the shelf above the mantelpiece. They had an aspidistra sticking up between them, and your da always said it looked as though he'd married it, not yer mam.'

They were laughing again, but carefully. Sarah wondered when they could stop doing things carefully. Three times eight is . . .

'Nearly there,' Roy called. 'Top layers off, ambulances here, waiting. Soon be a cuppa in your hands, but the docs have to check you. That's after me and Simon get at yer.'

Fran called, 'Do you hear that, girls? Come on, tell me you hear it, one at a time. Roy's going to get at us.'

They laughed, or some of them did. There had been thirteen, but there were probably fewer now, Sarah thought. 'I remember the photo, but I divint know if she's still got it, Fran. If not, your mam has one, hasn't she? Or Beth's mam.'

'Oh aye, because Beth were married in it – cut about a bit it was. Mebbe.'

'Aye, mebbe,' Sarah whispered. 'But what about yer mam, Fran, when we marry? She needs Stan's money.'

'Mebbe not. I'm working, she's at the Hall more often than not, and gets paid for that and her rugs. Howay, we'll sort it out between us all, eh? The thing is to keep breathing long enough to get up the aisle, lass.'

They laughed, but were too tired, too cold, hurting too much, and Sarah only wanted to sleep. She drifted, listening to the crackling of her mam's range, to the canaries singing, to Stan murmuring that he loved her. Then there was a crash. Roy called, 'It's all right, lasses. Just the last beam being chucked off. We're on our way to you now.'

There was scrabbling, bricks being thrown, curses, the revving of cars, the sound of buses as they left the site, the hooting. Aye, so it was the end of the aft shift, the beginning of the night shift. She called, 'What's the time, Roy?'

'Gone ten o' clock, lass. Overtime this evening, to make up for—' He stopped.

'Lost time, targets not filled,' she finished in a whisper.

Then she saw light and flinched. It seemed so bright. There were lights playing on the bricks. But what about the blackout?

She must have said it because Roy called, 'Ah well, we're

not just pretty faces. We set up awnings so we can see, but them buggers with the bombs can't.'

They were still moving bricks, she could hear them, and then a scream. 'Steady with her lads,' Simon said. 'Shift the machine gently. I need to be with her to stem the bleeding.'

Another scream. Fran started singing 'All or Nothing at All'. Soon all the girls were singing, out of tune, croaky, but singing. Roy joined in, discordant but wonderful, and soon there were more male voices, all singing as though they meant to bring down the awning. Slowly, the number of girls singing decreased as they were brought out. Then there were just Sarah and Fran, accompanied by male voices. Then only Sarah, though her voice was getting weaker. The breath in her body less and less, and the pain tore at her. Bricks were cleared, and a fireman peered down. 'Last but not bliddy least, bonny lass.' He was a Geordie. And Sarah wept, though she'd thought she had no more moisture in her body.

The bricks were shifted, thrown to the side, until she was staring up at the awning in the brightness of the lights. There were hands beneath her arms and Roy peered down. 'Steady as yer go, Sarah. Steady now.'

Hands were either side of her head, holding her still. The bricks beneath her tore into her skin, and she cried and cried. 'Stan,' she called.

Roy was guiding her on to the stretcher. 'Here we go.' She was carried down the heap of bricks, to the ambulance in which Fran lay.

Fran ached. She stared at the ceiling of the ambulance and forbade herself to cry. She didn't cry, not in front of her friends or her family. The ambulance tore round a corner, its bell ringing, and into and out of a pothole. Fran screamed, for the pain was so bad she couldn't breathe. Simon was looking down at her, shouting, 'Come on, Fran. Come on, breathe. There's a good girl, breathe.'

She was so tired, but the pain was still there, and she heard Simon say to Roy, 'She's in shock. We're losing her.'

Roy came and stroked her hair while Simon pushed on her chest and then Roy held her wrist. He shook his head, but she was still here, she was just tired. 'Come on, Fran, try. Breathe, for the love of Mike. Come on, you've a wedding to go to.'

Simon yelled, 'For God's sake, Timothy, get your bleedin' foot down and stop fannying about.'

The driver called, 'Shut your noise, we're doing our best. There's snow on the road.'

'But it's not bliddy good enough,' Sarah called then. 'This is Fran.'

All this Fran heard as she jerked and bumped. None of it mattered; she was too tired to try. Davey wasn't here, neither were Beth or Mam, and the war just went on and on . . .

Roy was close to her now, shouting into her ear. 'I haven't spent hour after ruddy hour digging you out for you to give up, Fran bloody Hall. You've a broken shoulder, you've sliced open your head and your arm, lost a lot of blood, but that's no bloody excuse, do you hear me?'

Fran wanted him to stop shouting. She wanted to rest, that was all. 'Don't you want to live?' Roy asked finally, his lips so close to her ear he was almost eating her. She laughed, inside. Laughed, for the girls on the bus would think it funny too. And Mrs Oborne would say, 'Get some bliddy gumption, our Franny.'

But she'd say, 'I'm too bliddy tired and I miss my Davey, and this bugger's eating me bliddy ear.'

Simon shouted then: 'Don't be so bliddy feeble, Fran. We're all bliddy tired, and it's not time to sleep, there's a war to win. And Viola, your mate's, lost half a hand, so

266

who's going to hold the other one, eh, to help her along, if not you? Because I hear you're the strong one, Miss Franny Hall.'

That's why she was tired, thought Franny. 'I'm tired of being the strong one.'

But Viola wouldn't go away, her sweet pale face, her freckles, and her hand. How would she play the saxophone? Oh no, how? 'How can she play the saxophone now?'

Roy said to Simon, 'What's she talking about? Look . . . I've got a stronger pulse.'

Simon sat back and stopped banging her chest. 'About bliddy time.'

As the bell went on ringing and the ambulance swerved round another corner, Sarah whispered, 'Viola can sing, Franny. There'll have to be four of us, a quartet, not a trio, and pet, you're not the only strong one. I am too, and I'm not afeared of anything, for I led the times tables, and it was me mam that taught me to do that – she'll be strong again an' all, or I'll have something to say about it.' She began, 'Four times eight is twenty-eight.'

Fran muttered, 'Don't be so bliddy silly, it's thirty-two, our Sarah.'

Sarah laughed and laughed. 'Got yer good. Course I knew that.'

The two girls said the eight times table together while Roy groaned to Simon, 'If I ever hear a times tables ever again it'll be too soon.' But soon they were joining in, and quietly Roy said, 'Not a bad trick to use another time, eh?'

Simon agreed, for there would be another time, if not here, wherever else they were posted.

Chapter Twenty

It was the next morning, and the co-op women latched a wooden trolley to Madge's bike. The trolley had been made up at the Hall by Alfie Biggins, Stan, Sid and Norm, all working together without too much shouting. There'd been some fairly cack-handed help from the whelp, not that anyone had said as much. They'd merely slapped him on the back, surprised, and said he'd done a good job.

In the Halls' backyard the wind was whipping the litter into a frenzy and Mrs Bedley peeled a page of newspaper from her leg. 'Howay, reckon the gales might be coming in after all. Tommo at the post office said he'd heard they was on the way.'

Annie Hall stood with her hands on her hips as Beryl stacked the last of the frames in the trolley. Audrey Smith covered them with the tarpaulin. 'Aye, happen you're right, but we could let the tarpaulin loose and we'll sail up to Massingham Hall quick as a wink.'

The women laughed, including the new lass, Cathy, brought along by Maisie's mam. Cathy was an embroiderer really, but a dab hand at rag rugs too. She was teaching some of the evacuee girls how to embroider their mams' initials onto the corner of a handkerchief as a gift for when they next saw them.

Stan had lent his bike to Cathy, and Mrs Bedley had passed on Davey's to Beryl on the promise that Ben and Stan could use Bob's, Beth's husband's. The women set off, Mrs Bedley in the lead, and the others followed, hoping that the new determination in the woman wasn't a pretence, but a real effort to finally stop the drinking. Aye, she still smelled of the stuff, but not as often, so as long as the effort built . . . And what's more, they'd not seen her like this, with gritted teeth, clean clothes and a clean scullery, since Tom's death. Aye, she was improving, and that was something. Indeed it was. Not enough, but something.

Beth was different too, her mam had said. It was as though having had to stand on her own two feet while her marrers worked elsewhere, as well as having to face up to the problem of Maud, had helped her grow up.

But what had helped them all more than anything was that Miss Ellington had spread the word when she'd arrived in Massingham after her fore shift yesterday that the girls would be home next Saturday. Almost definitely, which was as good as definite, well, they hoped it was, as there were sufficient replacements now.

They trundled along the back-lane cobbles, huffing and puffing, the frames rattling. They turned onto Main Street, bending over the handlebars into the wind, almost beyond speech before they'd even left Massingham. Madge adjusted her eyepatch as she rode alongside Annie, who talked of today's teaching list, which they had put together last night.

Madge had added in a cheese pie she thought they could make with the girls and the boys for their lunch today. Sophia had said yesterday that she felt the boys should be included again, after helping with the scones, because it would be good for them to be able to look after themselves. Mrs Oborne had called, 'Howay, the pitmen'd have a bit to say about that.'

Sophia had laughed and nodded. 'Well, I wouldn't want to have to cook after a day at the coalface, but these lads will need something in them to play well in the football match your son and his marrers have set up for the after-noon. They're forming a league, no less.'

Annie was laughing at the thought as they turned left, then right, enjoying going downhill, but dreading the rise leading to the Hall. But not even that was really a problem, for the girls were coming home, for the women had decided to be positive, no probable return about it. No. They *were* coming and her heart was singing, as Stan's had been when he left for the fore shift this morning. She reckoned he'd be cheering on his lads from the sidelines louder than usual.

'You'll need to keep a bit of an eye on the evacuees versus the local lads including some of the Sunday School boys. No fisticuffs between the two teams, please,' she'd told Stan before he'd left this morning.

He'd grimaced, then grinned. 'All your fault, us getting wrapped up in this, but by, it saves the three of us lying around all day eating peeled grapes and being waited on, with me thinking of me Sarah coming back.'

She shouted this to the co-op women now as they headed in through the Massingham Hall gates, puffing away. Yesterday, as they'd worked on their rugs in the kitchen, Sophia had said Alfie would pick them up this morning, but, as Mrs Oborne pointed out, 'Petrol's brought in by the lads on ships being torpedoed, so we should leave it for them who need it. We can use our legs, for pity's sake.'

Behind her back Beryl had pulled a face as she worked her hook, then muttered, 'Forget the legs, what about our arses? You're all right with your great sofa of a one, Tilly Oborne. Mine gets reet sore because it's a neat tiddler. Bit like the princess, I am, who'd feel a pea under a hundred mattresses, so delicate and pretty is my bum.'

Sophia had looked around at the gaggle of women, wondering if Mrs Oborne was going to be offended. Instead there had been a roar of laughter and Mrs Oborne had

270

spluttered, 'Aye, our Beryl, you've been listening to our Bert too closely.'

Annie was laughing at the memory as they cycled on the gravel surrounding the house. They parked their bikes by the garages and carried their frames across the yard. Alfie called after them, 'Lunch is it, ladies? I'll be there.'

'It's the bairns cooking it.'

Alfie pulled a face. 'Ah, but they wipe their noses on t'backs of their hands, or stick their fingers up them.'

Madge yelled, 'Well, yer best check each forkful carefully for bogeys.'

'I've me sandwiches,' Alfie muttered, wiping his own hands on an oily rag.

'Don't be daft, lad,' yelled Annie. 'We all wiped our noses when we were bairns, and I know yer did cos I saw you. They'll wash their hands or I'll want to know why. Come at twelve.'

Annie followed the others down the steps to the kitchen, hearing Alfie call, 'Wouldn't dare not, cos you witches'll come after me on yer brooms.'

'Aye, that'd be reet good. Save all this cycling, lad.'

The cheese pie was a success, with a bit of a fight to clean the dish where the crisp cheese had stuck. The boys had to help with the washing-up before heading out to meet up with Stan, Sid and Norm at the school playing field for the match, while the co-op and Sophia continued rug-making with the girls.

Outside, the wind was becoming wild, and Ralph clattered down the stairs into the kitchen, freshly bathed after a fore shift at the coalface. Sophia looked up. 'Oh darling, it sounds quite dreadful out there. I do hope you're not going out.'

'Only to the garage.' Ralph stopped when he saw the

271

women, and forced a smile. 'Ladies. How are you?' Without waiting for a reply, he continued, 'Do tell me that cook is preparing our dinner this evening, Sophia, and we're not having to suffer whatever pie the children made. The kitchen is full of the lingering smell of something.'

There was silence. The evacuee girls kept their heads low over their work, proggy and hooky tools in their hands. Annie Hall said quietly, 'It were delicious, Mr Massingham.'

'They did really well,' Sophia added. 'A lovely crisp top layer of potatoes and cheese.'

Ralph merely nodded, then turned on his heel. 'Maybe I'll just read the newspaper. The girls are singing this evening. One hopes that it's still on, given the weather. It's snowing heavily, to add to the misery.'

As he left, the telephone rang in the corridor. 'Would you, Ralph, please?'

Ralph snatched up the receiver. Before the war they'd had a butler. Perhaps when it was all over, they would again, but why? They could pick up their own ruddy telephone, surely.

He stopped, the receiver halfway to his ear. They? He realised he meant Father, Sophia, and himself, a family, his family, the ones he loved, the ones he had to protect by continuing to be the Ralph of old. He shook his head, thinking of the kitchen taken over by those homeless children, the cheese and potato crusts on the pies, and those women chattering around the table, their bikes cluttering up the garage so he couldn't get his car in. And it didn't matter. How could it ever have done? But he had to pretend it still did. He had to be Ralph Massingham, for who was watching and reporting to Tim?

'Massingham residence,' he barked into the mouthpiece.

'Oh, Ralph, it's Amelia. How lovely to hear your voice. Look, we're still booked for Smeaton, on the off chance that people will be struggling out to hear us. The villagers at least will, one would think. Heavens, though, what chaos – bins flying around the place, and the fence is down here, and not just in one place. Guards all over, but they can't patrol everywhere, so they're just choosing the tricky areas.'

Ralph said, almost in a whisper, 'Good heavens. What a do, eh? Is nowhere safe?'

'Seems not. Someone was saying they have to patrol where the woods come up close, in case anyone slips in that way because there are those Ander—No, I mustn't say. Though who on earth would be out in this? Even bad boys have more sense.' She laughed. 'But, oh dear, I'm going on. I rattle along like a train sometimes, I think it's because I'm tired. I work so hard. Anyway, enough of work – will I be seeing you?'

Ralph stared at nothing. He didn't want to see her, he didn't want to listen to this blather, he just wanted to stay here. He said, 'Oh, of course, for a short while at least. Don't really want to get stuck. So, dear Amelia, I will see you later. What a lovely thought.'

He replaced the receiver, then turned back, opening the door into the kitchen, peering in. He knew he shouldn't make the offer, for it wasn't what Ralph would say. But he said it anyway. 'Look, the weather is truly terrible, so perhaps, ladies, I should run you all home in shifts?'

They looked at one another. Mrs Hall said, 'Is it all right with you, Sophia, if we leave now? Stan and the lads will be bringing the boys back. Really, Ralph, that's reet kind, but we'll have the wind behind us by now, so we can manage on our bikes, truly we can. It won't be the first time, and won't be the last.'

Sophia shook her head. 'Yes, please, if it's worse you must go. The girls and I will get on superbly on our own, and show off our progress when you come tomorrow, but are you sure Ralph can't run you?' Sophia smiled at Ralph. 'Bless you for offering.'

Ralph looked around. It was calm and warm. More and more he found he liked being kind.

It was then that Mrs Hall realised Mrs Bedley had still not returned from her trip to the upstairs toilet, which Sophia had insisted was warmer. Sophia said, 'You pack up. I'll rally the troops.'

She set off upstairs, but the toilet was empty. She stood, not sure where on earth Mrs Bedley could be, but then heard a sound in the drawing room. She crossed the hall and opened the door to see Mrs Bedley standing by the side table lifting the brandy decanter with one hand, and holding the stopper in the other.

'Oh,' said Sophia.

Mrs Bedley swung round. She looked at Sophia. 'It's not what you think, Mrs Massingham. I were testing myself. I shouldn't be in here, I know I shouldn't, but yer cat were shut in and meking a fuss, so I let it out and it scuttled down the stairs. I saw the brandy. I wanted it, so I went to it. I stood telling meself the need weren't there. I thought of Beth, for she's been staying. We have a pact.'

Sophia looked from her to the decanter. 'Then that is a huge success, and you should be proud. This is between us, our shared moment, but treasure what you have done today, and God bless Beth. Soon her friends will be back, and Sarah will be so proud of you. So very proud.'

The two of them walked downstairs together, and Sophia could smell the brandy on the woman's breath and wanted to shake her till her teeth rattled. But the co-op had said there was an improvement, so that's what they all had to hold fast to. Sophia waved them off from the yard. She hadn't told the others – what was the point?

The women hardly had to pedal, and laughed their way

home as the snow fell and whisked away their words, feeling like bairns as they lifted their legs and seemed to freewheel all the way, hanging on to their hats and calling into the wind, 'Howay, howay, the lasses are on their way.'

Maud licked her lips as the chanting finished. All she could think was that just a nip hadn't hurt. Just the one, but then one wasn't enough, and then the lass had come. Mrs Massingham had believed her. She had, hadn't she? Perhaps she hadn't, and that's why she'd waited, so they could leave the room together? Maud had known she shouldn't, and now, as the snow fell faster, she knew she mustn't drink at all, for even one sparked the need. But none was too harsh, course it was. She cycled round a frozen clod. So, all she had to do was keep it to one nip. Grit her teeth, and keep it at that.

The wind was cold, the clouds building. But how could she keep the drinking a secret when Sarah was back? Well, the lass wouldn't find the hidey-hole in the netty, and she'd just tell her she'd stopped, that's all. And she could comfort herself with the thought that she'd always know that if she just moved two bricks and reached through, there would be Norris Suffolk's bottles, and this time he'd said he'd keep the interest down. Aye, it wasn't comfortable in the netty, but she didn't care; a nip was enough to keep her going, and Sarah *was* coming back, even though she'd written in her cross note that she might not.

Maud pedalled on, seeing in her mind's eye her daughter's note propped on the bedroom mantelpiece. When she woke in the night, her mouth dry, imagining the sherry, the beer, the wine, anything alcoholic that would ease the longing, she would grope for the torch and shine it on Sarah's note. She also thought of Beth, with her own battles, sleeping in Sarah's room, and all of that made her wait till morning. And that were a real achievement and deserved a reward, and it was good, for now she waited till after her breakfast cup of tea for that reward. And then it was just one nip. And another after her dinner, another . . .

Would Beth tell Sarah she was improving? Course she would. Would it be enough for Sarah? Course it would, and she'd be proud of her mam, and soon she'd stop, soon.

Ralph was crossing the hall after dinner when the telephone rang. His father called, 'Would you mind, Ralph?' just as Sophia had done earlier. They were so alike, so normal, so familiar, and how could he not have seen their value in his life?

He lifted the receiver. 'Good evening, Massingham residence.'

Tim said, 'Well, lad, cometh the hour, cometh the man. John 4:23?' There was a pause. Ralph clenched the receiver. This was the code for him to get some sabotage done. Tim must know about the fence. Well, of course he did. Amelia had so carelessly pinpointed the store and the fence in her most recent chatter. And Tim's other bloody ears on the ground would know, damn them.

Tim continued: 'Mustn't talk much more on your dear papa's phone, because he's such a busy sort that others might be trying to get through. I just heard about the weather and did hope you felt able to continue with your ramble. Probably best if you avoid the woods and keep to the moorland. Anyway, you'll know best. Good luck to you. Let me know you've returned safely. Can't have you turning into a snowman, eh?'

Ralph felt his stomach twist. He understood the message completely. Don't go through the woods, go over open terrain.

He couldn't stop himself asking, 'How did you know? I've just found out myself.' Then cursed at Tim's reply.

'Me to know, you *not* to try and find out.' The pips were going. There was a click, then nothing.

'All right, Ralph?' his father called. Ralph pressed down on the receiver, drawing in a breath. At that moment he realised that it *was* all right. This was his chance to try, and to fail, and no one would be any the wiser, not in this weather. He sent up a silent prayer. Please, God, let it get them off me and my family's back.

He found his way to a village called Smeaton and the Dog and Duck, where Amelia and the girls were performing.

As always the pub went quiet when he walked in, because the whelp wasn't liked. He dug his hand in his pocket and bought a round for everyone there – why not? If bloody Tim mentioned it, he'd say he was—He stopped as an old boy lifted his tankard of weak beer and called, 'Thank you kindly, Mr Ralph.'

Amelia, Brenda and Rosie were singing and now she waved. He pointed to a chair by the fireplace. She nodded, and off they went singing 'Begin the Beguine'. He gathered three other chairs around the table, as per usual, stretched out his legs and tried to snooze. Fat chance, because there was the break-in hanging like a cloud, and the cries of Tom and Joe beneath the coal, and the knowledge that Tim's eyes were probably on him.

He heard Beth and Valerie then, calling across the singing, 'Thank you for the drink, Ralph.'

He lifted a hand. 'My pleasure, girls.'

Beth's smile was strained. He longed to ask how Fran and Sarah were, and when they were coming home. Was it definite it was in a week, as he'd heard Sophia tell his father? On and on the singing went, and the snow was probably still falling. Would he manage to grind his way home in the roadster?

The singing was over at last, and he signalled for three glasses of elderberry wine. They came. The girls too, sitting down around him. He said, 'Good singing, girls. A nice lot of clapping too.'

Brenda lifted her sherry glass. 'Thanks, Ralph.'

Valerie and Beth were gravitating to the fire, and why not? Amelia had said something, and nudged him. 'Did you hear? The snow has stopped, Valerie's just said. Good thing too – another fence went down today. The patrols by the woods have been doubled, poor dev—'

Rosie nudged her. 'For heaven's sake, Amelia.'

Ralph couldn't believe Amelia's foolishness. How many times had she been told? But he merely said, 'Sorry, I missed all that. I was miles away. I liked your rendition of "All or Nothing at All" almost more than "Begin the Beguine" . . .'

The evening dragged on until finally he drove the girls home and, last but not least, dropped Valerie and Amelia outside Valerie's house in Sledgeford. He gave Amelia a quick kiss, tasting the wine on her lips, as Valerie made her way to the front door. 'Quick,' Ralph said, as Amelia pouted her lips for another. 'You'll let the cold in and the heat out of the house, then her mother will be displeased. You don't want to have to look for new lodgings.' He leaned across and shoved open the passenger door. Almost before Amelia had slammed it shut, he was off as fast as he could on the slippery roads, hating the pretence, hating himself, not daring to think of where all this was leading.

Chapter Twenty-One

That same evening, Stan, Sid and Norm were in the Canary Club shed with Cyn Ellington and Simon Parrot.

They were talking of the lads' football match in the afternoon, and how the lads had mobbed Mrs Massingham when she clambered out of the car. Abraham had reached her first, launching himself at her, wrapping his arms around her gardening mac. 'It were a draw, Auntie Sophia. A right belter of a goal. Tommy did it. Good right foot he's got.'

Sophia had laughed along with the muddy urchins, and then shared a wink with the three pitmen. 'Muddy and happy, it couldn't be better, and just as well I brought a blanket for the back seat.'

The boys were clamouring around her, telling her how the wind had taken the ball, and just at that moment the wind had taken her green velvet hat and tumbled it across the pitch, with them in hot pursuit. She'd thanked Stan, Sid and Norm, pressing a pound into their hands for the odd drink or two, waving away their protests. 'No, I am so immensely grateful. What would I do without you three and the co-op? Absurd to take on so many children, and little beggars they are too, lots of spirit, and one needs spirit . . .' She'd trailed off.

Stan laughed now as they downed Simon's home-made beer. 'She were right, little beggars they are, but Abraham's right, that Tommy's got a good right foot on him. I reckon there's more good than bad in 'em.'

Norm raised his glass at Stan. 'Which weren't what your da said about us, half the time.'

Stan put down his beer and dipped his hands into the seed mix, letting it run through his fingers. Da? Memories were everywhere. 'Aye, you're right there, I reckon.'

Outside they could hear the gale still buffeting. Norm sank the remains of his beer. 'Reckon I'll get on. I don't know, down in the pit one minute, the next standing on the edge of a footie pitch yelling orders that nowt listen to. Meks a bloke reet hungry, so back to Mam's vegetable pie.'

Cyn Ellington was drinking a cuppa from her flask, nodding at something Simon had said. She turned to Stan. 'So, the wedding? Getting on with it, I hope? Made a date?'

Stan pulled a face. 'Not easy when the lass has been somewhere, heaven knows where, doing summat, heaven knows what. But you're right. I reckon before the spring would be good, eh? Then we can see the buds burst together. I'm trying and trying to make meself believe they're really on their way home. It was supposed to be temporary, but here we are at the end of January and I miss the lass. Can't you find out that it's for definite they're coming back, Miss Ellington?'

Her smile was smug. 'Aye, that's what I was leading up to. I asked, and Swinton said, "For the love of God, woman, stop mithering it. Between you and me, I wouldn't have been tipped the wink unless it were certain." So here I am, telling you, and I'll have to kill you if you give me away.' She roared with laughter. 'But tell your mam and the others, eh? So Saturday they'll be here, so no more ifs, buts and maybes, eh?'

Stan felt a release of tension, a relaxation and an utter sense of joy. At last, he thought. At last, and of course he'd tell his mam, who'd tell Mrs Bedley. But then the thought that was always niggling caught him, for how could he keep two houses going? And what about a dress, the food? Had they enough coupons?

Simon was pushing chickweed through the wire and the canaries were looking at him as though saying, 'Is there nowt else?'

Norm stood in the doorway, looking out across the allotment. 'Reckon we're going to lose more fences, and the bliddy compost heaps are all over the place. The slag heap's got a right smoulder on itself, whipped up it is.'

He was holding on to the door, struggling to keep it still. Stan and Sid looked at one another. 'Reet,' Sid muttered, 'I'm off. At least we have a lie-in tomorrow. Not needed, surplus to requirements, and the bliddy rest of it, thank the Lord.'

They tipped their caps at Simon Parrot and Miss Ellington, and as he passed her, Stan whispered, 'You could always make it a double one, yer know, share a parachute to mek the dresses, maybe Fran an' all – mek it a trio of couples.'

Miss Ellington just raised an eyebrow. 'Not so much beer for you, lad. Meks yer silly, as does the news yer lass is almost on her way. Get on home to yer mam now, like a good little boy.'

Stan's laugh was snatched away by the wind as he stepped out. He reached for his cap, but had to chase it along the path, while Sid cursed because the Woodbine he was smoking had been snatched from his mouth and tossed into the snow building up against the shed.

Stan, Ben and their mam had eaten their meal in silence. Stan had called Sarah from the public telephone box as usual, but there'd been no reply. Sometimes there wasn't if they had to do overtime, but on the other hand he didn't like the thought of the gale whipping around his lass, for she was so slight it could almost tumble her along the street.

And what's more, he wanted to talk about the wedding, wanted to hear the joy in her voice that she was coming home. Once the tea had been cleared, they settled for the evening, with Ben sitting on the stool in front of his mam's armchair, mithering, 'Why me, not Stan?'

'Stan's done his fair share in t'past, lad,' said Annie. Ben grumbled under his breath, the hank of wool which she had found in the attic stretched between his hands as she wound it into a ball. 'Howay, Stan, give her a call tomorrow,' she said. 'Anything in particular yer needed to say?'

Stan stretched his legs out in front of the fire, not sure how to put it. 'I want to marry Sarah, Mam.'

'Ben,' snapped Annie, 'keep them arms wide, lad, you're sagging.'

'Not bliddy surprised,' muttered Ben.

Together, Stan and Annie said, 'Language,' and Ben huffed.

Stan and his mam shared a glance and smiled, and she said, 'Well, we know you want to marry the lass—' She stopped. 'Or do you have to, is that what yer saying? If so . . .'

Stan shook his head. 'Course not. I want to, Mam. I want to get wed soon as she comes back, to see in the spring together.'

The last of the wool had been wound and Ben stretched his back and shook his arms, saying, 'So, where'll you live? No room here. There is at Mrs Bedley's, but ye'll have to put yer pay their way if yer do that, or some of it, for she'll be yer wife, and Mrs Bedley's her mam.'

Stan stared at the lad. This was the problem and he hadn't known how to say it. But Ben was chattering on as he picked up the stool and put it back by the dresser. 'So, thinking on that, I've news I was waiting to tell yer both.' He was struggling to sound casual. 'I've sold a crossword to the magazine and Mr Halford says I can do more. I divint want to tell yer in case ... Well, in case nowt happened. That Mr Halford says it's good for lads to set 'em for the children's column.' His smile was so wide by the time he'd finished, Stan thought it would split the lad's face.

Stan rose and went to him. He picked him up, turned him upside down while he struggled, then turned him back the right way, giving him a grand hug. 'Yer're a right canny lad, you are, Ben Hall, and I'm proud of yer, and our da would be, an' all.'

Annie was holding out her arms. 'Come and give yer mam a kiss for I'm so proud I could burst. But you're both forgetting while you're sorting out Stan's pay that I'm getting money for the rugs, and for the work with the bairns at the Hall. If Franny can help, that'll do nicely, so stop yer mithering, Stanhope Hall. It's high time you wed yer girl. That copper wire'll be getting dull as ditchwater soon. They might well not send a married lass hither and yonder either, so it'd be good if Fran could wed Davey soon an' all. I know I said it were too early, but . . .'

Ben said from the kitchen table, where he'd fled after giving his mam a kiss, 'But Davey's miles away.'

Stan was sitting again, looking from one to the other, for his little brother and mam were talking away like two old hens, putting the problem to rest. At last he said, 'Howay, Davey hasn't even given our Fran a piece of copper wire on her finger.'

His mam said quietly, 'He doesn't have to, them two have been together since they were born. They'll get wed when time permits, I reckon, and for now all's well, for the lasses will be back, aye, that they will.'

They sat on, all three of them, as the wind whistled, shrieked and crashed around their house. Finally they headed for bed, Stan and Ben to the attic they shared, his mam to her double bed, alone. Before they slept, each of them, separately, thought of the wedding and smiled, for it was good news, nice news, happy news.

It was in the early hours that the battering of the wind penetrated Stan's sleep, banging and banging a gate somewhere. He checked his watch: three in the morning. He cursed and Ben woke. 'A door must be unlatched. Who's getting up, our Stan? Well, 'tisn't me. You're the man of the family, and I'm just a wee bairn.'

Stan lay there, drugged with tiredness. 'Bugger,' he muttered, finally getting out of bed and dragging a blanket round him. 'And shut yer noise, bairn. In days gone by you'd be scunning up chimneys earning your keep, not writing fancy crosswords. Gone to yer head, it has.'

Ben's snigger followed him down the attic ladder. Their mam's door opened. 'I'll sort it, Mam,' said Stan. 'Just something banging.'

'Not something, lad,' said his mam. 'Someone – at the front door, an' all.'

Stan realised that she was right. The front door? He took the stairs two at a time. That door was only used in an emergency, or for someone like the Massinghams. Behind him came Ben and then his mam, who said, her voice strong and firm, 'Stand aside. I will answer.'

Mrs Annie Hall opened the front door and there on the step was the telegraph boy, the wind pulling at his uniform, but he wasn't a boy, he was a middle-aged man. In the war, the other war, they had all been boys. It was a boy who came to her mam's front door that night, a mere lad who had handed over the buff envelope in 1917 and hurried away, for he had delivered too many, far too many, and knew what they contained.

Her mam had not flinched; she had brought the telegram into the kitchen, unread, telling her daughter to sit at the table. Annie had sat while her mam read out the words that seemed to drop heavy and slow, words that told them with regret that Stanhope Hall, Annie's brother and her parents' son, was dead. 'He were nineteen and died a hero,' her mam had said. 'But he were always a hero to me, you and yer da,' she had added, and made a pot of tea, refusing help.

Silently, Annie, all of eighteen and just married, had watched her as she brought the kettle to the boil and her world became dark and cold. She had counted as her mam spooned tea into the pot from the caddy – three teaspoons, more than usual. She watched as Mam had poured on the water, and as she stood while it mashed, her mam's hand had gripped the brass towel rail so hard her knuckles showed white, even in the dull light of the oil lamp. Mam had poured two cups of tea, leaving the third empty, and had said, 'That's fer our canny Stan, to see him on his way, so he knows he's not forgot.'

Annie had sat, weeping, breathing in her mam's strength, growing tall in it, expanding to be like her, and finally they had talked of Stanhope, and how he had started as a putter, pushing the trolleys, and ended up one of Massingham's best hewers. They talked of Joe at the front, and her mam said, 'There'll be no more deaths in our family, for one per war is enough, and I'll not be having it.'

Her mam had been right, in that war. But this was a different one.

Annie Hall only knew that she'd been staring when the telegraph man said, 'Annie, here yer are, and I remember I brought your brother's an' all, when I were a sight younger.'

He tipped his telegraph uniform cap and cycled off into he gale. She called, making sure her voice was strong, 'Thank you.'

Chapter Twenty-Two

Annie Hall held the telegram to her, seeing nothing, though the gale tore at her dressing gown and screeched down the terrace. It could only be Fran. Franny. Precious Franny Hall. Sister of Stan. Of Ben. Fran who was to marry Davey. Annie gripped the telegram, pressing it harder and harder against her heart.

She did as her mam had and turned, to see Stan and Ben on the stairs. She walked to the kitchen and opened the vents on the range, placed the kettle on the plate and said as she heard the two boys enter, 'Sit. I'll mek a cuppa.'

She turned and opened the telegram. She read it, then said, 'Our Franny has been injured in an accident and transferred to Glasgow Royal Infirmary.'

Her voice was as steady as her mam's had been, and it was because Fran was alive, injured, but alive. She wondered yet again, as she had done over the years, how her mam had been so very brave. She looked from Stan to Ben, both of whom were shocked, silenced, confused. Ben shouted, 'But alive, she's bliddy alive, our Fran is.'

Annie nodded, turned to the range and swallowed before reaching for the caddy. 'We'll have fresh tea leaves, so we will, for we have plans to mek.'

She put two spoons into the pot, her vision blurred, but no tears would fall. She would be like her mam, who had stayed strong.

Stan was standing now, pale as a statue. 'Sarah?' he whispered.

Annie said without turning, 'Yer get dressed and out to Maud Bedley, Stan. Check and see if they've had one an' all. Then there's Davey to be—'

She was interrupted by a pounding at the back door. Ben flew to it, while Stan stared as though the door held the world's worst secrets. Perhaps it did. Stan clutched his blanket around himself as Maud Bedley entered.

'Did you get a telegram, our Annie?'

Annie held it up. 'Fran's injured.'

'Then they're in hospital together.' The two women looked steadily at one another, and as far as anyone would think, they were waiting to cross a road.

Annie said, 'That's all reet then. Tek a chair, our Maud. Then we'll sort out what's to be done now, and what's to be left till morning.'

Stan was still standing, even paler.

Annie said softly, 'Best get yer clothes on, Stan and our Ben, for the pair of you prancing about in yer pyjama bottoms and blankets as we telephone the hospital from the phone box isn't going to be the best sight in t'world. Now, our Maud, do you feel you need just a tiny nip, as 'tis a difficult time?' She pointed to the top of the dresser, then at Maud. 'I know you still need it,' she said, 'though 'tis better, and you're to be praised for that.'

All the while she was speaking she was thinking that if the news of her daughter didn't stop her marrer, nothing would.

Stan waited by the kitchen door and looked from Maud to Annie, puzzled, and then the realisation broke, and he stood straight, the anger visible in his face and in the bracing of his shoulders.

Annie's words echoed in Maud's head while her face showed that she knew the truth of Maud's lies. Maud looked at Stan and recognised his shock. She swung back

287

to Annie, and saw her friend's need for an answer as she stood full square, the tea scoop steady in her hand. Time seemed to stand still. There was only the faint hiss of the range, the click of the clock's second hand, and Maud knew that today, this minute, was one of the most important in her life.

Annie waited for her answer. Maud felt the power of her own disgust at herself, at her pain that Sarah was hurt, at her lies. At last, long last, she really felt it.

She looked at Stan again. 'Aye, lad, you have every right to be angry that I, Sarah's mam, have been lying, that you were hurt trying to sort our Norris and I have still bought from him after that.'

She stared at Annie, parched. She looked at the bottle of elderberry wine on top of the dresser, which was where they'd kept the booze in her own house until she, Maud Bedley, had hidden it behind the netty. The netty, for God's sake. But, aye, that's how drunks behaved.

She sighed. Well, Maud Bedley, what else are thee? That's what I'd like to know.

Still everyone stood, still the range hissed, the clock clicked.

She said, 'My Sarah's in hospital, hurt, perhaps dying. What have I been thinking? Where has me head been, and what about me heart?'

No one answered. She went on, her voice rasping because the call of the drink was strong and it had dried her mouth. 'Yes, I feel I need a drink, our Annie. I 'spect I'll always feel I need a drink, but I'm never, ever having another. Never, for 'tis time to stop pretending, to meself, to everyone. 'Tis time for it all to stop. My poor wee bairn is hurt, but I've hurt her an' all, in her heart, even more'n her body. I lost meself, but it's over, right now. Finished, done with.'

Annie merely added another spoon of tea leaves to the

pot as the steam sang in the kettle. She poured the water into the pot of tea, turned and said, 'I'm proud of you, Maud. Proud.'

Again, they looked at one another, and the years of friendship laid down the rules. It was over, the lies, the drink, the self-pity. They nodded, for Annie saw again the steel in Maud that had been lost. Stan saw it too, and his shoulders relaxed. Maud clenched her hands. 'Aye, well, 'tis all over. It's the bairns that are important.'

'Beth?' asked Annie.

'She's gone on round to Audrey, saying her mam'd want to be here with us. Not sure she'll come out into this gale with a smile on her face, though.'

Annie brought the teapot over to the table, while Maud brought cups from the scullery, concentrating on the shine on their rims, not the dryness of her mouth. Ben was still sitting at the table, looking from one to the other, tugging at his pyjamas, then leapt to his feet, shouting, 'You're both wittering on, then getting bliddy tea to drink. Don't you bliddy care our girls are hurt? Don't you want to see them?'

Annie ruffled his hair, but he pushed her hand away. She said, 'Howay, our lad, we care, but if'n our lasses'd been dreadfully cut about, the telegram'd have said in all likelihood get here quick, or words to that effect, and by now we'd be running along t'road on our way to Glasgow town. So instead we need to be strong and mek a plan, so we'll sit and work out how to telephone the infirmary to find out what's to do, and then do it, quick as a wink, if t'news is worse than we fear.'

There was a silence, and then Stan answered from the doorway, 'Aye, we can find the number from the operator. She'll know.'

The women pushed across a cup. Maud ordered, 'You

two bairns get yourselves changed.' They went, and the women sipped, saying nothing, just smiling at one another. There was a rush of feet on the stairs and both returned, dressed after a fashion, the clothes slung on them both. Stan came to the table and sipped his tea. He wore his after-work clothes and a muffler. 'Davey?' asked Maud.

Ben looked up from his tea, calm now, learning to be strong. 'They'll be on shifts where he is, bet yer. So, why don't we telephone Mr Massingham? He'll know who we should call at the main place, because he knows everything. Or Davey told me we could telephone the Foreign Office, or summat like that, if there was a coal fall. Or we can tele-graph the landlady, because he whispered her address, didn't he mam? Where'd you put it? But Mrs Wotsher-name's lad's been ill so I'm not sure if we should.'

Audrey and Beth came in then without knocking. Both were windswept and snow-covered. Audrey said to Ben, 'Shove over, lad, and Beth, fetch up another chair for yer-self, or tek the armchair. Stan, don't just sit there like a gormless Gertie, fetch a couple of cups, if yer please.'

Stan looked around the table. 'You're a bliddy nightmare, you women.'

'Language,' said Beth, bringing over another chair, then whispering to Ben, 'Howay, lad, what news?'

He pointed to the women. 'They said if we needed to get in a stress the telegram'd have said to get there quick, so they're planning what's to do. Meks sense.'

As the women downed their tea and worked out how to pay for the fares once they'd made their call, Stan wondered who to talk to about time off. Ben would need a letter for school if he came too. There was another knock, but at the back door again. Beth snatched a look at the clock. 'By, it's three forty in the morning, for heaven's sake. Anyone'd think it was Newcastle Town Moor fair day.'

'Sid or Norm?' queried Stan.

'They'd not have heard yet, even in Massingham, and they'd be in by now, stamping about,' muttered Ben, pulling a face at Stan. 'Got no more manners than you, Stan.'

Annie answered the door. 'Mrs Massingham, what—'

'No, it's Sophia, remember. And Reginald is here too. What we're doing is seeing what we can do to help. Heavens, the co-op's helped me so much recently, it's fair do's.'

'Mebbe a cuppa for you both?' Maud asked.

Ben sighed. 'Shouldn't we be phoning the hospital?'

Stan nodded. 'In a minute.' He slipped through to the scullery, coming back with two more cups.

'And here's me still in me dressing gown,' muttered Annie.

Stan opened the hall door. 'Why not go and change, Mam, while we chat to . . .' He trailed off.

Sophia grinned and sat on Annie's chair, while Stan pointed to his own. Reginald sat, putting his homburg on his lap.

'But how did you . . . ?' asked Mrs Bedley.

'Know?' answered Sophia, her own green velvet hat scrunched in her hand, her hair awry. 'I happen to know Donald the telegraph "boy".' She paused and smiled. 'All to do with both of us working with the evacuees. He knows I'd want to know immediately if he delivered bad news to any of the co-op. I had the temerity to telephone the hospital and was told that no one is critical, but of course, no details. Those are for your ears.'

By the time Annie returned, plans were afoot to deliver them by car to Newcastle station to work their way cross-country by train. 'So, Alfie will pick up Stan, Ben and Annie from here, and Beth and Mrs Bedley from the Bedleys'. If necessary, some will have to sit on the others' laps. We happen to know there is a train you can take if you leave here at 4.30.' It was Sophia orchestrating things, while Reginald Massingham looked on, nodding.

While Maud filled in Annie with the news that no one was critical, Mr Massingham wrote down the number of the hospital on the back of his business card. He would put in a call to one of his friends, Professor Smythe, who knew everyone worth knowing who could facilitate any situation. Plans would be made to make sure that Davey knew all the ins and outs where he was posted, and to pass on the infirmary's number too. The ways and means of his arrival in Glasgow would be sorted.

Sophia stood. 'And now we'll leave, while you call the infirmary for details and let them know that you are on your way, though I imagine that a cavalry charge such as the combined Halls, Bedleys and Smiths is more than enough to gain admittance, night or day. It just so happens, though, that the redoubtable Sister Newsome, as she was when she looked after Davey at the Royal Victoria Infirmary after the roof fall, is now married to the equally redoubtable Dr Wilson, who has contacts here and there. Reginald will therefore be in touch with him just to clear a way. Isn't that right, darling?'

Reginald Massingham stood and with a wink at Stan said, 'If you say so, my dear, it will be done, as usual, and one wonders if we should call Sister Newsome by her married name?'

Sophia raised her eyebrows at Annie, who was watching the exchange with glee, for Mr Massingham didn't stand a chance, and what's more he knew it. How Fran would be laughing. Her heart seemed to stop. Franny. She must phone the hospital, immediately. She had to know exactly what the situation was. She looked across at the range, suddenly seeing her mam. She sat again. They had the number; they had a plan arrived at while she dressed. It was not just up to her.

Sophia continued: 'Tickets for the train journey will be waiting at the station. If you need to stay there for a few days, let us know so we can help. If we don't know, we can't do much, can we? But this standing about won't do, Reginald, so do come along, we must head back and release cook, who has left her apartment door open to hear if any of the children wake.'

She headed for the door. Reginald Massingham followed, but stopped halfway. 'Thank you kindly for the tea, and try not to worry. I feel that though your daughters might be bloodied, they will be unbowed, and with all of you in their corner, how can they not be well soon?'

At that, they stepped out into the gale. It was only when they reached the gate that the Halls, Bedleys and Smiths galvanised themselves to rush to the door, and in a hushed voice so as not to wake the neighbours, Annie called, 'How can we thank you?'

Mr Massingham hesitated, then half whispered back, 'There is no need, I am forever in your debt for making the life and work of my wife considerably easier.' He started to shut the gate behind him, then reappeared. 'Of course, if you should happen to trip over some young woman who would like the role of nanny in our household, I would be grateful. At least then Sophia might get a few undisturbed nights and so might I, which is something that quite appeals to me, if I am honest. Stan, I'll sort your leave of absence. Perhaps you'd drop a note in to your marrers, just for old Elliott's files. A stickler for paperwork, but then a manager should be.'

This time he left, and Stan waited a moment, then shut the door, pushing hard against the wind, while Annie Hall said, 'For two pins I'd put our girls up for the job if it kept them close at hand and away from – well, whatever it is they do.'

Maud Bedley and Audrey Smith joined her, their hands gripping one another's. 'Coats on, ladies, and out into the storm. We've a phone call to make.'

Chapter Twenty-Three

Fran awoke and stared around. It was so light. Where was she? Too light – had she died? A cool hand touched her wrist, a woman in a white cap leaned over her. 'There you are, Miss Frances Hall. Back again, and you don't know where you are, do you?' Fran just stared, her eyelids so heavy, her arm hurting, her ribs, her head, everything. The woman smiled. 'Well, you're at the Glasgow Royal Infirmary, in our capable hands, and have just been in the operating theatre where a rather difficult broken lower arm has been nailed together and a badly behaved shoulder has been sorted out.'

Fran followed her words. Nailed? The woman laughed. 'I'm Sister Morris, and "nailed" always gets some attention. But let's just say mended like the leg of a chair.'

'Then don't let anyone sit on me,' Fran murmured.

Sister Morris roared with laughter. 'Oh, you'll do. I was led to expect this from Dr Wilson, who telephoned through. He looked after your man Davey, apparently.' Sister Morris was checking her watch, which was pinned to her uniform, her fingers still on Fran's wrist.

'Davey? Where's Sarah? Viola? The others?'

'Later, wee lassie. That can all wait till later, but yer family is on its way, and if my phone doesn't stop ringing asking for news of one or the other of you, I will have tae lie in a darkened room. There's a Mr Swinton who was on, and a Mr Bolton, not to mention a Miss Ellington . . . And a Mr Massingham . . . I canna go on – too many.' Sister Morris patted her hand, letting her watch fall against her breast. 'Aye, nice steady pulse, and the pills will help the pain, though I daresay a nice malt whisky might also help . . .'

She moved to the next bed. Fran turned her head slightly and there was Sarah, watching Fran, her head on her pillow, mucky blonde hair lying on the pristine white pillowcase, and she was smiling.

'Howay, Franny. We got out – or Simon, Roy and the others got us out. You've not long been back from surgery. I've just had me cuts sluiced and stitched. Not as neat as the stitching after Mam's wallops, but they'll do. The load squashed a lung or somesuch, but it's all right now, and I've a few stitches on me ribcage where they shoved something in or pulled something out to get the lung working. I canna remember what they said.'

Fran smiled back, feeling some pain, but not too much, and the plaster on her arm felt strange. Perhaps people would sign it as they had signed Davey's when his leg was broken in the pit. Would they be as rude?

Sarah grinned. 'Probably not, they're not pitmen here.'

So, Fran had spoken aloud. 'Viola?' she whispered.

Sarah whispered back, 'I divint know, yet. And she has no one coming. No one to tell, so we're the lucky ones, Franny, because from what Sister Morris said, the bliddy cavalry is on its way, from all points of the compass.'

'Davey?'

'Oh aye, so says Sister Morris, who I think is from the same womb as Sister Newsome. She's expecting 'em all: yer mam, my mam, Mrs Bedley, Ben, Beth – but Beth's going straight back, owes it to the Factory, to Swinton – Stan and Uncle Tom Cobley an' all.'

Fran smiled, for Davey was coming, and Mam, Ben and Stan too. She asked again, 'But we need to know about Viola.'

Sarah tried to sit up, failed, and instead called, 'Sister Morris, is Viola back from surgery yet?'

Sister Morris, who had been checking the clipboard hooked onto the bottom of the bed next to Fran's, nodded, a finger to her lips, another pointing at the patient. It was only then the girls realised it was Viola, lying so still, so pale, her hair shorn on one side, her skin scorched. Fran lifted her hand towards Sarah. 'Oh no,' she whispered.

Davey and Daniel spread the usual dab of margarine on their toast, drank the weak tea and talked of Daisy, and the eggs they would take to her today. They'd tell her to ask her landlady to whisk them up for an omelette this evening. 'At least she's stopped being sick,' Daniel whispered, for Daisy was still hiding her ever-increasing bump and thought she was almost eight months.

'Aye, and she's less grumpy, but your da still hasn't found a place, has he?'

There was a knock on the front door, and Mrs Siddely was heard heading for it, muttering that she'd paid the milkman on Friday as usual.

Daniel sank his teeth into his toast. 'He will. He always does, and we'll tell her that, again.' He sighed, then looked up at Davey. 'How did we come to be mother hens, anyway?'

Davey laughed as Mrs Siddely came into the dining room, pale and worried. 'Davey, come into the hall, please, right now.'

'Oy, oy,' called Martin. 'You've been a bad boy from the sound of it, laddo.'

'Do be quiet, Martin,' snapped Mrs Siddely, turning on her heel.

Daniel looked from the doorway to Davey, confused. Davey gripped the napkin and hurried into the hall, his mind racing. Had she heard of Daisy and misunderstood. 'Yes?'

Mrs Siddely pulled him into the kitchen, a place that was normally out of bounds. 'Sit down.' He did. She drew the telegram from her apron pocket. 'It's just arrived.'

Davey just looked at it, not understanding. She said, 'Read it, lad. Little wretches in buff envelopes don't open themselves.' She was scrabbling in her pocket again and drew out a packet of Woodbines, lit one and placed it in Davey's mouth. 'Go on, read it. We won't know what's what until you do, and until we do, we can't do anything about it.'

Now at last Davey's mind caught up with events. Fran? Sarah? The Factory? Stan? The pit? Mam? The drink? He tore it open and read it. And then again. Fran and Sarah. It was Franny, his love; Sarah, his sister.

'Right, lad, bad news. Let me have a dekko.' Mrs Siddely took the telegram from his limp hand, scanned it, then lit a cigarette for herself. 'Right you are. Up you go, pack a few things. It says a taxi has been arranged to get you to the station.' A quick glance at the clock showed he had ten minutes.

'Quick, quick. The Park has been told, it says. And it puts the times of trains. You've got money? And you're lucky, for you've certainly got friends.'

Davey was taking the stairs two at a time on his way to the bedroom. 'Yes, enough. Yes I have. Please tell Daniel an' all.'

There was no need because Daniel was in the hallway, talking to Mrs Siddely. Colin and Martin had taken up position at the gate to wait for and hold the taxi. Daniel called after them, 'Throw yourselves in front of it, if necessary.'

'Bugger off,' shouted Colin.

A mother passing with two young children bound for school tutted.

Within half an hour Davey was on the train. It would take hours, and all the while his Fran was hurt, and Sarah

298

too, though neither was critical. What the hell did that mean? Not critical, but hurt. The girls were hurt. Poor Beth, it was her marrers. The thought stopped him short. Yes, poor Beth, poor mams, poor bliddy everyone, but especially his Fran and Sarah. His heart ached for them. Could 'not critical' change to 'critical'? They weren't pitmen, they were girls. He leaned back, listening to the wheels rumbling over the tracks, thinking of Fran and remembering everything about her. And as he did he settled into himself, for of course his Fran might not be a pitman, but she was a good match for any one who was, and . . . and . . .

He sat now, reading his newspaper as the wheels drummed along the tracks. Though the Japanese were having things all their own way, he read that the Germans were still in retreat as Stalin counter attacked. There was also a small piece about the December success of the British in North Africa being put down to the Germans running out of ammunition, though that problem must have been solved as Rommel was into his stride again, and firmly on the attack. So, their munitions workers had been chivvied up, had they? Well, they're not the only ones, he wanted to shout out to the world.

He listened to the clickety-click of the wheels over the points, and they chimed with the clickety-click of the decoding machines. He felt despair wash over him. Fran. Sarah. Fran, Sarah. Yes, maybe they weren't critical, but they'd bliddy go back into it all, because that's the sort of girls they were, so there was no end in sight.

In the infirmary Sarah was sitting up against banked pillows, looking at the clock again and picking at the starched sheets, so different to her own stemming-stained ones, and Beth's. Beth had said on one of their calls that she'd been put back there because Mr Swinton had said she needed a break from the more dangerous work. He'd sent Mrs Oborne into the sewing section.

Beth had ended with, 'He still seems so changed, so, well, almost nice. I thought it might fade, but it hasn't. I wonder if your da's and Mr Hall's funerals made him think he might go to hell unless he got a bit of a sprint on to try and get into heaven.' Fran had been squashed into the phone box too and all three had laughed, but kindly.

Sarah found herself staring at nothing, because she couldn't hold a thought, or a memory. Sister Morris had said it was the shock or the anaesthetic, or she was just going daft. Sarah grinned. Sister Morris and Sister Newsome were so similar it helped her and Fran feel safe. She looked around the ward. There were eleven other patients apart from the three of them. Some were young, some old, some in between. None were from the factory, for those not badly hurt had gone home; another had died at the hospital. That was Deirdre. So far they had lost Fiona, Deirdre, the new girl and the security officer. She couldn't stop seeing Fiona's and Deirdre's faces and didn't want to doze, for then she heard their voices too.

Fran asked Sister Morris, who was checking their charts, when they could go home.

'Not until you're tip-top enough to be transferred to Sister Newsome's tender care,' she said.

Sarah laughed when Fran of course grimaced and muttered, 'I don't remember much about her care being tender.'

To which Sister Morris, now busy tucking in Fran's sheet, said, 'I'll tell her that, and let's see what she has to say about it, shall we?'

Fran begged and begged her not to, but Sister Morris sailed off down the ward, calling back that it would depend on how angelic her behaviour became. Sarah could imagine Beth's face at that thought, and wondered if she would have yellow skin when she came today. Beth, dear Beth, who had looked after her mam. How could she ever have thought the worst of either her marrer or the man she loved?

She had kept the letter her mam had written telling her that Beth had been a pillar of strength and Stan had barely any cause to call on them now, because she was so much better. Yes, those were her mam's words, but Sarah wasn't sure what 'so much better' meant. She wasn't actually saying that she had stopped? But of course she had, she must have done, for no one had told her otherwise. Perhaps it needed someone outside the family to help sort it all out? She smiled at the thought of her mam and Beth, together as a team, bridging the generations. Just imagine.

Fran called, 'What's that smile for, bonny lass?' only to be hushed by Sister Morris, who pointed to Viola. Worry overwhelmed Sarah, for although the drugs were wearing off and the pain was biting, she hadn't lost one side of her hand. The machine had crushed Viola's. Neither was she burned, scorched a bit, as they all were, but not burned like the lass.

She eased herself on the pillows. She'd broken a rib. She now knew she was also stitched across her back, but she'd be fine, Nurse Rogers had said this morning as she took her pulse for the hundredth time. Yes, she hurt, but she was alive, and Beth, Stan and her mam were coming. She realised with a start that she'd put her friend before the others.

At six o clock the visitors started streaming in, and as they did so Viola stirred at last. Nurse Rogers left her chair at the nurses' table in the centre of the ward and was by her bedside in a flash, taking her pulse and listening to her chest. She called Nurse Standing to help her sit Viola up a little. They helped her to drink water from something that looked like a teapot.

'Och, that's a good drink for a wee lassie,' Nurse Standing almost crooned.

Viola smiled weakly, whispering, 'I'd rather have a beer.'

The two nurses laughed as they eased her back down onto the two pillows. Nurse Standing said, 'No sitting up just yet. But soon.'

Nurse Rogers smoothed the sheet and tucked it in, saying, 'Sister Morris warned me about the other two, but said nothing about you being of the same ilk, madam.'

Viola turned her head a little and Sarah waved, Fran too. The hand Viola raised was bandaged, seeping blood, and only half what it should be. Nurse Standing supported the injured hand. 'Best not to move it yet.'

Viola muttered something. Nurse Standing and Nurse Rogers looked at one another. It was Nurse Standing who said, 'Och, I think you'll have more than enough fingers tae make rude signs, and if not, you'll use your other hand. You factory girls are as tough as old boots, that you are.'

Fran and Sarah heard Viola say, 'So some are left, and how much of my hand?'

Nurse Morris traced a line on her own left hand. 'Are you right-handed?' she asked Viola. Viola nodded. 'Then you're fine and dandy. You'll be able to write love letters. Would you like me to tell you why it had to be removed?'

Viola waited for a moment. 'Two times two is four,' she said, as though her mind had wandered somewhere else.

The two nurses looked around, about to call for Sister Morris, who was talking to a patient's parents at the end of the ward. Sarah called out, 'She's building her strength. Give her a moment. It's what we did, under—'

'It's what you showed us to do, bonny lass,' Fran called. 'I reckon it kept us going, and it took us somewhere else, for a minute, anyway.'

Sister Morris was leading the parents of the patient at

the end of the ward out to her office. The mother was weeping. Sarah watched, relieved it wasn't any of the factory girls, but even so, the end bed held someone's lass. Perhaps the lass was dying? She didn't want to know. Instead she concentrated on Viola, who was saying, her voice stronger now, 'Aye, well, Roy and Simon warned me when they cleared the rubble from me that it were the machine that were trapping me hand and stopping me from moving, but they also said that the bliddy lump of metal had stopped me bleeding fit to die. I'm a lucky lass, so I am, and that's what Roy said an' all . . .'

Fran peered from Viola to Sarah, for this was gumption and even Mrs Oborne would be impressed. As the visitors began in earnest, Fran replied to Viola, 'Aye, so you are, bliddy lucky, because you have us as your marrers. What more do you want?'

Viola looked at them now and smiled. 'Nowt, for we three made it, at least.'

'Oh aye, reckon the three of us charging the pearly gates were a bit too much for St Peter, but sweet lass, you had the worst of it,' Fran called.

Viola was touching her hair and bandages now, but Nurse Standing drew her hand away. 'Never fear, most will grow back. It's what we call a superficial burn—'

Sarah laughed as Fran called out, 'It might be superficial to you, Nurse Standing, but I reckon it feels like a mighty big 'un to our lass.'

'Ignore your friend,' Nurse Standing went on, 'she's all mouth and no trousers. We had to cut those off.' Viola was smiling. The nurse continued. 'What doesn't grow, you can hide using the rest of your auburn locks, eh? Now, best close those eyes for a while. You've had a big operation. Sleep while you can for these other two can talk the hind leg off a donkey.'

But Viola was already asleep and not long after that the Massingham contingent arrived, dishevelled and creased from the journey. It had been long, with frequent changes and fussing on the tracks, or so the girls heard as Sister Morris met them in the doorway, insisting on two at a time.

Stan and Mrs Bedley surged into the ward, heading for Sarah, with Stan waving across to Fran. Annie Hall and Ben headed for Fran, with Mrs Hall calling, 'Davey'll be here soon and let this be a lesson to you girls. You'll go into the office or I'll swing for you. Audrey's staying to support the co-op at Massingham Hall and Beth's in work. Poor old beggar Swinton's juggling staff, looking too tired to stay on his feet, and our Beth offered to stay.'

Sarah and Stan smiled at one another as he gripped her hand while her mam sat on the other side, stroking her hair. Stan muttered, kissing her forehead, 'Aye, I can't go through this again, lass, nor can your mam. What d'yer reckon, Mrs Bedley?'

Sarah looked at her mam, who was calm and did not smell of the drink, and whose eyes were tired. 'Howay, lad. She'll do as she pleases, whether she's to become Mrs Hall the second on the first of March or not.'

Sarah laughed out loud. 'The first of March?'

Her mam patted her arm. 'Oh aye, it were all decided on the journey here, the food an' all. Just need Reverend Walters to read the banns and his sister to find some flowers and we're there, even if you say no and we have to shove you up the aisle. But I reckon yer'll probably run, eh? Now I'm off to sit wi' that poor lass, Viola, who Sister Morris whispered has no one to visit her and no home, and a burned scalp, and half an ear, which as she said, is a sight more than Van Gogh was left with. All that, as well as no home. Well, we canna have it, that we can't. She's to come to Massingham, if she wants to. Miss Ellington said Swinton said she could. But mebbe she can't work in the factory if she's bad hurt?'

Her mam bustled off and Sarah watched her while Stan kissed the back of her hand. 'She's back to being me mam,' Sarah whispered.

Stan grinned. 'Oh aye, took a bit of time. She got better bit by bit, and I'll tell you now, Beth helped, by did that girl help, but it were you being hurt that I reckon's really hit the nail on the head.' He moved his chair closer. 'How do you really feel about the first of March?'

Feeling the tightness of his grip and seeing the anxiety on his face, a face that was so dear, so tired, so embedded with coal, and still healing from the bashing Norris had given him, she said, 'I'll have to give it some thought, lad. I have so many princes hacking their way through the briars to tek me away from all this, a lass's spoilt for choice.'

He laughed, loud and long, then kissed her lips, saying against them, 'Yer seem different, more . . .' He sat back down.

She was the one to kiss his hand now. 'Oh, I reckon being stuck under a heap of bricks gives yer time to grow up, eh? But you must know, for you've been caught under coal yerself.'

They shared a long hard look, and knew that at last they understood one another's worlds. 'So,' she said, 'the first of March will be a good day, eh? Bit scratched by the briars, are yer? Well, mebbe I'll just have to kiss 'em better.'

She lay back on the pillows, thinking not just of their future life together, but of the road her mam had had to travel to stop drinking completely. Did she believe she had really stopped? She had to, for there had been real love in her mam's eyes. She smiled, at peace.

Chapter Twenty-Four

Mrs Bedley sat beside Viola's bed, touching her arm, her heart breaking at the sight of the seeping bandage on the lass's damaged hand. 'Poor bairn,' she whispered. 'When will this bliddy war end? Why did that madman tramp his bliddy great boots and thugs into all those countries which were minding their own damn business?'

Viola murmured, 'Who knows, but he did, and we have to fight him and his thugs . . .' She faded.

Mrs Bedley was startled, for she'd thought Viola was sleeping. She stood and eased Viola's pillows a little, being careful with her poor bandaged head. She swallowed, stroking the girl's cheek. 'Aye, well, you've done yer fighting for the moment, precious bairn.'

'My mam used to call me that,' Viola whispered.

'Well, I'm Sarah's mam, and so I've a mind to call her friends that an' all.' She sat again. 'And how are you, inside yerself, bonny lass?'

Viola just looked at her for a moment, and then said, 'I were buried before, with me mam and da. They died, I didn't, and this time I didn't but them others did. So I'm lucky.'

Mrs Bedley's confusion must have shown, for Viola explained, 'You see, we got caught in the bombing in Newcastle, so being buried weren't such a change, but howay, I don't want a third go at it, that's for certain.' Viola tried to lift her injured hand, but gave up and, using her right hand, gestured towards her burned head. 'Me ear hurts, really hurts, more'n me scalp. Best they cut it off like they did part of me hand. I'll have to tell them.'

Mrs Bedley looked around for a nurse. What should you tell a patient, if the nurses hadn't?'

Viola said, 'If they did, then—' She stopped as Mrs Bedley bit on her lip. 'Tell me,' Viola whispered.

Maud wished she hadn't come over, wished it wasn't her who had to tell the bairn. She needed a nip in the face of all this. Her mouth was dry, and she wanted to run out and find some. But she gripped her hands and, looking from Viola's hand to her ear, said, 'It's . . .' She stopped, swallowing.

'Tell me, please, if you're me friend's mam, for me own mam would.'

Maud Bedley would rather have faced a million Hitlers or a trillion Norrises, but she held Viola's arm, well clear of the bandages, and leaned towards her. 'Remember that you have beautiful hair that can cover the burn while your scalp heals.'

Viola nodded. 'But?'

'Aye, there's a but, for it'll have to do a bit more of a job, for the top . . . no . . . half your ear is gone. What's hurting, I suppose, is where the machine cut into it, but not your head. Aye, it could have been your noddle, but, well . . .' Maud was squeezing the girl's arm. 'You'll live, you'll have a future. You three are survivors, and that's saying summat big.'

Viola muttered, 'Three times two is six, four times two is eight.'

Mrs Bedley stared at her, remembering: her bairn, on the floor, and the pain in Maud's hand from the blow that had put her there, and that wee voice saying, 'One times two is two, two times two is four.' Yes, it was all clear as day, as it had not been before. She drew in a deep breath, for her shame knew no bounds, and she sat back on the visitor's chair more determined than ever not to drink.

Viola had reached 'Six times two is twelve.' Then she breathed deeply and murmured, 'Sarah said she learned this when she were young, to take her away from what was happening, and glad she had to an' all, she said, because under the bricks it kept us calm. And one day she'd tell whoever it was who made her need it that it saved us, and made her strong.' Viola swallowed. 'Have you a handbag mirror, Mrs Bedley? For I'm ready to see me face.'

Maud was staring at but not seeing her. She was winding back the words and listening again. She wanted to rush to Sarah and hold her. But this one here, with the auburn hair and grey eyes, had need of her, so this was not the time to be considering her own affairs. But she hesitated to dig in her bag for the mirror. What if it was too much of a shock? Should she ask the nurse?

'Don't be afeared for me, Mrs Bedley,' said Viola. 'You say the times table and it'll keep yer calm and strong, so if I need help you can be there, eh?'

Maud dug in her handbag and she did indeed think of the two times table as she drew out the mirror, saying, 'Are you sure?'

Viola nodded. 'If you stay by my side?'

'Oh aye, for as long as yer need me, I'll be here, at your side, till the sky falls in.' Because she hadn't been for Sarah, or Davey, when things were bad. But that was all over.

Viola smiled and reached for the mirror. She looked. Her eyes filled with tears, but they did not drop. She handed back the mirror, then Maud stood and patted her cheeks with her own handkerchief for now the bairn's tears *were* falling. And why the hell shouldn't they?

Reaching up, Viola stayed her hand. 'Let me. You sit. You've come such a long way. I just get silly sometimes. I don't know where I'm to go, you see, to get well.'

Maud smoothed the sheets, but carefully. All the time

308

her mind was racing and finally she said, 'Beth, the girls' marrer, stays with me right now, but will be returning to her home, for 'tis time. And Sarah and Stan will be marrying and we've all decided that'll be on the first of March. They will either stay wi' me or have their own pitman's house, but you will also live wi' me, or us, whichever it is. We have the small bedroom that was Sarah's. If they live with us they will take the front room. Neither I, they, nor any here' – she gestured to the families of the two Massingham girls – 'will have you being alone, and besides, there's always room for another friend for the three girls.'

Viola was lying back on her pillows, exhaustion lining her face, and for a moment Maud wondered if she was asleep, though it didn't matter. She would stay here until someone else was free to take over.

But Viola opened her eyes. 'That'd be reet nice, Mrs Bedley, that'll be really grand, like a dream . . .' She faded, and slept, and still Mrs Bedley sat, for here was someone who needed her help, just as she had needed Beth, Stan, the co-op, Massingham, but most of all Annie Hall. She pulled out her knitting from her bag; it was to be a scarf for Eva, one of the evacuees, whose ears ached in the cold weather.

Her needles clicked, one knit, one pearl, one knit, one pearl, and she watched Viola. She turned to check on the other two from time to time, and soon Davey would come to be with his Fran, and Mrs Hall could sit here with her and watch over Viola. She reached the end of the row, and began another, one knit, one pearl, and it was this that worked for her, as the times table had worked for the girls, but she wouldn't have had her needles under all that lot, so she'd just have designed a pattern. Aye, that's what she would do if the bombs fell or calamity prowled around them all yet again.

She eased her shoulders, but never missed a stitch, and then she heard his footsteps, her son's, and there he was, cap in hand, standing in the opening to the ward. Tiredness drained his colour, his blue eyes were desperate and his blond hair windswept. Though he was now an office worker, he still had his pitman's scars on his forehead and his hands were still hard and strong.

He saw Maud, their eyes met. He started towards her, but Maud nodded towards Fran instead, giving her permission with a smile. Aye, and that was as it should be, Maud thought. But how time was passing; how the bairns were growing up. But they were already grown up, and the mams were no longer needed to kiss a hurt better or make the world right. No, that was for the men to do for the lasses, and the lasses to do for their men.

Davey slowed when he saw Fran leaning back on her stark white pillows, her face almost as pale. Well, pale but with blue bruises and red-stitched wounds, and his heart ached. He saw her plastered arm and remembered the pain of his own mangled leg.

Mrs Hall held his Franny's hand, while Ben stood at the near side of the bed, writing on her plaster. Further along, in the next bed, was his sister, Sarah, with Stan sitting at *her* bedside, gripping her hand, but smiling at Davey. Oh God, how he'd missed them and longed to belong again, longed never to leave his family, his marrers, his Fran, whom he should have protected, somehow.

He edged closer to Fran's bed and then she saw him. She reached out a hand. 'Oh Davey, oh, Davey.'

Ben grinned and stepped away, making room for him. 'Howay, bonny lad, and not before time, but not too much kissing, downright soppy 'tis,' he said as Davey bent to hold Fran and kiss her hair.

Annie Hall was moving away. 'You, Ben Hall, hush. No one wants to listen to your smart-alec remarks.'

Ben tutted and slouched after his mam, grumbling that no one ever wanted to listen to him, but Davey heard the red-haired girl in the bed one along from Fran call in a thready voice, 'Talk to Mrs Bedley and me, Ben. Tell us about your crossword setting. Me da used to do those.' Ben turned on his heel and made his way to her bedside. Davey smiled as he kissed Fran's dark hair again, seeing the shaved bit where her scalp had been stitched.

'Darling lass, if I could take yer pain into meself, I would, you have to know that.'

Fran's reply was a mumble against his coat. He eased her back against the pillows, his heart catching at the deep-set eyes, her scorched scalp on the left side. He touched her cut lips, her swollen cheek and half-closed eye. She smiled. 'Howay, lad, you've cold fingers.'

'Aye well, it's snowing fit to burst, and there're more gales to come, so I'm not bliddy surprised. Best get me mam to knit me some mitts, eh?'

'Aye, and sew 'em on to elastic and run it through yer sleeves so yer don't lose them.' She stopped. 'Or better still, lad, use the elastic for yer drawers, eh?' They were both laughing now, and Fran was wiping her face with the back of her hand, but he leaned across and finished the job with the ends of his scarf. She caught his hand. 'By, lad, it's such a long way to come for such a short time.'

He held her hand gently, as though it was the most fragile thing in the universe, and to him she was, and it broke his heart. 'Mrs Siddely's found some elastic, and now me drawers canna fall down, Franny Hall, but I'll tek it right back out if you divint move to an office. You have to, for I canna stand it.'

Her frown was deep. 'Don't tek on so, Davey. I'm alive,

311

others aren't. This is how we women feel when you're in the pit and being as careful as yer can be. Accidents happen wherever you are, and whatever you're doing.'

He stared at her. 'I've never heard such bliddy rubbish in the whole of me life. Look where you work?'

Fran just smiled at him. 'Aye, and we get to wear trousers.'

'Oy, oy,' shouted Ben from beside Viola's bed. 'She'll be wearing 'em at home an' all at this rate, because they're to be worn at your old Factory an' all, Franny. Or so Beth says. Socks too, she says, nice and warm under them trouser overalls. Dungarees, really.' The lad stood on his tiptoes, peering past Fran's bed to Sarah's. 'You hear that, our Stan. After the first of March you watch our Sarah, she'll be after checking you're behaving, so bossy she'll be. Best get 'em back into a skirt, that's what I say.'

Sister Morris appeared at Viola's bed. 'And you say a mite too much, young sir, and too loudly. Hush, hush, whisper it, eh?'

Davey and Fran laughed as Ben subsided as though he were a balloon that had been punctured. Davey whispered to Fran, 'Has Sister Newsome a sister?'

Fran was laughing quietly. 'Aye, makes yer wonder. Out of the same drawer, I reckon. Best nurses there are, those two. But Davey, how long have you got?'

'I can be here two hours, then I have to get the night train down. It's worth it, but I meant it, Franny, what's to be done? I need you safe, I need you to marry me an' all. What's this first of March they're talking about?' Fran told him. He grinned and called to Stan, who was deep in conversation with Sarah, 'Fancy a double wedding, our Stan?'

Before Stan could answer, Fran waved to him. 'He's joking, our Stan.'

Davey looked hurt and whispered, 'No, I'm not. I want to marry you, soon. I want to know that if this happens again, I have a right to be with you. Don't yer see, we've always known since we were babes that we should be together. Why not a double wedding?'

He was jogging her arm. She winced. He cursed himself, but whispered, 'Why not, Franny? 'Tis time.'

She reached across with her good hand, and he gripped it. She said, 'Who will give Sarah away, eh? You. You can't be standing there with a flower in your lapel, dodging about from her to me, lad. Can you imagine, for Stan would have to give me away, so you'd be tripping over one another and one of you'd end up in plaster again. No, no, let them have their day, and then we'll have ours. How does that sound, for to me it sounds grand.'

'When?' was all Davey said, smoothing back her chestnut hair.

'A month later?' Fran whispered, sounding so tired.

Davey wanted to scoop her up and take her back to Massingham as Sister Morris checked her pulse. Davey said, 'Aye, the first of April it is, then.'

Sister Morris stared from Davey to Fran. 'That's a joke.'

Davey looked up at her. 'A joke?'

Sister Morris grinned. 'I'd make it the second of April if I were you, lad. Remember April Fools' Day? It's on Wednesday this year, and you might well ask how I know that? Well, and I whisper this – we always plan a few surprises for the doctors – and have had our thinking hats on for a while, let me tell you. The second is Thursday so you could get wed and have the weekend for a bit of a honeymoon, all while she's probably still on sick leave, so not bothered by shifts.' She patted Fran's hand, made a note on the chart, and walked off, calling quietly over her shoulder, 'That's my contribution. The rest is up to you two, but quietly if you please, all of you. Visiting finished over half an hour ago.'

It was then they all realised that a different nurse was at the table in the centre of the ward. A doctor entered and beckoned to Sister Morris. They spoke, she nodded, he left and Sister Morris spoke quietly to Stan and Sarah, who nodded and then smiled as though Christmas had come. She moved back to Davey and Fran. 'I should tell you before you go, Davey, as I heard you say you only had a couple of hours – the girls will be transferred to Newcastle Royal Infirmary possibly tomorrow, if not the next day, all being well, of course. We feel it would be best that these two are in their home territory, with everyone around. And Dr Wilson has been on the telephone. It appears Sister Newsome quite welcomes having them under her control.'

She walked on, but was called back by Annie Hall. They talked quietly together, then Sister Morris double-backed to the end of Fran's bed. 'Viola will be transferred with you, for it seems the mothers have decided that she is tae be one of the family, or should I say families? Either way, I gather the Massingham umbrella is to be held over her. That's nice. I'm pleased.'

Davey shook his head as she proceeded to Viola's bed. 'Yes, definitely out of the same drawer as Sister Newsome, or should we call her Wilson?'

Fran was smiling as she said, 'Howay, lad, don't yer fret. She'll tell us soon enough.'

They spent the rest of the two hours planning the wedding, just as they could hear Stan and Sarah doing, but before Davey left, Fran asked, 'And Daisy? Has Daniel's father found a place for her?'

Davey shook his head, adding, 'Better find it soon, or it'll be here. She just seems to be ignoring the whole thing. I

314

reckon Dan and I do more worrying about it than she does, or at least we worry about the bairn.' He reached for her hand, and kissed it. 'Oh Franny, we're lucky, we have one another. Won't you find an office job?'

The shake of her head was enough. 'There's a war on and work to be done,' she said.

Chapter Twenty-Five

The next day the weather turned colder and the gales grew stronger.

Ralph slipped out of the house at dawn, though Sophia called from the landing, 'I thought I heard you, but you're on aft shift, dear Ralph?'

'I know, but I'm restless.' He'd managed a piece of toast, too sick with tension. For the Hall and Bedley girls were hurt, and it was all worse: the dreams, the screams, the guilt.

He tramped across the yard, the wind whipping snow around and over him, and stepped into the quiet of the garage. It was almost warm out of the storm. He'd decided yesterday to go to the village and telephone Tim Swinton to tell him to sod off, he'd changed his mind, he couldn't turn a game into reality, couldn't kill his own people, but he'd been too scared of the consequences, and that disgusted him. A killer and a coward. But why tell Tim? Why not just do something that was harmless, to everyone else? It was only he who might be caught and suffer the consequences.

He started to pull up the hood on the roadster just as Alfie came down from his quarters above the garage. 'Morning, Mr Massingham.' Alfie tipped his cap. Ralph never knew if he was cheeking him or showing respect.

'Morning,' he muttered.

'Off into the storm? It's blowing a lot of snow along with it. Bit late for the fore shift aren't we? Dawn's well broken and you're usually long gone.'

Ralph snapped, 'We're not late, I'm on aft-shift, which is when you'll be here, driving a nice warm car for my father. Whereas I'll be down in the depths helping the war effort, but now I'm just having a bit of a drive, see how she handles in this sort of wind.'

Alfie just shrugged and Ralph hated himself, for the lad couldn't help his club foot, whereas he, Ralph Massingham . . . Ralph closed his eyes, then shook his head. He had to continue to be the Ralph Massingham everyone knew. But what was the lad doing up already?

What Alfie was doing was helping with the hood. 'There you go, sir. Take it easy on the roads. It'll be a bit of peace at least, for the little beggars won't be going to school in this, eh?' He was laughing and for a moment Ralph joined him. It felt so good, so comforting, normal.

Alfie gave a half salute. 'Need a bit of breakfast, then your father will want to be on the road too, I daresay.' He disappeared upstairs again and Ralph backed his car out into the gale, which was blowing even heavier snow before it. As he drove towards the munitions factory, the wipers screeched under the weight of their load and he swallowed.

'For the cause,' Tim had toasted last year at a pub in London. 'It's not a bloody game,' Ralph would yell now. 'You kill, and then it haunts you, and rips you apart, every minute of every day. You can't un-kill. You can't go back.' But would he really have the courage to say that? He'd seen Tim, knuckle-dusters glinting, as he waded into dissenters at meetings before the war, seen the satisfaction in his eyes.

He was leaving Massingham far behind, taking it slowly, for he had to reach the environs of the Factory. If Tim had eyes on him, as he seemingly had, he'd know by the end of the day if he'd tried, but even his people couldn't actually witness the deed. He took the hill steadily, in second gear.

Amelia had let slip yesterday evening that those on patrol had dogs. The girls had been warned not to touch them.

Apparently, the fence had been re-erected in places, especially those skirting the woods. He was taking the track alongside the woods, heading to the north of them. He wouldn't be seen.

Once in, he would leave a wrench, free of fingerprints. It would be discovered and there would be talk and proof enough that he had tried, but no damage done. The wind was shifting the car, and perhaps it would blow him off the road. Perhaps he'd freeze and that would end it all. Would Alfie tell his father he was out in it? Well, that was all right, he'd said he wanted to see how the car handled under these conditions. Or was Alfie one of them, Tim's men? As he skidded slightly on the bend Ralph realised he'd thought 'one of them', not one of 'us'.

He peered through the snow, seeking the track, his face stiff with cold. On and on for another three miles, and now he was almost crawling, the engine spluttering. Was it the cold or was he driving too slowly?

He saw the track he had in mind and turned right. The snow had drifted to one side, so the way was clear, and in the lee of the woods it was quieter. He kept on, and was free of the woods quite suddenly, so he backed up and swung the roadster into a passing area, parked, then decided to turn the car so a quick escape was possible, if need be.

He parked, found the wrench beneath his seat, and tramped along the edge of the wood to the moor, praying the snow didn't stop, for how could the guards see in this? How could the dogs find a scent? And more to the point, how could his car be seen or his tyre prints traced when they were covered with snow? He reached the downed fence and could see and hear nothing. He moved at a crouch, stepping over the posts that had been blown over, and made his way towards the buildings, straining to hear. Then he just stopped. This was his plan. Stop, turn and leave, for he could not blow up another living thing. He bent forward as the wind heightened, and then he heard the whistle, the barking . . .

'Oh God.' He turned, dropped the wrench and fled, back through the posts, catching his side on something . . . what? It didn't matter – get up, get up.

He scrambled to his feet and ran alongside the woods, clutching his side as the barking drew nearer. Had the dogs been let off? Oh God. The cold seared his throat, the snow was in his mouth, his heart was pumping and the snow was dragging at his feet. On and on he ran until he reached his roadster and leapt in, firing the engine. It caught, and died. Oh God.

. He could hardly breathe. The wind had changed and was shifting the car. He fired the engine again, this time it held and he was off, not daring to speed. 'Steady, steady,' he said. Then shouted, 'Steady.' For a dog was bounding along behind, he could see it in his mirror. He roared now to the end of the track and back along the road, taking the next turn, and working his way towards Massingham along the back roads, for so few knew these roads as he did.

He arrived back at Massingham Hall, swung the car into the garage and just sat there, hearing the ticking as the engine cooled, over the thumping of his heart. He tasted vomit, and bit down on his lip. His side hurt. It bloody hurt, but at least he could say he tried.

But it had been so close, those dogs, the whistles. Thank you, God. The snow would cover his tracks, or blow them clear away. He'd done it, but not done it. He leaned back, then jerked upright as Alfie knocked on the window.

'Good journey, sir? Shall I clean her up?'

*

319

At lunch at the Factory, Beth ate with Mrs Oborne, who asked what news about Fran and Sarah? Beth had waited by the phone box that morning and Stan had telephoned through to say that it wouldn't be long before they were at Newcastle Royal, and Sister Newsome would set them straight in time for the wedding on the first of March.

All of this she told the table and was able to smile along with them and listen to the talk of what they would wear and, more importantly, what Sarah would wear. 'Aye, well, get your thinking caps on, for 'tis Fran and Davey's on the second of April and we'll have to get stuck in again.'

Then the chatter knew no bounds as they wondered what they had hanging in their wardrobes. As they talked, Beth thought of her own wedding day, in her mam's old wedding dress, but it were in shreds now.

She smiled, for at least her marriage wasn't torn apart. Bob was coming into Grimsby and would try to get to her. Stan was marrying Sarah, and she and Mrs Bedley would stand together with the mams. She said then, 'They're bringing a lass called Viola to Newcastle an' all. She lost her parents in the Newcastle bombing, so Mrs Bedley's teking her in when she's able to leave the hospital.'

More chatter, and now Cyn Ellington was here, tapping her watch, a light in her eyes. Beth found herself wondering if there would be yet another wedding. She hoped so.

She saw Amelia strutting along the rear of the canteen, a clipboard under her arm, and hurried after her. 'What was the alarm about, Amelia? We heard the whistles and the dogs . . .'

Amelia was wearing her high heels as always. 'Aren't you perishing, lass?' Beth asked.

Amelia pursed her lips. Her legs were blotchy from the cold, but she wasn't about to admit it. Instead she said,

'Appearances are important, Beth. You wouldn't see me dead in those trouser overalls you've all taken to wearing. Whatever is the management thinking?'

'Sense, I daresay,' said Mrs Oborne as she swept past. 'Boots, socks and trousers make for warm legs. Yer should try it one day. I reckon you've a few chilblains on the way and I doubt you'll get wintergreen any more.'

Valerie merely looked at Amelia as she followed Mrs Oborne, then swung round and came back. 'You must be quieter when you come in at night, yer know, Amelia. Aye, you might have been out with the whelp, but tell him not to rev his bliddy car, and best you keep your mouth shut an' all. Who knows, whoever tried to get in today might have heard you yammering about the fence – where it was repaired, where it wasn't. You were giving it a bit of a go, showing off at t'pub in between your singing. "Keep Mum" is what the poster says.'

Amelia flushed as Valerie stalked on. Beth sighed, for Amelia had been shouting the odds – she'd heard her. She said, 'Think on, Amelia. If whoever did it says he heard about the fence in the pub, and it's known it were you, your feet won't touch the ground when they fling you out, or worse, into a cell. Grow up, or you'll get yerself into a heap of trouble, and I don't want to see that. You're not bad, you're just bliddy silly. And if I were yer, I'd choose me friends more carefully, for yer drink too much with the whelp, who has no interest in you. You know that, I know that. Any more than you have in him, except for what he can do for you.'

Amelia shifted the clipboard. 'I know nothing of the kind, and neither do you.'

Beth wanted to walk away, but someone had to save the girl from herself. 'Mebbe you're reet, but I'll say again, be careful. If Valerie and I noticed, who else did? Shut your mouth, except to sing. Just do that for me, and the rest of us. We divint want you in trouble.'

Beth moved on as the tannoy drifted to 'Begin the Beguine', and not for the first time she wondered what those words really meant.

As Ralph walked along the main seam at the start of the aft shift with Sid and Norm, he remembered to pick up his feet and none of them coughed as much. He'd plugged the cut in his side with cotton wool and tried to pull the edges together with plasters when he returned from the Factory this morning. Then he'd bandaged the lot to hide the blood. He winced as he tripped and jolted the wound.

Sid peered at him. 'Bit pale and interesting today, Ralph? Been on the beer, lad?'

'Sherry actually, old son.'

The other two laughed, and it was as though they were all beginning to accept and understand one another. Or was it just that at last he had the hang of the pick and the pit? It had all happened quite suddenly. He looked down, welcoming the pain, for why should he not feel some? Two dead men and now their daughters in hospital. How the hell would they cope? Especially the Bedleys, with Davey gone from the pit and no money coming in from Sarah for as long as she was laid up.

He'd spoken to Sophia over lunch about what news there had been from the hospital. As he waited for her answer he saw that Tommy was using a knife and fork, and Abraham too. Little Eva was still having trouble, but at least she was trying, instead of using her fingers. He wondered if there was a way of cutting down the size of the knife and fork. Maybe he'd ask the pit blacksmith.

'They'll make a full recovery, even the girl with half her

hand amputated,' Sophia had said, helping Janet cut her spam cutlet.

'But until then, what?' he'd asked. 'The girls have no money coming in?'

Even now, in the dust and darkness of the pit, he could picture the surprise on Sophia's face. 'Why, Ralph, how very thoughtful.' Then she'd flushed, embarrassed to point out what a pig's ear he'd been most of his life, he supposed. Well, she was right, and here he was, changing to someone he almost didn't recognise, or was he just trying to buy his way towards some forgiveness, or perhaps some bloody sleep?

They were passing the entrance to Bell Seam, where Joe Hall and Tom Bedley had died. He tripped again; his legs felt too heavy. Sid clapped him on the back. The pain almost made him faint and he was glad of it, for it stopped his mind. Sid said, 'Howay lad, we've the shift ahead of us, don't fall on yer face just yet, we need you on yer pick.'

Norm laughed, and Ralph did too, but it died, for what would they say if they knew what he'd done? Bury him in his turn? Norm said, 'I saw Beth, who heard from Stan about the girls. They'll be sent to Newcastle soonest, and he and Sarah'll be getting wed on the first of March. They'll be living at the Bedleys' and bugger me, Davey and Fran'll be next in April.'

Once at the coalface, the other two stripped off, but Ralph worked in trousers and shirt. Norm called, 'Howay, our lad. Off to a meeting are yer? Yer shirt'll be black as the pit. What's the matter with yer?'

He ignored him, for what would they say about the cut? It had to be seen as a pit injury. He threw his pick at the face, nuzzling it into a crack, working it until the coal fell. Sid called, 'Where the bliddy hell's the putter? We need this coal cleared.'

323

Ralph flung down his pick. 'Before you buggars take pleasure in pointing the finger, I'll step forward just for today.'

They laughed and he shovelled the coal into the tub, then pushed it along the seam, stooping low to get beneath the overhang. Once he was past, he held the tub still, ripped his shirt, tore off the bandages and stuffed them to one side. Almost before he'd done that, the blacklocks and rats were after the blood. He tore his shirt above the cut, grabbed a handful of coal dust from the ground and rubbed it in the wound, gritting his teeth against the pain. Now he relaxed, for he could pass it off as a pit wound.

He shoved the tub to the main seam, and only when he reached the face again did he swear and rip his shirt off. Norm saw, watching as Ralph peered at his side. 'Howay, Ralph, that's a bugger of a slice. Reckon it needs stitches. Where'd you do that?'

The blood was dripping, black-stained, onto Ralph's trousers. Ralph held up his shirt so they could see the tear. 'Beyond the overhang. My own fault.'

He twirled his shirt around several times, then tied it against the wound. 'That'll stop the bleeding. Come on, targets to reach.' He picked up his pick and went to work, with Sid calling, 'You're on yer way to being a pitman, lad.'

Ralph grinned. 'So, do I get a badge?'

Norm, hacking at the coalface, grunted. 'Nay, lad, you buy the drinks.'

Cycling home from the pit in the snow at the end of the aft shift, Ralph stopped at the telephone box and called Tim as arranged. When he answered Ralph said, 'I had to abort. The dogs were on me in no time.'

Tim's voice was cold. 'Aye, I heard. Another time then, but not yet, for they'll be waiting for a second attempt. You left yer wrench, but as well you didn't leave explosives. I'll be in touch. Best get that cut seen to, eh.' There was a click as the receiver was replaced.

Ralph put the receiver down, feeling a cold deeper than the chill of the snow. How the hell did Tim know about the cut?

Chapter Twenty-Six

A Few Days Later at the Newcastle Royal Infirmary

Sarah, Fran and Viola were neatly tucked up alongside one another in Sister Newsome's ward. She was eyeing them for progress as she made her way around the ward in the company of Dr Wilson and his minions. At last they stopped at Fran's bedside, Dr Wilson checking her notes, Sister Newsome taking her pulse.

'Still alive, am I, Sister Newsome?' asked Fran.

Sister Newsome was checking the watch pinned to her breast. 'For now, Fran Hall. For now, but so much depends on how one behaves.'

'Best measure you up for yer shroud, then, Fran,' called Sarah from the next bed.

Viola, from the bed the other side of Fran, added, 'Will you smother or poison her?'

Dr Wilson looked from one to the other. 'You have a cure, I believe, Sister Newsome, for troublesome patients?'

'Oh no, not the enemas?' Sarah groaned.

Sister Newsome nodded. 'Got it in one.'

Dr Wilson moved on to Viola, his minions standing by quietly as he talked to her while Sister Newsome and Nurse Ogden rolled back her bandage. Viola was so intent on Dr Wilson she seemed not to notice, and that, thought Sarah, showed medical teamwork. Did Dr Wilson and

Sister Newsome talk about work as they washed the pots at home? It wouldn't surprise her.

She and Fran watched anxiously as Dr Wilson took over and eased off the final dressing with what looked like tweezers, dropping both into a steel kidney bowl with a clang. He looked at the healing hand, then smelled it. He straightened. 'No sign or smell of infection. I'm really pleased with this.' He checked her scalp and ear. 'Yes, like Fran's noddle, this is doing really well too. I gather you are going to stay with Mrs Bedley?'

Viola nodded as her hand was dressed and bandaged by Nurse Ogden while Dr Wilson and Sister Newsome moved to the foot of her bed. Dr Wilson made notes on the chart and put his pen in his breast pocket. 'Good, then we'll have you all discharged and in Massingham very soon, for I hear there are wedding plans to be finalised.'

He swept on to the next patient, Sister Newsome in his wake, but not before she'd wagged her finger at all three of them and said, 'Behave, or you'll stay here for longer, and no one in their right mind wants that, certainly not the staff, eh, Nurse Ogden?'

It was already lunchtime and the girls ate on trays, feeling frauds, for they felt remarkably well, but even with food inside them they barely had the energy to drink their cups of tea before they fell asleep. Sarah dreamed of Stan and the dress she, Fran and Viola had thought could perhaps be made from an old sheet. Then she dreamed of Deirdre and Fiona beneath the rubble, and so did Fran. Sarah woke to Fran's cry of, 'We'll get you out.'

Sarah dozed again. This time she was walking down the aisle in her dress. It started off feeling light and airy, but as she walked it grew heavier and heavier. She looked back and found she was dragging several blankets and a couple of pillows down the aisle, in a mockery of a train, and then she saw Deirdre lying on it, making it just too heavy.

She was glad to be woken by the visitors' bell, and pushed herself up on the pillows, feeling guilty – she had survived but the others hadn't. She concentrated on the people who came through the double doors, all searching for their wife, mother, auntie or whoever. The girls weren't sure whether to expect anyone, for they'd only arrived at midday, having travelled overnight in the ambulance. It depended on shifts, whether Stan would be free; that was if Sister Morris had stayed true to her word and phoned through to Massingham Hall from Glasgow to ask them to spread the word.

As Sister Newsome and Nurse Ogden busied themselves doing this, that and the other, Sarah heard the chatter of children, then the clap of hands and Sophia Massingham's voice saying, 'Any more noise and you stay out in the corridor, or worse, Sister Newsome will have something to say, and she's really fierce.'

Sarah and Fran grinned as they heard a girl ask, 'Does she bite?'

Sister Newsome was at the double doors now, and every word was as clear as a bell. 'Oh yes, I do,' she said. 'And I draw blood.'

There was a sudden silence from the children, though there were titters in the ward. A crocodile of children led by Sophia entered, with Annie, Audrey and Maud in the lead. 'Howay, do you see who I see?' Fran said, for bringing up the rear were Mr Swinton and Miss Ellington.

They waited, bracing themselves for both the children and Swinton, but there was no need. Mrs Smith sat with Viola, introducing herself and gathering around a few of the children. Mrs Hall sat with Fran, and Mrs Bedley with Sarah, each with a few boys and girls, while Sophia fluttered from one bed to another and Miss Ellington and Swinton stood about awkwardly.

Sister Newsome came to them. 'Do shove in beside one of the beds. You're making the ward look untidy.'

Mr Swinton was fingering his cap, and when Miss Ellington threw back her head and laughed, he smiled weakly. Cyn Ellington took his arm and headed for Fran. Over the top of the children's heads she said, 'We had to come, we've been so worried, and are so glad that you're back now.'

'Aye,' Mr Swinton said. 'Need to know what shift to put you on, is all.'

Fran stared. Oh, so he was back to the man he always used to be, she thought. How stupid to think otherwise.

Miss Ellington was laughing and nudging him. He broke into a smile. 'A joke,' he said. 'Just wanted to say, we miss thee. Come back when you can, but only then. It'll be sewing section to work your way in, Sarah, an' all. Can't rush it. There, that's done. Best be off.'

He turned, but Fran called, 'Oh, do stay, just a bit, Mr Swinton. We've missed you. You trained us well, they all said that at . . . well . . . at the factory. But I was careless, I should have seen it . . . We would have done better under your care. I were slack. We didn't check one another carefully. Not till too . . .' For she could still see the new girl, the danger man, Fiona, and she felt she'd killed them.

He said, his voice rough, 'Nay, that's the thing, 'tis a fact that accidents happen. Accidents is a way of life, 'tis those that you suspect aren't accidents that yer canna forgi—' He stopped, shook his head slightly. Fran and Cyn Ellington looked at one another, confused. Mr Swinton saw. 'Oh, I'm reet tired. Ignore me, eh?'

Miss Ellington bustled with him across to Viola's bed, to talk about this and that, and Fran saw her showing Viola her handless arm and heard her say, 'An absent hand makes life perfectly doable, so half a hand is half the loss. Buttons are a nuisance, 'tis the only thing, but you've yer thumb and a couple of fingers.'

The children had collected around Miss Ellington, fascinated, and Eva said loudly. "Ow do you pick yer nose?'

Sophia darted across, hushing her, but Miss Ellington squatted beside the child. 'With the other hand.'

Mr Swinton was standing, looking from the children to Miss Ellington as though he'd never seen such strange beasts before, and then he nodded. 'Aye, yer listen to Miss Ellington. Not sure what she'd be like with two hands. I reckon they'd use her in the war to bang heads together, which would bring it to an end sharpish.'

Viola roared with laughter, as did Miss Ellington and Sophia. Sarah called across to him, 'Keep the first of March free, Mr Swinton, for Stan and me is to wed, so best bib and tucker, eh. St Oswald's it'll be, but what I'll be wearin', heaven knows? We were thinking one of the sheets . . .'

Her mam said, 'Don't worry about that now. We're trying to sort something.'

Sophia had been sharing herself out between the children gathered beside the beds, tapping this one's head, finger to her mouth to another and helping yet another read a book. She looked at Sarah. 'No, no, not a sheet. The summer nursery curtains are the answer, ladies. They're a sort of white brocade, which looks good at the windows, but would be much better walking down the aisle. What do you think, you mothers? Could you work some magic?'

Mr Swinton took a step towards Sarah's bed. 'Is that an invitation, Sarah? Is yer sure? I mean, that's right kind.'

Sarah smiled and Fran waited, not sure if Sarah was pleased, for perhaps she was just being polite. Sarah lifted herself from her pillows, leaning forward, resting her arms on her knees, calling past Fran, 'I am sure, Mr Swinton. You and Miss Ellington are the ones I reckon have taught us to be careful, and probably saved our lives a few times without us ever knowing, and you're not as bliddy-minded as you used to be, seems to me.'

There was a horrible silence as the women looked anywhere but at Mr Swinton, who eventually laughed. It was a strange, dried-up sound, as though it had been woken up from the depths. 'Aye, well, that'd be grand, and I were going to say that if your mam sorts a pattern, perhaps Mrs Oborne could put it together on one of the sewing machines in the Factory. Not sure if you have one of yer own?'

None of the co-op did. 'I'll have a word, then, with Tilly,' Mr Swinton said.

'Tilly?' whispered Fran's mam. 'Tilly Oborne? Good grief, has the man had a heart exchange?'

Fran hushed her. 'Oh Mam, the poor beggar's worked off his feet, surrounded by a load of women to sort out and . . . Well, the war. It changes us all. Stan says even Ralph's half human now.'

Her mam said, 'Aye, well, that's true enough. Let's face it, the lad's a sticker, an' all. Pick work's coming on and the targets are met, and – oh well, mebbe the lads are just getting used to one another. Teks time, as in all things. Mark yer, Sophia said the lad came home early from the fore shift today. Burning up he was, caught himself on an overhang, it seems, and says he hasn't time to see a doctor. He said pitmen don't fuss.' She laughed.

Fran thought of Dr Wilson sniffing Viola's hand. She told her mam, who raised her eyebrows. 'Ah well, usually it's enough just to look, but maybe he was after the start of gangrene or summat?'

Sister Newsome called as she was passing, 'Another doctor missed just that. They're all more cautious now. Just had a call from Stan, Sarah. He'll be in later. But you others will have to go. It's like a ruddy fairground in here. Half of you outside, if you please.'

The co-op ladies arrived on their bikes as usual the next morning, Saturday, with poor Madge towing the trailer that contained their rug frames. Annie Hall, however, also carried sphagnum moss and bandages in her bag just in case Ralph was still home and feverish, because gangrene was the beginning of the end, especially on the torso.

Alfie was busy in the garage and waved to them as they puffed and panted their way into the yard. Madge grunted, 'All very well for yer to be smiling, lad. You haven't icicles hanging from your nose and hair, not to mention yer eyepatch.'

He laughed. 'Neither have you, Madge, so stop making a fuss.'

Mrs Smith leaned her bike against the side of the garage. 'Dangerous talk, lad, when you're stuck in here in the warm.'

Alfie limped across and helped Madge with the trailer, handing out the rug frames to the women. 'I canna feel that it's that warm in here, Mrs Smith, with a raging draught whistling around me. And howay, soon you'll be in the kitchen, brewing a cup of tea, and will I have one? Unless of course . . .' He left it hanging.

Beryl grinned and tightened her scarf around her head. 'Unless of course some kind, beautiful maiden finds it in her heart to bring you a mug?'

Alfie grinned. 'Took the words reet out of me mouth.'

Maud said, 'So which of us would that be, our Alfie?'

Alfie looked stumped for a moment as they all waited, staring out at the frozen yard and the snow that was beginning to fall again. Finally he muttered, ''Tis so hard to choose one from such a bevy of beauties.'

The women laughed. Annie said, 'Well recovered, lad. Come to the kitchen door in ten minutes, because no one's trekking out with it, no matter how much you blather.'

As they headed across the cobbles, using the path to the basement steps that Alfie had sanded, he called, 'Mrs Hall, just a word.'

She turned, retracing her steps. 'Aye, lad?'

'Your Stan says you're a dab hand with the moss, after using it in t'other war. I reckon the whelp's in need.'

Annie looked up, surprised, for she hadn't heard Ralph called the whelp for a while. Alfie was going on: 'He looked reet bad when he came home early from the pit yesterday. I've seen it before, what with those bright eyes and a reet colour on him, and he had a pitman's cut that happened a few days ago, or so Sid said at the club. Sid reckons it should have been stitched, but he never went to the doctor. Reckon he's showing a bit of ... Well, not sure what. Gumption, mebbe?'

Annie nodded. 'Aye, thank you, Alfie. I had heard, so I have some moss that'll draw it if need be, so let's see how things are today, eh?'

Annie and Sophia climbed the stairs together after a cuppa. The little girls had been set to work on their own frames, which Alfie had knocked together. The boys were across in the garage now, booted and coated, learning the parts of an engine, which Alfie had said was by way of doing his bit. He also said he'd be sending them back in for a top-up for his cuppa, since a day off school didn't mean they stopped learning, and keeping a bloke supplied with a cuppa was part of the learning.

'I'm just so glad you're here, Annie,' Sophia said. 'I think you'll be strong enough to insist he lets you have a look, whereas he's just too embarrassed with me. Silly boy.'

Annie slid her a look. 'By, he's no boy, lass, certainly not t'boy you nannied.'

Sophia gripped her arm. 'Men're all ruddy boys, Annie, you know that.' They were laughing as they reached Ralph's door. Sophia muttered, 'I'll stay outside. He was very cross yesterday, and again this morning when I took him in a drink and said I'd get a doctor. You'd think I had offered to pull his fingernails out for the sheer pleasure of it.'

Annie Hall knocked on the door, imagining Ben or Stan in there. She called, ''Tis Mrs Hall, Ralph, and I'm entering whether you're ready or not. I've seen it all before, lad, and you're nowt special.'

All she heard was a croak. She entered, walked to the curtains and pulled them back, opening the window a little. 'There,' she said. 'No point in you stewing in yer stale air. Let's be having a look at yer, lad.'

She sounded stronger than she felt, for this was Ralph Massingham, who had caused trouble, who had been arrogant and rude, who had caused her lass pain—No, she thought to herself, this is someone just like Ben or Stan, being silly.

Ralph was lying there, only his eyes moving. He spoke with the sheet over his mouth.

'Move the sheet down, silly lad,' she said. 'Then I have a chance of hearing you.'

She was at the side of the bed now and ripped the sheet and blankets away, revealing his bare chest, then his pyjama bottoms. 'Over yer go, onto your side, quick, quick. I haven't all day. Let's get it sorted, eh?'

Stunned, Ralph obeyed, muttering, 'I don't need help.'

Annie stared at the wound, which was filled with coal dust and pus and was swollen red around the edges, with streaks of red leading from it. 'Yer need a doctor,' she insisted.

'No, not a doctor. I'm a pitman.'

She laid down her bag and drew a deep breath. She went to the door, hoping Sophia was still there. She was, and nearly fell into the room because she'd been pressing her ear so hard against the door. 'I have sterile water in a bottle with me, Sophia, and dressings, and cloths. Would you sterilise a bowl, and add boiled water in case I need more? I need to clean the wound and then I'll be using repeated moss dressings to draw the poison. I will have to sit with him, probably for twenty-four hours. I'd be grateful if you'd let Stan know – perhaps Alfie can?'

Sophia paled. 'Oh no, he's really poorly? I'll phone the doctor.'

'I'll have no interfering doctor, you hear.' Ralph's voice was little more than a croak.

'He has a right to his own decisions, Sophia. He says no. I've seen worse, much worse. Just bring me the water, please.'

Annie shut the door and returned to Ralph. She slopped water from the bottle she'd brought onto a cloth and held it to his forehead. 'We need to get this temperature under control, lad, so we'll use t'water to cool yer, then I'm going to clean yer wound with sterile water and dress it wi' the moss, which'll draw the infection. I'll stay here for twenty-four hours, so yer best get used to me hovering. I'll change the dressing frequently. But if I canna mek yer better I will call the doctor, do yer understand? I canna have yer dying. I divint allow such things.'

Ralph said nothing, but his eyes followed her as she sponged him, then sat beside the bed, and he shivered as the cold air blew into the room. Annie said, 'I'm here. I won't leave. I will tek care of yer.'

He whispered, 'How do you know how?'

'I nursed much worse than yer in t'other war, lad. Most

lived, some were too far gone. You are not. Together we'll sort it, all reet. You have to trust me, fer Doctor Brown, the army doctor, did.'

Though her words sounded firm and full of confidence, in her heart she wasn't so sure, but it was her or no one, for once a lad had set his mind on no, no it was.

Ralph lay hour after hour, shivering, dreaming and sweating. Either Mrs Hall or Sophia was there the whole time, watching, caring.

Mrs Hall sometimes sang. She had the voice of an angel, and it was hymns she sang, in particular 'Oh God, Our Help in Ages Past'. She sang and his heart seemed to slow, his breath grew stronger. When she stopped, he'd turn slightly and say, 'Thank you.'

She would say, 'I like to sing.'

Then, as the night deepened and the cold wind blew in the window, the fever fought the caring, and he moaned with the heat and the pulsing pain. Mrs Hall shooed Sophia away, telling her she would be needed by the bairns in the morning and must sleep. 'I will guard Mr Ralph.'

It was Mrs Hall who placed cool cloths on his forehead, who felt his pulse and patted his hand, murmuring, 'There, there, bonny lad. My friends and I'll not leave you till you're well. There, there, now, bonny bairn.'

Her face was kind, her voice too, and her eyes were firm. He trusted her. He knew that this woman would fight for him. In the early hours Mrs Bedley came, breathless from cycling. She insisted that Mrs Hall take the armchair and she put a stool beneath her feet and wrapped her in a blanket of knitted squares that she had brought. It was Sarah's mother who took over the nursing, crooning 'All or Nothing at All', and the click of her knitting needles was a comfort. Hour after hour she sat, sometimes checking and changing the dressing. There was no smell of drink, which the gossips said she'd turned to when her husband was killed, by him.

He looked at her, and said, 'I'm so sorry.'

Mrs Bedley laid down her knitting and patted his hand. 'Nothing to be sorry about, lad. Pitmen get hurt.'

'I didn't mean that.' But she didn't hear for she was knitting again.

Mrs Smith came as dawn broke and sat with Mrs Bedley while Mrs Hall made tea in the kitchen. She brought it up, and the three of them sat by him, guarding him, talking in whispers about the weddings, then checking him and changing the dressing.

When his father slipped into the room later in the morning, Mrs Hall said, 'The fever's not gone, but the pus and infection are in retreat. It would be helpful, Mr Massingham, if you would take these dressings and burn them in the range.'

Ralph smiled. His father looked at him and winked. Then came to stand by him. 'Nothing to eat?'

Ralph shook his head. His father touched his hand. 'Well, I have my task, and I will do that, then return and sit with you while your nurses have some food.'

So that's what happened.

The day wore on, and Mrs Bedley went home to sort out things for the wedding. Then Madge with the eyepatch came, and Mrs Adams, while the three mothers visited Fran, Sarah and Viola.

And so it went on, and the co-op examined the dressings and nodded each time. And each said, 'Aye, lad, the dressing is clearer, it has drawn as it should, the smell is better.'

Beryl came and read to him, taking a book off the shelf. It was *Black Beauty*, his favourite. Mrs Bedley, Mrs Hall and Mrs Smith came back and Ralph thought them all angels, and he'd killed the husbands of two of them.

He didn't know how many days had passed when Sophia came with chicken broth as the light was fading. Mrs Bedley and Mrs Hall were there, and the three of them eased him up onto the pillows, for his temperature was lower. He couldn't eat, but Sophia held the spoon to his lips. 'Just a sip, sweet boy. For me.'

He sipped.

The children were shouting. He heard Madge hush them, then come in, and she took the spoon from Sophia. She had a purple eyepatch this time. 'Let me. The evacuees need you.'

'I'm Madge,' she said again, as though he could forget. 'And just take another sip. One down the hole for Mrs Hall.'

Ralph did, because Mrs Hall was an angel.

Madge said, 'And another sip, for Mrs Bedley.' He did, for Mrs Bedley was an angel.

'You are all angels,' he said. 'And I never knew.'

Madge laughed and wiped his mouth with a clean handerchief that smelled of lavender. 'Far from angels, bonny lad, but we make good rugs. Aye, that we do.'

Ralph slept and woke again in the dead of night, and there were Mrs Bedley and Mrs Smith. He hadn't killed Mr Smith, at least he hadn't done that, and he wept. The women soothed him, wiped his tears. 'There, there,' they said. 'You'll be better soon, but the infection makes you weak, so never mind the tears. Tears are good, they release the soul from fear.'

The morning brought Mrs Hall, dear Mrs Hall, the angel. It was she who read more of *Black Beauty* to him, in the shaded room, and held the glass to his lips so that he could sip, and she said, '*Black Beauty* is Sarah's favourite, and I can see this has been well loved.'

'It's my favourite, or was. I had forgotten about it somehow.'

'Well,' she said. 'We do forget things, because we don't realise their importance, eh? You must drink,' she added. 'You must cleanse your body of the infection.'

She changed his dressing, the smell was so much less, his heart didn't race so much, the wound didn't hurt as it had. His father knocked and crept to his bedside. Mrs Hall moved as though to rise. His father placed a hand on her shoulder. 'You are an angel,' his father said. 'You and your friends, and I don't know how to thank you.'

Mrs Hall said, as Ralph watched her in the gloom of the curtained room, 'There's nowt to thank us for. We're all Massingham people, we look after our own.'

Ralph and his father shared a look. Their world had changed. They belonged.

And Ralph had killed Mrs Hall's and Mrs Bedley's husbands.

Chapter Twenty-Seven

28 February 1942

Sarah and Fran sewed the last few overalls, sat back and smiled at one another. The shift was over, their backs ached, their injuries too, but nothing mattered for the wedding was tomorrow. Fran muttered, 'Amazing what yer can do with plaster on yer broken arm, never mind a cracked shoulder. I'm a bliddy tornado on the sewing machine.'

Valerie, sitting opposite, called, 'It should be a required tool. I'll get Mr Swinton to put in a requisition, eh?'

'First he'll have to break our arms,' Beth said, 'and I reckon these days he might not fancy it, for it might not suit his emerging halo. Once upon a time he'd have rushed to get the hammer.'

'Aye, that'll be right, and he'd have had one for each hand,' Mrs Oborne added.

'And one between his teeth,' was Maisie's contribution.

They were all laughing, but kindly, when from the doorway Mr Swinton shouted, 'Howay, Beth Jones, I still know where the hammers are, I'll have yer know, and you should be on yer way, Bert's waiting with the bus. You've tomorrow off for the wedding yer lot, but not the next day. Shame is, not even Sarah and Stan will be off then.' He put up his hand to quell the protests, which he'd already heard, several times. 'Answer's still t'same: 'ave a word with Mr 'Itler, eh. By t'way, Sarah, how did the dress wash? Water barely warm, like I said? Brocade don't tek kindly to boiling.'

Sarah eased herself up from the chair. 'Perfect it is, Mr Swinton, but you'll see it yourself tomorrow. I reckon I should write Mrs Oborne's name on it, so everyone knows how clever she is as I walk down the aisle, and yours an' all, for letting us use the machines.'

The girls were following him down the corridor now because the aft shift had already taken their places. Fran linked arms with Beth, but didn't have an unplastered one for Sarah. 'I can hardly breathe for excitement, Sarah, and you too, Beth. The mams'll be meking the food today. It'll keep in the meat safes, and after the wedding Sarah and Stan can nip off to the Rising Sun and Bert'll collect you on Monday for the shift.'

They reached the changing room where they stripped free of their overalls, dressed and were checked by Cyn Ellington, who whispered to Sarah, 'See you there. Just enjoy every minute.'

Sarah smiled, for how could she not? She was to marry her Stan. Davey wouldn't be there, unless the gods looked kindly on him and he was given a twenty-four-hour pass, and neither would Bob, but that's what life was like now.

'And what about you and Simon Parrot, eh?' asked Fran. 'Wedding bells or not?'

Miss Ellington grimaced. 'That's for me to know, and no need for you all to find out.'

As they were about to leave for the gate, Amelia came in with Brenda and Rosie, all three of whom had permission to take their places in the sewing shop tomorrow. They carried a box that held a bottle of Stevie's elderberry wine and two antique wine glasses.

'They're not new,' said Brenda, 'the glasses were me mam's, and we thought you two should have them, in repayment for all our bookings when they should have been yours.'

341

Rosie was nodding. Amelia's lips were pursed, but then she tried to smile. There was also a small package wrapped in what looked like a piece of the brocade used to make Sarah's dress. Amelia muttered, shamefaced, 'Our fees for the last two bookings, for the three of you. To help towards costs while you were laid up.'

Everyone was watching, but no one was moving. Amelia looked at Beth. 'I've been a right fool. Maybe now is the time to put it behind us all?'

Into the silence Miss Ellington said, clapping her hands, 'Bus is waiting.'

The women started to leave, but Beth, Fran and Sarah waited. The six girls stood quietly until Sarah finally took the box. 'Thank yer, 'tis really kind, and we're reet pleased that we are working together ter win this war.'

They left, and as they walked down the icy path and headed for the gate, Fran muttered, 'Yer sound like a bliddy politician – hot air, but saying nowt.'

Beth nudged Fran. 'Aye, she should stand for Parliament, eh? But Amelia can't just wipe it all out, though mebbe's she opened the door a crack. Maybe she'll go on opening it and if she does, then that's right and good.'

They all turned as Amelia called after them, standing in the doorway, her arms crossed, shivering in the cold wind: 'The bookings are yours now. They've dried up for us, and I no longer see Ralph, just so you know, Beth.' With that, she turned back inside.

Fran began to laugh as they headed down the path. 'So, has she dumped Ralph because the bookings dried up, for goodness' sake?'

Beth told them then of the attempted break-in after Amelia had blown her mouth off at the pub ... well, several pubs ... spouting on about where the fence was weakest. 'I took her to one side, so I did, and told her to keep her bliddy mouth shut or end up in prison. Maybe she can't trust herself, so has backed out; maybe she went off Ralph, he's been reet poorly. Oh I divint care, just as long as she keeps out of me way.'

Sarah puffed as they hurried through the gate, only to be called back to have their bags searched. 'Still bringing the water bottles, I see?' Jimmy the guard said.

'Always,' Fran answered.

They ran as Bert drove the bus forward, hooting. 'Yer'd better not be late tomorrow, lass,' Bert yelled. 'The church'll be perishing and we'll be in a rush to get to the victuals.'

Mrs Oborne called down the bus, 'Hush yer noise, you old fool, and tek us home. I have me hair to wash and need time to mek meself beautiful.'

Bert shouted back as he turned the bus and headed home, 'There aren't enough years for that, you old besom.'

Sarah smiled, loving them all, as she sat at the back with Beth on one side and Fran on the other, for this is how they travelled now – the three were back together, and had sworn they'd never be separated again.

Sunday had dawned cold but fine, St Oswald's was full, and the four girls waited in the covered porch, their macs around their shoulders. Fran, Sarah and Beth had included Viola ever since she had recovered sufficiently. Beth adjusted Sarah's veil, Fran her hair, and Viola retied the bundle of greenery that made up her bouquet, using her two and a half fingers and thumb. 'It's the thumb, yer see. Meks things possible.'

As Sarah smoothed her dress, Beth whispered, 'Howay, lass, it looks a mite better on you than a nursery window.'

Sarah whispered back, 'Do my shoes show?' For she only had her brown court shoes.

Fran checked. 'No sight and hardly a sound.'

Viola grimaced. 'Sound? What d'yer mean, sound? They don't squeak, do they?'

Fran muttered, 'As for you, young lady, yer look pretty as a picture in my mam's frock, and no, they don't squeak, yer besom. Just thought we'd get you going.' They were all laughing. 'But I reckon the mice'll be having a bit of a go with all these people. They like a crowd, they do.'

They were all helpless with laughter now as the organ wheezed and squeaked. Beth spluttered, 'Well, even if yer shoes did squeak, they'll think 'tis the blooming music, so hush yer worry. 'Tis just if one of the little beggars teks it in its mind to run up a leg. Then there might be a bit of a do.'

They were leaning against one another now, gasping, desperate to stop laughing because it was hurting their injuries so much. As they drew breath they heard a frantic hooting from the bottom of the hill. They peered out and down the hill to see Davey slamming the taxi door, slinging his carpet bag over his shoulder and running up the path as fast as his leg would allow.

Fran shrieked from the doorway, 'Davey, oh Davey,' loud enough for him to hear.

'Probably drowned the organ,' Viola laughed, for the wedding march was playing.

'Howay, that means your brother can walk you down the aisle to give you away, our Sarah, just when we were all looking forward to being the ones to palm you off on Stan,' Beth grumbled.

Viola and Sarah both slapped her, then they all turned to watch Fran rush down the path to meet Davey, who dropped his bag as he took her carefully in his arms, kissing and hugging her while she said, 'I didn't think . . . Oh Davey, aye, they'll let you come on the second of April for ours an' all? Say they will.'

He was too busy kissing her to answer and when he

344

stopped, he said, holding her face, 'Let them try and stop me, lass.'

They hurried together to the church and Davey hugged Sarah, swinging her round as the others dodged out of the way. 'Come on, then, time to go.' He tore off his coat and hat, nipped a piece of greenery out of Sarah's bouquet and stuck it in his lapel, ignoring her yelp of 'Oy.'

'Hush, lass. Got to hold my end up, eh?'

Sarah slipped her arm through his, and the girls lined up behind, Beth and Viola together, with Fran bringing up the rear, whispering, 'All ready to mek an honest woman of yerself, Sarah Bedley, though by the end of the next twenty minutes yer'll be a Hall.'

'An honest woman, eh?' said Beth. 'Our Sarah? Not so sure about that.'

Davey turned and grinned. 'There's no hope now there are four of you lasses on the rampage. Best Stan and me head for the hills while us still can.'

Fran and Sarah said together, 'We'll hunt yer down.'

They were all laughing as Davey reached forward and pushed open the doors. Heads turned, including Stan's and his best man Ben's. Stan looked at Sarah, and all the love a man had ever felt for a woman was in that glance. As they began the walk down the aisle he saw Davey, and there was almost as much love in his look for his marrer. Davey heard his mam call, 'Oh, Davey.' That was all, and it was worth all the rushing, all the begging and pleading and overtime. Sarah had said Maud never ever touched a drop, and never smelled of it either, and the bottles had gone from the hidey-hole in the netty.

They held a steady course up the aisle, smiling back at their Massingham community and the Factory girls, with Bert standing amongst them. They passed Simon Parrot and Cyn Ellington. Davey winked at Simon, but didn't

345

know the two young men standing next to them. Sarah whispered, 'The medics, Simon and Roy. They laughed at Simon Parrot being in charge of the Canary Club, felt it should be a parrot club. Right kind they were, and saved our Viola's life, I reckon.'

'Our Viola, eh?'

'Oh aye,' whispered Sarah, 'she's one of us now.'

There was Mr Swinton, next to Steve and Tilly Oborne and their lad, Colin, and Maisie too, though Mrs Adams was with Mrs Bedley, Mrs Hall, Mrs Smith and Madge, in a sparkly gold eyepatch, all sitting in two rows of pews alongside the rest of the co-op gang, which was how the girls thought of them now. To the right sat Sophia and Reginald Massingham, and someone Sarah didn't know. Next to him was Ralph, looking much better thanks to her mam and the co-op, who had nursed him for several days and nights. Behind them were the evacuees, who had made a rug for Sarah and Stan's bedroom, which was to be the front room of the Bedley house.

The thought caught at Sarah, held her. *Their* bedroom. Quite suddenly, she didn't want to spend tonight at the Rising Sun; she wanted to spend it in Massingham, with her husband, amongst her family.

They were almost there and Reverend Walters smiled at Sarah and Davey as they stopped before him. The organ, played by Miss Walters, the reverend's sister, also stopped with a squeal and a squeak. Sarah heard the giggles from the other three, and soon all four were laughing yet again, and Davey was no help as he concentrated on trying to control himself.

Stan looked at her, raised his eyebrows and whispered, 'I'm not even going to ask, but have you a mouse under that dress?'

That did it. They were all helpless, even Reverend Walters.

That was until his sister took it upon herself to thunder down on the keys and restore order.

'We are gathered in the sight of God and the whole congregation . . .'

Before they walked back down the aisle, Beth, Fran and Viola, who had collected her saxophone from Mrs Bedley, moved to the front and Reverend Walters cleared his throat. 'Before we head off for the photographs, we have just one final moment. It's wartime, and we can ring no bells, but listen, please, to "It Had to Be You".' He stepped to one side and held out his hand to the girls.

Viola manipulated her devastated hand to play the introduction and the girls came in, their voices pure and resonant. The saxophone soared, the voices too, as The Factory Girls' choir stood and sang, with Valerie and Mrs Oborne making up the staccato drumming. 'For nobody else gave me a thrill . . .' Sarah and Stan moved to the music, and then danced, close together, in the aisle. Viola missed two notes, though they were barely noticeable, but her courage was, and after the last lines – 'It had to be you, wonderful you, it had to be you' – had echoed, silence fell. If it hadn't been a church, applause would have echoed endlessly.

As they walked back down the aisle, now man and wife, Stan held Sarah's hand tightly, for he'd never ever let her go. They smiled at their friends – so many of them – and Sarah grinned at her mam and wondered if she would stay off the drink, but they'd have to hope until she had regained their trust. She and Stan walked on, and as they did so the door into the church opened and in came Bob Jones in his naval uniform and his cap with no name, for secrecy in wartime was everything. He slipped into the back pew, next to the pit blacksmith who at Ralph's request had made a smaller knife and fork for Eva, and Norm and Sid.

Stan heard Beth sigh, 'Oh Bob, you came.'

Stan sighed too as he saw Sid and Norm pass little packets over the shoulders of those sitting in front. Confetti, but how? There was a war on ... As though reading his thoughts, Sarah said, 'The evacuees. Mam said they'd been colouring and cutting.'

'That's all reet then, if it's the bairns, for we'll have some too, one day.'

They smiled at one another as they drew alongside Stan's marrers, who slipped out after them with Bob, who joined Beth.

They had thought they'd have to don their coats to stand outside, but the cold wind had dropped a little, though only a little, and at least the sun was out so that Stan and Sarah didn't feel the cold. The marrers and Bob threw confetti, Stevie from the Rising Sun bent over, tucked his head beneath the cloth of his tripod camera and called, 'Smile, for the love of God. Oh, sorry, Vicar, but I've a howling gale blowing up me arse. Smile, please.'

It was hard not to, and while he took photos of just the bride and groom, Mrs Hall, Ben and Fran, along with Davey and Mrs Bedley, walked to their fathers' graves, and little Betty's, and laid some of the confetti on the mounds. 'One day we'll be able to afford headstones,' Mrs Hall soothed Ben.

As Fran put her arm around the lad she thought of Fiona and Deirdre who shared the bedroom next to theirs at the hostel, and the new girl and the danger man. These were the four she dreamed of, crying beneath the debris. Sarah's dreams had stopped, but it was Fran who should have seen the kirby grip sooner, and then they would still be alive. It was her error, her guilt. She sighed, longing to speak of it, but there was no one who understood, and no one who realised that her world seemed darker.

Sophia and Reginald Massingham chatted to Professor Smythe, who not only handled the Massingham scholarship scheme, but also taught at Oxford and had fingers in many secret pies. Professor Smythe lifted his face to the sun, then looked around. 'Just look, slag heaps, pitheads, all producing energy to fuel the heart of the nation – our industries, which so many think of as inferior to their legal briefs, their accountants' figures, their political utterances. Here, all around us, is our crucial beating heartland.'

Reginald raised an eyebrow. 'Oh, do put the lecture back in your pocket, Auberon. Just admire the scenery, you old buffer. You'll come to the wedding tea, of course? It's to be held in the Miners' Club, courtesy of the co-op, whom you have yet to meet. When you do, stand by to repel boarders, they take no prisoners. And I do believe Eva and the other children are to wait on us?'

He cocked his head at Sophia, who pulled a face. 'Annie Hall thought it worth a try, though we fear the worst, mayhem in fact.'

They were laughing as the photography session finished and the bride and groom led the guests down to the two buses that Bert and Cecil would drive to Massingham and the club. As they walked, the evacuees took to the graveyard, running amok and pretending to be airplanes, shooting down one another with loud whoops and bangs.

Sophia sighed. 'Oh well, let's hope they'll get it all out of their system now.'

As Ralph walked slowly and unsteadily behind them, Mr Swinton came to join him. He said, 'Please, Mr Ralph, if you see my son, tell him I must talk to him. I must find out . . . Oh well, I must see how he is.'

Ralph looked at the tired, worried man walking alongside and all he could say was, 'I never see him, Mr Swinton. Our paths don't cross. But if I should, I will. I promise. Try not to worry.'

Mr Swinton was scooped up by Maisie then, and chivvied about his silk buttonhole, while Ralph so wished that what he had just said to the old boy was true, that their paths never crossed, for looking around simply confirmed what the days and nights of his illness had embedded in him. Here, as Smythe had said, was the beating heart of the nation, but even more than that, here were the people who were strong, resolute and melded to one another.

These people were fighting with all they had to survive, as they had always done, trying to defeat what he had once thought was exciting and new. Something that might bring order and make trains run on time, but which actually wrought mayhem, pain and disaster. Here, there were people like these girls, singing, playing, one with half her hand missing, but playing nonetheless when the pain it gave her was obvious. How could he not have seen all this before?

He continued walking in his parents' wake, and now Mrs Hall came and kept him company. 'How are you, Mr Massingham?'

He tipped his hat. 'Thanks to you, Mrs Hall, and your friends, I am recovered, or as good as damn it. And it's Ralph, or the whelp, please.' He grinned.

They were almost at the bottom of the hill when Mrs Hall said, 'Oh, Ralph it is, lad. No longer the whelp around Massingham. You're a pitman now, working yer way to being a hewer, remember. You were a brave lad when we nursed you, not just brave, but a good patient when many wouldn't have been with the pain. Aye, you've the makings of a fine man, a fine hewer, a pitman who can hold his own with the rest of them.'

Fran was waiting by the bus, beckoning to her mother. 'Mam, come on, hurry.'

Ralph tipped his hat at her too. Fran, feisty Fran, who was so far above him as to be unobtainable, except to someone like Davey.

He watched as they all clambered onto the bus, and couldn't altogether bear to appear at the Miners' Club, not now, not after . . . The loneliness of his guilt caught at him, for Bedley and Hall still came to him at night and he so admired their wives – no, more than that, he loved them – for their goodness, kindness and support.

He turned and almost tripped over Professor Smythe, who looked from him to the buses. 'Quite a gathering, eh?'

Ralph nodded. Professor Smythe gestured to Ralph's parents' car. 'There's room for you there, as the children are on the buses, or I could drive you into Massingham.' He pointed to an old Buick. 'I am inordinately fond of my motor car, old though it is. It has quirks and secrets, but one learns how to negotiate such things and put them to good use with the proper guidance.'

His tone was so strange, his gaze so powerful, that Ralph couldn't drag himself free. So mesmerising was it that neither did he want to. As he had lain ill, but cared for, he'd thought that perhaps Professor Smythe could be his route to salvation. It was he who had the contacts that had placed Davey at some decoding facility, and who, his father had hinted, was far more than he seemed. And who else could he ask?

'Yes, I'd like that.' He drew a deep breath.

The remnants of the snow still lay where it had drifted up against the drystone walls. The crows were squawking, the sheep were baaing and seeking shelter against the wind. He realised that they had reached the Buick. It was red, and old.

Professor Smythe was looking at the sheep, the car keys in his hand. 'Ah, hiding from the wind, eh? Sometimes one needs to do more than hide, don't you think? Sometimes one needs to take on the foe.'

Again, that look. Ralph held it, hearing the sheep, feeling the wind, and drew a deep breath, for this could be his death knell – the hangman's rope – or salvation. He said, 'You see, I need to talk to someone who can help me extricate myself from a situation that at one time seemed attractive, but which now I see is the road to hell. Face the foe, perhaps. But how?'

It was as though it was the answer Professor Smythe had been seeking, because he turned and patted the car. 'My beautiful Buick. A dear old friend. Sometimes one's friends turn out to be less than we thought, young Ralph. Come with me, Ralph Massingham, and we'll talk in the car, and consider John 4, verse 23, "Cometh the hour, cometh the man".'

Ralph froze. Those were Tim's words. Professor Smythe was jangling his keys. 'Ah yes, I see you remember. You see, we have been monitoring your calls for some while, *quite* some while. Though we'd love, indeed we'd be ecstatic, dear boy, to hear the calls from and to telephone boxes, it's still somewhat beyond our ken. The change in you has been noticed, however, on the heels of that deadly deed. And oh, Ralph Massingham, you do need to redeem yourself, my dear old lad, and in the doing, who knows, dire consequences could be diverted, eh, and nightmares vanquished?'

Ralph stared up at St Oswald's. Never had it looked so appealing, so timeless, and he so unworthy. Yes, dire consequences were what he deserved, but not what his parents should suffer. And how could he possibly face Mrs Hall and Mrs Bedley, or any of the family, if the truth came out?

He dug his hands deep into his pockets. The wind blew and brought a few flakes of snow. The crow flew off. Professor Smythe continued at last. 'Your sincerity is for others to assess and, depending on that, your abilities to be honed. If it is felt that your sincerity is lacking, then – and do not doubt this – you will be thrown to the wolves.' Professor Smythe patted his arm now. 'Of course, should you pass muster, it will enable you to work for, rather than against, your own nation. It is a nation that, given the support of our American allies, has a chance of surviving and indeed triumphing. One mustn't be thankful for tragedies such as Pearl Harbor, but one is, rather.'

He was opening the car door. 'Get in.' It was an order.

Ralph obeyed. Did his father know his telephone was being monitored? Did he know of his son's crimes?

He watched Professor Smythe walk round the front of the car and get into the driver's seat, pulling on string-backed driving gloves as he did so. Smythe settled himself and looked ahead.'What we do feel, Ralph, is that you are involved enough in this particular cell to be able to sink deeper, which would be to our advantage. It would enable you to provide us with information to thwart and cripple those who would do us down. Only then would we be able to discuss redemption. You do understand this, for espionage is a dirty business with consequences, Ralph?'

Ralph continued looking at St Oswald's. He felt his arm being gripped, and the strength of the elderly man surprised him.

'Let's talk on our way to the celebration, old lad, about shoes and ships and sealing wax, and cabbages, saboteurs and kings, eh?' Ralph was aware he was being led towards a choice: a chance to change the things he had done, or pay for them.

At that moment the buses passed them and it looked as

though the girls were kneeling on the back seat, with Stan, Davey and Bob standing behind them.They waved. Professor Smythe waved back, and Ralph did too.

'Such splendid young people,' Smythe said, sounding almost wistful.

Ralph nodded. 'And the co-op. Lord, they are all really quite something.'

Smythe continued to wave and smile, looking after the bus.'We'll make something of you yet, Ralph Massingham. I thought not at one time, but now life has intruded, you'll perhaps do well.' He gripped Ralph's arm again. 'If, of course, you are acting even now for someone else, then it will not bode well for you, for this is not a game and we are enormously good at what it is.'

'I'm not acting,' Ralph said, in little more than a whisper.

'We shall see,' replied Professor Smythe. That was all, but the grip on Ralph's arm loosened.

On the bus, the four girls sat back down while Stan told them about Professor Smythe and how he couldn't stand Ralph, feeling that the Massingham apple had fallen far from the tree.

Fran grinned at Davey. 'I hope he wasn't giving the lad too hard a time – the whelp seems to be growing up a bit. He gave Mam a present for all her care, and the others too.'

'Well, don't leave it there,' said Davey, 'what was it?'

'He paid for the drink for the wedding, obtained by a friend of Reginald Massingham's, and commissioned a couple of rugs that he wants made to a design for Sophia, and magically there's a two-week tab at Mrs Adams' shop been set up for the co-op families.'

'Huh,' Beth muttered, 'he'll have to grow up more than a bit to get into my good books.'

Mrs Oborne was calling from the middle of the bus, 'Get

yer foot down, Bert. Dilly-dallying about won't do when we need to get the happy couple into t'club.'

'Never ever is there a moment of quiet when you're on the bus, you old witch.'

'Steady on, Bert,' called Mr Oborne. 'That's me auld besom you're talking about.'

There was the sound of a slap and then a gruff male voice. 'Ouch.'

Over the laughter Mrs Oborne called, 'Let's have a song, you four lasses. Perhaps Viola could play saxophone for the others. "All or Nothing at All", I reckon.'

Viola shook her head. 'Me hand's a bit sore. I'd rather sing.'

Stan kissed Sarah. 'Which probably means it's agony, pet.'

The girls began, but as they drew into Massingham the whole bus was singing and the girls stopped to listen to them, these wonderful women, some with their menfolk. The girls knew that there was nowhere else they would rather be, ever, than with all their friends and family.

Welcome to

Penny Street

where your favourite authors and stories live.

Meet casts of characters you'll never forget,
create memories you'll treasure for ever,
and discover places that will stay with
you long after the last page.

Turn the page to step into the home of

ANNIE CLARKE

and discover more about

The Factory Girls . . .

Dear Reader,

'Let's go to Beamish Living Museum and see the world we remember,' I said, 'The one where slag heaps dotted the countryside and communities were as they were in the days of *Heroes on the Home Front*, and kitchens had ranges, and airers that hung from the ceiling.'

'What about the netty in the yard?' said Kathleen.

'Oh, aye, I remember that well,' said I.

My friend, Dr Kathleen Thompson (author of *From Both Ends of the Stethoscope*) and I had met up in Newcastle for an away weekend, as we do from time to time, and being old ducks with bus passes, we leapt aboard one destined for the Beamish Living Museum of the North. We LOVE bus journeys, chatting away to complete strangers and getting ideas for other books – which of course I've stored away for subsequent books in the Factory Girls series. Once at Beamish, we found the bus stopped right outside the museum – fabulous.

I've been before, but it seemed so much more this time. We rode on and off trams, with rain whacking on the windows and headed for the colliery village Beamish have imported and rebuilt, stone by stone, and brick by brick.

I knew when we were nearing the mine, as the evocative smell of my childhood was everywhere, (we used to stay with my uncle in school holidays) and there I was, back in mam's pit village in County Durham, and not just that, but

to the earlier 30s and 40s my mam talked of, and which I have re-imagined for the Factory Girls series.

We darted about into the sheds of the colliery, seeing the train and gear, smelling the coal…

On to the school rooms chatting to the school master – and then, and then – the colliery houses where the ranges were burning.

The proggy and hooky rugs were lying as though just put down while Mam made a cuppa. You can just see the back of one, and the untrimmed ragged 'right' side, and then there was the smoother hooky.

See the range, with the rail for tea towels, and this and that where we chatted to the lass dressed as she would have been, 'back then', full of information as she darned socks (remember the mushrooms our mums used? Ours were green.).

The back is the heart of the house.

See the netty which was NOT the heart of the house, but a necessity. Argh, tip-toeing out in the dead of night, unless you kept a po under the bed. Fabulous, wonderful, sad, thought provoking.

How my Factory Girls, Fran, Sarah and Beth would have been chattering in real life, and the co-op too, catching up on gossip, or sorting out problems, and hearing the men clomping along the cobbled back lane, to or from their shift at Auld Hilda – as they do in *Heroes on the Home Front*.

You can see the cobbled streets. There's a chemist, assorted shops including a photographer, where they explained why mum and her brother, Stan, looked so smart when they were as poor as church mice – the photographers would have provided the clothes. The photo of Mum and Stan on the next page must have been taken soon after her mum had died, and sent as a comfort to their da, out in the First World War, somewhere.

You simply must go and show the children, or grandchildren the reality of life, back when times were hard. When communities clung together. When the smell of coal filled the air. Visit www.beamish.org.uk to find out more.

Annie x

Turn the page for a sneak
peek into my new novel

Wedding Bells on the
Home Front

1 March 1942

Bert drove the bus carrying half Stan and Sarah's wedding guests from the church to the reception in Massingham pit village. He was following Cecil, who drove the other half who would be first in for the food and drink, clustering round the buffet like gannets, Fran Hall thought, laughing to herself. The wind carried gusts of snow that settled on the wipers, stalling them until they screeched, but somehow they always picked up steam again. Was it because Bert's language was becoming worse and worse?

She sat on the back seat with Davey's arm around her, listening to Beth and Viola, the other two bridesmaids, chatting alongside her while the bride and groom were squashed together at the end, though they'd be sitting close as could be whether they were tight for space or not. All three bridesmaids' outfits were a bit of a hotchpotch, but Sarah's brocade dress, once the Massingham Hall nursery curtains, was a picture.

Fran called to Sarah, 'By, lass, I reckon them photos Stevie took outside St Oswald's will be something to keep on the mantelpiece for many a year. We three girls in our mams' summer dresses and you in yer finery.'

Stan, Fran's brother, huffed, 'What about the

bridegroom in his best bib and tucker, shiny boots and come-hither smile, I'd like to know?' Sarah slapped him. 'Ouch.'

''Tis yer *only* bib and tucker,' called young Ben, who was sitting on the seat in front of them.

Stan flicked the lad's cap. 'Enough from you, little brother.'

Viola sighed. 'I couldn't get over the confetti – all that colouring and cutting by the evacuees. Must have taken an age.'

Fran raised her eyebrows, grinning. 'Aye, it made me laugh when Mrs Massingham said we're to have a wedding every month because it keeps the bairns busy and quiet after school—'

Beth butted in, laughing. '*Quieter* is what she said, bonny lass.'

Sarah turned away from stroking Stan's hair. 'Aye, quieter, for it were Stan, Sid and Norm kicking the footie with the boys down in the Massinghams' meadow that sorted the lads out. Too puffed out to be anything but quiet when they came back.'

'And the bairns were too,' giggled Beth.

Sarah shouted over their laughter, 'Aye, well, you took me joke, for I were going to say the same thing.'

They were all laughing now, and it took Stan to roar above it all, 'We weren't puffed, course we weren't. We're pitmen, after all.'

Fran conducted while the girls pretended to play

violins until her fiancé, Davey, waved them all to a hush and said, 'Me mam told us they turfed you out with them an' all, later, when Ralph Massingham were getting better from that cut he got down t'seam. Septic it were, Mam said, made all his body sort of septic—'

Viola groaned. 'Oh, belt up, pet. That's reet disgusting, and we've food to eat. I were raving with hunger – till now.'

They were all laughing again, and Fran looked down the aisle of the bus towards her mam and the rest of the Proggy Rug Co-operative. Aye, those women were worth their weight in gold. They had learned in the last war how to use sphagnum moss to suck out poison. Her mam reckoned Ralph, the pit owner's son and heir, would have died otherwise.

Fran sat back, thinking yet again about Ralph and how strange it was that ever since her own father and Sarah's had died in a roof fall down Bell Seam before Christmas and then this cut, he'd been nicer. Her mam had even said they weren't to call him the whelp any more, saying everyone had the right to grow up.

Fran shrugged, for she'd loathed the bugger with his airs and graces from when they were bairns, and for his bullying once they were adults. So why should she forget all that, just because he'd gone into the pit 'to do his bit'? Did he think a few blue scars would make him one of them? Never mind an infected cut, which were as common as the day was long. Daft beggar.

As though sensing her daughter's stare, Annie Hall turned and waved. Davey hugged Fran to him, kissing her and whispering, 'Well, lass, since you told me over the phone about our mams' using the moss on Ralph I've been thinking, and I reckon more might have been sucked out than the infection. It's as though summat deep that were making him a dark bugger has gone. But can we trust it? Could be he's still just a bit under t'weather.'

'How did you know what I were mulling?' Fran lifted her face to him, loving her blond, blue-eyed boy as much as Sarah, Davey's sister, loved Stan.

Davey kissed Fran again, saying against her mouth, 'Because I love you so much, and know you so well. Howay, I've been able to guess your thoughts since we were wee bairns, don't forget.'

'Yer mean you can decode her, I reckon,' Beth whooped, then put her hand over her mouth, whispering, 'By, when we're all together in the gang, I forget . . .' She raised her voice, trying again. 'After all, you do them decoding crosswords, so I reckon you can solve anything.'

They were coming into Massingham, and Bob, Beth's husband, sitting in the seat in front, leaned over, took off his naval cap and fanned her. 'Calm yerself. No one heard but us, and we know you're a dilly-dally dafty—'

Bob's 'Ouch' was loud enough to make Stan's marrers, Sid and Norm, sitting on the other side, swing round. 'Man up, Bob, she's only a bitty lass—'

Just then there was a shriek of brakes and they were flung forwards, then back. The men swore, but Bert was loudest, and then he bellowed, 'Bliddy hell, it were a cat just ran across in front.'

'Black one, I hope?' boomed Mrs Oborne.

Maisie, who worked at the Factory with the girls, had a window seat and yelled, 'Aye.'

'That's all reet then,' shouted Mrs Oborne, 'for 'tis good luck for us all, so come on, Bert, stop making a meal of it and get yer foot down. We need to get to the victuals before Cecil's bus loadseat the whole bliddy lot. He's got the rest of the co-op and the Factory girls on board, aye, and some of the evacuee bairns, and it'll be gobs open and no holds barred.'

'Aye, and you could do to shut yer gob an' all, Tilly Oborne, or I'll turf yer off.'

The passengers were screaming with laughter, and Bert's tirade ended on a great guffaw as he did indeed put his foot down.

Sitting with Stan, feeling his body pressed against hers, Sarah didn't think she could be any happier than she was this minute. She linked her arm carefully through Fran's plastered one. The three of them, Viola, Fran and Sarah, the new Mrs Hall, had survived the accident at the Scottish explosives factory, and had brought the orphaned Viola back with them. So now the three Factory girls were a gang of four, and one was married. Suddenly she said, 'Here I am, Sarah Hall, yes, Hall, not Bedley any more.' She stopped and laughed. 'No, I'm not a Bedley, I'm the wife of Stan, one of the best hewers in t'pit, and a scholarship lad who's been to Oxford, an' all.'

Fran leaned against her. 'Someone's happy today, eh? And aye, Mrs Hall, me brother is one of t'best.'

Sarah just grinned. 'Well, in a month you'll not be Fran Hall any longer, but Fran Bedley when you wed that galumph of a brother of mine. It's like a roundabout, isn't it? Hall, Bedley, Bedley, Hall, and if you don't have a black cat running across in front of yer bus, then we'll share mine. Oh Franny, it's all so wonderful.'

Stan was laughing, and she leaned against his shoulder. He was so strong, so brave, so certain. Well, so was she now, especially after the dreams – or perhaps nightmares would be a better word – had stopped. Night after night they'd come, dreams of lying beneath the debris in the accident, the one that had seen her, Fran and Viola in hospital and then back home, to Massingham, and to Beth, who had not been transferred north with them.

Massingham, with all the familiarity of its back-to-backs, the slag heap, the pithead, the clop of pitmen's boots in the early morning, had soothed and put her to rights. She snatched a look at Fran, for she was too pale, too short of sleep, and still heard Fiona, Deidre and the new girl, and the safety inspector too, crying out from under the rubble before they'd died, even though they hadn't, in truth, done much of that, for three of the four were already dead, so it was said.

Fran turned. 'So, not feeling any of yer aches and pains today?'

'Aye,' Beth called across, 'she's tripping the light fantastic, so she is.'

They braced themselves as there was another shriek of brakes, followed by a call from Mrs Oborne. 'For pity's sake, Bert, get a bliddy grip.'

'Aye,' came Bert's reply, 'and the grip'll be round that big gob, you old besom. Open yer eyes, lass. We're here.'

Everyone had been too busy talking but now they looked out of the windows and saw that they were parked behind Cecil's bus, about twenty yards this side of the Miners' Club.

'All off the charabanc,' yelled Bert. 'And I'll have no more cheek from yer, Tilly Oborne, or I'll lock yer in the luggage hold and your old man'll not stop me, so yer can settle back down, our Steve.'

Steve sat down with a thump, laughing. Then he was up again as his wife shouted orders and they joined their friends moving slowly towards the pavement, the club and the victuals.

At the back Viola waved Fran to go ahead, and then Davey too. Fran smiled, and slipped out after Sarah and Stan. Davey said, his breath on her neck, 'Don't fret, lass, the dreams will stop soon. It's yer mind's way of shifting the thoughts. Stan and I were the same in t'pit when our legs were buggered.'

Fran nodded, as they shuffled forward. The debris that had fallen on Stan and Davey was a natural fall, but the one at the Scottish factory hadn't been. That had been the result of a kirby grip falling into the explosives, causing a spark, and she had been too slow in calling out a warning, too unsure that it really had been a kirby grip glinting in the new girl's hair, the new girl with a freckled face. A kirby grip that they should have all seen when they checked one another in the changing room. Well, she and Viola and Sarah had checked one another, and someone should have double-checked the inexperienced new girl. Perhaps someone had, but it had been hidden too deep in her hair.

She, Fran Hall, had seen a glint in the workshop

though, but had waited, looking, peering forward to make sure. Waited too long, for it had fallen into the machine, killing four people, taking half of Viola's hand and ear, and hurting others.

Fran had already told her friends and her mam that she'd thought she'd seen it but hadn't called the warning in time; they just interrupted, every time, and would not let her say she felt so guilty. Instead, as though they didn't want to hear, they said: 'Hush, these things can happen. It's not your fault.' But she felt it was. So what do I do about that? she wanted to scream. Just let me say it.

Ahead of her the bridal pair were laughing at something, as Davey murmured, 'Cheer up, lass, think of some'at else, they're only dreams.'

She felt rage sweep her – he had said he knew her, could read her mind, but he couldn't. No one could, so no one could help. Her mam could almost understand, because she'd been in the First War. Almost. But not really.

'Come on, down you come.' They'd reached the bus steps and Fran eased herself onto the ground, Davey following, slipping his arm around her waist, careful not to jog her cracked ribs, her fractured arm, damaged shoulder. She looked ahead to the club where bunting hung over the doorway, each triangle of cream wallpaper coloured by the evacuees. Some of the red had smeared in the wet of the snow, and looked as though they'd been weeping.

Beth followed Viola along the bus aisle and waited while the lass eased herself down the steps in Davey and Fran's wake. Aye, and I'd ease meself if I'd cracked a rib or two in the explosion, thought Beth, as well as lost some of me hand, and ear, and burned me scalp. It would hurt for a while yet, poor lass. Once down, Viola called after Fran and Davey, 'Wait for us.'

As Beth followed, with Bob behind her, Bert said, 'Leave a spam sandwich for me, lass.'

'Aye, I reckon there'll be pheasant ones too, a contribution from the Massinghams. I'll try and tuck some to one side, Bert.'

He smiled, tiredness dragging at his face. Well, she thought, he was about sixty and drove the bus to and from the Factory, delivering the shift workers at all hours, so of course he was tired. But then there was a war on, and everyone—

Bob tapped her on the shoulder. 'Howay, lass. Let's get going, or there'll be nowt left, and I have to get going at midnight, back to me ship, or I'll turn into a pumpkin. See you in there, eh, Bert?'

'Aye, you will, lad. Be rough at sea today, so 'tis best you're here.'

They set off, Viola hurrying after Fran. Ahead of

them, beyond the allotments, snow lay on the hills, and in the easterly wind the slag heap was smouldering, as it often did when the wind grew cruel.

As they walked, Bob pulled Beth along. 'Howay, pet. Let's get a wriggle on, I need more'n a few dances with me lass. Tommy'll pick me up from the telephone box on his motorbike. He's been up near the Scottish border and we've to get to Grimsby by dawn, but I'll have to kill yer if you tell anyone that's where we're headed.'

She leaned into him and laughed. 'I'll not say a word, as long as you swear to tek care, eh?'

'Always do.' They followed the long crocodile into the warmth and light of the Miners' Club hall, where the food was laid out on trestle tables. The co-op was bustling about, whipping the greaseproof paper off plates of sandwiches. Beth knew exactly where the pheasant ones were laid out since she, Fran and Viola had helped sort out the victuals at dawn, slipping along with Beth's mam to help prepare for the reception. Sid and Norm had put up the bunting, which had been a grand effort, given the hangovers they both had.

Norm had said, winking at her, 'Had to commiserate over a pint or two, for it's not every day we get to offload our marrer into the wedded state . . . Poor devil.'

As they headed for the tables, Bob yawned, still

tired after his dash to get to the church, a bit late for the wedding, but in time to throw confetti. Beth saw that the cardboard cake was laid out on a card table in front of the stage. Underneath the cardboard was the tiny cake Beth's and Sarah's mams had made with ingredients supplied by anyone in the pit village who had a twist of sugar or flour to spare from their ration.

Sarah and Fran, who had been waiting for her, turned to Beth, who grinned. Standing alongside, Viola called, 'Is the cake real?' There was wonder in her voice.

Bob nudged Beth and answered, 'As real as you want it to be, Viola. That's the thing to remember.'

Beth put her arm around Viola and whispered, 'Stevie'll tek a photo, getting all rattled and shouty as he did at the church because no one's standing still, and we lasses will look at the photo in years to come, alongside the one of the happy couple, and laugh, and be bliddy glad the war is over and that our own lasses can have a proper cake. This cardboard one lifts up, yer see, and there's a tiddler underneath.'

Viola smiled and just then young Ben put a record on the gramophone player, which was on one side of the stage. It was a waltz. 'Coats off,' he yelled. 'Let's warm the place up with a bit of a dance while the mams get the urn on for tea. First waltz for the new Mr and Mrs Hall, but no kissing. It's disgusting and too much of a shock for a twelve-year-old. Come on, all of you, get yerselves sorted and warm up the place, it's bliddy freezing.'

'Language,' shouted his mam, the girls and most of the hall.

Ben scowled and gestured them all to be quiet, or that's how it could be interpreted, perhaps. Beth and Viola were laughing, leaning against one another, and Fran muttered, 'Nothing changes.'

Viola looked from one to another and smiled. 'I'm beginning to see that.'

Quietly, Fran said, 'But, let's hope some things do.' No one heard.

Beth edged up closer to Viola, saying to Bob as he tried to get her to dance, 'Let the newly-weds take to the floor first, lad,' she said. Bob nodded and Beth murmured to Viola, 'Howay, lass. It must be hard, both yer parents gone in the Newcastle bombing, but as we said when the other two dragged yer here from hospital, yer home's in Massingham with me and Mam now, so never think you're alone. As long as we girls stick together, nowt can break us, see?'

Behind them, coats were being thrown over the chairs that lined the room, or hung on the pegs against the door. The walls were painted dull green and the usual noticeboards and notices were also festooned with bunting for the day. Stan was dragging Sarah onto the floor and into his arms. They moved to the music, Sarah's brocade wedding dress shimmering, Stan's suit dark against it, his black hair against her blonde chignon. With a look to Ben, and a wink, the only kiss he gave his bride was one on the forehead and there was as much love in that as there would have been in anything more.

A steady flow of other couples joined them, but first on were Fran and Davey, as in love as the other two, and now Norm, Stan's marrer, escorted Viola into a dance, holding her wounded hand as gently as if it were cut glass.

As Beth looked on, loving the sight of her friends and neighbours, she felt Bob's arm slide around her.

'Yer all reet, lass? Must be strange to see yer old boyfriend wed to yer marrer?'

Beth was so startled she swung round and pulled him to her. 'No, yer daft thing, no stranger than Stan being at our wedding. Bob Jones, you know that I love you, deep through to me core.'

He drew her even closer. 'I love you, an' all. I just want this bliddy war over because it makes things so bliddy difficult, such a bliddy mess.' He paused, then repeated against her hair. 'Aye, I love you, reet enough, my lass.'

'Howay, are you trying to convince yerself, bonny lad?' Beth laughed.

'Course not. It's just . . . Oh I don't know. Give us a dance, lass.'

They danced for just a moment, but then Beth saw Bert enter and groaned. 'The pheasant sandwiches.' She flew to the trestle tables, gathered up several sandwiches – pheasant and spam – onto a side plate and tucked it on the counter behind the hatch. 'These are for Bert,' she called to her mam and Sophia Massingham, the boss's wife. 'He's looking reet worn out.' She spun round and almost banged into the whelp.

Ralph stepped to one side. 'So sorry, Beth.'

Reminding herself that her mam had said he wasn't to be thought of as the whelp any more, for there was a sea change under way, she smiled uncertainly.

'It was a lovely service,' said Ralph, and leaned in closer. 'But did I hear a mouse? There was a definite squeak.' He winked.

She laughed, surprised, and looked around to check that the organist, who was the Reverend Walters' sister, was nowhere near. 'Ah, Ralph . . . Sometimes there's a problem with the organ's wind, and we get a squeak.'

They both looked at one another, and burst out laughing.

'Well, not quite like that, but . . .' she said.

Ralph nodded. 'But something like that, then, eh?'

Beth scurried off to dance with Bob again and told him of the conversation, and when Bob had stopped laughing, he said, 'Aye, well, t'pit's a hard taskmaster, and p'raps our whelp's met his match.'

Beth shook her head. 'On top of being poorly, I reckon that Bell Seam roof fall shook him. Probably never seen death up close before.'

Behind Bob, she saw the professor who had mentored Stan after he'd won the Massingham scholarship to Oxford University – or had until Stan returned to the pit. Professor Smythe finished chatting to his old friend Reginald Massingham, Ralph's father, who had set up the scholarship. She watched as he began to wind his way through the tables and the groups of guests towards Ralph, who was taking his coat down from one of the pegs near the door. What? she thought, it's only just started. But then the lad had been ill. She shrugged and turned back to Bob, kissing his cheek.

'Going already?' Professor Smythe murmured, almost in a whisper to Ralph. 'I had hoped I might have your answer before I left?'

Ralph swallowed, his coat over his arm. He glanced around nervously, but everyone was dancing, or sitting at tables some way away. He replied, just as quietly as the Professor, 'I need a bit more time. I'm not sure I can do it.'

'Well,' the Professor said, under the cover of a cough into his hand, 'Counter-espionage is a dicey task.' He lifted his head, and his eyes were steely now, as the two stood together, and surveyed the room. 'Smile, lad, look as though we're enjoying a few pleasantries, eh.' He laughed, and Ralph managed to produce a semblance of the same. The Professor continued. 'You'll need to keep your wits about you, but you'll be taught. The thing is, you are the one who approached me, dear old lad, outside the church, once I'd dropped a few openings, admittedly. It was apparent then that you were desperate to make amends for causing, quite deliberately, the roof fall that inadvertently killed those two fathers. You told me you had to get out of the whole damned mess you have created for yourself.' Professor Smythe's voice was little more than a breath, but his laugh was hearty, and he patted Ralph's arm, raising his voice, 'Yes, indeed, those sandwiches do look good.'

Ralph forced himself to nod, and to smile. 'You really should try the pheasant, as well as the spam. Best to tuck in, Professor, as you have a way to go but delightful to see you, not to mention catching up on the news from Oxford.'

He looked around, again – it was what he found himself doing a lot now, for who knew who might be a member of the Fascist cell he had joined while still at school? Back then it had been so different from anything else, so exciting, and had felt like a bit of a rebellion. But now he had at last come to his senses.

Professor Smythe continued, 'Yes, pheasant, so delicious, I can hardly wait. Spam does pall, doesn't it?' He lowered his voice again, though no one was in the vicinity, and Ralph strained to hear. 'I do hope you *do* decide to work with us, for I repeat, it will put me in the most dreadful fix if not, dear boy. One thinks of the monitored calls between you and Tim Swinton . . . For they prove beyond all doubt you have committed treason through the mere fact of sabotage in time of war, and I do believe you could deceive quite adequately. Pheasant as well as spam . . . Nicely done, if I may say—'

Ralph interrupted, and he too was speaking quietly, so terribly quietly. 'No, you don't understand. I mean, pheasant and spam are one thing, but I really don't think I'll be able to do it. To pretend . . .' he looked around as he whispered '. . . when I don't want to be near the bastards, to be part . . .'

Professor Smythe nodded. 'Indeed, but what options have you? Shame, disgrace, and the rope or—' He laughed, clapping his hands as a dance ended. 'So wonderful to be young.'

Ralph followed the Professor's lead, though his mouth was dry with terror at his words, true though they were. 'Well, I should get myself on the floor too, but I need to sleep. I find I get whacked easily and *am* on the fore shift tomorrow.' He waved to Mrs Hall, who smiled back, as she left a plate of sandwiches at one of the tables. Ralph laughed as she mimicked drinking a tankard of beer, shaking his head, and pointing to the door. She nodded, and he murmured to the Professor, his voice shaking, 'I so need to reclaim some honour. I—' Smythe put up his hand and whispered a warning: 'Wait.'

Davey was weaving through the tables, heading towards them, and Fran, feisty Fran, daughter of Mr Hall. Mr Hall, who was Mrs Hall's husband. Mr Hall who had died beneath the coal, which he, Ralph brought down with an explosion, oh so cleverly placed behind a prop. Mr Hall, who he didn't know would be surveying that seam. Oh God.

Fran seemed pale, and Ralph remembered hearing her mother talking to Beth's in his bedroom after they'd dressed the wound everyone believed was a pit injury. They had been worried about Fran blaming herself for not spotting the kirby grip sooner, blaming herself for the four deaths. They had agreed then not to let her speak of the dreams in which she heard them crying out in the rubble, in the belief that it would help her to put it all behind her. Ralph suspected, that like him, she probably wouldn't.

Ralph stepped to one side as Davey shook Professor Smythe's hand. 'Good to see you, Prof. Thought you'd like to know young Ben's doing some crosswords for the London magazine that commissioned mine. How's your RAF son? Promoted to an instructor was the last Stan said he'd heard. So more or less out of it, I suppose.'

Professor Smythe's face changed, just a fraction. 'Sadly, dear boy, went back to flying sorties, and failed to return. We wait for news, or rather, I wait for news. His mother is, alas, no longer of this earth.'

There was a silence between them, and Davey flushed, 'Christ, I'm so—' Fran reached forward and gripped the professor's hand. 'You wait, he could well be found in a prisoner-of-war camp. You just wait, d'yer hear me?' Her voice was low but fierce.

While the music flowed and the dancers swirled, Professor Smythe covered her hand with his own and nodded, for a moment unable to speak.

Ralph noticed his father beckoning to him from the buffet table, where he chatted to Mrs Hall, who was busy filling a platter with yet more sandwiches. As Ralph reached him, his father excused himself to Fran's mother, who nodded towards the coat over his arm. 'So glad to see you being sensible, lad, and heading home. After an infected cut you need to tek care. Don't you keep him long, Mr Massingham.' She headed towards another few tables.

'So, Ralph, we've had our orders,' his father winked, and added, 'Nice to see our Stan and Sarah married. Pleasant service, eh?'

'Yes, yes, of course it was. Well, it would be with those two,' Ralph replied, pausing. 'But Father, I need a word later this evening, if it's convenient?'

Reginald Massingham studied his son, then nodded. 'Yes, that would be good. Auberon has apprised me of your discussions, dearest Ralph.'

That was all, but it was too kind.

Ralph walked back, shrugged himself into his coat, and reached for the door, but then spun round for a last look at the joy and happiness, almost knocking into Fran, who stood slightly apart from her fiancé, her face drawn and strained. Ralph stepped nearer.

'The cries are a manifestation of a sense of guilt, Fran. You mustn't go down that path. I heard your mother, you see. You did all you could. You might think you didn't, but you did. Frances Hall, the dead don't want your sorrow. They want you to live – for them. You tried. That's what's important. You tried.'

He turned, stepped towards Professor Smythe, interrupting his chat with Davey. 'Yes, do telephone me tomorrow, Professor. Three, after the fore shift sounds a good idea?'

Smythe hadn't suggested it, but it felt good for Ralph to take back a tiny bit of control when his life was spiralling out of it. The professor held out his hand and shook Ralph's. 'I will,' he said. His eyes searched Ralph's as if looking for the correct decision.

Ralph slipped from the hall, wondering if he would have the courage to stay, but knowing he couldn't ever run away because Tim Swinton had made it quite clear that he would hurt Ralph's father and stepmother if he faltered.

As he walked, he wondered if Fran would put her demons to one side, for he would willingly carry them for that young woman for the rest of his life if she would allow him, or if such a thing were possible. If only life were that easy.

He walked on back to the main road. Darkness had fallen, the moon was high. The pit workings sang, carried on the wind, and nearer Massingham Hall he would be able to hear the owls in full voice. As he walked past the phone box it rang. He hesitated, chilled, fearing it would be Tim Swinton. So, had someone indeed been watching? He breathed deeply, and waited for someone to come to the telephone box, someone who had arranged for their son, or daughter, or husband to phone at a particular time. No-one came, and the ringing continued.

He waited just a moment longer, thanking the skill of the professor in showing him how to intersperse life and death discussions with laughter and banality. God, he hoped it had worked. He suspected that was why the man had spoken to him in the main hall, and not walked outside with him. It was a test and a lesson, for the future, if indeed to fight back against the Fascists was to be his decision.

Still no-one else came and he knew he must answer. He swallowed, pulled open the door and reached for the receiver. Once this world had been exciting, before he killed two men he knew and admired.

He lifted the receiver. 'Well, Ralphy . . .' came Tim's voice.

WANT TO KNOW WHAT HAPPENS NEXT?

Wedding Bells on the
Home Front

ANNIE CLARKE

ORDER YOUR COPY NOW

Hear more from

ANNIE CLARKE